MW01152501

Other Books by MJ Duncan

Second Chances

Veritas

Spectrum

Atramentum

Symphony in Blue

Heist

Pas de Deux

prologue

Mallory Collingswood pressed her violin case behind her hip and held the door to Higher Ground open for the young mother who was shepherding a small child ahead of her. The little girl had a smaller version of her mother's teal and white patterned takeaway cup in her hands, and she beamed as she lifted her cup and shared quite proudly, "I got hot cocoa with whipped cream!"

Even though it was the end of June, the weather was especially dreary, and Mallory smiled at the girl as she replied, "That sounds marvelous. Make sure you mind your step, then, so you don't spill."

"I will," the girl promised as she turned and began walking away with her cup clasped tightly between her hands.

"Cheers," the mother murmured as she hurried to catch up to her daughter.

"Of course," Mallory replied with a nod before she ducked inside the coffee shop.

She had discovered Higher Ground by accident after she had returned to London roughly ten months ago when her train had broken-down two stops into her journey to work, and she had been forced to look for alternate transportation to the Barbican. The sky had opened up the moment she stepped onto the sidewalk outside the Covent Garden tube station and, instead of waiting for a taxi in the deluge, she'd hurried across the street toward the warmly lit coffee shop.

The soft jazz that had been playing through the speakers hidden behind the rough-hewn rafters overhead and the exposed weathered brick on the walls combined to give the shop a laid-back, urban-bohemian vibe that she had fallen in love with before the front door had completely closed behind her. She'd been immediately drawn to the large gallery-styled framed prints of dancers on stage at the nearby Royal Opera House that filled the walls. The beautiful lines of the dancers' bodies and the composition of the lighting were such that she often found it difficult to look away. She knew nothing about ballet beyond vague memories of the time her parents had taken her to a performance of The Nutcracker before she began at The Royal Academy of Music, but there was no mistaking the artistry or the skill captured in each frame.

All she had been looking for that day was shelter, a place to wait out the squall until she could order a cab, and instead she'd found what had quickly become her favorite place in all of London.

She had been stopping by on her way into work ever since for a cappuccino and a positively sinful, homemade turtle croissant.

She had always been a creature of habit, and after having what felt like her entire life yanked out from under her roughly ten months earlier, she had greedily grabbed on to the security a daily routine provided her.

Routine, after all, unlike people, wouldn't break her heart.

"Hey, Mallory," Lena Black, one of the owners of Higher Ground, greeted her when she made it to the counter. Lena was positively tiny in both stature and frame, with short black hair, keen green eyes, and a pointed chin that Mallory would sometimes tease made her look like one of Tinkerbell's friends from those newer films she had seen when she was helping Will watch his niece. "Your usual?"

"Please." Mallory smiled and nodded as she reached for her wallet inside the leather Zegna briefcase that usually acted as her purse.

"Thank you."

"Of course. Hey, I've got the place staffed tonight—you want to go out to dinner?"

"I'd love to, but I can't. It's the last night of the season. Maybe next week?" Mallory handed Lena her card. "I have the next ten days off before we leave to go on tour," she added wryly as she tucked her long blond hair behind her ears and made a mental note to schedule an appointment with her stylist before she left the country.

"Sure. Let me see what the employee schedule looks like, and I'll let you know what days work for me. You lot are going to America, right?"

Mallory nodded and counted off the stops on her fingers, "Boston, New York, Atlanta, Chicago, Denver, Seattle, and San Francisco." She would have preferred to avoid California altogether, but at least they weren't going anywhere near Los Angeles.

"Sounds fun." Lena grinned and handed Mallory her card back.

"It should be," Mallory agreed as she slipped it into the fold of her wallet. She would put it away properly later. "Though, by the end of those seven weeks, I am going to be more than ready to come home."

"I'll bet. As much as I enjoyed touring, there was nothing better than sleeping in my own bed when it was over," Lena commiserated. She had been a dancer with The Royal Ballet before her ankle had decided it'd had enough of being en pointe, and they had spent many a morning chatting idly about the many similarities between dancing and music. Today wasn't going to be one of those days, however, because Lena glanced apologetically at the queue of customers forming behind Mallory. "I can't wait to hear all about it. Make sure to share pictures on your Instagram so I can live vicariously through you."

"I will," Mallory promised with a smile as she moved out of the way to allow the person behind her to approach the register.

"I'll have Clark bring your order out once it's ready." Lena tipped her head toward the back of the shop where Mallory always sat.

"Cheers, darling," Mallory murmured.

Lena winked at her before she turned her attention to the gentleman who had been waiting.

Mallory made her way toward her favorite spot near the electric fireplace. It was the quietest spot in the shop, far enough from the traffic flow that it was almost its own little world. She sighed contentedly as she slipped her violin case and briefcase from her shoulder and set them beneath the table so they'd be out of the way. Even though it was June, there was still a bit of a nip in the morning air—or perhaps it was just that her blood had yet to properly thicken after returning home from Los Angeles—and she angled her chair in a way that let her feel the warmth of the flames against her back.

Her cappuccino and scone were delivered by a fresh-faced university student not long after she had made herself comfortable, and she murmured her thanks as the boy wiped his hands on his jeans and turned to leave. She glanced at a couple a few tables over as she moved the scone to the side and pulled her coffee closer, and relaxed in her seat as she retrieved her phone from the pocket of her jacket. With an hour to kill before she needed to get back on the tube to head over to the Barbican for her final rehearsal of the season, she opened her Twitter app as she reached for her coffee.

While her bosses at the London Symphony Orchestra didn't require quite the level of a social media presence as she'd had in Los Angeles, they still expected her to post something a few times a week. If she were to be honest, her thoughts on their performance this evening ran more along the lines of, *I made it a whole season without breaking down!* and *hopefully next season will be easier*—but that wasn't exactly the kind of sentiment the board would appreciate. She was supposed to be engaging and upbeat, representing the LSO in its best possible light, so she instead typed out a quick, *Last performance of the season is tonight! You lot are going to LOVE it!*

Obligation fulfilled, she scrolled through her feed to see if any of her old friends or colleagues had tweeted anything about their performance the night before. She smiled when she saw a dozen or so tweets clustered together in a way that made her think the Phil's first violins had gathered together backstage after their show and fired off their tweets all at once to punctuate the end of their season. They were all pretty standard and nearly identical to what she would be tweeting later that evening—*What a great year, can't wait for next season!* or some similar sentiment of fondness for the season they had just wrapped. She liked each of their tweets and replied to those few friends she still kept in touch with, offering her congratulations, but it was the tweet from LA Phil's official account that brought her scrolling to a complete stop.

@LAPhil is proud to present 'Symphony in Blue,' a modern masterpiece composed by our very own Gwen Harrison! Click the link for the video…

She frowned as she reread the tweet slowly, and then a third time, lingering on the shape of each letter to make sure she was reading the words correctly. A leaden feeling, cold and bitter and impossible to ignore settled in her stomach as she stared at those ellipses for the fourth time. Her chest tightened as the truth sank in, making it hard to breathe.

Gwen—the woman she had once thought she would marry—wrote music.

And she'd had absolutely no idea.

God, had she even known her at all?

Mallory put her coffee back onto the table and pushed it away. Just the idea of drinking the bitter brew was enough to turn her stomach, and she instead reached for the wireless headphones she kept in her bag. Really, she should have just kept scrolling. Or closed the app altogether. She didn't want to tarnish what remained of her fond memories of her time in Los Angeles, but the bright blue YouTube link at the end of the tweet was a siren's call she was helpless to resist.

As soon as the headphones connected to her phone, she pressed her thumb to the link. She glanced up at the sound of a bag hitting a chair at the next table and watched as the owner of the bag slipped gracefully into the chair opposite it. The woman was young, just barely into her twenties at the most, with flawless olive skin and wavy dark curls streaked with auburn highlights that tickled her chiseled jawline. The woman yawned as she stretched her long, lean legs beneath her little café table, unexpectedly defined muscles flexing against the tight fabric, and shook her head as she tugged at the sleeves of the pink, long-sleeved tee that clung to her petite frame. She looked both fragile and impossibly strong at the same time, and Mallory was grateful for the sound of her old conductor's voice coming through her headphones that forced her to look away before the woman caught her staring.

She willed herself to ignore the almost haunted-looking reflection of her pale blue eyes on the screen as she focused her attention on the video. It clearly began toward the end of Rhode's introduction because he was turned toward Gwen with an outstretched hand and a hint of a smile visible beyond his shock of wild curls. She held her breath as she watched Gwen set her bow on her music stand and pass her cello to Roland Yves before she pushed herself to her feet, and her throat tightened with emotion as she watched Gwen make her way across the stage to where Rhode was waiting for her.

With her dark hair pulled back into a loose chignon, drawing her delicate features and stunning blue eyes into even sharper focus, Gwen was more beautiful than her dreams remembered; and even after close to a year of no contact, the sight of her smiling shyly as she fiddled with the microphone made her heart ache. But if she thought the sight of Gwen was painful, then listening to her speech was pure agony. The way she spoke about her new partner, Dana, with such obvious love in her voice and expression, was a dagger to the heart Mallory hadn't realized she could still suffer.

For all her faults—and she was painfully aware that she had many, many of them—she had truly loved Gwen Harrison.

She sucked in a deep breath and blinked away the sting of tears at the backs of her eyes as Gwen's introduction ended and she made her way back to her seat. Anger flared in her chest when she spotted Luke grinning at Gwen and giving her two cheesy thumbs up as the camera panned over the musicians seated on stage. Knowing how close he and Gwen were, she had tried so damn hard to win him over when she and Gwen had started dating, but he had never warmed up to her, and after close to six months of trying, she had given up. Part of her couldn't help but wonder if it was her inability to gain his trust that had ultimately contributed to the downfall of their relationship.

The camera thankfully panned out from his impish, annoying face to take in the entire stage, and she blew out a shaky breath as the anger she felt toward Luke was replaced by an icy sadness of just how much she had lost.

She swallowed thickly as she watched Rhode take his place on the rostrum, his hair even more unruly than she had remembered, and held her breath as he lifted his hands to ready the orchestra. There was a long pause as he looked over the musicians before his hands dropped—a move she *knew* was designed to give Gwen a moment to gather herself—and then the music began, and she was sent reeling.

The symphony Gwen had crafted was rich and layered and nuanced in a way that brought tears to her eyes. Not just for the love she had lost, but because she had never been allowed to see this part of her. Had never once been shown even the slightest hint that such depth and complexity and undiluted talent existed within Gwen.

Because the music she was listening to was truly phenomenal.

Each note, every bar, flowed together so perfectly and conveyed so much emotion that it was all she could do to keep the tears that threatened at bay. Even after listening for only a few minutes, she knew that the tweet that had led her to the video had not been exaggerating in the slightest. *Symphony in Blue* was a masterpiece in every sense of the word, and her heart broke all over again as she watched Gwen's body move as she played, her face that beautiful mask of concentration she had found so much comfort in seeing across the stage when they had performed together.

She ached to reach out and brush the errant strand of hair away from Gwen's brow, to tuck it behind her ear and lay the softest of kisses to her lips. But she wouldn't ever have that opportunity again, because she had lost her. And Dana—god, how she wished she could forget the blonde's name but she couldn't, just like she couldn't forget one word that she and Gwen had said the night her world had come crashing down—Dana had found her.

But maybe it was a good thing; because Gwen seemed more alive than she remembered ever seeing her. Even through her mask of concentration there was the slightest hint of a smile playing on her lips, and she looked tanned and healthy and happy. And for as much as she hated knowing that Dana was undoubtedly the cause of that change, she was also glad to see it. Glad to know that Gwen was loved and taken care of.

Even if she wasn't the one doing it.

She wiped at her eyes as she turned off the video, unable to bear watching any longer even though, by the tracker on the bottom of the screen, there were still close to twenty minutes left of the performance. She had thought that she'd finally begun to move past everything she had left behind in California, but this video and the near-crippling ache it elicited in her chest was proof that she hadn't.

Part of her wondered if she ever would.

She had long since accepted her own role in the demise of their relationship—the painful words Gwen had spoken that night had landed with enough weight that it had taken her a good few weeks to feel like she had her feet back under her—but this was just too much. Listening to the woman she had loved play the notes she'd written for another was one injustice too many to suffer, and she wasn't strong enough to watch the video until it ended. She bit the inside of her cheek as she wiped away the evidence of her distress, and shook her head as she removed her headphones and tucked them back into her briefcase.

Someday, she hoped, she might be strong enough to listen to the full piece.

But not today.

The woman she had noticed earlier at the next table caught her eye as she straightened, and Mallory sighed when the woman did not look away. She forced a tight smile that she hoped conveyed that she neither needed nor wanted the attention, but some of the turmoil she was feeling must have shown through because the woman's warm brown eyes softened with concern.

"Are you okay?" the woman asked.

Mallory dipped her head in a small nod. "Yes. Of course."

The woman smiled kindly and, instead of taking the hint—probably because she had the sweetest-sounding American accent and the gods clearly thought the video wasn't enough for Mallory to suffer through for one day—pressed on. "Of course you are," she murmured, a hint of a drawl slipping into her voice as she raked a hand through her hair that glinted red and gold in the overhead lights. "Stiff upper lip and all that, right?"

Mallory hummed and took a pointed sip of her cappuccino.

The woman chuckled, the sound so low and rich and melodious that, were it any other day, Mallory would have smiled back. "Sorry, my friends tell me that I can be a little too nosy sometimes." She pursed her lips thoughtfully. "You probably don't want to spill your heart out to some random stranger, right?"

Mallory tipped her head. "No. Not especially."

"Completely understandable." The woman rolled her eyes as her phone buzzed on the table in front of her. "So much for a late start." She nimbly unfolded herself from her seat, grabbed her kit bag, and slung it over her shoulder. She motioned toward Mallory's phone and added, "I hope everything works out okay."

"Me too," Mallory murmured.

The woman smiled and, with one last lingering look, made her way toward the door, her long, long legs carrying her elegantly through the sparse crowd gathered near the register before she disappeared from sight.

Mallory sighed as she looked back at her coffee and pastry, and pocketed her phone. The idea of eating made her sick to her stomach, and she needed to work off the melancholia that threatened to pull her under. Music had been her lifeline these last ten months, helping to keep her from drifting away into thoughts that were so cold and dark that it was nearly impossible to find a way out, and she could only hope that it would do so again this morning.

She gathered her things with shaking hands and hurried toward the exit. As she crossed the street to the underground entrance, she couldn't help but lament the fact that what should have been a fun, exciting day was now going to take every ounce of strength she possessed to see it through to the end.

one

"You're back! How was your tour?" Lena greeted Mallory with a wide grin.

Mallory smiled as she approached the register at Higher Ground. Lena's hair was longer than it had been on her last visit but, otherwise, everything seemed the same as it had been before. After seven weeks on the road and then the last whirlwind of a week that she had spent catching up on everything that had been neglected during her time away, she felt herself finally relaxing as the normalcy of the sounds and the smells and the brightness of Lena's smile assured her that she was finally home. "The tour went well, but it felt like it was downright interminable there at the end."

"I'll bet," Lena chuckled. "That's a long time to be living out of a suitcase. You want your usual?"

"Please." Mallory nodded and reached for her wallet. "How was your summer?"

"It was pretty much business as usual around here." Lena took Mallory's card and waved it toward the violin hanging off her shoulder. "I thought you lot didn't start rehearsing again until next week?"

"We don't. However," Mallory sighed, "I have a full day of meetings at the Barbican with a couple hours off around midday, so I figured I may as well get started on the bowing notations for the season during that time."

"Ouch," Lena commiserated as she handed Mallory her card back. "So much for a break, huh?"

"There's no rest for the wicked, I'm afraid," Mallory agreed as she tucked her card back into her wallet.

"Well, rest now, then." Lean pushed herself up onto the counter to peer toward the back of the shop and nodded as she dropped back to her feet. "Your table is free. Go get comfortable, and I'll bring your order just as soon as I get the coffee made. I'm guessing your meetings start around your usual ten o'clock?" When Mallory nodded, she added, "Good. So no work for the next forty minutes. Play on your phone, stare at the wall, grab a magazine from the stack on the fireplace hearth, whatever. But just let yourself relax and breathe until you really have to start your day."

Mallory ducked her head to hide the shy smile that tugged at her lips. Maybe it was because she spent the majority of her days making one decision after another, but there was something especially freeing about just doing as she was told. "You are a saint, Lena Black," she murmured.

"Bet your ass I am," Lena agreed with a little laugh. "I'll have your order out as soon as I can." She made a shooing motion with her hands. "Go hide from the world for a bit."

"Thank you."

"My pleasure, hot stuff."

Mallory took a deep breath as she turned toward the back of the shop, and slipped her briefcase and violin from her shoulder. She laid them on the chair that faced the wall and pulled her phone from the bag, and sighed as she settled into the chair opposite it that provided a relaxing view of the flickering electric fireplace. The flames were dancing as if it were the middle of winter instead of late August— though the weather outside was particularly dreary for a summer day.

It was almost enough to make her miss the dry and sunny weather of Los Angeles.

She blinked away the melancholy that still threatened to overwhelm her whenever she thought of her old life and forced a small smile when Lena appeared at her side with a white ceramic mug and a matching plate.

"One cappuccino and a freshly baked turtle croissant for the beautiful lady," Lena declared as she set them onto the table.

Mallory shook her head. "You are a terrible flirt; you know that—right?"

Lena shrugged. "Do you want me to stop?"

Mallory huffed a laugh as Lena's husband came out of the back room. "Your wife is flirting with me again," she shared with a smile that came easier and felt far lighter than any that had curled her lips in the last few weeks. God, it was good to be home. "Can I keep her?"

"You're not supposed to tell the usband-hay about the irting-flay," Lena lectured in a mock whisper.

"My apologies, darling," Mallory cooed, patting Lena's hip.

"She's all yours if you really want her," Dmitry laughed.

"Dmitry Petrov!" Lena turned on her husband, her emerald green eyes flashing with mirth. "That's how that fine arse of yours ends up sleeping on the couch."

"Yes, well, you're not snoring out there, so…" Dmitry teased as he danced away from the playful kick she aimed at him, looking so graceful that it wasn't hard to imagine him on stage at the Royal Opera House. He had never risen above the rank of first soloist in his time with the company but, according to Lena, that was more because he'd had the unfortunate luck of dancing during the tenure of two disgustingly talented male principals. He had stayed on with the company for a year after Lena's injury forced her to call it quits, but had decided to hang up his shoes after that. Apparently, it just wasn't the same for him without her there.

Mallory smiled. "Well, if she snores, then I'm afraid I don't want her anymore. I'm too old to not get a good night's sleep."

"You two are awful, and I hate you both," Lena grumbled.

Mallory shared an amused look with Dmitry as she reached out to wrap an arm around Lena's waist and pull her close. "I apologize, darling. I can buy earplugs if I need to."

"At least she loves me," Lena pouted at Dmitry.

He smirked and waggled his eyebrows. "Lucky you."

Lena gasped and was poised to respond when the bell above the door jingled, and the lightheartedness of the moment disappeared as they all looked toward the front of the shop where a woman had just entered. "Right, well, back to the salt mines for me," Lena announced with an exaggerated sigh as she wiped her hands on the narrow black apron tied around her waist. "Dmitry, go bug somebody else." He snapped off a limp salute and laughed as he turned to make his way toward the front counter. "As for you, beautiful—no work until you get to work. Got it?"

"I got it," Mallory assured her with a smile. "Thank you."

Lean winked and nodded as she gave Mallory's shoulder a light squeeze before turning to join her husband at the counter.

Even though she was tempted to watch them for a few minutes longer, Mallory turned her attention to her cappuccino. While she enjoyed her friends' playful dynamic, it was also a painful reminder of how alone she truly was. The last time Lena had caught her watching, she had tried to set her up with a friend of hers, and while Mallory appreciated the thought, the last thing she needed or wanted was to fall into another doomed relationship.

She had her friends and her work, and that was more than enough.

Even if she sometimes found herself wondering if maybe, just maybe, with the right woman, she might be able to find...

She shook her head. Nothing good ever came from letting her mind wander into the realm of what-ifs. She had survived her first season as leader of the LSO well enough, and she was determined to try to actually *enjoy* the coming year. And to do that, she needed to pull her heart out of the clouds and focus on the tangible aspects of her life that brought her joy—like music. And her friends.

That was what all the self-help books she had read while touring had said, anyway.

She dragged the tip of her finger through the foam atop her coffee and wiped it off on the napkin Lena had left behind. Her cappuccino had cooled to the perfect temperature while she had been chatting with Lena and Dmitry. She was convinced that Lena made the best coffee in all of London, and she hummed contentedly under her breath as she set the mug down and reached for her croissant. The turtle croissant looked like heaven on a plate, and after two months of going without, she was quite looking forward to enjoying her favorite treat.

She practically swooned at her first bite, and smiled to herself as she chewed. This was, without a doubt, the absolute best way to start the day.

"Hey, it's you," a sweet southern drawl interrupted her internal reverie.

Mallory looked up at the woman that had spoken and frowned as she hurried to finish chewing. The petite brunette was beautiful—even though her leggings and baggy sweatshirt made her look like a university student that had only just rolled out of bed—and seemed vaguely familiar, though she had no idea where she might have met her before. "I'm sorry?"

"Right. Sorry," the woman apologized. Her smile was kind, if a little hesitant, and Mallory tilted her head to the side as she waited for her to continue. "I saw you in here"—she waved her left hand toward Mallory's table as she hefted the strap of her kit bag higher on her shoulder—"a few months ago, I guess. Anyway, you looked upset," she continued, looking perfectly contrite, as if she somehow knew that Mallory wouldn't appreciate being reminded of her very public moment of weakness.

"I did?" Mallory murmured, her brow furrowing as she tried to recall the interaction the woman was describing.

"Um...a little? You were watching a video or something on your phone?"

Ah. That. Mallory nodded as she remembered how upset she had been when she had first seen the video of Gwen's symphony. She had been unforgivably short with the brunette who had, now that she was recalling the details of the interaction, been perfectly polite in inquiring about her well-being. "I'm so sorry about that. You caught me at a bad time, I'm afraid, and I…"

"No, you were fine," the brunette insisted with a kind smile. "I just…kind of kept wondering if you were okay." She shook her head as she played with the strap of her bag. "But then I didn't see you all summer so I couldn't ask you and, I mean, it's not like I was even *here* a lot, because of work, but I still—"

The woman's rambling was adorable, and Mallory couldn't help but smile as she interrupted to explain, "I was out of the country for most of the summer. I only got back last week."

"Oh." The woman blushed and nodded. "Right. Of course. That makes perfect sense."

The brunette was utterly charming in her awkward sincerity, and Mallory bit the inside of her cheek to keep from chuckling as she extended her hand. "Mallory Collingswood."

And, oh, it was a good thing she was still sitting down because the way the woman's face lit up as she shook her hand set her completely back on her heels. She could not remember the last time someone had smiled so openly at her like that. "Addison Leigh."

Mallory spotted Lena approaching them with a pleased smile curling her lips, looking very much like the cat that had caught the proverbial canary, and motioned toward the empty table beside her own. "I believe Lena is bringing your drink now."

And, okay, it wasn't exactly an invitation to join her, but it would be an unnecessary hassle to move her things from the chair across from her when the tables were close enough that they could comfortably converse without raising their voices.

"Oh. I wouldn't want to intrude…" Addison began.

Mallory chuckled as she refrained from pointing out that Addison had, in fact, already done just that. Though she was surprised to find, given how much she cherished these quiet moments before her day began in full, she didn't mind it at all. "I don't mind, honestly. And, considering Ms. Black here has forbidden me from working"—she shot Lena a playful glare that turned into a fond smile when Lena responded by sticking her tongue out at her—"I wouldn't mind the company. That is," she hastened to add, "assuming that's something you would like as well, of course."

"I would like that," Addison murmured, ducking her head as a soft smile curled her lips. She glanced at Lena as she pulled the chair that was effectively next to Mallory's from its table and shook her head at the way Lena grinned at her.

"You're in early," Lena observed as she set a takeaway cup and a breakfast sandwich in front of Addison.

"God, don't remind me," Addison groaned as she reached for the cup. "Her royal highness has summoned me to the studio before class today because I'm going to be in Kent tomorrow for an outreach thing and she has something she needs to talk to me about that can't wait until this afternoon."

"Any idea what she wants?"

"Nope. All I know is that I am to arrive 'prepared to work,'" she enunciated in a clipped Cambridge accent as she waved her free hand in the air dramatically.

Lena laughed. "Sounds about right."

"Right?" Addison sighed and shook her head.

Mallory looked between the two women. Their easy banter and seemingly abstract comments seemed to be perfectly understood by the other—much like herself and her colleagues at the LSO—and she realized that Addison must be a dancer at The Royal Ballet.

"Hopefully it's just a few more hours," Lena pointed out with a wry look.

Addison sighed and nodded as she rapped her knuckles on the table. "Yeah. Hopefully."

Lena gave her shoulder a light squeeze and smiled at Mallory. "I'll go bug my husband and let you two chat. Mal, remember what I said…"

"No work until I get to work," Mallory intoned, holding her right hand up as if swearing an oath. Her gaze drifted toward Addison, truly seeing her for the first time. She was petite, yes, but there was an undercurrent of strength in her posture, even when relaxed. There was also an unmistakable aura of confidence about her that was utterly enchanting. Maybe it was because she was a dancer, used to using her body as an instrument for her craft under the scrupulous gaze of an audience, but whatever it was, it looked good on her.

"Good girl." Lena winked at her and then, with one last smile, turned back toward the front of the shop where the line at the register had begun to reform.

"She's a handful, isn't she?" Addison mused, smiling fondly at Lena's retreating form.

"She certainly is that," Mallory agreed with a little laugh. She cleared her throat and looked away as she took a sip of her coffee. "How long have you been with The Royal Ballet?"

Addison smiled and leaned back in her chair. "How do you know I'm with The Royal Ballet?"

"Besides the fact that neither you nor Lena were speaking in complete phrases, and yet you understood each other perfectly…"

Addison laughed. "Point taken. This will be my fourth season with the company. How about you? Where do you play?" she asked, pointing at the violin case opposite Mallory.

"Keen eye," Mallory murmured. "This will be my second season with the London Symphony Orchestra."

"Fancy," Addison drawled. She grinned when Mallory laughed, and picked up her sandwich. "I'm sorry, but I'm going to be rude and eat while we talk because I don't want this to get cold. I have a feeling that I'm going to need my calories this morning."

"Go right on ahead." Mallory waved her on and picked up her own croissant.

"What do you do at the LSO?" Addison asked before taking a bite of her breakfast sandwich.

"Some days, it feels like everything," Mallory admitted. She smiled at the way Addison, cheeks puffed out as she chewed, arched a brow and nodded encouragingly for her to elaborate. "I'm the leader of the orchestra." When Addison's brow furrowed, she added, "You Americans call the position the concertmaster." She smiled as Addison's brow smoothed in understanding. "So, you see, I have many responsibilities beyond just showing up and playing."

Addison swallowed and shook her head. "So that's why Lena was telling you 'no work before you get to work.'"

"Or it could have just been Lena being Lena. She does love to boss me around."

"It's not just you," Addison shared, glancing toward the front counter where Lena was tending to a customer.

"Well, now I'm offended," Mallory drawled, feigning hurt. "I thought I was special."

Addison laughed and reached across the narrow gap separating them to give Mallory's arm a light pat. "I'm sure you are incredibly special, Mallory Collingswood."

Mallory was so unused to anyone who wasn't Lena or Will touching her that her breath caught in her throat at the feeling of Addison's fingers curling around her wrist. She looked away as she felt her cheeks begin to warm, and murmured, "That's kind of you to say."

"Yeah, well, that's me. Full of sweet Southern charm," Addison replied with an exaggerated drawl.

Mallory chuckled softly. "That's some accent."

Addison smirked as she replied in the same exaggerated drawl, "Glad you approve, Sugah." She took a deep breath and let it go as she shrugged. "Honestly, I'd probably still sound like that if I hadn't moved to New York when I was a kid."

"Oh, your family moved when you were young?"

"No, they stayed in Georgia. It was just me," Addison explained, her smile sheepish even though shoulders rolled back just a bit, making her look like she was torn between being embarrassed about rehashing her history and proud of it at the same time. "I won a position in The School of American Ballet when I was ten and a half and moved to New York to train just before I turned eleven."

"Did you dance in New York? Professionally, I mean…"

"For a few years. I was promoted from the school to the corps when I was sixteen."

"That seems young," Mallory couldn't help interjecting. She'd been carrying around the label of prodigy since she was barely out of nursery school, but even though she was performing with the LSO and other prominent symphonies around Europe as a guest soloist well before she had even entered her teens, she still finished a full course of studies at the Royal Academy of Music before officially beginning her career and continuing her education elsewhere.

"Oh, it was," Addison agreed with a little laugh. "I felt so out of my league that it was honestly ridiculous, but I learned a lot more dancing in the corps those first couple of years than I would have in school. Anyway, I danced with the NYC Ballet for a couple years, started to make something of a name for myself, and when a position opened up over here, I decided to throw my pointe shoes into the ring and see what happened."

"And the audition went well," Mallory said, no question in her tone. Even though she had no idea how old Addison was, she was obviously still in her early twenties, and if she was beginning her fourth season with The Royal Ballet, there was no other possible outcome to the audition in question.

Addison tipped her head in a small nod. "The audition went very well. They offered me a job, and I packed up all my things and moved to London two weeks before my twentieth birthday." She shrugged. "Anyway, yeah. That's me. How about you?"

"In a way, I guess you could say my career took a similar

approach," Mallory began with a fond smile. She told Addison about becoming a boarder at the Royal Academy of Music when she was nine, briefly touched on a few of her more memorable solos, and then her decision to go to America. She spoke of her time in Chicago, Boston, and Los Angeles—okay, she all but glossed entirely over that final chapter of her life abroad—and was in the middle of telling Addison about how she came to find herself back in London when her phone rang.

She glanced at the screen and sighed. It was Max Cole, the LSO's Music Director. And, while she hated to do it, she gave Addison her most apologetic look as she murmured, "Sorry, but I'm going to need to answer this."

"Nah, go on ahead." Addison waved her off as she sipped at her coffee. She made a face as she tilted the cup and shook her head as she set it back down. "Ugh. It's cold. What time is it?"

Mallory glanced at her watch as she lifted her phone to her ear and groaned. "It's a quarter till ten." Shite. She was going to be late. "Yes, hello Max," she answered the call in her most professional voice as she pushed herself to her feet and began gathering her things. She hated to run on Addison like this, but she hoped she would understand.

"Are you almost here? I need to speak with you about something before the music selection meeting with the Board."

"Barring transportation issues, yes," she lied as she shouldered her bag. If the train was at the underground station when she got down there, it would still be close to half an hour before she got to the Barbican Centre, but it would still be faster than hiring a cab for the trip. "Where would you like to meet?"

"Come to my office when you get here. If we're a little late getting the board meeting started, it will just give them more time to come up with even more complaints about there not being enough Mozart on the calendar," Max replied, sounding almost giddy at the idea of keeping the Board waiting. His devil-may-care approach to music had drawn the Board's ire on more than one occasion, but he was dealing from a position of power as their

ticket sales had only gone up the last couple years when most of the arts were suffering.

"I'll be there as soon as I can," Mallory promised before hanging up. She shook her head as she looked at Addison. "I'm terribly sorry," she apologized as she grabbed her violin and slung the strap over the same shoulder as her purse, "but I completely lost track of time and am going to be late to work."

"Go, go," Addison insisted, waving her off. "Maybe we'll run into each other in here again soon."

"I look forward to it," Mallory murmured.

Addison smiled that wide, beaming smile that once again made Mallory's breath catch in her throat as she replied softly, "Me too."

two

"You're late!"

Mallory glanced around the lobby of the administrative wing of the symphony's main offices, looking for the familiar face that went the teasing voice, and rolled her eyes when she spotted her best friend in the entire world, Will Adrian, smirking at her from one of the chairs in the corner beneath a potted ficus. His black trousers and dark blue shirt were a more masculine version of her own outfit, and his light brown hair was its usual unkempt style that he insisted made him look dashing despite all the times she tried to tell him it only made him look like he didn't know how to use a comb.

Even though she was already running later than expected—there was, of course, some kind of mishap at King's Cross that delayed her train to the Barbican—she still made her way over to where he was sitting. "You think I don't bloody well know that?" She hefted the straps of her briefcase and violin higher on her shoulder once she was close enough to speak in a normal voice. She had been so worried about getting to Max's office as quickly as possible that she honestly hadn't been paying too much attention to her surroundings, and as she glanced over her shoulder at the sound of laughter, she realized the lobby was much busier than it should have been considering the first of their meetings on the day was supposed to have started twenty minutes ago. Never mind the fact that, as the players' representative to the Board, Will should have been in the conference room already. "What are you doing out here?"

"The first meeting's been postponed an hour. I guess something came up that Max needed to take care of." He shrugged. "So, you're good still." He waved at the chair beside him. "Have a seat and catch your breath."

Mallory shook her head. "Unfortunately, I don't have time for that. While I have no idea what's going on, Max wants to speak with me before the meetings. So I'd wager that whatever it is that's holding things up, I'm somehow involved."

"Any idea what's going on?"

"None." She ran a hand through her hair and sighed. "Save me a seat in the conference room. I'll fill you in later."

Will nodded. "Sounds good. You better get going, then."

"Right," she muttered. "Wish me luck."

He grinned. "Break a leg, you sexy beast, you."

She laughed and flipped him off as she turned on her heel and started for the stairs to Max's office, grateful for his knack of always knowing just the right thing to say to lighten her mood. Of course, now that she had nothing to distract her from this break from the schedule for the day, her thoughts returned to trying to figure out just what, exactly, was going on. Nothing Max had said over the phone gave her any kind of clue as to what she would be walking into.

She had been expecting the impromptu meeting to be just the two of them, so the sight of Clara Martin, her favorite of the LSO's two principal guest conductors, leaning against the edge of Max's desk, and Joseph Hayes, the Managing Director of the LSO Board, lounging on the sofa in the small seating area that fronted Max's desk gave her pause. A meeting between herself, Max, and Clara wasn't unusual, but the addition of Joseph Hayes to the mix was enough to make her wonder just what in the hell was going on. She plastered on her most professional smile and knocked lightly on the doorframe, drawing their attention as she swept into the room.

"I apologize for my tardiness. The trains weren't cooperating this morning." She sounded appropriately contrite even as she shot Max a curious look. His answering smile was both apologetic and cryptic, and it set her stomach abuzz with nerves. Had she done something wrong? Was she being fired? Or, worse, demoted? It was only her many years of experience keeping a straight face in front of an audience no matter her nerves that kept her expression from showing just how much this surprise meeting, with the Managing Director in attendance no less, affected her.

"Ah, here's the woman of the hour," Hayes greeted her with a smile as he heaved himself to his feet, grunting a little with the effort. His left hand drifted toward his midsection, where his navy blue blazer curved around his stomach, as he offered her his right. "Ms. Collingswood, it's a pleasure to see you again."

"You, as well, Mr. Hayes," Mallory replied as she shook his hand.

"You were exceptional on tour this summer," Hayes declared as he released his grip and motioned for her to sit.

"Thank you, sir," Mallory murmured, as she slipped her violin and briefcase from her shoulder and lowered herself primly to the edge of one of the chairs that faced the group.

"So, Max, Clara—now that everyone's here, would one of you please explain why it was so imperative that I push the meeting back an hour?" Hayes asked.

Max waved a hand at Clara and pushed himself up so that he was sitting on top of his desk. His lips twitched with a smirk at the small huff of disapproval the move got from Hayes. Though, to be fair, Hayes' disapproval could have also been for his bright blue Cookie Monster socks that were decidedly unprofessional but perfectly Max. "I'm going to let Clara take this one," he said as he leaned back on his hands to listen.

"Ta, Max," Clara drawled, smiling as she ran a hand through her long, dark hair, and Mallory felt some of her panic begin to ease when she turned her smile onto her. Despite technically being her boss, Clara was also a friend, and Mallory was reassured by the knowledge that she didn't seem worried about whatever this meeting was about. "Nina Devereaux over at The Royal Ballet called me yesterday. As you know, I promised to work with the Royal Opera House at least once this season, and she wanted to discuss a ballet that she is looking to produce. Now, I will be the first to admit that everything I know about ballet is drawn from my time conducting at the ROH, so I'm by no means an expert, but she is an uncontested genius in the ballet world, and she proposed an interesting endeavor—if we're willing to help, that is."

"Help how?" Hayes demanded.

Clara turned her sharp brown eyes onto Mallory and gave her a look that was half-apology, half-pleading for her to be heard out. "She would like to borrow Mallory for a new production." She held up a hand to cut off the argument Hayes was so clearly poised to make. "Now, she assured me that she is not looking to, and I quote, 'steal Ms. Collingswood's talent from the LSO,' but she was rather insistent that there is literally nobody else who can fill the role."

Hayes scoffed. "Is she serious?"

While Mallory was slightly offended by his comment, she nevertheless nodded in agreement. The violin was one thing, but the ballet was something completely different. This had to be some kind of elaborate prank.

"Nina doesn't joke around when it comes to her company, so I can assure you that she is quite serious," Clara declared. She had spent close to eight years early in her career conducting at the Royal Opera House, and it was clear that she was still quite fond of the principal ballerina-turned-artistic director. She spared Hayes only the briefest of glances before she looked back at Mallory and continued, "But she also understands that Mal is committed to the LSO and, as such, has sought our permission"—she waved a hand between Max, Hayes, and herself—"to approach her about the role. All she's asking for is a chance to meet with Mallory to pitch this grand vision of hers. If Mallory isn't enticed by the idea, she will accept that and move forward with, and I quote again, 'a less talented violinist who will surely force the ballet to be shelved entirely.'"

Max chuckled. "She sure has a way with words, that one."

"And an impeccable eye," Clara agreed as she arched a brow at Mallory.

Mallory blinked as she tried to wrap her head around this whole thing. It was flattering that the artistic director for The Royal Ballet would ask for her personally, but it didn't make any sense.

"So you want the Board's blessing for this meeting?" Hayes surmised.

"Max and I wanted to at least sound you off on it. If Mallory agrees, we will, of course, go to the Board for approval."

Hayes turned to Max. "As Music Director, you support this?"

Max shrugged. "If Mallory is interested in the project, I have no problem with it as long as it doesn't conflict with any major LSO performances. I don't know Nina Devereaux as well as Clara does"— he shot Clara a look that was a little too smug and earned him a rather impressive glare in return—"but her reputation is stellar, and her productions attract a lot of critical attention. I want to see the details first, of course, but offhand, I have to say that a collaboration between our companies, with the implication that only we can supply Mal's caliber of talent…"

"Yes, well…" Hayes mused, nodding slowly. "It would be excellent PR for the LSO."

"But I'm not a dancer," Mallory pointed out, staring imploringly at Clara.

"She wants you for your skill with the violin," Clara assured her with a little laugh, "and seems to feel that she can teach you to handle whatever movement the role would require well enough."

"Well, it certainly sounds like it wouldn't hurt to at least hear her proposal," Hayes said, slapping his hands on his knees for emphasis.

"Let's mention it during the meeting, Max, but provided she understands that Ms. Collingswood's obligations to the LSO come first, I see no reason why the Board of Directors would have an issue with this if you're all on-board with the whole thing."

Mallory bit the inside of her cheek as she looked from Max to Hayes to Clara, who were all staring at her, waiting for her decision. Part of her wanted to tell them exactly where they could shove this whole crazy idea—she had not spent her entire life honing her skills to be made a fool of—but there was also something intriguing about it all as well. Maybe it was because she spent her mornings at Higher Ground, surrounded by stunning photographs of dancers on stage at the Royal Opera House, or perhaps it was just because she was flattered that Nina Devereaux had called to ask about her, but whatever the case, she was interested enough to at least meet with the renowned artistic director. "So long as I'm under no obligation to accept her proposal," Mallory started, and she waited until she had nods of agreement from them before she continued, "I will meet with Ms. Devereaux to hear what she has to say."

"Excellent," Joseph Hayes declared as he pushed himself to his feet. "Well, now that that's settled, I'm going to go get a cup of coffee before the meeting starts." He checked his watch. "I'll see you in the conference room in fifteen minutes."

"See you then," Max confirmed.

Clara smiled at Mallory as Hayes made his way toward the door, muttering something about inmates running the asylum. "Thank you, Mal. Nina will meet you at Neo at five tonight."

Mallory huffed a laugh and shook her head. "You were that certain I'd agree?"

She shrugged. "Not especially. But she insisted on setting a time in case you did."

"I'm surprised you didn't just bring her here to make the pitch herself," Mallory mused as she got to her feet.

"Nina can be very forceful when she has an idea, but she didn't want to ambush you. And before you ask, she didn't give me much more than the broadest idea of what she has planned. She was quite adamant that if you were to agree to the role that it would be of your own volition and not because you felt pressured to accept it."

Mallory smiled, suddenly feeling much more comfortable with her decision to meet with Nina Devereaux.

"Right, well," Max declared as he pulled on his blazer, "I think coffee sounds like an ace idea." He smiled at Mallory and Clara. "Don't rush out of here on my account. I'll see you ladies down there."

"We won't," Clara assured him with a smile. "Thanks for having my back on this."

"Always." He winked and then, whistling softly under his breath, gathered his leather folio and strolled out of the room.

"Sorry to have cornered you with Hayes like that," Clara spoke up once they were alone. "Max and I didn't want to tell him why we wanted the morning meetings pushed back until we'd spoken to you in case it wasn't something you were interested in but, Hayes being Hayes, he demanded he be a part of 'whatever was so important that *his* meetings needed to be postponed.'"

Mallory shook her head. "Not surprised, really. He likes to be the one in control of everything."

"Typical public school white male," Clara agreed wryly. "But I want to make sure that you know you're under no obligation to accept the role. I know last year was rough for you, and if you're on the fence about it or just don't want to deal with the extra stress or whatever, tell her no—okay? Your mental health and well-being are more important than any artistic production."

"I understand," Mallory assured her. "Thank you."

"Thank you for agreeing to meet with her," Clara countered as she gathered her leather portfolio notebook from the desk and waved it toward the door before tucking it under her arm so she could use both her hands to secure the buttons on her black blazer. "I haven't heard her this excited about a project in a long, long time."

Mallory glanced down at Clara as she took the hint and began making her way toward the door. "You're friends with her, aren't you?"

"Nina?" Clara asked.

"No, the Queen," Mallory teased with a laugh as she waved goodbye to Leanne, Max's secretary. "Yes, Nina. You've mentioned her a few times. You were close when you worked over there, weren't you?"

"We were," Clara murmured, a soft, almost wistful look crossing her face. She sighed as they turned toward the conference room at the end of the corridor where there was a small crowd milling about the door. "She's...special. Definitely not the kind of woman you meet every day. Or even every decade." She chuckled. "And she's also brash and demanding and doesn't mince words at all, but I swear that woman has the most refined eye for talent that I have ever seen in my life. If things do work out, this could be quite an opportunity for you, too."

Mallory smiled. "Should I call you tonight, once I've met with her?"

"I would greatly appreciate that, yes," Clara replied in a low voice as the crowd parted for them and they poured into the rapidly filling conference room. Being on the taller side of average for a woman, Mallory was always struck by the way Clara—at only five foot three—always managed to command a room without a word. It was hard enough being a half-Singaporean woman in a profession dominated by white men without the added disadvantage of being so petite, but Mallory had never seen *anyone* challenge Clara's authority. It was honestly beyond impressive given the size of the egos that filtered through the hall, and she and Will often joked about getting Clara a shirt with Shakespeare's famous line, "though she be but little, she is fierce," printed on it.

"Of course." Mallory spotted Will waving at her from the corner of the room furthest from where the board and Clara would sit and lifted a hand to let him know she saw him. "Is there anything else?"

"There always is," Clara sighed. "But, for now, you should

absolutely go hide in the corner with Will." She rubbed a hand over the back of her neck. "Lord knows I'd love to join you lot back there, but I've got to go sit by Max and Thad," she muttered, waving toward the front of the room where Max and the LSO's other principal guest conductor were holding court with a handful of board members.

Mallory laughed. "Sorry, Clara. No kids' table for you."

"Oh, bollocks," she grumbled, shooting her a playful smirk as she made her way toward the front of the room.

"So…?" Will prompted as soon as she'd taken her seat beside him.

Even though everyone in the room seemed to be engaged in their own conversation, she still leaned closer to him as she shared in a low tone, "The artistic director for The Royal Ballet wants to meet with me about a possible collaboration."

His eyes widened much the same way she was sure her own had at the news. "Seriously?"

She nodded. "Yeah."

"Damn," he murmured.

"Exactly."

"Do they know you can't dance for shit?"

She elbowed him in the side. "Oh, shut up." She was certainly no Ginger Rogers, but she had at least a modicum of rhythm.

"Well, I can't wait to hear what all that leads to, then." He smirked and bumped their knees together. "I was surprised you were late this morning. You're usually at least half an hour early. Is everything okay?"

"Everything is fine. I just lost track of time."

"And what, pray tell, caused you to lose track of time like that?"

She sighed, knowing that he would only become more insistent if she tried to avoid the topic altogether. "If you must know, I was talking with a woman at Higher Ground."

"Nicely done, mate!" He grinned.

She huffed a laugh. "Thank you."

"Does the beautiful woman have a name?"

"How do you know she's beautiful?" Mallory challenged. She

sighed at the way he just shook his head and stared at her, clearly intent on waiting her out, and muttered, "If you really must know, it's Addison."

"Pretty."

"Yes, she is," Mallory agreed quietly, more to herself than him.

Will must have heard anyway, because he pumped his fist and cheered, "I knew it!" He grimaced as a handful of people in front of them turned to see what the commotion was about. "Sorry," he apologized, ducking his head and holding a hand up for emphasis.

"I swear, I can't take you anywhere," Mallory muttered.

Once their audience had turned back toward the front of the room where Joseph Hayes was now trying to get everyone's attention to start the meeting, Will whispered, "You gonna see her again?"

"I have no idea," Mallory answered just as softly. "Besides, what does it matter?"

"You were late because you were talking to her. You're never late. Ergo, this Addison must be something special."

"You're ridiculous," Mallory scoffed, even as her lips curled in a small smile.

"Maybe," he agreed as he slumped in his seat, trying to make himself comfortable. "But you're smiling. And you look like you mean it for a change."

She shook her head. "I'm just glad to be back."

"Yeah," he grumbled as three old guys at the front of the room started arguing about whatever the first motion on the day was. "Aren't we all. Right lovely party, this is…"

three

Mallory's eyes swept over the dimly lit, upscale cocktail bar as the door to the underground lounge closed behind her. A large bar anchored the center of the space, rimmed by comfortable-looking tufted chairs, while long leather benches and tables and chairs lined the perimeter. Soft light was cast upward against the natural rock that lined the walls, creating a warm and elegant ambiance. She had never been to Neo before but, as she looked around, she made a note to visit again soon with Will and his wife Siobhan and some of her other friends from the LSO.

Goodness knows they needed a better place to go to after their performances than the corner pub they usually frequented, where pints were spilled with alarming regularity and they had to all but shout to be heard.

Thanks to a bit of Googling during her lunch break, she was able to spot Nina Devereaux almost immediately, sitting at a secluded corner table, toying with the stem of a martini glass as she scrolled through her phone. Despite the fact that Devereaux had asked for her by name, she hadn't wanted to presume that she would be recognized on sight, and she had to admit that the professional headshot on Nina's Wikipedia page—while stunning—paled in comparison to the woman in front of her now. Even though she had stepped away from the stage close to fifteen years earlier, Nina Devereaux exuded all the poise and confidence Mallory would expect from a former principal ballerina. Her arms and legs held the faintest hint of a tan and were perfectly toned, and her shoulder-length black hair caught the light in a way that made it seem to glow. Her black dress was classically cut, dipping low enough at the throat to reveal the sharp line of chiseled collarbones while remaining elegant and tasteful, and it hugged her body and draped around her thighs in a way that commanded everyone around her to look.

Judging by the barely-there quirk to her lips, she knew it, too.

Mallory toyed with the aluminum clasp at the base of her violin case as she started across the bar toward Devereaux, and wished she had worn something dressier than slacks and a blouse to work today. Although, she thought as she approached her table, she had a feeling she would have felt entirely inadequate next to her even in her fanciest blacks.

Nina Devereaux looked up from her phone just as she approached, and she smiled as she set the phone face-down on the table and pushed herself to her feet. "Ms. Collingswood." She held out her hand. "Thank you for agreeing to meet with me."

"Of course," Mallory demurred as she shook her hand. There was no missing the once-over she was given before her hand was released, and she smiled politely as she slipped her briefcase and violin from her shoulder. "Though I'll confess that I am not quite sure why you seem to feel so strongly that I am the person you need for your project."

Devereaux nodded as she gracefully retook her seat. "I'm well aware that this is a rather unconventional request," she said as she turned just enough to comfortably cross her right leg over her left, "but what I'm trying to do is anything but conventional."

"That was the impression Clara gave me, as well," Mallory confirmed as she settled into the chair opposite her. "Do you mind?" she asked as she motioned toward the menu sitting in the middle of the table.

"No. By all means." Devereaux waved for her to go ahead with her left hand as she picked up her drink with her right.

Mallory hummed her thanks as she opened the long, thin leather-bound book that was heavy on the cocktails and light on the food choices. She was keenly aware of sharp eyes watching her as she perused the menu, the weight of her gaze so intense that she knew there was very little—if anything—that the woman did not notice.

A server in black slacks and a silk black button-down blouse appeared at her shoulder the moment she set the menu back onto the table. "Are you ready to order?"

Mallory nodded. "I'll go with the rusty nail."

"Excellent choice." The server turned her attention to Devereaux and nodded toward her half-empty glass. "Can I bring you another?"

Devereaux shook her head. "Not quite yet."

"Of course. Can I get any appetizers for you ladies?"

Mallory was actually halfway to starving but, since she had no idea exactly how long this meeting was going to last, she thought better of speaking up about it.

Devereaux tapped a finger on the tabletop thoughtfully and nodded. "The vegetarian platter."

"To share?"

Mallory nodded when Devereaux looked to her with an arched brow.

"Please," Devereaux said, the single word both a confirmation and a dismissal.

"I'll be back shortly with your drink," the server murmured, ducking her head in a small bow as she turned toward the bar.

"Was the board meeting this morning as dull as Clara dreaded it might be?" Devereaux asked conversationally once they were alone.

Mallory chuckled. "I'm sure she would say that it was, yes."

"She always did hate the business side of the arts," Devereaux murmured fondly. "Though, I can hardly blame her. It's so much easier to go out on stage and perform than it is to feign interest in numbers and politicking and making sure everyone feels like their ass has been sufficiently kissed."

Mallory bit her lip to keep from laughing but, judging by the way Devereaux smirked around the rim of her martini glass, her reaction was exactly what the artistic director had been going for. Their server reappeared just then to set a lowball glass in front of Mallory before quickly and efficiently making herself scarce again.

Now that Mallory had a drink as well, Devereaux seemed to take that as her cue to get down to business, because she uncrossed her legs and sat up just that little bit straighter. "I don't want to bore you by repeating details you already know, so may I ask what Clara told you about my project?"

Mallory shrugged and reached for her glass, noting the way the lounge's lighting highlighted the golden-ochre color of the drink, making it look both darker and lighter than the mix usually appeared. "Honestly, very little beyond the fact that you inquired about me for the production."

Devereaux smiled, and it wasn't hard to see how pleased she was that Clara had left it to her to present the ballet herself. "What do you know of ballet?"

"My mother put me in the usual childhood dance classes before I was accepted at the Academy, but I essentially know nothing about ballet," Mallory confessed. "Which is why I don't—"

Devereaux arched a brow in playful challenge. "Have you lost any of that remarkable talent of yours with the violin over the summer holiday?"

Mallory huffed a laugh and shook her head. "No."

"Then you have all the innate skills I require. The rest of what I need from you can be taught."

"While I appreciate your confidence, won't your music director have a problem with you bringing someone in from outside your organization for this?"

"I don't consult the music director on my casting decisions,"

Devereaux scoffed. "Nevertheless, I imagine Henry will find some insult in the decision, especially if Clara agrees to conduct one of the performances." She paused and leveled Mallory with a pointed look. "Let's not pretend to ignore the obvious, Ms. Collingswood. You are the very best in the world at what you do, and though you might not be a dancer, you are the only person who can make this vision of mine come to life. I would rather shelve the idea altogether than produce a substandard version of my ballet."

There was a fierceness in Devereaux's gaze that said she wasn't exaggerating, and Mallory nodded, her interest sufficiently piqued by Devereaux's conviction that she was the right choice. "I'm flattered. And curious as to how, exactly, I fit into this grand vision of yours."

"You and your music will be integral to it," Devereaux murmured thoughtfully, almost more to herself than to Mallory as she twirled the stem of her glass between her thumb and index finger. "You and the principal I have in mind for the project will create a most striking pair," she said in a stronger voice.

"And I will be playing the violin?"

"Yes. And doing a bit of dancing"—she waved a hand dismissively—"though the bulk of that work will fall to your partner. You'll be mostly…moving with them. A dip here, a spin there, letting them use you like a living barre as the dance cycles from solo to adagio and back again. It isn't until the pas de deux at the very end that you'll be fully dancing with your partner."

Mallory tried to picture what Devereaux was describing. "Could you describe the ballet a bit more?"

Devereaux nodded. "*Evolution* will be presented in two parts; though, in all actuality, it will be a presentation of two entirely different ballets. The first will be a traditional ballet in every definition of the word. Tutus and tights and romanticized shirts for the men. Hair pulled back in pristine buns. A simple story that relies heavily on the corps with a handful of short solos and a single, relatively brief pas de deux. It's the ballet you picture when you hear the word 'ballet.' It will be beautiful and evocative and leave all the uptight traditionalists in the seats clasping their pearls and sighing wistfully about how much they love ballet."

Mallory chuckled. They had a few regulars at the LSO that perfectly matched that description.

"The second part—your part—will be a perfect evolution of the first half of the ballet. And ballet in general. Flowing, lightweight dresses instead of tutus, a more modern edge to the music, the movement, though nothing so gauche as truly 'modern' dance, updated. Faster. A little bit sharper, a little less steeped in the traditional *de rigueur*. It will be a glimpse of ballet as it can be that will leave even the staunchest classicist in awe and on their feet at the final curtain, applauding until their hands literally sting from the effort of it all."

"And you honestly believe that I have the skills to help pull that off?" Mallory asked.

"We wouldn't be here if I didn't," Devereaux answered, her gaze strong and unflinching.

The server returned with a platter of grilled and roasted mixed vegetables, slices of ciabatta, and what looked like a traditional olive oil and balsamic vinegar dip. Smaller, oblong plates and silverware wrapped in black cloth napkins followed, and she smiled politely at their murmured thanks as she backed away.

"Please, help yourself." Devereaux motioned toward the plate between them as she unrolled her silverware and laid her napkin over her lap.

Mallory did the same as she asked, "So what, may I ask, does this thoroughly modern ballet entail?"

Devereaux spooned a mixture of veggies onto her plate, completely ignoring the bread that had been served alongside them. "Each half of the ballet will run somewhere between forty and forty-five minutes. It depends on how things look once I get everyone into the studio for rehearsals next week when the season starts. You don't need to concern yourself with the first part, but the vision the second half is

38

based around is at once simple and striking—just you and my most talented principal on a stage blanketed by the faintest wisps of smoke, moving together in a way that highlights both of your talents in the most involved pas de deux the ballet world has ever seen. Imagine, if you will," Devereaux murmured, a small smile curling her lips as an inspired twinkle flickered in her dark eyes, "the two of you moving together as you play—gliding, spinning, pausing...her movements so perfectly attuned not just to yourself but also your music that you appear to be two halves of a whole."

Mallory arched a brow in surprise at the feminine pronoun but did not dare interrupt. Though Devereaux had said the ballet would be modern, a pas de deux between two women was a step or six further along that scale than she had imagined.

"If you're the type that needs a story behind the dance," Devereaux continued with a small shrug and a dismissive swish of her hand, "you can think of it as a dance between an artist and her muse—a physical representation of not just inspiration, but also creation."

Mallory nodded. "It sounds intriguing."

"Yes," Devereaux hummed. She cleared her throat and blinked, her expression losing the softness that had made her appear almost enthralled by the very idea she was presenting. "It is also incredibly ambitious, in that you would need to perform the entire thing from memory. And with the exception of the *entrée* where the corps sets the scene, you will be on stage for the entire ballet, drawing the audience in with your music. The dance will be beautiful and evocative, but there is no *Evolution* without you and your violin. Ballet and music have always been intertwined, but it is this marriage of the two mediums on stage that will make this a groundbreaking performance."

"Have you chosen the music?" Mallory asked, getting to what she saw as the heart of the matter. It was, after all, why she was meeting with Devereaux in the first place

"It will be a collection of pieces by Katja Halonen. Not a full ballet score, of course, because she tends to work in shorter pieces, but it should be—"

"Incredible," Mallory murmured as a frisson of excitement ran through her. Halonen was on her way to becoming one of the biggest names in modern classical composing, and she had never had the opportunity to perform the Finnish genius' work.

"Exactly." Devereaux grinned. "That's also why I'd like Clara to conduct at least one performance. She's fantastic with modern composers."

"Will the orchestra be accompanying me, or will the entire thing be a true solo?"

"Yes." Devereaux smiled, clearly responding to both parts of her question. "The orchestra will accompany you for most of the ballet, but even when they are providing some depth to what you are doing on stage, you will still be the one doing the heavy lifting. Especially during the pas de deux. I'm not going to lie to you, Ms. Collingswood, what I'm envisioning will be no easy task to pull off, but if we do..." She sighed and shook her head. "It will be a performance people will be talking about for the remainder of our careers. Any more questions?"

Mallory leaned back in her chair as she mentally ran through everything she had just learned of Devereaux's plan. "Assuming I agree to this, will you be able to work around my obligations to the LSO?"

"Of course. As I told Clara, I have no desire to steal you from them. We should be able to find a rehearsal schedule that is amenable to all parties involved. Clara seemed to imply that afternoons would work best with your schedule there?"

Mallory nodded. In the past, she had filled the time between morning rehearsal and evening performances with recording work for musical scores for films, television, and video games, but if she decided to take the role Nina was offering, it wouldn't be difficult to substitute ballet rehearsals for the contract work in her schedule. "Afternoons are best for me, yes. Though, depending on my performance schedule with the LSO, that could change."

"Perfectly understandable. That won't be a problem," Devereaux assured her. "I'm envisioning a run of four performances spread through the back half of the season—from January through June. Nothing is set in stone yet, of course, but that would translate to roughly six-to-eight-weeks between performances. This will lessen the impact on each of our respective institutions' regular schedules while simultaneously keeping interest high as there will not be a performance every week. People want what they can't have, after all, and doing a short run spread over several months should drive up ticket sales."

Mallory took a deep breath and let it go slowly. She was interested, of course, there was no way to not be after what she had just heard, but the project was daunting. Not just in terms of the music she would be required to perform—which was, in and of itself, a formidable task— but combined with having to actually dance... It would be the most challenging project any musician had ever undertaken. And committing to something like that required more than a few minutes' consideration. "When do you need an answer?"

Devereaux picked up her glass. "Within the week? I understand that this is something you will need to think about. But I also think I know of a way to help make your decision a little bit easier."

"How so?" Mallory asked as she reached for her drink.

Devereaux smiled, an almost predatory gleam settling in her eyes as she leaned forward. "Come by Covent Garden tomorrow, Ms. Collingswood. Let me *show* you what we could do together."

Mallory took a sip of her drink and nodded as she set the glass back down. She was intrigued by the project, and she didn't see a reason to pretend otherwise. "I have a meeting at ten tomorrow morning with my section leads to go over the music selections for the beginning of the season, but I can do something in the afternoon."

"Say...half-past three, then?"

"Sure," Mallory agreed. She had planned to spend the afternoon trying to plow through the small mountain of work she needed to do to get ready for the LSO season, but if the meeting with her section leaders went as quickly as she hoped it might, she would still have a few hours to herself before she needed to be at the Royal Opera House. She much preferred to work at home but, she figured, it would probably do her good to be seen around the Barbican before the season began, anyway.

"Excellent. Do you know how to find our stage door?"

Mallory shook her head. "I'm guessing it isn't on Bow…"

"No, it's not. It's on Floral, not far at all from the underground entrance. It's under the bridge that connects us to the school next door and is clearly marked, so you really can't miss it."

Mallory nodded as she fixed the location Devereaux was describing onto her mental map of the area. "Perfect."

four

The stage door to the Royal Opera House was exactly where Devereaux had told Mallory it would be, and she glanced at her watch as she reached for the handle on the unassuming metal and glass door tucked into a shallow alcove off Floral Street. The back entrance to the theatre was only a few minutes' walk from the Covent Garden underground station, and she filed that information away for later in case she actually ended up accepting Devereaux's offer.

There was a small office just inside the entry, with a wall of wooden mail cubbies that ran along the length of the space, and a television mounted near the ceiling toward the furthest corner that displayed running security footage of everyone who entered the building. The walls were a soft off-white, the linoleum a gleaming industrial gray, and there was a small black sofa pushed up against the wall opposite the doors. It was not unlike any of the other artists' entrances she had used during her life—though she was willing to wager that this one saw far more traffic from fans after performances than the ones at the symphony—and the nerves she had been pretending didn't exist all morning calmed at the familiarity of these unfamiliar surroundings.

She took a deep breath as she schooled her expression to one of professional expectation, and made her way toward an opening in the windows. A brunette in a cute summer dress noticed her approach, and she smiled politely as the woman made her way over toward her.

"May I help you?"

"Yes, hello. I'm Mallory Collingswood. Nina Devereaux should be expecting me."

"Right, I remember seeing something about that," she murmured as she picked up a clipboard. "Collingswood, you said?"

"Yes."

"Thank you, Yvette, but I've got her," a new voice called out, and Mallory instinctively reached for the strap of her violin case. It was something of a nervous tic, a subtle way to ground herself in an unfamiliar situation, and she bit the inside of her cheek as she turned to face the new arrival. The woman appeared to be in her late twenties, with dark red hair that draped flatteringly around her shoulders. Her impeccable makeup, black pencil skirt, jade green blouse, and four-inch black heels looked like they had all been pulled directly from the pages of a fashion magazine, and she smiled warmly as she offered Mallory her hand. "Serena Bowers. I'm Nina's assistant."

"Pleasure," Mallory murmured as she shook her hand.

"Right, well, Nina is just finishing up a call at the moment, so she asked me to come collect you and bring you up to Fonteyn Studio, so you weren't kept waiting." Serena motioned toward the hallway behind her. "Shall we?"

Mallory nodded. "After you."

"You'll enter through the stage door every day," Serena explained as she began leading the way along a narrow hallway that eventually sloped into a slight decline to take them below street level.

"Right," Mallory murmured as she looked at the framed photographs on the wall. They were strikingly similar in lighting and composition to the ones at Higher Ground which, she figured, made sense given Lena's former profession.

"We'll take the lift up to the rehearsal studio," Serena explained as she pushed her way through a set of swinging doors to a more utilitarian section of the theatre and made her way toward a set of lifts with gleaming steel doors.

Mallory nodded as she followed Serena into the lift and made her way to the back of the car. Once the doors closed, she had nothing to distract her, and she bit the inside of her lip as she waited for the lift to reach the fourth floor.

"All of our rehearsal studios are on this level," Serena shared as she turned left out of the lift. The hallway was wide and empty—a rare moment of tranquility that was sure to be lost once the season began in earnest the following week. She led them past the first empty studio and around a corner and, after passing three more closed doors, said, "Here we are." She waved demonstratively at a set of white doors painted to match the corridor that had narrow windows running the length of them near the handles. "Fonteyn is one of the smaller studios that we usually utilize for solos and pairs rehearsals," she shared as she pulled the door open and motioned for Mallory to go on ahead of her.

"Wow," Mallory breathed as she took in the space. The first thing she noticed was the room's high ceiling and the absolutely stunning skylight that took up the majority of it, filling the room with as much natural light as possible. Sconces were set above the mirrors that lined every wall of the studio—no doubt to compensate for London's typically overcast weather—and she was surprised to find that the floor was a pale gray linoleum instead of wood. An upright piano occupied the corner of the room furthest from the door, making her wonder if live music was really a standard part of the ballet company's rehearsals.

"The floor is sprung," Serena explained as she gave a small jump, which was impressive given her heels, "so you will notice a bit of a bounce to it, but it's more to cushion the impact from jumps and save our dancers' joints than to propel anyone into the air."

"Right…" Mallory was in the middle of saying when the door to the studio opened, drawing both of their attention. Her eyebrows lifted in surprise as she watched Nina Devereaux glide into the room. She hadn't really known what to expect from this meeting, but it certainly wasn't to see Devereaux in a leotard and track pants with a pair of black ballet slippers on her feet. Between the clothes and the way she had pinned her hair back just so, to keep the shorter strands from falling into her face, she looked like she was prepared to take the Covent Garden stage that night and set the world on fire with her brilliance.

"I'm sorry for keeping you waiting," Devereaux apologized as she strode across the studio to a small sound system. "Please, feel free to set your things anywhere beneath the barres," she continued as she began fiddling with the dials.

"Do I need my violin?" Mallory asked as she made her way toward the side wall.

"Not yet." Devereaux nodded once to herself as the distinctive pop of speakers turning on echoed from the four corners of the room and spun the small remote that Mallory guessed worked the sound system in her hand as she turned toward her. "I believe I promised you something of a demonstration, did I not?"

Mallory nodded. She set her things on the floor against the nearest wall and nudged them beneath the barre. "Where should I...?" Her voice trailed off as she looked around, unsure as to what was expected of her. Was she supposed to take part in this demonstration, or just stay out of the way and watch?

"There is fine. I want you to get an idea of the bigger picture, so we'll adjust to you." Devereaux smiled and looked at Serena. "Could you take a position like we discussed earlier and pretend to be Ms. Collingswood?" When Serena nodded and bent to pull off her heels and set them aside, she turned her attention back to Mallory. "I had hoped my principal you would be paired with would be back by now, but I'm afraid you'll have to settle for me," she said with a playful, self-deprecating sigh.

Mallory chuckled and dipped her head in a small nod. She had looked into Nina's career a bit more after their meeting the night before, and she had no doubt that there were hundreds of ballet aficionados who would give their right arm to see the Queen of London Ballet dance again.

Her response seemed to please Devereaux, because she winked and asked, "Shall we?"

Mallory waved her right arm as if to say, *The floor is yours.*

Devereaux used the remote to turn on the music, and Mallory leaned back against the barre as she watched her direct her assistant with a look and a small wave of her hand. Her steps matched the deep, throaty notes of the violin that cascaded over the room, and it wasn't hard at all to imagine her commanding the main stage at the Royal Opera House. Everything from the lift of her chin to the set of her shoulders and the outturn of her feet was regal, poised, and almost otherworldly, and Mallory found herself holding her breath as she stopped behind Serena.

The tempo of the music shifted to just below a full allegro, drums and woodwinds taking the focus off the violin yet still allowing it to shine. Devereaux's chest lifted with a breath, and then she began to *dance.* Her left hand stroked the length of Serena's arm that was extended away from her body, fingers lightly curled around the invisible neck of a violin, her shoulders and hips moving in opposite directions as she became the human embodiment of the melody.

Even if she hadn't done any research into Devereaux's career and had walked into the room knowing absolutely nothing about the woman, she would have known, just by watching the way she moved now, that she was in the presence of greatness.

It was so, so easy to be swept into the music and the movement, her eyes and ears taking everything in at once. Devereaux's hand curled around Serena's as she pushed up onto the ball of her left foot, her right leg lifting behind her. Serena, who had been standing on flat feet that were about hip's width apart moved then, joining the dance as she slid her right foot behind herself, initiating a turn for both Devereaux and herself as the music slowed and deepened.

Mallory's jaw dropped as she imagined what just that one turn would look like on stage, with an actual violinist playing and a ballerina on pointe—because she had no doubt that the dancer would absolutely be on her toes for this—being led into the turn.

It would be fucking incredible.

They made a full circle before Devereaux's heel dropped, and then leaned forward, their left arms reaching away from their bodies in a strong line from their shoulders as Devereaux's right hand found Serena's back shoulder. She popped up onto her right foot in a way that suggested the dancer would, once again, be on pointe, her weight shifting with a slow roll of her hips and shoulders to guide her upright.

The dance continued, Serena supporting Devereaux through a series of turns and holds and pauses exquisitely timed to the music. Mallory was reassured to see that, in this preview, at least, there did not seem to be anything too complicated required of her stand-in. It would be a step beyond her comfort zone to be so animated while playing, as she usually moved just enough to cue the orchestra to follow but, with enough practice, she knew that she could do it.

And, as her eyes traced the shapes and lines Devereaux and Serena were creating together, she found herself eagerly anticipating the opportunity to do something like it herself. This was an entirely sublime fusion of art forms, dance and music married in a way to enchant both the eyes and the ears, the heart and the mind, and she wanted in on it as much as she had wanted anything in her life.

The movement in front of her slowed as the pair reached what must have been the end of the prepared demonstration, Serena's shoulders relaxing as her arms fell to her sides and Devereaux spun away from her to level a pleased smile in Mallory's direction.

"There will be no lifts, obviously," Devereaux said as she pulled the stereo remote from her pocket and turned off the music. "And there will be sections where you two will be moving separately, but the majority of the time you will be together. It's all about the lines, you see, and as your hands will be occupied with your violin, it will fall to the other parts of your body—your shoulders, hips, elbows—to support the dancer." She set her hands on her hips. "What do you think?"

"That looked amazing," Mallory replied honestly.

"Do you envision any issues with the idea I'm presenting here? I will be the first to admit that I know very little about the violin beyond how to dance to it."

Mallory pursed her lips as she considered the question, appreciating the opportunity to offer her opinion and grateful that—so far, at least—this project seemed like it would be a true collaboration. "The bowing will need to be adjusted to the dancer's position so that she's not getting stabbed in the face. The holds off the support arm—the one holding the neck of the violin—could also be difficult depending on where they land in the music, but otherwise, it's absolutely do-able."

"And, if we incorporate those changes and remove any other obstacle that might hinder you…?" Devereaux arched a brow, the left side of her lips quirking with the beginning of a smile.

"I think I would be a bloody idiot to turn this opportunity down," Mallory admitted with a little laugh.

"I think so, too," Devereaux agreed with a triumphant smirk.

"And you're sure you can work around my LSO obligations?"

"There is very little I'm not willing to do to see this ballet make it to the stage." Devereaux looked at Serena. "Did Thierry bring up that contract I asked him to draft yet?"

Serena nodded. "It's on your desk."

"Excellent." Devereaux turned back to Mallory. "Shall we head down to my office, then, to discuss the finer details of the project?"

"Of course," Mallory agreed as she bent to gather her things.

Devereaux's office was on the floor below the rehearsal studios. It was large and airy, with oversized windows and soft white walls that amplified the natural light. Mallory took a seat at one of the upholstered armchairs that faced the expansive mahogany desk that was littered with paperwork as Devereaux made herself comfortable in the leather executive chair opposite her.

"Now, where…" Devereaux murmured as she shuffled through the papers on her desk, *ah-ha*-ing softly when she found what she was looking for. "I know we didn't discuss specifics with regard to salary and whatnot, but"—she handed Mallory the folder—"you can take a look at this, and we can go from there."

Mallory nodded as she accepted the folder and obligingly opened to the top page. It was a fairly standard contract, far more straightforward than the one she had signed with the symphony a year before. The salary compensation was in the final paragraph, and she arched a brow in surprise when she saw the number. Not that she needed the money, really, she had negotiated a more than generous salary when she had signed with the LSO the year before, but the offer she was looking at seemed painfully low given the amount of work she was sure the project would require.

"I'm afraid we don't have the budget you're used to at the symphony," Devereaux spoke up apologetically. "But that is comparable to what a dancer in our corps makes in a season. And, given the cuts we've had to take on for the year, this is, unfortunately, the best offer I can make you."

Mallory blinked as she looked up at her. Granted, she was the leader of one of the preeminent symphonies in the world, but even first-year second-violins made at least three times this amount. It was clear by the look on Devereaux's face that she was telling the truth, and Mallory shook her head as she looked down at the paper. "They must love dancing."

"More than life, most of the time," Devereaux confirmed softly.

"This is only for rehearsal time and the performances that we talked about? Then the money isn't an issue for me," Mallory said, hopefully putting what seemed to be Devereaux's biggest concern to rest. She nodded when Devereaux's shoulders relaxed ever-so-slightly in relief and pulled her briefcase onto her lap. The page she was looking for was pinned safely between her tablet and binder of sheet music, and she smiled as she offered it to her. "I printed out a summary of my LSO rehearsal schedule."

Devereaux picked up a pair of black-framed glasses and slipped them on as she looked at the paper. "You're dark on Tuesday? How odd…"

"In a way," Mallory agreed. Most theatre-type companies were dark on Monday. "But working Monday gives us a chance to go over our performances from the weekend while they're still fresh."

Devereaux nodded. "No. No. This is great. Sunday is the only day of the week we don't do class, so it won't impact our schedule here at all," she muttered as she plucked a paper from her desk. Her eyes moved quickly over the page, and she smiled as she slipped it behind Mallory's printout and set them onto her desk. "Okay"—she leaned forward to pick up a pen—"so here's what I'm thinking…" Her voice trailed off as she began scribbling on the bottom of Mallory's LSO schedule.

While Devereaux worked, Mallory pulled a pen from her bag and quickly flipped through the contract she'd been offered, marking a few places that she wanted to discuss with Max, who would probably refer her to somebody from the LSO's legal team. She was especially glad that she did not have to rely on this outside work to make ends meet, though. It was honestly criminal how little dancers were paid given the beating their bodies took.

"All of this is subject to change depending on performances and whatnot," Devereaux said as she dropped her pen onto the desk and handed back the paper she'd been writing on. "And once the ballet has been learned, we can back these hours down, but these times would fit into the breaks in your schedule, allowing plenty of time for you to get back and forth between here and the Barbican."

Mallory nodded as she looked over the paper. Two hours of rehearsal every day of the week except Tuesday—which Devereaux had given three—with weekends off. It was more rehearsal time than she had been expecting, but given that Devereaux said the time would lessen once she had learned her role, she couldn't find fault in the schedule. If anything, part of her was worried that this wouldn't be enough time for her to learn everything she needed to learn.

"Like we discussed last night, it will be a run of four performances over the back half of the year. The first will be sometime in early January. I don't have a date nailed down yet, but I'll talk with Clara and try to schedule each of the performances for a weekend where the LSO is either not playing, or where she would be okay going without you for a night."

"Both Clara and Max, our Music Director, are keen on the idea of this collaboration, so I don't envision you getting too much pushback from the LSO."

Devereaux smiled wryly and took off her glasses. "One can hope."

"I do need to have this contract reviewed by the LSO's lawyers, though, before I can sign."

"I would expect nothing less."

Mallory nodded. "Once they give me their approval to sign, assuming there aren't any changes they want to make to the contract, I'll have them send it back via courier, so you have it before we begin rehearsals."

"Perfect."

"Do you have copies of the music?"

Devereaux hummed and nodded as she picked up a thin black binder and handed it to her. "It's all in here, in the order it will be performed for the ballet."

"Excellent," Mallory muttered as she opened the binder and began flipping through the pages.

"How long will it take you to learn the music?"

Mallory blinked as she looked up at Devereaux. "All of it?"

"Say the first three pieces? We can work in stages, of course, so you don't need to memorize the lot at once, but you will need a working knowledge of the music before we begin so we can match the steps I'm seeing here"—she tapped her temple—"with what will actually work."

"I..." Mallory looked back down at the binder on her lap. She leafed through the first three pieces of the ballet, and was grateful, at least, that Halonen tended toward symmetry and repetition in her work. "I should be able to get a fairly competent working knowledge of the first three pieces in two weeks. Would that work?"

Devereaux nodded. "Of course." She grabbed a spiral planner that had been laying open atop a small stack of files. "Two weeks from today would be the fifth of September. I'm guessing you don't have any performances scheduled that early in the season; are you lot dark on Tuesdays when you're not performing?"

"We're not, but I should still be able to get here by three."

"Brilliant. Do you have any further questions for me?"

Mallory took a deep breath as she glanced at the folder of music on her lap and let it go slowly as she looked back up at Devereaux. "I don't think so. Not right now, anyway," she added with a small, wry smile and a little shrug.

"Well, if you think of anything, here's my contact information." Devereaux slid a business card across the desk. "I get to texts most quickly, and return calls throughout the day when I have time, but if you need something urgently, call my office number and Serena will handle it. Oh, and if you leave her your shoe size as well, I'll make sure we get appropriate footwear for you for your first rehearsal. You won't be en pointe, of course, but you'll still need a quality slipper."

"Got it." Mallory nodded.

"Excellent. And please make sure to leave your information with Serena before you leave." Devereaux got to her feet and extended her hand. "I look forward to working with you, Ms. Collingswood."

"Mallory, please," Mallory insisted as she shook her hand.

"Of course. And, please, call me Nina."

Mallory nodded. "I guess I will see you in a fortnight, then."

Nina grinned. "I look forward to it."

five

"Thank you all for your work," Clara said as she laid her baton on her music stand and stepped off the rostrum. "We will meet here again tomorrow morning at ten. Please make sure you're up to speed on the Bartók piece, as we will be re-visiting it first-thing." She was addressing the group as a whole, but Mallory was sure the words were intended for the new cellist who had mucked up enough of the music that morning to result in an extended rehearsal for the rest of them while he worked out his nerves.

As the rest of the musicians murmured some form of understanding, Clara ambled over to Mallory. "Today's the day, right? You ready?"

Mallory glanced at her watch and sighed. It was closing in on half past one, which meant that she had roughly an hour and a half to grab a quick lunch and get over to Covent Garden. Two weeks had never passed so quickly in her life. "We'll see," she murmured as she began gathering her things. She nodded to Charlie Fong, her second-chair, as he eased past them, and wasn't at all surprised when Will promptly took his seat.

"You ready?" Will asked.

"I just asked her the same thing," Clara chuckled. She gave Mallory's shoulder a light squeeze. "I'm sure you'll be fine. And you should know that the Board is quite chuffed with the whole collaboration idea. Hayes already has them trying to figure out ways to parlay it into increased media coverage for the LSO."

"Wonderful," Mallory drawled.

Clara laughed. "Tell Nina that I said hello, and I will see you tomorrow."

Mallory nodded. "I will."

Once Clara had left, Will nudged her with his elbow and asked, "So, are you ready?"

Mallory shook her head. "Not at all." She had thought the fortnight would be enough to let her learn enough of the music to feel prepared, but she didn't. Her thoughts were constantly haunted by the melodies of the songs she was supposed to learn. She had been seeing the music in her sleep for more than a week now, and any time she was without her violin in her hand she found her fingers working the notes of whatever section of music was stuck in her head against her leg. Her phone. A water bottle. And then there was the evening she'd been idly fingering the pole beside her seat on the tube as she made her way home after an afternoon of meetings that followed on the heels of a particularly tiring four-hour rehearsal, and the guy sitting across from her had thought she was hitting on him.

Part of her felt bad for the way she had laughed in his face when he tried to chat her up, but it was a very small part. Mostly she was still annoyed that he had dared to interrupt her when she had been finally making sense of a transition that had been giving her fits.

"You said it was, what? Like ten minutes of music?" Will dropped into the chair to her left and laid his oboe across his lap as he studied her. "Surely you have it memorized by now."

Mallory pursed her lips and shrugged. Memorizing the notes was the easy part. Learning the music was another problem altogether, and he knew it. "Eh. I mean, I have it memorized okay, but I don't feel like

I have a real handle on it, and I'm supposed to be able to not just play but also dance while doing it. I just…" She blew out a loud breath and resisted the urge to bury her face in her hands. "Why did I agree to do this again?"

Will laughed and looped a brotherly arm over her shoulder. "Because you seemed pretty wowed by the whole thing. I'm pretty sure when you called me after your little meeting at Covent Garden that you said the whole thing was going to be 'fucking brilliant,' yeah?"

"If it comes together like Nina thinks, then yes, it will. But I still…"

"Breathe, Mal. You've got this."

"Do I?" Mallory asked, a hint of panic creeping into her tone. "Because music is one thing, but the idea of dancing too…"

"Let Devereaux worry about that. That's her thing after all, yeah?"

"Well, yeah, but…"

"But nothing. It'll be fine. Honestly, it's good to be a little unsure about stuff every once in a while. Means you're pushing yourself."

"It does, huh?" Mallory drawled.

"Absolutely. Tell me, when was the last time you were this nervous about something?"

"Oh, you know, about a year or so ago when I proposed to Gwen. And look how well that turned out for me…"

Will sighed and pulled her in closer. "This won't be like that, I promise."

"You don't know that. It could be just as big of a flaming failure. Or worse, really, because at least then I was humiliated in private. This will be on stage, for all the world to witness."

Will pressed a light kiss to her temple. "I have faith in your ability to pull this off, and I'll wager that when the curtain comes down on your final performance that you'll have a good laugh at how worried you were about all of this."

She took a deep breath as his confidence took some of the edge off her panic. "I don't want to make a fool of myself," she whispered.

"So don't," Will replied, as if it were the easiest thing in the world. "Just go in there and try your best. I'm sure they won't put on the show before it's ready, so just have fun with it."

Mallory sighed and nodded. All of this was an exercise in futility anyway, because she had signed the contract and agreed to do the show. "You can't laugh at me if I'm awful."

Will chuckled and gave her shoulder a quick squeeze before pulling his arm away. "Bollocks. I absolutely can. But I won't have to, because you're going to be brilliant."

six

Nina's assistant Serena was chatting with the women behind the counter by the stage door when Mallory arrived at the theatre, and she smiled as she asked, "So, you ready?"

Mallory nodded even as she silently wished people would stop asking her that. "I believe so."

"Brilliant. I'm to show you to your dressing room, and then bring you by the shoe room to try on a few different pairs before your rehearsal," Serena explained. "Yvette, this is Mallory Collingswood, by the way. Have you met? She's collaborating on Nina's new production."

The brunette Mallory had noticed on her last visit smiled and offered her a little wave. "It's a pleasure, Ms. Collingswood."

"Mallory, please," she insisted.

"Mallory," the woman agreed with a small nod. "And I'm Yvette. If you need anything, please don't hesitate to ask."

"I will. Thank you," Mallory assured her.

"Yvette is the secret keeper here," Serena explained as she began making her way down the hall. "Knows everyone and everything and she's a vault, so if you have any questions that you don't want to ask Nina or myself for whatever reason, go to her. Odds are good she'll be able to help you out."

"Good to know," Mallory murmured as she adjusted the strap of her gym bag on her left shoulder so that it stopped bumping against her violin case. She was glad that she hadn't been left to her own devices to try to find her way through the massive building's maze of corridors. She usually had a decent memory for directions but, with her head so full of new music and apprehension of what was to come, it was nice to be able to just follow Serena and not have to worry about whether or not she was on the correct path.

Serena waved at a closed door to the left of the lifts as she pressed her thumb to the call button. "That's the main changing room."

Mallory nodded. She couldn't help but wonder where they were headed then, because the slacks, blouse, and sweater she was wearing were not at all appropriate for a ballet rehearsal, but she obediently followed Serena into the lift.

They only went up two floors before the lift stopped and the doors slid open, and Mallory grasped the strap of her violin case as she stepped into an entirely new corridor. There was a window at the end that let in a fraction of natural light to offset the fluorescents overhead, but it was so far away that Mallory couldn't see out it to gather her bearings. She had a feeling they were on the southern side of the building, but without a landmark to judge from, they could have been on the moon for all she knew.

Serena made her way past a handful of closed doors before stopping at one near the middle of the corridor. "You're in luck," she said as she pushed the door open. "One of our principals is out for the year with an injury, so you can use her dressing room for the length of your run. It's not much," she apologized as she motioned Mallory inside, "but it's private, which is a luxury in this business. Do you need anything?"

"I…don't think so?" Mallory murmured as she slipped past Serena to take a look at the room. The first thing she noticed was the dressing table that stretched along the wall opposite the door, with a long mirror framed with lights for hair and makeup. There was a small sink opposite the dressing table, next to the door, and a twin-sized bed pushed up against the wall beneath a large square window that, she saw when she got close enough to look through it, overlooked Covent Garden Piazza.

"I'll let you get changed, then. Showers and toilets are just there"— Serena waved toward the direction they'd come—"so I'll show you those before we head up to the studio."

Mallory nodded. "Thank you."

"Of course. I'll be right outside," Serena replied with a kind smile as she backed out of the room and closed the door after herself.

Not wanting to keep Serena waiting, Mallory quickly changed into the black capris leggings and maroon tank she had packed for the afternoon and left the slacks, blouse, and sweater she had worn to the LSO folded on the dressing table beside her duffle bag. She combed her fingers through her hair to pull it back into a simple ponytail, slipped her feet into a pair of Brooks trainers, and pulled on her favorite zippered hoodie. She took a deep breath as she pulled the folder of music for the ballet from the bag and picked up her violin, and gave her reflection one last *what the hell have I gotten myself into* look before turning toward the door.

Serena was leaning against the wall across from the door, tapping at the screen of her phone, and she looked up with a smile when Mallory exited the dressing room. "Here's the key, by the way." She handed Mallory a key on a simple key ring.

"Thank you." Mallory locked the door after herself.

Once she turned around, Serena pointed at a large opening to her left. "Not that it matters for the time being, but there is a set of stairs that lead down to backstage through there," she said as she pushed off the wall and turned toward the lifts. She waved at a closed door three down from Mallory's dressing room. "Toilets and showers are in here. Do you want to have a look?"

"I'm okay for now," Mallory assured her.

"Excellent. Then up we go!"

They took the lift to the top floor this time, and the first thing Mallory noticed when they exited the lift was the handful of insanely pretty, incredibly young and fit dancers milling about the corridor. She was instantly self-conscious of the fact that she was at least a decade older than the lot of them, and that those extra years had added a softness to her frame that her Pilates classes couldn't quite fight.

"Shoe room is this way," Serena said, waving to a few of the dancers as they passed. "I had Greta pull a few different shoes in your size for you to try on."

"I'm sure anything would be fine," Mallory protested, not wanting to make trouble.

"Trust me," Serena insisted as she pulled open a door and ushered Mallory inside, "you want shoes that are comfortable. It helps that you won't be on your toes, but you'll still be up and moving *a lot*, and you don't want a poor-fitting shoe. We'll find something that is passable for the time being, and if any modifications need to be made, we can do them here after the order comes in."

Mallory nodded as her eyes swept over the shoe room. It was long and narrow, the left wall taken up by gorgeous dark wood cubbies labeled with dancers' surnames that were absolutely stuffed with shoes and what looked like a workspace at the back of the room.

An older woman with perfectly silvered hair and half-lenses hanging from a chain around her neck appeared from the back of the room, and she smiled as she motioned toward a small bench that Mallory only just noticed opposite the cubbies. "You must be Mallory Collingswood," she said as she gathered a handful of black ballet slippers from a cubby. "I'm Greta. And you're an eight and a half. Yes?"

"Yes." Mallory nodded.

"Sit, sit," Greta insisted with a little wave. "Let's get you kitted out."

Even though the first pair of shoes Greta handed her were more than fine, the shoe mistress insisted she try on each of the half-dozen pairs she had pulled to make sure she found the best fit. And she was glad for it, too, because the last pair she slipped on felt like they had been made specifically for her. It must have shown in her expression, because Greta chuckled and patted her shoulder.

"Freed it is then. Is there anything about the shoe you'd like changed?" When Mallory shook her head, Greta smiled and nodded. "Unfortunately that's the only pair in your size that I have here, but since they're flats, they should last until the order comes in."

Mallory nodded and gathered her discarded trainers. "Thank you."

"Of course, dear." Greta winked.

"Right then," Serena drawled as she glanced at her watch. "Let's get going, shall we?"

Mallory nodded again, feeling utterly overwhelmed, and obediently followed Serena out of the shoe room and down the hall to the Fonteyn rehearsal studio. She was glad to see the studio was empty when they entered—she would have hated to have kept people waiting on her first day—and she immediately made her way toward an area of the barre that seemed like it would be out of the way to set her things. She wedged the folder with sheet music between her violin case and the mirrors and dropped her trainers beside the case.

She had just flipped the latches on her case open when a quiet murmur of voices filtered into the studio, and she hurried to grab her bow and violin. There was no mistaking the barely-suppressed panic in her eyes when she looked at herself in the mirror, and she took a deep breath as she pushed herself to her feet.

Not that she had seriously considered backing out, but the time to do so had now well and truly passed. It was time to put on a brave face and, as the old saying went, fake it till she made it.

The new arrivals were standing in a small huddle near the door, with Nina Devereaux holding court as Serena and the other three people who'd arrived with the artistic director listened. Mallory was grateful for the opportunity to just observe for a moment. All of this was so new that even this little bit of time to find some kind of equilibrium was a blessing.

Nina looked like she was ready to model for a fitness magazine in her silver leggings and oversized white, scoop-neck sweater that hung in a way that highlighted the sharp line of her collarbones and made her look effortlessly glamorous. The man to Nina's right was blond and fair and incredibly pretty, with bright blue eyes and chiseled jaw that was shadowed with a dusting of whiskers. The muscles in his arms were defined, though not in the bulky sort of way that was achieved by weightlifters. He was dressed to move in a pair of black track pants and a fitted tee, and looked perfectly at home in the studio as he rested his right hand on the barre.

A dancer. Or a former dancer, at the very least.

The man on Nina's left looked like a caricature of an absent-minded professor with his long, almost floppy brown hair brushed up away from his forehead and a full beard that was in desperate need of a trim, and she wondered what his role in all of this was given that his loafers, plaid sport shirt, and trousers were clearly not meant for dancing.

Surely Nina wasn't bringing in people to observe already? She shook her head. Even though she was new to this world, she had a feeling that the men weren't here to judge her. Oh, they would, of course, everyone does when they encounter someone new in their profession, but perhaps they were a kind of support staff to help her get this idea of hers off the ground.

Yes, that made much more sense, she decided as she turned her attention to the final member of the group—the woman she would undoubtedly be performing with. She was taller than Devereaux but shorter than herself, with short, dark hair that was held away from her face with a wide, blue and white patterned elastic headband that paired perfectly with her sky blue leggings and white sleeveless leotard. The woman's legs were long—almost impossibly so—and though her muscles were lean and her frame slight, she looked powerful.

Strong.

Competent.

And, while Mallory supposed she should have felt some kind of reassurance knowing that her partner was all of those things, it really just made her feel glaringly, impossibly inadequate.

And old.

Not that thirty-nine was old, exactly, but looking at the obviously young dancer, she felt positively geriatric. And sorry that she had skipped Pilates the last two weeks to focus on learning the music for this project.

Serena broke away from the group first, offering Mallory a reassuring smile and a thumb's up as she made her way toward the door. A moment later, with a twist of her hips and a dip of her shoulders, the dancer turned to look at her, and Mallory's eyes widened as she recognized her.

"Addison?" Mallory swallowed thickly in an attempt to force her heart, which had leapt into her throat the moment she recognized the dancer, back where it belonged.

Addison laughed and nodded as she made her way across the studio to where Mallory stood, too surprised to do much more than gape at her. "Yeah. I'm afraid you're stuck with me."

"Oh." Devereaux's expression turned curious as she waved a finger between them. "You know each other?"

"We've run into each other at Lena's place a couple times, yeah," Addison explained, her eyes crinkling with her smile. Her smile softened as she stopped in front of Mallory, and she added in a quieter voice, "I'm glad Nina was able to persuade you to take this on."

Mallory nodded as her nerves from earlier returned with a vengeance. Addison was looking at her like she was utterly chuffed about this arrangement, and Mallory just prayed that she was able to live up to whatever stories she might have heard about her. "Me too," she murmured.

Addison beamed, looking for all the world like her day had just been made. "Good."

"Well, let's finish our introductions so we can get on with it, shall we?" Devereaux drawled. When she was sure she had both of their attention, she nodded and motioned toward the blond man standing to her left. "This is Toby Doubek. He's going to help me with the choreography. And this is Paul Roxon, our resident notator," she continued, half-turning toward the professor-looking gentleman on her other side. "All, this is Mallory Collingswood, leader of the London Symphony Orchestra."

"We're going to be trying a lot of different things," Addison explained in a low voice, "so the notator will keep track of every step in relation to the music so that, once a decision is made as to how, exactly, the dance is to go, we'll have a record of it all."

Mallory nodded, the gesture at once a signal that she'd heard and understood Addison's explanation and an unspoken gesture of greeting to the two men who were regarding her with analytical expressions that assured her she was absolutely about to be judged.

God, why in the world had she ever agreed to this?

"Mallory, if you would, please…" Devereaux motioned toward the center of the room. "You'll, of course, have to make an entrance of some kind, but for now could you play the pieces you learned for today? To bring everyone up to speed with where you're at?"

Mallory nodded, her heart fluttering into her throat as she made her way to where Devereaux wanted her. Addison remained off to the side of the room, next to the barre where she had dropped to the floor and had begun pulling on a pair of pointe shoes, as Devereaux made her way toward the sound system and the choreographer and notator retrieved a couple of stools from the back of the room.

Once it appeared that everyone was ready, she lifted her violin and waited for further instruction. She watched as Devereaux fiddled with the stereo, and took a deep breath when the distinctive rumble of a bass spilled through the speakers. Devereaux nodded and arched an expectant brow that made her think that this was some kind of test, and she took a deep breath as she waited for her cue. The music swelled and dipped, and she closed her eyes as she lifted her bow and put it to strings.

She played through the first two pieces she'd learned and was preparing to launch into the third when the accompanying music fell silent.

"Very nice," Devereaux declared. Mallory blinked her eyes open and let her bow fall to her side as Devereaux continued, "Addison, thoughts?"

Addison's expression was awed as she shook her head and murmured, "Wow."

Mallory felt her cheeks warm at the open appreciation in Addison's voice, and she ducked her head as she smiled shyly at her.

Devereaux smirked and turned toward Toby and Paul. "Well?"

Toby grinned. "This is going to be fun." He hopped off his stool, his gaze thoughtful. "I think it would be better for her to make her entrance playing. It doesn't need to be anything fancy—just sort of..." His voice trailed off as he began making his way toward the center of the room where Mallory stood, his steps light and his stride long as he seemed to float on the balls of his feet. It was elegant yet without fanfare, and Mallory was relieved that it looked like something she would be able to do. "Like that."

Devereaux hummed and nodded. "Yes, I think that will work. No reason to make things more complicated than they need to be, after all." She turned to Mallory. "Can you try that, please?" She motioned toward the side of the room where Addison was still standing. "Just playing your part without the background music?"

Mallory nodded and moved to where Devereaux wanted her. She lifted her violin and waited for a sign to continue, and then took a deep breath as she split her focus between the music that was still too new to play entirely without thought, and her feet.

"Too stiff," Devereaux declared once she'd stopped near the spot she'd stood before. "You don't need to be dancing, but you can't look like a soldier marching in a parade. Again."

The next time, she paid more attention to her footwork and less to the music, but the result was the same as Devereaux shook her head and announced, "Again."

Mallory bit the inside of her cheek as she returned to her start position. This time she began without waiting for a cue and, when she reached her mark, waited for Devereaux's assessment.

"Again. Lighter in your frame."

What the hell did that even mean? Mallory took a deep breath and, though she had no idea what Nina was asking for, lifted her violin and tried again.

"No. Again," Devereaux dismissed and directed her with a quick flick of the wrist back to her starting point.

Fourteen tries. Fourteen failures. The furrow in Devereaux's brow was practically a chasm at this point, and her tone was barely concealed frustration.

"If you could just—" Mallory bit out, dangerously close to losing her temper, but was interrupted by a soft hand curling around her elbow.

"Relax your shoulders as much as you can while still being able to play," Addison murmured. "Let your feet turn out with each step. Walk on the balls of your feet and let the tip of your toes drag across the floor. Your heels can drop to the floor if you need to for balance, but allow them to do so only briefly. It will feel weird, but it should give the look she seems to be looking for."

There was no judgment in her tone, for which Mallory was eternally grateful. "Thank you," she whispered.

"We'll get it," Addison replied just as quietly with a confident smile.

Mallory took a deep breath and closed her eyes as she pictured the adjustments Addison suggested, and then let it go slowly as she blinked her eyes opened and once again lifted her bow to strings. Allowing the front of her feet scrape across the floor was easier than trying to step gracefully, and she knew when she reached the center of the room and looked at Devereaux that Addison's refinements had done the trick.

"Acceptable. For now." Devereaux nodded and tapped a finger against her lips thoughtfully as she turned to Toby. "So where do we have Addison come in?"

"I have an idea," Addison spoke up. "If I may?"

Devereaux nodded and took a step back, gesturing with a small wave of her hand for Addison to proceed as she told Mallory, "From the top, if you'd please. With the entrance."

"Of bloody course," Mallory muttered under her breath.

Addison laughed. "Come on. It's not that bad. You've got it now."

Mallory closed her eyes and took a deep breath to steady herself before she blinked her eyes open and attempted her entrance one more time. Devereaux's expression was a mask that she interpreted as meaning that she had somehow screwed up again, even though she was nearly positive that she had repeated her previous attempt perfectly, but she wasn't stopped when she reached her mark and found herself breathing easier as she continued to play. She turned her attention to Addison's reflection in the mirror as she waited for her entrance, curious as to what she had in mind, and it took all her years of experience not to lose her place in the music when Addison began to move.

She had known, intuitively, of course, that Addison would be exceptional given her youth and position within the ballet, but that knowledge didn't entirely set in until she watched her dance.

Addison took three long strides that looked like a carbon copy of how she'd instructed her to move, before her hips and shoulders dipped and twisted in opposite directions. Her arms lifted and extended, elbows bending and straightening as her entire body flowed in graceful lines that emphasized the music Mallory was still somehow managing to play through muscle memory alone because lord knows her thoughts were focused entirely on the beautiful creature in the mirrors.

Though Mallory was watching Addison with rapt attention, she was still startled when a soft hand landed on her shoulder, long fingers curling around the joint in an almost possessive sort of way. She took a shaky breath as she closed her eyes and focused only on the music, willing herself to ignore the feeling of Addison's fingers trailing lightly across her upper back.

Mallory was grateful that she was the only one who could hear the way her pulse tripped and stumbled over itself when Addison's touch glided along the length of her arm that was holding her violin. Three fingers became two as she rounded the curve of her elbow, which became one when she hit her wrist, and Mallory blinked her eyes open when the touch of that lone finger disappeared. She was grateful that all eyes were on Addison, whose arms had lifted above her head now as she did a little spin on the tip of her right shoe, her left leg bent and extended behind her, and her arms moved slowly lower as she repeated the move three more times as she finished her circuit of Mallory to end where she had begun—just behind her right side, with a gentle hand wrapped around her shoulder.

It was clear from the way she dropped to the flats of her feet and arched a brow at Devereaux that she had finished, and Mallory obligingly stopped playing and lowered her arms to her sides to await the artistic director's decision.

"Very nice," Devereaux murmured with a small, pleased smile. She glanced at Toby, who nodded his agreement, and then to Paul. "Did you get that?" When Paul nodded, she turned to Addison. "Can you do it again, exactly like that?"

Addison nodded. "Should be able to, yeah."

"Mallory…" Devereaux's voice trailed off, and she pursed her lips thoughtfully as she made her way toward her. "I need you to look a little less terrified when Addison touches you," she continued in a low tone. Mallory figured she should be grateful, at least, that Devereaux seemed to want to spare her the embarrassment of having her correction heard by everyone in the room. Though, really, the fact that Addison had heard it was more than mortifying enough. And, well, if she had to pick an emotion—terror would be the complete opposite of what she'd actually been feeling.

"I'm sorry?" Mallory asked.

Devereaux clucked her tongue as she shook her head. "Shoulder your instrument? Is that the correct cue?"

"It works." Mallory murmured as she lifted her violin, placing the butt of the instrument against the side of her neck and lifting her shoulder to cradle it. "Like this?"

Devereaux hummed and nodded as she placed her left hand on Mallory's elbow and her right on her at the base of her neck so that her thumb and ring finger pressed into the muscles on either side.

"Soften your shoulders," Devereaux instructed, pressing her fingertips into Mallory's muscles indicatively. "Relax." When Mallory did as instructed, she murmured, "Very good. Just like that. Now, chin up a bit."

"I need my chin on the rest to hold the violin in place," Mallory argued. "So if you want my shoulders down, then the chin has to come down more. It's impossible to play otherwise."

Devereaux sighed and combed a hand through her hair. "Can you get one of those lifts then? You head being bowed like this"—she ducked her head in a gross exaggeration of Mallory's playing posture— "throws off the lines. You need to appear elegant, regal…"

"You mean a shoulder rest?" Mallory clarified.

"Yes. That," Devereaux said, waving her hands imperiously as she stepped back and gave Mallory a thorough once-over, nodding to herself as if confirming her own suggestion. "Can you do that?"

Mallory blew out a soft breath. While she knew plenty of violinists who used shoulder rests, she never had, and she had no doubt that it would affect her playing until she got used to it. "How imperative is this change visually?"

"Incredibly."

Of course it was. Because why should any single element of this endeavor be comfortable for her. "I can pick one up and try to get used to it, but I've never actually used one before, so…"

"Good. Good," Devereaux said. "When can you get one? Can you have it before rehearsal tomorrow afternoon?"

Mallory bit the inside of her cheek and nodded. There was a shop she knew of not far from the Barbican that should have something that would work. "I should be able to find something before tomorrow."

"Excellent." Devereaux clapped her hands twice. "Now, let's do it again. And try to relax into Addison, this time. She's your muse, after all. You shouldn't be afraid of her."

"Yes, of course, because I'm apparently Lindsey fucking Sterling, now," Mallory grumbled under her breath as she and Addison returned to their starting position.

"I wouldn't give her any ideas if I were you," Addison chuckled.

"Right," Mallory drawled. She rolled her head counter-clockwise to try to loosen her neck to try to meet Devereaux's exacting standards, and sighed as she straightened. "Any other words of wisdom?"

"Yeah." Addison smiled and bumped Mallory's arm with her shoulder. "Try and have fun."

Mallory grit her teeth to keep from pointing out that there was nothing about the experience so far that she felt came even remotely close to 'fun.' It wasn't Addison's fault that she was miles out of her depth and struggling to stay afloat. She had already disappointed Devereaux, the last thing she needed was to put herself at odds with her partner in all of this as well. "Right. I'll see what I can do about that."

seven

"No, no, no." Devereaux waved a frustrated hand in the air. "Stop. Just stop."

Mallory cursed under her breath as she let her arms fall to the side, her shoulders slumping under the weight of Devereaux's latest criticism that was, no doubt, about to be flung at her. After close to three hours of genuinely *trying* to meet the expectations leveled upon her and— judging by the scowl that seemed permanently etched on Devereaux's face and the near-constant head shaking from Toby—failing spectacularly, she was ready to run away and never show her face in Covent Garden ever again.

She grit her teeth as she waited for the blow to land, her jaw tightening even further when Addison relaxed beside her, eyes wide and expectant, as if eagerly awaiting whatever critique was about to be leveled at them.

"Addison, you need to really extend your allongé on that arabesque, and make sure you hold until Mallory's bow begins to move toward you," Devereaux instructed. "Then you turn to face her, left hand moves from her wrist to her forearm, working leg into attitude devant, hold, and let Mallory guide the turn."

"Got it." Addison nodded, not at all bothered by the critique. If anything, she seemed to almost *enjoy* it.

Which was at once infuriating and enviable.

Every time Devereaux stopped them, Mallory was torn between wanting to throw her violin at the woman and demand she do the job herself—which she would never do, if only because her violin would most likely be broken beyond repair, and she would break her own arm before she purposefully destroyed a 1779 Lorenzo Storioni—and crying in frustration—which was an equally unpleasant idea, because she absolutely loathed the idea of letting anyone know they had gotten to her so completely.

If she had the strength to keep it together in the face of Gwen telling her about Dana, she could damn well do so now. All she had to do was make it through the rest of this positively hellish rehearsal, and then she could go home and just let go.

She took a deep breath to steel herself as Devereaux's attention turned to her. *Please just let whatever she wants to be fixed be something simple for a goddamn change.*

Devereaux sighed and shook her head. "Mallory, I know we're pushing you, and that your main responsibility in this section is leading that spin while supporting Addison, but I need you to relax and actually move with her. You're entirely too stiff."

Mallory clenched her jaw and nodded, not trusting herself to speak. It was much safer, and much more professional, to take the criticism in silence than to risk opening her mouth and snapping at Devereaux. She had been doing her best to 'move with Addison'—and she had been much more demonstrative than she would have had she simply been playing a solo—but there were things she just could not do while playing.

"Good." Devereaux took a step back and waved a hand toward the center of the room. "Again, please," she instructed as she pulled her phone from the pocket sewn into her leggings and frowned at the screen. "From the end of Addison's entrance," she continued distractedly as she tapped out a reply to whatever message couldn't wait until after rehearsal.

Mallory closed her eyes and nodded. The first time she had been instructed to begin playing in the middle of the piece as if she were a machine that could be cued without effort, or someone blessed to have sheet music in front of her, she had nearly lost it, but she was getting used to the command now. Annoying as it was, there was something strangely comforting in the confidence Devereaux had in her to just know where in the music to begin.

And the fact that it further cemented her knowledge of the piece wasn't a bad thing, either.

"How are you doing?" Addison asked softly as they took their positions.

"Fine," Mallory lied.

Addison smiled and shook her head. "It will get better, I promise. It's always brutal in the beginning. Maybe try and close your eyes this time around. Just let yourself go and really *feel* the music, let it guide your movement."

Mallory bit her lip as Addison's words reminded her of another time and another place, when she'd been given a nearly identical suggestion. Her gaze turned unfocused, the rehearsal studio replaced for the briefest of moments by a clear blue sky, a slowly filling amphitheater, and a comforting arm draped over her shoulders. The illusion was shattered, thankfully, by a pair of worried brown eyes and a warm hand on her wrist.

Addison squeezed her wrist gently as she leaned in to murmur, "I'm sorry. Did I say something wrong?"

"No. I... Somebody else told me something similar once, and it just..." Mallory's voice trailed off, and she shook her head. "Old memories. I'm fine."

"You're sure?"

"Of course." Mallory did her best to look like she meant it. Judging by the way Addison's lips tugged down in a small frown, though, she had failed just as miserably at that task as she had everything else that afternoon.

"Jasmine Lewis is in my office and is apparently rather adamant that she speak with me immediately," Devereaux announced with a heavy eye roll. "It's past six anyway, so let's just go on and call it a day. We'll pick up here tomorrow afternoon," she added as she turned toward the door, sparing the briefest of glances at Toby and Paul, who watched her go with matching grim expressions.

Grateful for the fact that her bruised and battered ego was spared for the rest of the day, Mallory let herself relax as she watched Toby and Paul hurry after Nina. Once the door had closed behind them, leaving her and Addison alone in the studio, she asked, "Dare I ask who Jasmine Lewis is?"

"A ridiculously wealthy donor whose granddaughter is in her final year at the Upper School," Addison explained, motioning vaguely in the direction of Floral Street. "She wants the girl to be promoted to the corps before graduation, but the kid isn't ready. She's a decent enough dancer, of course—you don't get accepted to the Upper School if you're not—but she's nowhere near as talented as her grandmother would like to believe. If she makes the jump here, she'd probably never advance beyond the corps. Honestly, she would be better off starting her professional career on a smaller scale somewhere, but…"

Mallory grimaced. "Sounds like a right headache."

"And then some," Addison agreed with a rueful smile. "Add in the fact that our funding took a serious hit this season and that one cheque from Lewis is enough to keep the entire company in shoes for a year…" Her voice trailed off, and she shrugged. "I wouldn't trade places with Nina for all the money in the world right now."

"No, I don't imagine I would, either," Mallory murmured.

Addison nodded. "Anyway, how are you feeling? Do you want to work through this one more time before calling it a day?"

"Not particularly," Mallory admitted with a small shake of her head, "but I probably should, given how problematic Nina seemed to find my performance."

"You did fine," Addison insisted with a kind smile that only grew when Mallory scoffed and arched a disbelieving brow in response. "Seriously. For not being a dancer, you managed today incredibly well. And your playing…" Her voice trailed off as she tilted her head, her right shoulder lifting ever so slightly to follow the movement. "You're amazing."

It was a compliment Mallory had heard many times over her career, but for the first time in years, it made her smile. She looked down at their feet and took a deep breath to try and calm the blush that was beginning to warm her cheeks. Knowing her reaction was ridiculous only seemed to make it worse, and she shook her head as she whispered, "Thank you." She blinked as she lifted her head, unsurprised to find Addison's warm, earnest brown eyes smiling at her. "You're pretty amazing yourself."

"Oh, I know," Addison replied with a laugh and a little wave of her hand. It was clear she was trying to lighten the mood, but the way her smile softened as she held her gaze conveyed just how much she appreciated the sentiment. "So, are we dancing, or are we calling it a day?"

It was startling how well Addison could read her mood and somehow know just what to say to make everything easier, and Mallory smiled as she dipped her chin in a small nod. "We're dancing." And, oh, the way Addison smiled at her then—her so eyes full of joy and her cheeks dimpled with happiness—made her heart flutter up into her throat so that she had to clear it softly before being able to speak. "From the beginning? Or the end of your entrance, as Nina had suggested?"

Addison shook her head. "We can just start from here," she said, tapping the padded block at the toe of her shoe on the floor.

"Okay." Mallory nodded and lifted her violin. She smiled at Addison in the mirror as she watched her take her position just off her right shoulder, and asked, "Ready?"

"When you are, maestro," Addison replied with a wink.

Mallory took a deep breath as she lifted her bow, and began playing the last couple bars from Addison's entrance to help get them onto the same page. She let herself soften into Addison's touch as the ballerina lifted onto her toes, and closed her eyes as she surrendered to the feeling of warm fingers against her skin, letting that and the music guide her instead of her thoughts.

It was easier this way, she realized as the muscles in her back relaxed ever so slightly, and she leaned with the fingers dragging across her upper back. Her focus was split so completely between the notes she was playing and Addison's touch that she couldn't spare a thought about what she was doing with the rest of her body. Instead of worrying about how she looked, she just went with the music and Addison, letting them take the lead, her body simply an instrument that moved and bent to each as her hips shifted and her feet slid across the smooth linoleum so she could keep Addison's fingers against her skin. The spin still gave her trouble—she hadn't quite figured out how to generate the power that she needed to turn them both given that she was starting essentially from a standstill—but she knew even before she reached the end of the section and blinked her eyes open that it had been a much better effort.

And, judging by the way Addison was looking at her—her eyes crinkled with happiness and her smile full of sunshine—she felt the same way. Still, she couldn't help but ask as she let her arms fall to her sides, "Better?"

"My god, Mal!" Addison laughed as she threw her arms around Mallory's neck and pulled her into a happy, bouncing hug. "That was it!"

Mallory smiled as she wrapped her arms around Addison's waist, pressing her wrists into the small of her back to keep from poking her with the violin and bow still in her hands as she returned the embrace, and laughed in relief. If Addison was this pleased with what she had just done then maybe, just maybe, she might actually be able to pull this whole thing off. "Thank you."

"For what?" Addison asked as she let her arms fall and took a step back to look at her.

Mallory switched her bow to her left hand and lifted her now empty right hand in a vague wave. "I don't know. I just…I just felt like I needed to say it."

Addison's smile softened in understanding. "You're welcome, then. Could you tell the difference in what you were doing? Did it feel better to you?"

"It did. I could definitely tell that I was moving more, I just…I hope I didn't look too ridiculous."

"No." Addison shook her head. "You…" She huffed a soft breath as she shook her head again. "You looked perfect," she whispered.

There was something in the way Addison was looking at her now that made Mallory's stomach flip, and she sucked in a sharp breath as she looked away. It felt like a lifetime had passed since the last time a woman had looked at her like she was something special and, while she was sure it could only be because Addison was pleased with how their attempt had gone, it was still nice to feel like she was *seen*. "Okay. Good."

Addison's voice carried the slightest husk when she agreed, "Yeah." She cleared her throat softly. "So, you ready to get out of here?"

Twenty minutes ago, Mallory would have gladly sprinted for the door, but she found herself suddenly reluctant to leave, lest this sliver of magic that was beginning to form disappear. Still, they had no reason to stay any longer because they would be back at it all the following afternoon, so she forced a small smile as she nodded. "Sure."

"All right." Addison took a deep breath and let it go slowly as, with one last lingering look, she turned toward her kit bag.

Mallory fell into step beside her, the silence between them at once comfortable and palpable with something she dared not try to identify. She knelt to stow her bow and violin as Addison sat down a few feet away to begin unknotting the ribbons crisscrossing her ankles, and once her instrument was secure, she too took a seat to switch out her new ballet slippers for her trainers.

She looked up from tying her shoes when Addison sighed softly beside her as she tossed her pointe shoes into her bag and wiggled and stretched her toes as wide as the tape around them allowed. Her expression was the familiar one of relief any woman would recognize after a night out in heels, and Mallory couldn't resist asking, "Does it hurt to dance like that?"

Addison chuckled and shook her head. "Not at all," she insisted as she pulled a pair of worn, wooly slippers that looked sinfully soft from her kit bag and slipped them on. "I mean, it helps that I have a ridiculously high pain tolerance but, as long as there's nothing going on with my feet, it's really no different than walking regularly for me at this point. It is nice to free the toes, though."

"I can imagine." Mallory pushed herself to her feet and gathered her dance shoes in her left hand as she slung the strap of her violin case over her head and across her chest with her right. Once Addison had zipped her bag shut, she offered her a hand to help her up.

"Thanks." Addison smiled as she took her hand. It was almost unfair how graceful she looked as she rose to her feet, and she tilted her head toward the door once she'd picked up her bag. "Shall we?"

"We shall," Mallory agreed with a small nod.

There were only a few dancers in the corridor when they exited the studio and, though they were all incredibly young and in even more incredible shape, she took some solace in the fact that each of them looked more tired than she felt. Of course, hers was more of a mental exhaustion where she had no doubt theirs was physical, but still…

Small favors were still favors, and at this point in the game, she would take anything she could get.

She pulled up short at the feeling of Addison's hand on her elbow and arched a brow as she turned to look at her.

"Hold on a sec?" Addison waved at the large, crimson rectangle lined with super-sized binder clips and sheets of paper. "I need to check the boards before I head out."

"The boards?"

"Rehearsal schedules," Addison explained as she leaned in closer to study one of the pages. After a minute, she nodded to herself and turned to Mallory with a smile. "Okay. No changes for tomorrow," she shared as she looped a hand around Mallory's bicep and turned toward the lifts.

"What would cause a change?" Mallory asked as she happily allowed Addison to lead.

"This early in the season, when the schedule is still months from changing, usually it's an injury that prompts a reshuffling of assignments. But then if Nina or one of the other instructors aren't happy with how rehearsals for a show are going, they'll change things up too." Addison let go of Mallory's arm to call the elevator. The doors opened immediately, and she shook her head as she continued, "There are no set rules for any of this—it all just comes down to making sure we're prepared to go on stage."

"That makes sense," Mallory murmured as she moved to the back of the car and turned to lean against the wall.

Addison glanced at her as she pressed the button for the second floor. "So, Serena said they gave you Regina's dressing room?"

Mallory shrugged. "She just said that the dancer it belonged to was out for the season with an injury."

"Yeah." Addison grimaced and crossed her fingers. "Here's to hoping." She shook her head at the questioning look Mallory gave her. "Hip. Her doctor capped the joint with titanium instead of doing a full replacement, but it's still too early to tell if it's something she'll be able to come back from."

"Oh..."

"Yeah. Ballet's brutal like that." The elevator stopped at the second floor, and Addison held an arm over the gap in a clear motion for Mallory to go first. Her stomach growled loudly just as Mallory passed, and she laughed as she stepped out of the lift. "Apparently I need food. How about you? You have time to maybe go grab a bite? It'd give us a chance to get to know each other a little better since we'll be working together so much…"

Mallory pulled her phone from her bag to check the time, and pursed her lips as she considered the offer. This was the first ten-plus hour day of what would be *months* of working herself to the bone, and she knew she should beg off so she could go home and get some sleep, but she couldn't resist the hopeful glimmer in Addison's eyes. "Sure. What did you have in mind?"

"There's a nice little place just over in Neal's Yard that I like. It's only like a five-minute walk from here so it wouldn't put you too far from the underground."

Mallory smiled. "Sounds wonderful."

"Yeah?"

Mallory laughed softly and nodded. "Yeah."

"Okay." Addison took a deep breath and waved at the door on her right. "This is me, by the way. Would you want to meet down by the stage door? I just need to grab a quick shower before we head out, but I swear I'll be downstairs in fifteen minutes, tops. Did Serena show you where the showers and stuff are if you need them?"

"She did. And feel free to take your time. I didn't work up much of a sweat, so I think I'll just change, but I don't mind waiting. There's no reason for you to rush on my account."

"That's sweet of you, but I was raised better than to keep a pretty girl waiting," Addison replied with a smile and a little wink as she unlocked the door to her dressing room and shoved it open. "I'll be down in a jiff—promise," she added as she ducked inside.

Too surprised by the flirty little comment to formulate a coherent response, Mallory simply nodded at Addison's back as the young dancer disappeared into her dressing room. The slamming of Addison's door snapped her back to her senses, and she blinked twice as she shook her head and turned toward her own dressing room.

She was too brain-fried to even begin trying to make sense of what had undoubtedly been a simple bit of playful banter.

A boyish-looking man in a daring pink and purple paisley waistcoat smiled and nodded in greeting when she made her way down to the stage door area to wait for Addison. She motioned toward the small sofa as she told him, "I'm just going to wait here for Addison."

"Of course. I'm Josh, by the way. Are you new?"

"In a way? I'm not a dancer," Mallory explained as she set her bag on the sofa. "I'm just collaborating on a project with Nina."

"Yvette told me about that. And that would totally explain the violin case. Was today your first rehearsal?" When Mallory nodded, he asked, "How'd it go?"

"It went perfectly," Addison answered as she swept into the waiting area. Her wet hair was tucked behind her ears, and she had changed into a pair of jeans that were so faded they were practically white and nearly worn-through at the knees and a blue hoodie that had BLAKE emblazoned across the chest in black and white letters. Between the jeans and hoodie and the fluorescent trainers on her feet, she looked like she belonged on a university campus somewhere, and Mallory was struck once again by their gaping age-difference.

There was no way she would *ever* be confused for a student.

"Well, with you on the case, why wouldn't it?" Josh replied with a smirk. "You ladies done for the day?"

"We are. And we are going to dinner, so you enjoy the peace and quiet while it lasts, Josh-my-boy," Addison quipped as she looped a hand around Mallory's arm. "I'll see you tomorrow."

"Oh, I will," he assured her with a grin as he brandished his phone. "I just started the fifth season of *Person of Interest*."

"Dude, you're gonna love it," Addison enthused. "Hit me up tomorrow and we'll geek out properly over it, okay?"

"Deal." He waved his phone toward the door. "Now, get out of here while you can. Enjoy your dinner."

"Thanks, we will," Addison replied with a wink as she tugged at Mallory's arm. Her hand fell away once they had hit the pavement outside the stage door, and she adjusted her kit bag so the shoulder strap cut across her chest.

"So, what's Blake?" Mallory asked as they wove their way through a throng of tourists outside Higher Ground. She peered through the glass to see if she could see Lena, but the crowd at the counter was so thick that she could see nothing but the customers' backs.

"A small, private university in New Hampshire. My baby brother decided to do his Christmas shopping in the student bookstore last year, so the whole family got kitted out with Blake gear."

"How many siblings do you have?"

"Too many," Addison chuckled. She shook her head and elaborated, "I'm the fourth of five, and the only girl."

"Wow."

"It certainly kept things interesting growing up," Addison agreed. "How about you?"

"None for me." Mallory combed a hand through her hair and shrugged. Honestly, having gone off to boarding school as young as she did, she didn't feel as if she had missed out on anything by not having siblings. If anything, the quiet that awaited her at home when she returned for holidays was a blessed relief. "Are you the only ex-pat in your family?"

Addison laughed. "I'd hardly call myself an ex-pat, but yes. I mean, Asher's up in New Hampshire for school, but Andrew, Aaron, Austin, and their families all live near my parents."

"That's a lot of A-names."

"It is. Andrew was named after our grandfather, but as the story goes, he apparently never napped—he would randomly pass out places, but he never took a proper nap—so by the time my mom was pregnant with Aaron she said they were too exhausted to get past the A section in the baby name book. And then it just became a thing, basically."

Mallory smiled. "Will you move back to the States when you're done dancing?"

"Who knows." Addison shrugged. "I'm not going to tempt the Fates by planning too far ahead. And, honestly, I've been on my own for so long that I think moving back to Georgia and being around my family all the time would be too stifling."

Mallory nodded. "That's understandable. Not that my parents are very demanding of my time or anything now that I'm so close again, but there is something to the whole feeling like you've got your own space thing."

"Exactly." Addison shoved her hands into her pockets as they turned to make their way through the narrow gap in storefronts to head into Neal's Yard. Once they had made their way into the colorful central courtyard, she waved a hand toward a restaurant storefront with painted dark green window frames and a sign above the door that read 'Sprout.' "Here we are," she said as she pulled the door open and ushered Mallory inside.

The restaurant was more of a cafe, with small square tables spread in no discernible pattern throughout the space and a counter at the far end beneath a chalkboard menu that suggested one was to order first before finding a seat, and the moment the door closed behind them, a chorus of voices called out, "Addy!"

Addison shot an embarrassed look her way as she and waved at the guys behind the counter.

"Come here often, do you?" Mallory couldn't resist teasing.

"Maybe once or twice a week," Addison admitted with a wry smile. "My place is just up the way, there"—she waved toward the colorful blue and yellow buildings visible through the cafe's windows—"so when I'm too worn out from rehearsals to worry about cooking, I'll stop by on my way home."

Mallory arched a brow in surprise. Given what Devereaux had said while presenting her contract, she wouldn't have expected a dancer to be able to afford a place in the heart of the city like this. It would be impossibly rude to ask about it, however, so instead she offered, "There's a Thai place between the underground station and my flat that I'll stop at on those kinds of nights." She huffed a laugh and rubbed a hand over the back of her neck. "I have a feeling I'll be seeing them a lot more often, too, given how today went."

"Tired?"

Mallory hummed and nodded. "But I'm glad I agreed to take on the project."

Addison's eyes softened with her smile as she leaned in and whispered, "Me too."

eight

Mallory sighed as she looked around the elegantly dressed crowd milling about Sky Pod—the ultra-exclusive event space at the top of a towering glass skyscraper in the heart of downtown London—and wished, not for the first time, that she was playing with the small chamber group that was providing the ambient music for the evening instead of being forced to mingle with the crowd. She had never been a fan of glad-hand events such as this, but her attendance was non-negotiable given her position in the symphony. The fact that this was the LSO's largest fundraising event of the winter season, of course, only added to the importance of her presence.

Usually, she would be able to put on a smile and engage in meaningless small-talk with donors who possessed far less musical knowledge than they believed, but after two weeks of LSO and *Evolution* rehearsals, never mind meetings, private practice time, and the hours upon hours that were spent continuing to learn new music for the ballet, the task was even more arduous than usual. She was physically and mentally drained. Her feet, shoulders, and upper back ached almost constantly, and she was starting to get used to going about her day as if in a fog—trusting her body to move with minimal direction from her brain, which was too preoccupied with notes and bars and steps to focus on anything else.

But for as worn-down as she was from her grueling schedule, she was also energized by it, too.

Never in her life had she been pushed so hard so quickly, and she genuinely enjoyed the challenge *Evolution* provided. She still struggled to accept Nina and Toby's criticisms and critiques gracefully, but she was becoming more adept at it. Perhaps it was because of the way Addison would smile encouragingly at her whenever their individual or combined efforts were found lacking, or maybe it was simply a case of her becoming numb to hearing that she had, once again, messed up, but whatever the reason, she left the studio every night tired and sore but overall pleased with the progress they were making.

Honestly, it was more than a little shocking how quickly they were finding their groove and bringing life and sound and movement to the choreography that had previously only existed in Devereaux's mind.

"I was wondering where you'd disappeared to," Will drawled as he sidled up next to her. He snagged two flutes of champagne off the tray of a passing server and held one out to her. "I don't know about you, but I need a drink."

Mallory nodded and tapped the rim of her glass against his. "Cheers, mate," she murmured as she lifted the glass to her lips.

"So who are you hiding from over here in the corner?" Will asked as he turned to lean against the railing so they were shoulder-to-shoulder.

"Does it have to be just one person?" Mallory replied with an arched brow. She smiled when Will laughed, and shook her head. "Honestly, I'm not hiding from anyone. Everyone I've come across so far has been tolerable. I'm just tired. I would much rather be at home on the sofa than stuck here pretending that I care about whatever it is that these donors want to talk to me about."

"And next week we start performances," Will agreed with a groan as he scrubbed a hand through his hair.

"God, don't remind me." She covered a yawn with the back of her hand. "Sorry."

"You're fine." He nudged her with his elbow. "I'm beat after the last two weeks, and I'm not doing the whole ballet thing on top of all of this. I don't know how you're doing it."

"Neither do I, to be honest." Her phone buzzed in her clutch, and since she knew Will wouldn't mind, she opened the bag and pulled it out.

A small, soft smile tugged at her lips when she saw a text alert from Addison on her lock screen. *So, how's the gala?*

It was one thing to form a congenial working relationship with someone almost fifteen years her junior, but she honestly hadn't expected for them to become friends. Fifteen years was a significant age difference, and yet, whether it was because of their shared dedication to their respective crafts or something else, it wasn't. She felt immediately comfortable with Addison in a way that had only happened once before in her life—when she and Will had literally crashed into each other in the doorway of their first orchestra rehearsal at the Royal Academy of Music—and knowing that Addison was thinking about her when they weren't together made her heart flutter with joy.

Will had, of course, noticed this, and took great joy teasing her about it at every opportunity. "And how's Miss Leigh doing this evening?"

"Sod off," Mallory muttered as she unlocked her phone, the jab carrying little weight as she was still smiling. *Wonderful. Will and I are currently hiding from the masses.*

As they had made something of a tradition of going to dinner after rehearsals—meals that stretched longer and longer with each successive day—Addison had heard many stories about Will, and Mallory couldn't help but laugh when Addison replied, *Has he spilled his drink on anyone yet?*

"What?" Will rolled his eyes when Mallory turned her phone so he could see Addison's question, and shook his head as he muttered, "It happened one time."

"To the Duchess of Hanover," Mallory couldn't resist pointing out.

"I'm never going to live that one down, am I?" Will groused. "I can't believe you told her about that, by the way, but you can assure her that I haven't spilled a drop of champagne so far this evening."

Mallory laughed and typed out the instructed reply. "Is the Duchess here?" she asked Will as she hit send.

"She's an old friend of Joseph Hayes, so I'd wager she'll make an appearance at some point." He took a long, slow sip of champagne and sighed as he lowered his glass. "So, what is your new best friend up to this evening?"

"I haven't a clue." Mallory's phone buzzed, and she huffed a little laugh when she saw another text from Addison. "But if I had to guess, I'd say she's sitting at home, quite enjoying the idea of relaxing whilst I'm suffering here," she said as she showed him the message.

Will grinned and waggled his eyebrows. "You've been holding out on me, Mal. You never said you and Ms. Leigh were at the 'what are you wearing' point of your relationship…"

"I knew you'd get a kick out of that one," Mallory muttered, rolling her eyes. Really, she should have known better than to show him the text in the first place, but it was nice to let her life at the ballet filter into her everyday life at the symphony. It made it feel more real, in a way, to not have these two incredibly demanding halves of her life existing in their own individual spheres. "However, she asked what my dress looked like; not what I was wearing. I was still making up my mind when I saw her yesterday and—"

Will snatched her phone out of her hand with a smirk.

She gaped at him. "Just what do you think you're doing?"

"God. Just relax, Mal." He set his glass down and moved a few steps away. "The girl wants to see your dress, so smile and look pretty," he instructed as he lifted her phone.

"It's just a simple gown," Mallory grumbled as she glanced down at herself. Granted, the midnight blue fabric was so dark it nearly black while still managing to hold the faintest shimmer, but it was, in essence, a perfectly traditional V-neck, floor-length gown that wasn't all that dissimilar from what the majority of the women at the gala were wearing. "I can just say that…"

Will *tsked* and shook his head. "A picture is worth a thousand words and tonight, my friend, 'simple' gown or not, you look incredible. So why not send the girl a picture?"

"I know you enjoy teasing me about her for some reason, but—"

"That would be because she's the first woman to catch your eye since you moved back," Will interrupted, right eyebrow cocked in a way that dared her to contradict him.

"Yes, well, she's also fifteen years my junior, and my colleague," Mallory reminded him.

Will just arched a brow and gave her a look that clearly said he wasn't buying that argument.

"Look, I won't deny that she's a beautiful woman, or pretend that I don't enjoy her company, but this…this *thing* you seem to think is happening between us will never happen."

"How do you know that?" Will challenged.

Mallory pinched the bridge of her nose and shook her head. "Because even if she did fancy the company of the fairer sex—which I have no idea about one way or the other, by the way, so don't even bother—I am shite with women. One needn't look further than what happened with Gwen to see that. And Addison…" Her voice trailed off into a sigh, and she shook her head again. She might not have known her for very long, but she knew Addison deserved someone so much better than herself. "I'm happy with where my life is right now. Granted, I'm too busy to remember my own name half the time, but I genuinely enjoy my work, and I don't need anything else. Okay? So"— she held her hand out and crooked her fingers for him to give her the phone back as she spotted Clara over Will's shoulder, looking their way with a pointed *get your arses out here* glare on her face—"just let me reply to her text so we can get back to work. Clara looks about ready to march over here and drag us back into the crowd by the ear."

Will smiled and shook his head as he tapped at the screen of her phone. "This will be faster. Say cheese!" he instructed in a high-pitched, overly-enthusiastic tone of voice better suited to coaxing a smile from a toddler than a grown woman.

Nevertheless, Mallory couldn't help but chuckle as she muttered, "You're bloody ridiculous."

Will hummed and nodded as he turned her phone so she could see the screen. "Perhaps. But you're beautiful, Mal. And I like seeing you happy. Send her the picture."

A small smile tugged at Mallory's lips as she looked at the picture he'd taken. It wasn't often that she actually liked seeing herself in photographs, but whether it was the smirk she was wearing in the shot or the amused twinkle in her eyes, she couldn't find any of the multitude of faults she knew she possessed in the image. "Fine," she grumbled as she took the phone from him and attached the picture to the message thread. She debated adding some kind of comment to act as a caption of sorts, but every idea that came to mind seemed impossibly lame, and so she instead sent the picture on its own.

Because it was worth a thousand words.

Or something.

"There. You happy?" she asked Will as she locked the screen and reached for her bag. Before she could slip the phone inside, however, it buzzed with Addison's response. Nerves, light and fluttery, erupted in her stomach as her fingers tightened around the slim edge of the phone, and she held her breath as she flipped her wrist to see the screen.

"What'd she say?" Will asked, sounding impossibly pleased with himself.

There was no containing the smile that bloomed on her face when she saw the string of heart-eyes emojis that Addison had sent, and shook her head as she opened her clutch and dropped the phone inside. He might have prompted her to send the photo, but there was no way she was going to show him Addison's response. He would try and convince her that it meant more than she was certain it did, and the last thing she needed was his encouraging the quiet hope that blossomed in the back of her mind whenever Addison did or said something that blurred the line between friendship and flirtation. She had seen Addison with her friends in Covent Garden, had lost count of the number of hugs and cheek kisses that had been exchanged, and she didn't want to be forced to crush the whisper of *what if* that swirled inside her whenever that casual affection was turned her way by having to explain just how innocent Addison's response had been.

So, instead, she answered simply, "She liked it."

And Will, thankfully, didn't press for more as he smirked as he offered her his arm and tilted his head toward Clara, who was still staring pointedly in their direction. "Told you it was a good idea."

"You did," Mallory agreed as she tucked her hand in the crook of his arm and they began making their way back into the crowd.

Clara, who looked quite dashing in one of her trademark suits, nodded to them as they neared where she was stuck in conversation with a round-looking man in a tuxedo and his equally round wife in an unflattering peach gown and smiled at the couple as she waved a hand at them in turn as she introduced them. "Mr. and Mrs. Verne, may I introduce Mallory Collingswood, leader of the symphony, and Will Adrian, our bassoonist."

The couple's eyes betrayed exactly how star-struck they were as they all shook hands, and Mallory cleared her throat as she plastered a polite smile on her face and buckled herself in for what was sure to be a positively interminable evening.

nine

"Hold on a moment, please," Devereaux instructed, holding her hand up to stop Mallory and Addison.

Mallory turned to go get a drink of water as Nina and Toby fell into hushed conversation, only partially paying attention to the arms and legs moving in the mirror as the two talked. With almost four days down in her third week of rehearsals, she knew that now was the time to steal a sip of water if she wanted one, because as soon as the two choreographers agreed on whatever it was they were discussing, she would be directed back to one spot or another on the floor to try it all again.

They had introduced the fourth piece of music the day before, having gotten the steps for the first three at least adequately down, and so the rehearsal was back to the start-and-stop routine of the first two weeks as they worked out the kinks. Though, because the section they were working on featured Addison much more heavily than herself— she had been instructed to stand somewhere between center stage and up-stage center to give Addison more room to dance—there were noticeably fewer interruptions than when she was more actively involved.

The ultra-competitive part of herself was mildly irked by this, but mostly she was grateful for Addison's ability to quickly grasp the ideas being presented to her and turn it into a strikingly beautiful series of dance steps.

"So, what do you think?" Addison asked as she dropped to the floor beside their bags, which migrated further and further every day from where Nina, Toby, and Paul liked to stand. She stretched her legs out in front of herself as she pulled a metal water bottle from her bag and took a long swallow.

Mallory set her violin in her open case and retrieved her own refillable water bottle from the floor beside it as she sat down next to Addison. "I haven't the foggiest idea," she admitted with a small shrug as she watched the muscles in Addison's thighs twitch beneath the thin, almost sheer fabric of her white tights that she wore beneath a pair of royal blue running shorts.

The music had been building from the beginning, slowly becoming faster and more energetic to build to this part, but she wouldn't dare presume to even think that she knew enough about ballet to hazard a guess as to what Nina and Toby might be looking for.

Addison grabbed a towel from her bag and wiped at her forehead. She didn't look frustrated by the constant corrections, but she did look tired. The steps Nina and Toby had been directing her through were, to Mallory's untrained eye, at least, a blend of classical ballet and modern dance, and she had been spinning and leaping and jumping for close to two hours now. And, though she made it look easy, the sweat drenching her pale blue leotard was proof enough that it took a remarkable amount of effort to appear so effortless. "Yeah..." she sighed.

Mallory smiled and nudged Addison's foot with her own. "I thought you looked wonderful, though."

"Thanks." Addison rocked her foot to return Mallory's nudge and winked. She sighed and returned her small towel back to her bag and pulled out her phone. Her eyes widened as she looked at the screen, and she arched a questioning brow glanced up at Mallory. "We've gone over. It's pushing four o'clock. Don't you have a performance tonight?"

"I had a feeling we might have," Mallory admitted. There were no clocks in the room, but they had worked through the first ten minutes of the performance three times before bringing in the next part, a positively formidable seven-minute piece titled *Rise* that was not for the faint of heart to attempt, which they had gone through more times than she could remember. "It's fine. We don't go on until seven, and my pre-show meeting with Clara is at a quarter after six, so I have time. I brought my dress blacks with me because I wasn't sure if I'd have time to run home and change before I have to be at the Barbican, so I'll just grab a quick dinner at the canteen there and change in my office. Lord knows I'm only going to need a quick little warm up before I go on after this."

"I realize we've gone over for the day," Nina called out, interrupting them. "But if we could just work through this one more time before wrapping up, we think we have this bit figured out. Mallory, is that okay with your schedule?"

"Of course." Mallory nodded and set her water bottle back onto the floor beside her violin case as Addison all but floated to her feet.

"Here." Addison held out both her hands to help Mallory up, knowing that the violin would stay put until she was back on her feet.

They had taken to switching off helping the other to their feet after breaks, and Mallory smiled her as she laid her hands in Addison's, tensed her arms, and bent her legs to help hoist herself from the floor. "Thank you."

Addison grinned and rocked back on her left leg as she yanked on Mallory's hands.

"Addy!" Mallory squeaked as she was nearly lifted into the air.

"Sorry!" Addison laughed, looking entirely unrepentant as she deftly released Mallory's hands and grabbed her hips to steady her as she stumbled to find her footing. "Guess I don't know my own strength."

The warmth of Addison's touch was noticeable even through the material of the thin capris sweatpants she was wearing, and her pulse jumped at the way Addison's thumbs pressed against the point of her hipbones. "Bollocks," she muttered as she stared down into laughing brown eyes.

That made Addison smile even wider, and she looked so beautifully pleased with herself that Mallory couldn't help but smile back. It was, she was learning, all but pointless to try to even feign annoyance with her.

"I like it when you call me Addy," Addison whispered, her smile softening in a way that made Mallory's breath catch as she gave her sides a little squeeze. She sighed and cocked her head toward Nina and Toby as her hands fell back to her sides. "Right, well, back to the salt mines we go…"

Mallory cleared her throat and nodded. "Right…" She took a deep breath as she bent down to gather her violin and bow, and let it go as she straightened and turned toward the spot where Addison was being swept into conversation with Nina and Toby while Paul listened on.

She fiddled with the screws for the shoulder rest on her violin as a flurry of Franglais flowed back and forth between the choreographers and Addison, not really bothering to try and keep up with the exchange. The handful of words she knew in French did not translate to ballet, and it was so much less mentally taxing just to tune it all out and wait for the gist of what had been decided to be conveyed to her in proper British English.

"I can do that," Addison declared, drawing Mallory's attention back to the group.

"Excellent." Nina looked to Mallory and gestured toward the back of the room. "Mallory, could you take your previous spot, please," Devereaux instructed, the pitch of her voice lifting at the end of the statement even though it wasn't a question. "Maybe vamp the beginning few bars to let Addison find her place, and when she begins to move, just stay with her."

"Will do," Mallory agreed. She shouldered her violin as she neared her spot, and took a deep breath as her eyes locked onto Addison's in the mirrors. She waited until the small tip of Addison's chin assured her she was ready, and only then lifted her bow and began to play.

Even though Nina had only asked for the first few bars to be vamped, she played through about the first minute of the song before ad-libbing a bridge that took her back to the beginning. This time though, Addison's eyes fell shut as her shoulders, arms, and legs twitched in micro-movements to the music. The gestures got fractionally larger the third time around, and when she circled back to the beginning to start again for the fourth time, Addison's eyes blinked open as her left shoulder dipped and her right arm lifted and she began to dance.

Mallory didn't need to know the names of the steps Addison was performing to appreciate their beauty, but before she could get swept up in the moment and lose herself in the long, long legs lifting and stretching twirling in front of her, she pulled her gaze to the mirrors. It was, she had discovered over the last few weeks, so much easier to not get distracted by Addison's beauty and remarkable athleticism when she focused on the large-scale scene they were creating.

Toby catching her eye and wiggling his shoulders was all the instruction she needed to know that she had slipped into old habits and was standing too still, and she took a deep breath as she relaxed her stance and allowed herself to move with the music. Close to three weeks of practice had made it easier for her to become more demonstrative while playing—though it still took a conscious effort on her part—and the nod Toby gave her for her effort made her feel like she was flying.

She rode that high through to the end of the piece and, when the last note faded to silence, took a deep breath and squared her shoulders as she waited for Nina's verdict. In front of her, Addison seemed to be doing the same as she dropped from her toes, her heels smacking softly against the floor.

Nina seemed to enjoy toying with them as she studied them

seriously for almost a minute, tapping her index finger against her lips, but then the furrow in her brow smoothed and a pleased smile curled her lips. "We can work with that. Nicely done, both of you." She rubbed her hands on her thighs and nodded. "That's it for today, ladies. Thank you for your hard work. We'll pick up again tomorrow at one."

Mallory's eyes widened as Addison turned to her with a beaming grin. 'Nicely done' was high praise, indeed, when it came from Nina Devereaux.

Toby and Paul followed Nina from the studio as she and Addison made their way toward their things, the pleased tenor of their chatter the perfect way to end the session. All the frustration from their previous rehearsals was forgotten in the high of success, and Mallory felt lighter on her feet than she had since the first afternoon she had walked into Fonteyn.

Once the door closed after Nina and company, leaving them were alone in the studio, Addison laughed and looped a victorious arm around Mallory's waist. "We did it!"

"You did it," Mallory corrected with a smile. "I just made sure to stay out of your way."

"And played the most incredible music," Addison argued, squeezing Mallory's side for emphasis. She released her hold as they stopped in front of their pile of belongings against the side wall and gave Mallory a pointed look. "You do realize that none of this would be possible without you, right?"

"Yes, well..." Mallory murmured, lifting her right shoulder in a small shrug as she looked away. The rehearsal session had gone so much better than the ones where she had been expected to dance that she sincerely doubted Addison's belief that she was the only one who could handle the musical half of the equation, but she nevertheless appreciated the sentiment.

Addison rolled her eyes and poked Mallory's hip. "Don't even try and argue with me on this. Just accept the compliment, Collingswood."

"Pushy American," Mallory grumbled as she shifted away from Addison's finger and bent to set her violin in its case.

"Stubborn Brit," Addison shot back as she dropped to the floor and began changing out of her pointe shoes.

Mallory huffed a laugh and shook her head as she closed up her violin case. She was stubborn, usually to a fault, so she didn't see the point in even trying to argue that one. "Right, well, what do you have going on this evening? Anything exciting?"

"I've got one more rehearsal from four thirty till six to get ready for *Mayerling* in two weeks, and then I'm going to go home, toss a frozen lasagna in the oven to cook while I have a nice, long soak in the tub. Then I'll probably eat dinner on the couch with my feet in an ice bucket and turn on some old *Grey's Anatomy* episodes on Netflix to distract me from the cold."

"Minus the ice bath, that sounds heavenly." Mallory sighed as she tossed her ballet slippers into her bag and slipped her feet into her trainers, not bothering with the laces since they'd be coming off again as soon as she was in her dressing room. She was looking forward to officially kicking off the symphony's season—Clara had put together a program that she was sure the audience would love and they had performed it flawlessly in rehearsal that morning—but the idea of going home and giving herself time to recover from the day she had already put in was appealing, too.

"But the ice is the worst part!"

"Exactly." Mallory smirked and grabbed the lower rung of the barre overhead to pull herself upright. She rolled her head in a slow circle as Addison's bandaged toes disappeared into soft slippers, and tilted her head toward the door when Addison crossed her legs at her ankles and pushed herself to her feet. "Ready?"

"As I'll ever be." Addison gathered the strap of her kit bag in her hand and slung it over her shoulder. "Want me to send you a picture of my poor feet freezing away in an ice bath?" she asked as they fell into step beside each other, their bags bumping together as they walked.

"You know, just so you have proof that you weren't the only one suffering?"

Mallory shook her head as she pulled the door open and motioned for Addison to go ahead. "I don't need a picture of that, no."

"Come on, there's nothing sexier than feet that have spent the better part of the day en pointe," Addison teased. "I mean, the bruises, the chafed skin from tape being pulled off...what's not to swoon over?"

"Okay. You win," Mallory relented. "I'd love nothing more than to find a picture of your lovely feet waiting for me when I leave stage tonight."

"Kinky."

Mallory gave Addison's shoulder a shove. "You're the one who was insisting!"

Addison laughed. "Uh huh. Sure. But it's okay. I won't tell anyone."

"You're ridiculous."

"I'm in here next," Addison explained as she stopped beside the door to the De Valois studio. "And you know you love it."

Mallory huffed her best sardonic laugh and shook her head. "God, what does that say about me, then?"

"No idea. But I'm glad," Addison murmured. She cleared her throat softly as a young, male dancer in black track pants and a faded blue zip-up hoodie eased past them, muttering an apology for interrupting but that he needed to warm up. She shook her head as she helped the door close after him. "I guess it's time for me to get back at it," she sighed. "Knock 'em dead out there tonight, Mal."

"I'll try my best," Mallory promised.

Addison smiled and dipped her head in a small nod. "Well, then they're not going to know what hit them."

ten

"Do you have any ideas for how we might make a bridge between *Soar* and *Shift?*" Nina asked. "You and Addison will be mid-spin, leading into that dip we have been working on when *Soar* ends, so it needs to flow from one to the next without pause."

Mallory nodded slowly as she mulled the possible options. The past fortnight had moved their progress on *Evolution* forward toward the final third of the ballet, and for as much as she loved watching her collaboration with Addison come to life, it was moments like these that made her feel like she was actually contributing something valuable to the production they were creating. She was getting better at moving her feet and her body how Nina wanted, but this—discussing the music— was where she still felt most comfortable. The difficulty in joining the two lay in the fact that *Soar* ended a full octave higher than where *Shift* began, but...

"If you want it to be done quickly, to jump from one to the next without much in the way of superfluous notes, a portamento would probably be the most effective way to go at it." She lifted her violin to her shoulder and played the last few bars of *Soar*, drawing the final note to the extreme limit of her bow before angling it down and, in a single pull, taking the music from high-to-low and then seamlessly transitioned into the opening few bars *Shift*.

She was having to work long into the night, even after a full day of rehearsals and performances, to commit the remaining minutes of music for *Evolution* to memory, but the pleased smile that curled Nina's lips as she let the final note fade was evidence that the effort was worth it.

"Perfect." Nina nodded. "Yes. That will be perfect," she repeated, almost to herself as she moved her arms and shoulders in minute approximations of what she was, undoubtedly, going to ask them to perform. Still smiling, she arched a brow at Mallory as she asked, "Will you remember it?"

"I'll make a note on my music, but yes, I should be able to remember it just fine." Mallory glanced over at Addison, who was lying on the floor with her eyes closed and her arms flung wide from her shoulders while her legs extended above her, propped against the barre.

"Wonderful." Mallory turned her attention back to Nina, who was looking at Addison with a critical eye. Addison was clearly spent. Beyond rehearsals for *Evolution,* which were becoming more demanding by the day due to the fact that she was able to grasp the new ideas being presented to her so much more quickly, Addison was also pushing through final preparations for her turn in *Mayerling* and beginning rehearsals for *Swan Lake.* It was a schedule that would test even the toughest athlete and, thankfully, Nina was able to recognize and understand when her dancers needed a break. "We'll pick up with this transition tomorrow," she decided, making sure to speak loudly enough for her voice to carry to where Addison was lying on the floor. She smiled fondly at the little cheer Addison gave in response and shook her head as she instructed, "But, for now, try and get some rest. Go hit the physio suite—get a massage and whatever else you need to be ready for tomorrow. We'll work for only an hour or so, so Addison will have plenty of time to rest before her performance, but we can't afford to miss a day."

"One o'clock?" Paul asked as he began packing his things. It was just the four of them in Fonteyn, as Toby had left halfway through their session to assist with another rehearsal.

Nina nodded. "Yes." She patted Mallory on the shoulder. "Good work today."

"Thank you." Mallory dipped her head.

"How about me?" Addison called. She was still laying on the floor, though she did crane her neck in a way to be almost looking at them.

"Adequate," Nina declared, her lips pressing into a smirk.

"Love you too, Nina," Addison sassed as she resumed her previous position, face pointed toward the ceiling with her eyes closed.

Nina chuckled softly under her breath and gave Mallory's shoulder one last pat before she turned toward the door. Paul followed at her heels, offering Mallory a smile and a small tip of his head—he wasn't the most talkative fellow—and once the door had closed after them, Mallory sighed and made her way toward her things.

"Are you okay?" she asked Addison as she knelt beside her to begin packing away her violin.

"Just tired," Addison assured her through a yawn. "You?"

"About the same," Mallory confessed. "And I've still got a performance later this evening to get through."

Addison turned her head to look at Mallory and blinked her eyes open. "You should come to physio with me and get a massage. Not a full sports massage or anything that will leave you sore, but just a relaxing rub-down. Eve's massages are pure magic; she'll have you feeling like you can leap tall buildings in a single bound by the time she's done."

Mallory had to admit that a massage sounded wonderful, but it was already nearing three forty-five and she needed to be at St. Luke's—the LSO's auxiliary performance location—by half-past six to meet with Clara and the young girl who had been selected from a local youth orchestra to serve as a "guest conductor" for a couple of the pieces they would be performing that evening. As had become her routine, her concert blacks were hanging in a garment bag in her dressing room, and she had been hoping to steal a quick cat-nap to recharge her batteries a bit before having to head out. "I don't know, Addy. I mean, it sounds heavenly, but—"

"Trust me." Addy rolled onto her side and pushed herself to a sitting position. "What you need is to get on Eve's table. Her hands are seriously to die for," she enthused as she began unknotting the ribbons around her ankles.

"How do you even know she'd have time for me? And, if she's that good, why don't you go to her?"

"Whenever I can get onto her schedule, I do. But Gabs had her booked already, so I took a spot with Jason. I'm not picky, and he does a good job getting into my hip. But now Celine is out for a couple weeks with a tweaked hammy and Gabs has been slotted into her spot in the *Mayerling* rotation, so she'll be in rehearsal this afternoon instead."

Mallory nodded. While she had no idea who Celine was, she had met Gabriella "Gabs" Calvente, a first-soloist with the company and Addison's best friend, a handful of times. The beautiful Spaniard was just as friendly and outgoing as Addison, and though it was a little overwhelming to be caught in the whirlwind of so much combined energy, watching their easy friendship reminded her a lot of herself and Will. "Good for her."

"Yeah. So, anyway, take her spot with Eve."

"Addy," Mallory sighed and rubbed the back of her neck. Whether as an unconscious response to the suggestion of a massage, or simply a result of standing still long enough for the aches of playing as much as she had been lately to settle in, she was suddenly keenly aware of how tight her neck and shoulders were. "You're not going to let this go, are you?"

Addison grinned, clearly sensing victory was near. "Nope." She tossed her pointe shoes into her bag and grabbed her slippers. "Come on, Mal," she cajoled in a soft voice as she popped to her feet. "You've been here for a month now, it's about time you take advantage of some of the perks. Lord knows you've earned it."

"Okay. Fine. You win. Let's go see this magic-worker of yours."

"Yay!" Addison cheered as she grabbed Mallory's left arm and pulled her toward the door.

The curious looks that had followed Mallory the first few weeks she had been rehearsing *Evolution* had all but disappeared, and she appreciated being able to blend into the waves of dancers that ebbed and flowed between various rehearsal spaces. It was a nice change of pace to simply be a face amongst the crowd, not responsible for anything beyond herself.

The physio and massage suites were on the floor below the main rehearsal studios. What Mallory assumed was the main physio suite—a gym full of weight machines, ellipticals, treadmills, and free weights that looked like it could rival the fanciest of private health clubs—was closest to the lifts, and the woman working the desk outside the glassed-in room waved at Addison as they passed. Inside, there were a good dozen or so dancers putting the equipment through its paces.

Mallory leaned in close to whisper, "Surely there aren't that many injured dancers in the company?"

Addison chuckled and shook her head. "Most of the boys like to lift at least a few times a week because they need to be strong enough to throw us girls in the air, and a lot of us will come in and log some miles on the elliptical on lighter rehearsal days for the cardio. Of course, we all have our weak spots—ankles, hips, backs, what have you—and the therapists are always willing to help devise programs for us that will strengthen those areas. This isn't a job you can do if you're hurt, so we're all very proactive in making sure we're as physically strong as possible to lower the risk of injury."

"That makes sense."

"Which includes," Addison continued with a smile and a wink as she steered them around a corner that took them right up to a small desk that was situated at the head of a short hallway, "regular massages."

The man at the desk looked up at them and smiled. He looked to be in his early forties, Mallory guessed, with cropped salt-and-pepper hair and kind blue eyes. "Hey, Addy and friend."

Addison wrapped a hand around Mallory's arm as she leaned into her side. "Jason, this is my partner in Nina's latest attack on the old-school ballet establishment, Mallory Collingswood."

Jason nodded as he pushed himself to his feet and offered Mallory his hand. "Jason Collins."

"Pleasure," Mallory murmured as she shook his hand.

"She's going to take Gabs' spot with Eve," Addison explained.

"Gabs said you wanted us to hold the spot for you when she called down earlier." Jason smirked. "I was going to give you a hard time for just showing up and not calling ahead to cancel, but I guess all has to be forgiven now. Shame though, I had quite the dressing-down plotted for you."

Addison laughed. "Sure you did."

"You are not as cute as you think you are," Jason pointed out.

"Please, I'm adorable," Addison sassed.

Jason rolled his eyes. "Anyway," he declared, pointedly ignoring Addison as he smiled at Mallory. "If you're putting up with that one on a daily business, I can't believe we haven't seen you sooner."

Mallory pursed her lips to keep from laughing and lifted her shoulders in a small shrug.

"Oh, shut it. She loves me," Addison insisted. "I am an absolute delight to work with."

"Yeah, that's what all you superstars think," Jason jibed. "Mallory, Eve is finishing up a phone call and then she'll be out. And we"—he snapped his fingers at Addison—"are going to go dig into that hip of yours."

"No digging. I'm on tomorrow night."

"Don't be a wuss," Jason teased.

Addison arched a brow defiantly. "Excuse me?"

"Will you two knock it off," a new, distinctly female voice called out. The woman was tall and lean, all arms and legs in a way that

Mallory had come to associate with dancers, with wild red curls and the brightest green eyes Mallory had ever seen. She shook her head at Addison and Jason, who had matching playfully affronted looks on their faces, and extended her hand to Mallory. "They're as bad as children whenever they get together. Eve Burkstrand."

Mallory bit the inside of her cheek to keep from smiling and nodded as she shook Eve's hand. "Mallory Collingswood."

"You ready?"

"I guess?" Mallory glanced around the tiny reception area. The last time she'd visited a new masseuse, she'd had to fill out a brief medical history. "Are there any forms I need to fill out?"

Eve smiled kindly and shook her head. "Nope. We'll take care of it in the room."

"I'll wait for you out here?" Addison offered.

It wasn't necessary, really, Mallory was sure she would be able to find her way back to her dressing room without too much difficulty, but she couldn't help but be touched by the offer. "Sure."

"Excellent," Jason drawled, clapping a hand on Addison's shoulder and steering her toward a room. "Now, let's go. For as much as I'd love to go home after this, you are not the last dancer who is going to occupy my table today."

"Aww, poor baby…" Addison mocked as she turned into the room.

"You know, it's not a good idea to tease the guy who's going to be digging his thumb into your hip here in a minute," Jason pointed out as he followed her inside.

The door closed after them slow enough that they could hear Addison saying, "Yeah, well, you know it's not a good idea for you to do anything that will keep me from going on stage tomorrow night, so I guess we're at a stalemate here, aren't we, Bucko?"

"Wow," Mallory muttered once the door had clicked shut after them.

"Yep." Eve chuckled. "Come on." Once they were secured in the room beside the one Addison had disappeared into, Eve leaned against the door and crossed her arms over her chest. "Have you had any recent surgeries?"

Mallory shook her head as she set her violin and kit bag on the floor beneath a chair. "None."

"Points of pain?"

"Just a general discomfort in my neck and shoulders. But I do have a concert tonight. Addison seemed to suggest that wouldn't be a problem?"

"Not a problem at all. Do you want me to work on your legs too, or just the upper body?"

"I think my upper body would be more than sufficient."

"Okay then." Eve smiled and tipped her head at the sheet-covered table in the center of the room. "If you want, you can leave your sweats and underwear on. Shoes, shirt, and bra will need to come off. There's a heating pad under the sheet on the table that I can turn off if you get too warm, but just go ahead and make yourself comfortable on your stomach beneath the top sheet, and I'll be back in in a minute."

"Wonderful. Ta," Mallory muttered as she began toeing off her trainers. Once the door was shut, she quickly undressed and made herself comfortable on the table as Eve had instructed.

A few minutes later a light knock sounded on the door, which was pushed slowly open as Eve called out, "Ready?"

"Yes," Mallory answered through a yawn. "Sorry."

"No reason to apologize," Eve assured her with a smile. "Feel free to close your eyes and relax. Do you want me to turn on some music?"

Mallory shrugged. So much of her days anymore were filled with noise and people and activity that she had grown to cherish moments of quiet—even if her mind did seem to be constantly spinning. "I'm fine without it if you are."

"Perfectly fine," Eve assured her.

Mallory sighed as warm hands landed lightly on her upper back.

Eve chuckled. "When was your last massage?"

"God, a lifetime ago," Mallory muttered. "Maybe two years?"

Eve clicked her tongue disapprovingly. "When we're done here, we're going to put you on my schedule at least once a week. Is there a day you don't work?"

"Not anymore," Mallory groaned as Eve's thumbs found matching knots on her shoulders, one on either side of her spine. "Tuesdays are my day off at the LSO, and I have rehearsals here with Nina Monday through Friday, so…"

"We'll figure something out," Eve assured her in a gentle tone. "Now, just relax. Let me know if you need me to ease up anywhere, but I won't dig into anything I find too hard."

Mallory sighed as Eve's hands smoothed over her shoulders. "You are an angel."

Eve chuckled but didn't respond, and Mallory relaxed into the table. She made a mental note to thank Addison for talking her into this, but then all thought disappeared as her mind contented itself with focusing only on the heavenly push and pull of Eve's hands against her skin.

"Okay, you," Eve declared some time later, placing her palm flat on Mallory's back between her shoulder blades and giving a little shake. "Time to wake up."

"No thank you," Mallory muttered. She blinked her eyes open and smiled at Eve. "Addison was right. Your hands are pure magic."

"I'm glad I could help," Eve chuckled. "Feel free to lie there for as long as you want, and I'll be waiting at the desk once you're dressed, and we'll look at the schedule and find a time for you to come in every week."

Mallory nodded as Eve slipped out of the room, and sighed as she pushed herself upright. She would have loved nothing more than to stay on that table all night, but a glance at the clock on the wall over the door was enough to spur her into action. She had just over ninety minutes until she needed to be at St. Luke's, and she still needed to shower, dress, and find some kind of dinner.

"It was nice while it lasted," she murmured to herself as she reached for her clothes.

She found Addison sitting on the desk in the reception area talking to Eve and Jason once she'd dressed and gathered her things, and she smiled and nodded at the questioning look Addison gave her.

Addison beamed. "Told you."

"Hush, you." Eve poked Addison in the side. "I have an opening at six on Mondays. Would that work for you?"

Mallory looked at Addison. It was rare that the LSO had a performance on Monday evenings, but if she came down to see Eve after they had finished with their rehearsal, they wouldn't be able to go to dinner. "Do you have anything either in the morning or around midday on Tuesday? Our rehearsal doesn't begin until three o'clock, so I can come in any time before then…"

"I don't." Eve shook her head. "Sorry."

"You're early!" Jason announced with a happy smile as a lanky male dancer in baggy basketball shorts and a stretched out hoodie rounded the corner. "Let's get you on the table, my man."

"I'm your last appointment, aren't I?" the dancer laughed. He smiled at Addison. "Hey, Addy."

"What's up, Matt?"

"Nothing much," Matt replied with a shrug as he fell into step beside Jason.

Jason pointed at Addison. "I'll see you Saturday morning."

"Yes, sir." Addison saluted.

"Now *that's* the respect I like to see!" Jason threw back at her with a wink.

Addison shook her head as she looked back at Mallory. "Take the spot, Mal. If you don't, somebody else will…"

Mallory glanced at Eve, who was watching them with a small, speculative smile, and lifted her eyes to the ceiling as she murmured, "But we usually go to dinner…"

Addison smiled and shrugged. "I'll wait for you."

"You're sure?" Mallory couldn't help but ask.

"God, you two are cute," Eve interrupted. She laughed at the way Mallory's eyes widened in surprise and Addison's mouth fell open. "Sorry, but my next appointment should be here any minute; so if we could make a decision on this sometime today…"

Mallory blushed. "I will take the appointment. Thank you."

"Great. I've got you on the calendar. I'll see you Monday. Good luck at your performance tonight."

"Thank you," Mallory murmured as Addison hopped off the desk.

"Sorry about that," Addison apologized once they had rounded the corner and there was little chance of Eve overhearing their conversation.

"About what?"

Addison dragged a hand through her hair. "I don't know," she sighed after a moment. She shook her head as she drove her thumb into the call button for the lift. "Will you have enough time to get to St. Luke's?"

"I should."

"Good." The lift arrived, and they filtered inside. "So," Addison began as the doors slid shut, "do you have another performance tomorrow night?"

"No." Mallory tilted her head in a small shrug. She had been sure the topic had come up at dinner the other night, but perhaps she was mistaken. "We have a matinee and evening performance Saturday, so the scheduler saw fit to allow us a night off."

Addison nodded. "Would you maybe want to come to the show tomorrow night, then? I can leave tickets at the window for you."

Mallory smiled at the adorable way Addison was worrying at her lower lip. "That sounds lovely."

"Really?" Addison grinned. "Okay. Is there anyone you'd like to bring? I can get four tickets…"

"Maybe Will and his wife?" Mallory mused aloud. She shook her head and shrugged. "I can ask him tonight at our performance.

111

Otherwise, I'll just come by myself."

"You're sure?"

Mallory nodded. "I can think of no better way to spend my night off."

eleven

"Well, don't you look lovely!" Lena smiled at Mallory. "Hot date?"

Mallory smiled and shook her head as the door to Higher Ground closed behind her. "Thank you." She smoothed her hands over the lapels of the light gray blazer she wore over her favorite little black dress to combat the chill in the air. The weather had yet to take a significant turn toward winter, but it wasn't nearly warm enough to venture out without a jacket of some kind. She had spent far more time than she would ever admit deciding on her outfit, and it was a relief to hear that she had chosen well. "And, no. Not really."

"What does 'not really' mean?"

"Nothing. I'm just meeting Will and Siobhan over at Covent Garden to see the show tonight."

"And how is the stunning Miss Leigh doing?" Lena teased, her voice tinged with laughter.

Mallory rolled her eyes. Of course Lena would know that Addison was dancing tonight. "God, not you, too."

"Have I told you that she looks for you every morning when she stops in on her way to work?" She sighed dramatically and shook her head. "And on the days when you're not hunkered down at back there"—she hiked a thumb in the direction of Mallory's favorite table near the fireplace—"she looks like somebody stole her puppy."

"She does not," Mallory muttered.

"Well, okay, maybe it's not *that* bad, but her smile definitely loses a few watts." Lena looked at the large, circular wall clock hanging above a cluster of leather armchairs just off the front entrance, and waved a hand toward the front counter. "Curtain is in a little more than half an hour. Coffee?"

Mallory nodded. Though their rehearsal that afternoon had run just long enough for them to work through the transition they had been discussing the day before two times before Nina ordered Addison off to rest, she had made use of the unscheduled hours to begin working on the last few pieces for *Evolution* instead of relaxing as well. She figured she didn't need to—she had gone from a full rehearsal to her own evening performances without issue—but it appeared the lack of adrenaline that precluded a performance left her feeling dead on her feet and dangerously close to falling asleep. And she would be damned if she missed one minute of Addison's performance. "Please. The stronger, the better."

The mischief in Lena's expression softened into concern as they began making their way toward the front counter. "How are you holding up?"

"As well as could be expected, I think, given my schedule. I'm used to working long days, of course, but the physicality this new endeavor requires of me is something I'm still getting used to."

"Are you sorry you agreed to take on the project? Nina isn't an easy woman to work for."

"Nina's been great, actually. Demanding, of course, but it's my own fault for having two left feet and a penchant for standing far too stiffly for her liking." Mallory shrugged. "I knew taking on the ballet would make my days even more grueling than they already were, but I don't regret the decision."

"Full-caff cappuccino?" Lena asked as she slipped behind the counter, not even waiting for Mallory's response as she began loading a portafilter with ground espresso. She waved off the credit card Mallory tried to hand her. "This one is on the house."

"I can—"

"Just say thank you and be done with it," Lena interrupted.

"Thank you and be done with it," Mallory repeated obediently.

Lena shot her a playful glare as she turned on the machine and began pouring the shot. "Cheeky bugger."

Mallory did her best to look innocent as Lena pulled a gallon of milk from the fridge behind the bar and poured it into the stainless frothing pitcher. "Me?"

"Keep it up, Collingswood, and I'll throw in an extra shot or four that will keep you up all night."

Mallory held her hands up in defeat. "My apologies, darling."

Lena smiled as she powered on the steamer, letting her expression convey that the apology was accepted. Once the machine had quieted and she was pouring the drink into a paper carryout cup, she asked, "So did you send her flowers?"

"Addison?"

"No, the other woman you got all dressed up for. Yes, Addison."

Mallory nodded. "I did. I had Serena get me the number of the florist she prefers who services the ballet, and I phoned it in this afternoon."

"Good. You didn't cheap out on the bouquet, did you?"

Mallory huffed a laugh. "Hardly. The bloody thing cost me almost two hundred quid. I expect the flowers to be gilded at that price."

"Good girl. And did you include a card?" Lena handed Mallory her coffee. It was, thankfully, large enough that it would keep her awake for a few hours but small enough that she shouldn't have too much trouble finishing it in the time it took her to walk to the main entrance of the Royal Opera House.

"Of course. Dare I ask why you're giving me the third degree on this?"

Lena shook her head as she made her way out from behind the counter and pulled Mallory into a light hug. "No, you probably don't want to ask that." She brushed a kiss across her cheek and smirked as she gave her a gentle push toward the door. "You do probably want to get going, though, so you're not late. Enjoy the show."

Mallory took a deep breath and let it go slowly. "Okay. Thank you."

A crowd of people in suits and dresses emerged from the tube station as she exited Higher Ground, and Mallory sipped at her coffee as she merged with the pack. She spotted Will and Siobhan the moment she rounded the corner onto Bow and lifted her takeaway cup in greeting as she approached. Will, who had been scanning the crowd, smiled and waved back. He must have said something to announce her arrival because his wife, Siobhan glanced up at her and nodded, looking apologetic and harried as she turned her attention back to her phone.

"Hiya, sorry I'm late," Mallory apologized as she approached the couple.

"It's fine," Will assured her with a smile. "Siobhan's just finishing up some work."

"Everything okay?" Mallory asked.

"The steel for the Pikes project was delivered this afternoon, and when the foreman inspected it all, he found that half the beams had some kind of damage," Siobhan answered distractedly. She was a project architect at one of London's many firms responsible for replacing the old stone and character of the city with steel and glass. She sighed and hit send on the message she'd been composing. "So I'm just trying to put out fires before Quincy loses his shit."

"I see…" Mallory murmured. She had heard enough horror stories about Siobhan's boss to know that his losing his shit usually resulted in pink slips.

"Right." Siobhan shook her head. "But, enough worrying about work for one night. We are here to have some fun." She smiled as she pulled Mallory into a hug. "You look wonderful."

"You too," Mallory murmured.

"Please," Siobhan chuckled. "This is the suit I wore to work today.

I came straight from the office. Unlike this one"—she shot her husband a playful glare as she ran a hand through her loosely curled honey-blond hair that fell in waves around her shoulders—"who spent his afternoon lounging on the sofa, napping and watching footy."

"We've got two performances tomorrow!" Will argued.

"I wish I'd made the time for a nap," Mallory confessed with no small measure of regret. "But, instead, I have coffee." She motioned with her cup to the finely-dressed people making their way through the lower doors of the Royal Opera House. "Shall we go collect our tickets?"

"So do you just stop and stare at the building every day when you come for rehearsals?" Will asked as he gazed up at the gleaming white, Neoclassical landmark.

"If I entered here, I might," Mallory admitted as he pulled the door open for them all. "But I use the stage door that's just there," she explained, motioning to the narrow side street to their right as she slipped past him. She took a sip of her coffee and eyed the queue for the ticket window as the warmth of the small lobby swept over her. There were a good half-dozen people in front of her, and she sighed as she looked at Will and Siobhan. "You lot can go wander if you want. I'll collect the tickets."

Siobhan looked poised to agree when her phone chirped in her bag, and she swore under her breath as she dug into the purse to retrieve it. "I'm sorry, I need to take this."

"We'll just go over there"—Will gestured to the side of the lobby that was mostly out of the way with his left hand as he touched his wife's elbow with his right so she would follow—"and wait for you."

Mallory joined the back of the queue and sipped at her coffee as she busied herself with watching the people streaming through the main doors and idly listening-in to the conversations happening around her.

"I can't believe you managed to secure tickets to Addison Leigh's performance," the woman in front of her enthused as she looked around the lobby. She and the man on her left looked to be in their early twenties, and the lack of a ring on either of their left hands suggested they were on a date. Her accent had the distinctive tones and cadence of the North, and Mallory smiled as she wondered if they had made the trip down just for this performance. The woman must have noticed her smiling, because she turned toward Mallory and added, "I've heard watching her dance is positively life-altering."

That had certainly proven to be true in her own experience, and Mallory dipped her head in a small nod as she confirmed, "It is."

"Have you seen her dance before?" The woman's eyes widened.

"A few times," Mallory demurred with a kind smile. She had become so accustomed to performances being *work*—show up, tune, discuss particulars of the performance, file out, play, stand, bow, pack up, wash-rinse-repeat—that it was refreshing to be reminded that there were people in the audience who were genuinely thrilled to be there. "She is incredible. You'll be blown away by her performance tonight, I'm sure."

"Oh, I hope so," the woman replied, looking mildly embarrassed as she realized she'd been fangirling to a perfect stranger.

"Darling, we're up," the man beside her said in a low voice.

"Oh! Right!" The woman gave Mallory one last smile before turning toward the ticket window.

Mallory hovered at a discreet distance to not infringe on their privacy, and offered them a small bow once they'd left the window and began making their way toward the crimson stairs that led toward the main level of the auditorium.

She cleared her throat as she approached the window and offered the young man working the desk a polite smile. "Yes, hello. My name is Mallory Collingswood. Addison Leigh was supposed to leave tickets for me here?"

He nodded and reached for an envelope that was sitting atop a small stack of programs on the counter in front of him. "Here you are," he said as he handed her the envelope as well as the programs it had been resting on.

"Ta," Mallory murmured as she smiled at the sight of Addison on the program's cover.

"And these are your backstage passes for after the show," the young man continued as he held out another envelope. "Go to the end of the corridor nearest the stage on the orchestra level once the performance is over, and an usher will see you through."

Mallory nodded as she took the envelope. Backstage passes were unnecessary considering the fact that she could explore the stage area at her leisure whenever she wanted given her position with the company, but she quite liked the idea of seeing Addison after the show. While she more than understood that Addison needed to rest before her performance, she had missed the time they'd lost together that afternoon. "Thank you."

"My pleasure. Enjoy the performance," the young man replied with a smile.

"I'm sure we will," Mallory assured him, returning his smile with a small one of her own.

"All good?" Will asked once she rejoined them.

Mallory nodded and handed him the programs. "We are. And she also left backstage passes for afterward if you would like to go have a look around."

"That was nice of her," Siobhan murmured.

There was no missing the sly smile she and Will shared, and Mallory shook her head. "You are both ridiculous."

"So where are our seats?" Will asked as Siobhan slipped her phone back into her purse.

Mallory shrugged and opened the first envelope she'd been given. Her eyes widened in surprise. "Box sixty-eight," she shared as she pulled out a folded piece of paper that had been tucked behind the tickets. There was no containing the smile that curled her lips when she saw the message Addison had left for her.

Enjoy the show. Can't wait to see you afterwards. -A

She cleared her throat as she slipped the note into her purse where it would be safe from prying eyes, and wasn't at all surprised to find Will and Siobhan watching her with matching grins. "Sod off, the both of you."

"No idea what you're talking about," Will retorted as he motioned toward the stairs that would take them to the amphitheater.

"Must have been some note," Siobhan added, waggling her eyebrows. She laughed when Mallory only pursed her lips in response, and wrapped a light hand around her arm. "Come on, Collingswood. Let's go find the box seats your *friend* secured for you."

"I should have come by myself," Mallory muttered. She tossed her nearly-empty coffee cup in the rubbish bin at the foot of the stairs, and allowed her friends to all but carry her forward.

"Maybe." Will draped an arm over her shoulders. "But you're stuck with us. There is no excuse for one person to keep an entire box to themselves."

"I don't know. At this point, it sounds rather peaceful," Mallory quipped.

Will's arm fell away after a few steps, though Siobhan's fingers remained curled around her arm, and while she could have done without the teasing, she was glad to have her friends with her. A handful of ushers in black suits and crimson ties were spaced along the main foyer, and she handed Will the envelope with their tickets as they made their way toward the nearest one.

"Right away, madam," Will murmured.

"Welcome to the Royal Opera House," the usher greeted them with a polite smile as he looked at the tickets. He straightened slightly when he saw where they were headed, and motioned with a gloved hand toward the grand curving staircase on their left. "Your box in on the balcony level, stage right. Do you require any assistance in finding your seats?"

"No, thank you. I'm sure we'll be fine," Mallory assured him with a smile.

"Enjoy the show," he replied, his head and shoulders dipping in a small bow.

The box was easy to find once they had reached the appropriate level, and Mallory looked around in wonder as she stepped through the curtain. Built in the style of nineteenth-century Italian opera houses, the compact, horseshoe-shaped amphitheater was designed in a way that allowed every seat to have a clear view of the stage. A flutter of nerves and excitement bubbled in her throat as she drank in the lavish crimson velvet that blocked the stage, the lights and the gold leaf accents that made the space feel like it was from another era, and she swallowed them back when she stepped to the front of the box and looked down at the stage.

In a matter of months, she and Addison would be taking that stage together for the first time.

"Not a bad view, huh?" Will said as he waved a hand at the theatre. "Pictures really don't do this place justice."

"It's quite striking," Mallory agreed as she turned, her voice soft, as if speaking above a whisper would shatter the grandeur that surrounded them.

Will hummed in agreement. "You two go on and take the front seats, I'll stretch out in the back."

"Are you sure?" Mallory asked, tearing her eyes away from the gilded edge of the curtain to look at them. "Surely you'd prefer to sit next to your wife."

"Eh, this way I can fall asleep without getting in trouble." He waved her off with a laugh. His expression gentled as he added, "Addison didn't give you this box to hide in the back of it, Mal."

"I still don't know why she gave me a box at all," Mallory admitted.

"You're adorable," Siobhan said as she took the seat in the front row that was further from the stage. "She's clearly trying to impress you. You'll be able to see everything from here."

"I would have been able to see everything from any of the seats."

"Not like you will from here, I'd wager." Will pointed toward an empty box one level down and directly across from them that bore the royal coat of arms. "If the Queen sits there, this has to be one of the better seats in the house."

The sconces at the back of the box flickered and the music from the orchestra pit swelled, and Mallory shook her head as she obeyed the cue to take her seat. "It probably just hadn't sold, so the box office gave it to her," she argued.

"Or that," Will conceded as he dropped into the seat behind his wife.

His smirk negated his easy agreement, however, and Mallory pinched the bridge of her nose as she wondered just what she would have to say for people to understand that there was nothing going on between her and Addison.

"Behave," Siobhan chuckled as she turned in her seat to smack Will's leg with her purse.

"Of course, darling," Will drawled.

Siobhan rolled her eyes as she turned her back on him. She sighed as she grabbed Mallory's wrist and gave it a light squeeze. "Come on, Mal. The show's about to start."

Mallory took a deep breath and nodded as she sat beside Siobhan, and let it go slowly as she set her purse on the floor in front of her feet. She caught her lower lip between her teeth and worried at it as she turned in her seat so she could see the stage in its entirety without having to turn her head.

The hum of conversation quieted as the lights dimmed, and her lip slipped free of her teeth as she instinctively leaned forward. A flurry of motion in the pit led to an outward swell of sound as the orchestra began to play, ushering the curtain to rise as spotlights found their targets on the stage.

As a child, she had been awed by the entirety of the ballet in the way all children are swept away by theatre, but this time the stage could have been bare of any set decorations for all she noticed. From the moment Addison glided onto the stage to a brief burst of applause, the rest of the theatre—hell, the rest of the world—may well have disappeared, because all she could see was Addison.

The small smile that often curled her lips in rehearsal was gone, replaced by a steely focus and whatever expression was required for the story she was dancing to be properly conveyed. She commanded the stage with leaps and turns that seemed otherworldly, her body stretching and reaching, twisting and bending with such fluidity and ease that it was like watching a painting come to life.

It was, as the woman at the ticket window had said, a life-altering experience to watch Addison perform.

And that was even after spending five days a week in a studio with her.

"Goddamn, she is good," Siobhan murmured when the curtains fell for intermission and the theatre lights slowly brightened.

Mallory could only nod in agreement as she stared at the stage.

"How long is the intermission?" Will wondered.

"Fifteen? Twenty?" Siobhan guessed. "I imagine it will be like most other theatre performances."

"Fancy a drink?" Will asked.

"Sure. I could go for a glass of wine," Siobhan answered. "Mal?"

Mallory cleared her throat and shook her head. "No. Thank you." She blinked as she tore her eyes away from the stage, and wasn't at all surprised to find Siobhan watching her with a speculative look on her face. "But don't let me stop you, please. I'll just wait here."

"Water?" Siobhan offered as she pushed herself to her feet.

Really, all she wanted was for the curtain to rise and the lights to dim and Addison to reappear, but Mallory smiled and dipped her head in a small nod all the same. "That would be lovely. Thank you."

Siobhan's smile was soft and understanding as she gave Mallory's shoulder a light squeeze. "We'll be back."

"I'll be here," Mallory replied as she turned back toward the stage.

123

Will and Siobhan returned just as the lights began to flicker once more, and Mallory murmured her thanks as she sipped at the water they'd brought her. The lights dimmed after what felt like a lifetime of waiting, and she barely noticed when Siobhan took the small plastic glass from her hand as the music swelled and the curtains rose on the back half of the performance.

She was helpless but to surrender to the siren's call of Addison's presence on stage, a state she welcomed gladly as she allowed herself to be swept away by her performance. In what seemed like no time at all the story reached its end, and then she was on her feet with the rest of the audience, applauding the performance they had been blessed to witness as they waited for the cast to assemble.

The noise in the theatre when the curtains rose again was thunderous, and she ignored the flutter of her heart in her chest and the tears that stung at her eyes as she searched the faces at the back of the stage, looking for Addison as the corps took their bow. Next were the character dancers, the soloists, and then the prince, and then finally, finally, the bodies clogging the stage parted and Addison appeared, beaming at the audience as she glided toward the front of the stage. Her right foot slid behind her left as she dropped into a graceful bow, and when she stood, a young man in a black suit was making his way toward her with a positively enormous bouquet. Flowers balanced in the crook of her left arm, her co-star joined her at the front of the stage, and they bowed together.

Addison's eyes searched out the box where Mallory was standing, applauding so hard her hands were beginning to sting from the effort, and the beaming smile she'd given the theatre at large softened to something much more intimate as their gazes locked.

"You are so fucked, mate!" Will laughed in her ear as Addison turned to wave at the audience one last time before stepping behind the curtains that were beginning to drop.

Though the curtains remained down, Addison and her co-star slipped between the gap three more times before the applause finally began to fade, and once it became clear that they were not going to emerge again, Siobhan handed Mallory her purse and asked, "You ready to go backstage and tell her in person how incredible she was?"

"I…" Mallory nodded. "Yes."

Siobhan chuckled and wrapped a gentle hand around her arm. "Come on, sweetie," she murmured.

Mallory took a deep breath as she allowed herself to be led out of the box and down the stairs, and by the time they reached the main floor, she felt somewhat in control of herself once more. The usher who looked more like a bouncer studied both sides of their backstage passes before eventually waving them through.

The stage was empty, save for the crews that were busy breaking down the set dressings from the performance so they could set up for the opera the following day, and Mallory glanced at Siobhan and Will as she led them deeper into the wings. She spotted Addison and her co-star—who she now recognized as the dancer who'd arrived for his massage when they had been leaving the night before, though she could not remember his name—talking at a portable barre as they stretched in cool-down.

"Hey, you," Addison murmured when she spotted them.

Addison's co-star looked between them with a smile and shook his head as he lowered his leg and gave Addison's hand a quick squeeze. "Looks like your visitors have arrived, my dear, so I'll get out of your hair. Way to crush it out there tonight."

"You too, Matt." Addison smiled and lifted herself up onto the balls of her feet to pull him into a hug with the bar between them. "You were brilliant."

"Only because I had to keep up with you," Matt replied with a cheeky wink. He waved to Mallory, Will, and Siobhan, and then turned with a little hop to leave.

"So, what'd you think? Addison asked as she made her way toward where they were standing.

"Wonderful," Will enthused before Mallory could respond as

Siobhan chimed in, "Amazing."

"Thank you." Addison turned toward Mallory's guests and offered them her hand. "You must be Will and Siobhan. It's so nice to finally meet you, I've heard so much about you."

"All terrible, I'm sure," Will chuckled as he shook her hand.

"Only mostly," Addison corrected with a smirk.

"That's probably fair." Siobhan laughed as she shook Addison's hand. "It's lovely to meet you, as well."

Addison dipped her head in thanks as she took a step back, her attention and her body angling toward Mallory.

Keenly aware of the fact that her friends were watching, Mallory smiled and murmured, "You were wonderful."

Addison's smile was breathtaking as she whispered, "Thank you."

"Right, well," Siobhan declared, shattering the moment, "It's late, and I am practically dead on my feet, so…" She elbowed Will in the side. "We had probably best be going. Thank you for the wonderful seats. You really were amazing."

"It wasn't a problem at all," Addison assured her. "And thank you. I'm glad you enjoyed the performance."

"Mal, I'll see you tomorrow," Will said as Siobhan took his arm.

Mallory nodded. "Tomorrow."

Once Siobhan and Will left the way they'd come, Addison turned to Mallory and shook her head as she pulled her into a hug. "Thank you for the flowers," she whispered, her breath dancing lightly over Mallory's ear. "They're gorgeous."

Mallory wrapped her arms around Addison's waist and whispered, "You're welcome, darling." She closed her eyes as soft lips brushed against her cheek, and blinked them open when Addison's hold loosened and she began to pull away. "I'm so very glad you like them."

"I do." Addison smiled and arched a playful brow. "So, I know you've got two shows tomorrow, but I'm starving and wide awake. Would you want to maybe go grab a bite to eat?"

The caffeine from her coffee earlier had stopped working its magic not long after intermission, but Addison looked so happy that Mallory found herself willing to do anything to keep that look on her face. "I'd love nothing more."

twelve

The weeks that had passed since Mallory had watched Addison command the Covent Garden stage passed in a blur of LSO and *Evolution* rehearsals, meetings, and concerts and far, far too little sleep to be even remotely healthy. It was a good thing, though, because it kept her from thinking about what Will had said at the ballet that night. Because if she actually stopped to think about the way her heart skipped a beat when Addison had looked up at her from the stage, or the butterflies that had erupted in her stomach when Addison had kissed her cheek after the show, she would have to admit—to herself, at least—that he was right.

And she just didn't have the energy to deal with what that would mean.

It was so much easier to focus on symphony structure, learning new music, and trying to not trip over her own feet than to dwell, even for a moment, on the idea that she was developing an ill-fated crush on her much, much younger colleague.

And it was ill-fated.

Or, it would be, if she decided to acknowledge it.

Not just because of the whole age-difference thing—though that was absolutely the first nail in the hypothetical coffin—but because she was convinced that there was no way Addison could harbor feelings beyond friendship for her. She had seen Addison with her friends, had seen the way she and Gabs all but hung off each other whenever they were together, and she was more than old enough to know better than to read more into something that didn't exist.

So she worked harder than she ever had before. She woke before dawn and toiled well into the night, pushing herself to the brink of collapse day after day after day so that her professional life could be as perfect as the rest of her life wasn't.

And her hyper-focus on her work had paid off, as they were able to work their way through to the end of putting movement to notes and ideas for *Evolution*.

"And turn," Nina directed from the front of the studio, her soft voice a metronome to pace arms and legs and music despite the fact that they had long since adopted and embodied these final steps and made them their own.

Mallory's attention was focused more on her feet than the music as she spun with Addison, her right leg extending behind her and her toes drawing an invisible arc on the floor as she pulled her bow across the strings of her violin. She continued the movement of her arm as the bow cleared the strings, and barely resisted the urge to close her eyes as Addison's right hand lifted to cradle her cheek, turning her face from her violin that she no longer needed to hold in place. They moved closer as her bow hand fell away and the final note reverberated into silence, and her throat tightened with private longing and professional pride as she dipped her head to touch her forehead to Addison's.

"And hold," Nina whispered. "Beautiful. Stay just like that until the curtain drops. I want that to be the final image the audience holds in their memories of the performance." After a beat, she clapped her hands and declared, "Perfect. That's it."

Addison pulled Mallory into a hug. "We got it."

"We do," Mallory agreed as she wrapped her arms around Addison's waist and held her close. "You were brilliant."

"You were!" Addison argued with a little laugh as she pulled away.

"Yes, yes," Nina drawled, too pleased with how everything had just gone to hide her amusement as she smiled at them both. "You did it. And, come Monday, you'll get to do it all from the beginning."

Mallory nodded, while Addison threw her head back and, in a rather impressive impersonation of an aggrieved teenager, groaned, "Awesome."

"Indeed," Nina chuckled. She snapped her fingers and waved her hand as if to brush them toward their things to change. "And now we need to go see Ginny in wardrobe, because it's time to put together your costumes. So…shoes off, layers on, and I'll meet you down there. I'll go make sure she has everything I asked for laid out and ready for you both to try on."

"So how do these things usually go?" Mallory asked as they obediently moved to follow Nina's instructions.

"We go down to the costume department and basically become living mannequins for however long it takes for Ginny to put together an outfit that Nina approves." Addison shrugged as she sat down and began tugging at the ribbons around her ankles.

"That doesn't sound promising." Mallory glanced at her watch as she pulled up a bit of floor next to Addison. "I do have a performance tonight."

"It shouldn't take that long," Addison assured her. "I mean, Nina and Ginny have been going back-and-forth about sketches pretty much since we started rehearsing—so if they're ready for us to come in, they probably have a pretty good idea of what it is they're looking to do."

Mallory sighed, her thoughts evident in the soft, slow exhale. *I sure hope so.*

"It'll be fine," Addison insisted. "Worst-case scenario, we go back and do it some more tomorrow. What are you guys playing tonight?"

Mallory blinked at the abrupt topic shift. "It's a trio of Stravinsky pieces—*Firebird*, the 1974 *Petrushka*, and then *The Rite of Spring*."

Addison's eyes widened in recognition. "The *Firebird* ballet?"

"You know it?" Mallory shook her head and smiled apologetically.

"Never mind. Of course you do. I mean, you probably know the actual dance that goes with the music, that was—"

"Hey," Addison interrupted her rambling with a hand on her knee. "Yes, I know the ballet. It's kind of impossible for me not to be aware of it. But"—she squeezed Mallory's knee and then slowly pulled her hand away—"I've also been listening to more classical music lately."

Mallory paused in putting her violin away to gape at her. They had talked about music a few times in the past, but Addison had seemed more interested in the type of stuff one heard on popular radio channels than what was played at the symphony. "You have?"

Addison lifted her right shoulder in a small shrug. "Yeah." Her expression was shy and simmering with something Mallory couldn't quite identify, and she looked away to busy herself with stashing her pointe shoes in her bag as she said, "I mean, it only seemed fair that I expand my horizons too, considering everything you're doing…"

Mallory chuckled softly as she snapped her violin case shut. "You are aware that this isn't a competition, right?"

"Oh, I know. I just…" Addison's lips pressed in a thoughtful line as her head gave the tiniest of shakes. "You love it. So I wanted to learn more about it."

"You're adorable," Mallory murmured before she could censor herself. The words had been soft, but the way Addison's lips quirked in a small, pleased smile was enough to tell her that they'd been heard. "Anyway," she continued in a stronger voice, "have you found anyone you like?"

Addison nodded slowly, her gaze soft as her head tilted ever so slightly to the left. "I have."

Mallory smiled. "Brilliant. Wait… Please tell me it isn't Mozart. I mean, nothing against Mozart, of course, it's just that he's like the *only* name half the Board seems to know and for as much fun as some of his stuff is to play, it just gets old when there's so much other music out there."

"I… No." Addison pulled a pair of tapered fleece track pants from her bag and pulled them up over the bottom half of her legs. "It's not Mozart."

"Who, then?"

Addison shrugged as she angled her slippers over her feet, and let it slip free as she pushed herself to stand so she could finish pulling up her sweatpants. "I like the faster, more modern compositions."

"So…like what we're doing here? With Halonen's stuff?"

Addison huffed a little laugh. "Yeah. Like what we're doing here. Exactly that, really."

"I'll see if I can't think of any recommendations for you, then," Mallory promised with a smile.

Addison sighed softly and nodded. "Cool," she murmured after a few beats. "Thanks."

"Of course." Mallory changed her ballet slippers for the pair of flip-flops she'd taken to wearing up to the studio, and pushed herself to her feet. "So, shall we go see what costumes we'll be expected to wear?"

"We shall," Addison agreed with a small smile as they started for the door.

The smile didn't quite reach her eyes, however, and Mallory's heart dropped as she quickly set about replaying their conversation to try and pinpoint the moment she'd said something to upset her. Gwen had accused her of being too self-absorbed to even notice that something was wrong with their relationship—which she now recognized was true—and so she had been making a concerted effort to change. To do and be better, so her friends didn't feel like she was taking them for granted. The problem was, however, no matter how she looked at the conversation they had just had, she could not figure out what she had done wrong.

"May I ask you a question?" Mallory ventured in a soft voice as they waited for the lift.

"Of course."

"Did I…" Mallory fiddled with the strap of her violin case. She hated that she even had to ask, but if she didn't, the fear would only fester and grow until it was the only thing she could think about and she just didn't have the time for that level of an anxiety attack this week. Which was, in itself, selfish and self-absorbed, but it had to count for something that the root of it all was her concern for someone else—right? "Did I say something to upset you just now? In Fonteyn? I...I've been told that I can be rather—"

"No," Addison interrupted. She shook her head as she reached out to still Mallory's fingers. "You didn't say anything wrong."

"You're sure?"

"I'm sure, sweetie," Addison murmured, giving Mallory's hand a squeeze.

Both the touch—which Mallory hadn't even realized she'd been missing until right that moment—and the soft crinkle at the corners of Addison's eyes quieted the panic in her mind, and she nodded. "Okay." She licked her lips and looked away, at once relieved and monumentally embarrassed that her lingering insecurity had given Addison a glimpse at how broken she actually was. It was easy to pretend to be strong when her life had consisted of work and old friends who knew all her faults and loved her anyway, but it was so much harder when the friendship was new and she had no idea how fragile it might be.

She was busier than she had ever been in her life, but she was also happier than she could remember ever being as well, and the last thing she wanted was to sabotage it all.

"I'm sorry," she apologized.

"No reason to be sorry." Addison squeezed her hand again as the lift pulled to a stop. "You okay?"

"I'm trying to be," Mallory answered honestly.

Addison huffed a wry laugh and nodded. "Aren't we all." She gave Mallory's hand one last squeeze before pulling away, and she sighed as she motioned toward the doors that had begun to slide open. "Shall we?"

Mallory nodded as she fisted her hand around the strap of her violin case. It was partly to keep herself from reaching for Addison's hand, but mostly to ground herself. She had already made things awkward enough, but Addison had been kind and understanding, and she was okay.

The door to the costume department was only a few steps from the lift, and Mallory hurried to pull it open for Addison. She longed for the return of their usual easy banter, and forced the closest thing to a genuine smile she could manage as she tipped her head and motioned for Addison to go ahead of her. Her smile became more effortless when Addison's hand brushed lightly over her arm as she passed, murmuring her thanks, and she took a deep breath as she made to follow.

She could do this.

They were okay.

"There they are!" Ginny Sanderson, the tall, raven-haired seamstress who was in charge of the ballet's costumes declared with an air of mock relief when they finally found her and Nina at the back of the large room. Standing an inch over six-feet, Ginny was taller than quite a few of the male dancers Mallory had met about the halls, and while she claimed to have two left feet, she moved about her domain with just as much grace as the athletes she dressed.

Nina smirked and arched a brow as she made a show of looking at her watch. "Did you get lost on the way down here?"

"Something like that," Addison sassed as she tossed her bag onto the floor beside a small wooden stool. "What's up, Gin?"

"The usual," Ginny replied. "Sewing, sketching, waiting for diva dancers to show up for fittings…"

Addison laughed and pointed an accusing finger at the seamstress. "Not you, too! I thought we were friends!"

"We were, but then I met Mallory, and she's so much more charming than you…" Ginny's voice trailed off into a chuckle at the way Addison gasped and clasped a hand over her heart as if wounded, and shook her head as she turned to Mallory. "Hiya, Mal."

"Hello, Ginny," Mallory murmured, offering her a small smile as she set her things down with much more care than Addison had shown. They had met the week before when Nina had ordered her to go get measured, and she had immediately felt safe with Ginny—which was good, given the fact that there wasn't one inch of her body that had been spared the measuring tape. The most bizarre had been the "tip-to-tip" measurement, but by the time Ginny had gotten to the point where she was measuring the distance between her nipples they had settled into such an easy conversation that Mallory had been only vaguely aware of where the woman's tape measure was stretched. "I apologize if we kept you waiting."

"You're fine," Ginny assured her with a wink.

"Mallory has a concert this evening," Nina drawled, bringing their playfulness to heel, "so if we could start actually trying on the clothes…"

"Yes, your highness," Ginny muttered.

Mallory pressed her lips together to keep from laughing and shot Addison a *did she really just say that* look, but Nina just chuckled and gave Ginny a playful shove toward the rack of costumes that had been pulled toward the center of the room with a brusque, "That's enough, you."

Ginny smirked and turned to pull two dresses from the rack. One was the color of sun-kissed copper with a loose, uneven skirt that was made of layers of a soft, gauzy fabric in varying complementary shades of gold and crimson, while the other was a rich crimson knee-length number that was more tailored than the first but looked like it would be just as easy to move in. "I still have a bit to do with embroidery and such, but I want to make sure the dresses themselves are right before I set about making them ready for the stage." She waved the dresses at Mallory and Addison as she pulled a curtain to separate them from the rest of the workspace. "You heard the mistress, chop chop."

Mallory looked for a place to change as she took the hanger from Ginny, but realized what was expected when Addison grumbled something under her breath and immediately began stripping where she stood.

Ginny smiled kindly at her. "I can drag out another curtain out to create a changing room if you'd be more comfortable, but when it's just us girls we usually we just…" She waved a hand at Addison, who was working her leotard, sweats, and tights down over her hips.

Mallory shook her head. The idea of stripping down right here in front of everyone was enough to send her pulse racing, but she told herself it was just like being in a locker room at the gym. "No, no. This is fine."

She kept her eyes on the floor as she stripped, glad that the black bikini briefs she'd pulled on that morning at least matched the sports bra she had grabbed from her drawer without realizing they would be seen by anyone else. She considered it a victory that her hand didn't shake when she held it out for the dress she was to try on, and she nodded slightly at Ginny as she took possession of the crimson dress. The dress was gorgeous, even without embellishments, and she arched a brow when she saw that the back of the dress had a light-colored panel of fabric that was a perfect match to her skin-tone that, from the audience, would make it seem as if she were wearing a backless dress.

"We went for the elegant look for you," Ginny explained with a small smile. "Zipper is tucked into a flap under the seam on the left side of the back. You get it on, and I'll close you up?"

Mallory found the zipper and looked down at her chest as she pulled it down. "Bra off, then? Because this one won't work…"

"For now, if you don't mind. If you feel the bodice doesn't provide enough support, I can add some more, and if that still doesn't work, we'll find something that will go with the design. We should be able to build it in, though. You're not *that* much larger than most of the girls I usually dress."

Mallory's brow furrowed as she bit her lip and nodded. She had no idea how to even respond to that one.

"Welcome to ballet, the land of tiny titties," Addison drawled. She winked and added, "We do have great butts, though."

Nina laughed, though it sounded like she was trying not to. "Addison… Must you really?"

Mallory glanced up at Addison, whose devilish smirk belied her wide-eyed faux-innocence, and chuckled softly under her breath.

"We all know that I absolutely must really," Addison told Nina.

"Tell me again why I saw fit to bring you into my company?" Nina grumbled with a fond smile.

"You're a closet masochist?"

"That must have been it," Nina agreed with a little laugh. "Now, could you please finish putting on the bloody dress so Ginny can do her job?"

"It's all right, I'm quite enjoying the floor show," Ginny insisted.

Mallory smiled as she turned her back to the group and pulled off her bra and then slipped the dress over her head. The fabric, while opulent, was sinfully soft against her skin, and she took a deep breath as she turned to Ginny. "Well…?"

"I am a genius," Ginny replied with a grin. "That color is perfect on you. Turn around, now, so I can zip you up, and we'll see what we need to do to this thing."

Mallory hummed under her breath as Ginny closed the zipper. The dress fit like a dream.

"What do you think?" Ginny asked when Mallory turn back to face her. "Is the bodice supportive enough? Or does it need something more?"

She stretched her arms out and did a little twist before miming holding a violin, and smiled as she shook her head. The dress honestly provided more support than the sports bra she had just taken off. "No, I don't think it does. This is great."

"Brilliant. And how about you?" Ginny rounded on Addison, who had finished getting into her dress while Ginny had been tending to Mallory. "Is the skirt length okay? It's a bit longer than what we did for the showcase last year, but I tried to keep the length to places where it wouldn't get in the way. Move around a bit and let me know if it gets in the way of anything."

Addison obediently popped up onto the ball of her right foot and into a quick pirouette. After she'd moved through a few other steps, she reported, "Perfectly perfect, as usual."

"Just wait." Ginny winked. "Go stand by your leading lady, there, and look in the mirror."

"Pretty sure we're both the leading lady, Gin," Addison teased.

"Hush, you, with the commentary. I swear, everything takes five times longer than usual with that mouth of yours." Ginny held up a warning finger when Addison arched a brow and smirked. "Don't you even think of turning that into something dirty."

"Who, me? I have no idea what you're talking about."

Mallory laughed and grabbed Addison's arm to pull her closer. "If you wouldn't mind just doing what the poor woman asked, darling," she murmured as she turned them toward the mirror on the wall to their left, "some of us have to get to work after this."

"Sorry," Addison whispered, her expression genuinely contrite as she looked around the room for a clock. "Are you okay on time?"

"I'll be fine..." Mallory's voice trailed off as she looked at their reflection. She knew she was supposed to be looking at how well their dresses looked side-by-side—and they really did look great together, the brighter colors and more carefree cut of Addison's dress paired beautifully with the darker tones and more refined lines of her own—but all she could see was Addison curled into her side, smiling at her. She had watched their reflections dance together in the mirrors upstairs on the daily for close to two months, but this was different. This wasn't worrying about body lines or making sure she didn't poke Addison's eye out with her bow. This was just the two of them together. She had tried so hard to convince herself that she didn't want this, that she didn't need anyone, but she did want it. She wanted someone to hold, and to hold her, and her heart ached at the sight of Addison curled so perfectly into her side because she didn't just want *someone*, she wanted her.

If only… the little voice in the back of her mind whispered.

"Damn." Addison whistled and nodded appreciatively as she leaned her head on Mallory's shoulder. "We look good together."

Mallory nodded. "We do," she agreed softly.

thirteen

"This is me." Mallory pointed to a plain black door to a shallow alcove just beyond the windows of an upscale burger joint on Wardour Street.

Addison nodded as her eyes swept over the variegated blue tile that skirted the base of the limestone building beside the sidewalk. "I think I'd be in there eating my weight in burgers every night if I lived here."

Mallory smiled. The restaurant had initially put her off the property, but her real estate agent had convinced her to go upstairs to look at the penthouse apartment, and she'd fallen in love the moment she stepped inside. "I got enough of burgers when I was in America," she confessed as she punched the five-digit code into the lock on the door and ushered Addison to go ahead of her, "so I'm mostly only tempted when it's late and I'm just too tired to even think about making something to eat."

"Makes sense." Addison stopped at the base of the stairs and arched a questioning brow. "Where to, my dear?"

"Third floor. All the way up."

"Fancy," Addison drawled with a little laugh as she started to climb.

"Fancy would be having a lift," Mallory pointed out as she fell into step beside Addison. The two of them plus the bags hanging off their shoulders filled the width of the marble and hardwood staircase that looked like it belonged in a manor somewhere in Kensington, and she chuckled when Addison swayed into her. "Tired, Ms. Leigh?"

"Fucking exhausted," Addison admitted. "You?"

"About the same," Mallory admitted with a tired nod. They had gotten *Evolution* down from start-to-finish by Wednesday evening, so Nina had brought Henry Tonkins—the Royal Opera House's music director—into the preparation fold. He had spent the last two days watching, videoing, and taking notes, and because it was a rare Saturday where neither she nor Addison had a performance, Nina had added an extra rehearsal to their schedule so they could run through the entire thing with Henry and his orchestra. "Excuse me," she apologized as she edged ahead of Addison to unlock her front door.

"Not a problem," Addison assured her as she pressed herself back against the wall.

"Here we are, then," Mallory declared as she pushed the door open and waved a hand for Addison to go on in. Her flat had an unusual layout as the "front door" actually opened onto a wide hallway by the bedrooms, and she held her breath as she watched Addison interestedly take it all in. She had spent weeks choosing just the right warm gray paint for the walls to enhance the bright, pale blond hardwood floors, and the large framed photographs that lined the walls were prints made from pictures she had taken herself on her many travels. When Addison turned to her with a smile, she waved a hand at the door straight ahead. "If you'd like, you can leave your things in the guest room that's just there."

"Oh my god, this room is gorgeous," Addison murmured as she stepped inside.

Mallory couldn't contain her smile as she ducked into the smallest bedroom that she used as a practice room and study that was across from the guest room to put her violin in its usual place. They met up in the hall, and she smiled as she tossed her kit bag that was full of dirty clothes through the door beside the one Addison had just come out of.

"This place is incredible," Addison enthused.

"Thank you." Mallory ducked her head and smiled. "Bathroom is there"—she pointed to the open door beside her study—"and the main living areas are this way," she continued as she led them into the brightly-lit, open-concept reception room. While she would have much preferred her front door open to this space, she could not fault the architect for the floor plan when it left the main living areas on this side of the building where large, knee-to-ceiling windows flooded the apartment with light.

"Oh wow…" Addison breathed.

Mallory chuckled softly at the open appreciation in her voice. "I'm glad you like it," she murmured as her eyes swept over the slate blue rug that anchored the main seating area and the soft, ivory sofas and chairs that framed its edges. Gray and blue throw pillows added splashes of color to the furniture, and she was relieved to see that nothing was too terribly out of place.

She hadn't exactly been expecting to bring company home with her from Covent Garden when she had rushed out the door earlier that morning.

"It's amazing. Totally not what I was expecting from the street, either."

"That's what I thought when I first saw it, too." Mallory smiled.

"What is that a picture of?" Addison pointed to the oversized black and white print centered between two windows behind the far sofa.

"A cello, actually." Mallory dragged a hand through her hair as she looked at the print in question.

The bridge of the instrument was in sharp focus—the heart-shaped cutout in the center of the maple standing in stark relief to the bright white wood—and everything else was a black or gray blur. Gwen had given it to her for their first anniversary and, despite having always loved the shot, she had been adamant that it never see the light of day in London. She had scoured the local galleries for over six months looking for a piece of art to fill the spot where the picture now hung but nothing she found fit *her* as well as that print, and so one night, after half a bottle of wine, she pulled it from its packing box and leaned it against the wall to see if she could handle seeing it every day.

The reminder of what she had lost was a constant hurt there for a while but, eventually, that hurt eased until finally only a wistful hollowness was left.

It was only then that she decided to hang the print in the spot it seemed to be made for. Will had called her a glutton for punishment the first time he had seen it up on the wall, but she loved the picture as much as she had once loved Gwen, and most of the time she could look at it without seeing anything but the wood and the strings and the light and the shadows.

Two months later, of course, she had seen that damned YouTube video and had taken the picture down the moment she had gotten home. It spent the summer in the back of the guest room closet while she'd been touring—relegated from sight despite the fact that nobody was even in the apartment to see it—and she had only pulled it out again and returned it to its spot on the wall after their costume fitting the week before.

The blank wall had been driving her crazy anyway, and seeing the print every time she entered the room was a perfect reminder of why she could not allow herself seriously consider acting on her developing feelings for Addison. Shadowed wood and sharp strings seemed to slice into her every time she laid eyes on the picture, reminding her of harsh words and righteous anger and dark blue eyes filled with tears.

She had thought she had been giving Gwen what she wanted. Had thought Gwen wanted the distance that had developed between them, so she hadn't pushed for more. She hadn't even thought to ask for it, honestly. She had known, from their very first date, that Gwen was so far beyond her league that she had contented herself with what time and affection she had been given. Now, of course, she knew that she had been wrong. That Gwen had wanted more from their relationship just as much as she had. And that, perhaps, all the hurt and the anger and the heartbreak could have been avoided if they had only just talked to one another, but they hadn't, and she was still trying to pick up the pieces.

"A cello?" Addison stepped closer to inspect the photograph. She didn't seem to register the way Mallory hummed softly in confirmation, which made Mallory think it hadn't been a question so much as a statement, and she turned to her a moment later with a smile. "I love it. But why not a violin?"

"Because the woman who took that photograph is a cellist." Mallory shrugged. Not wanting to face further questions regarding the picture's origin, added, "And, honestly, stringed instruments are basically the same—just different sizes—so…"

"That makes sense," Addison agreed as she turned back toward the picture. "It really is cool, though."

"I think so, too," Mallory murmured. She cleared her throat softly and, in a desperate bid to change the subject, said, "Will and Siobhan should be here soon, I'd imagine. I know we stopped for smoothies after rehearsal, but would you like something to drink or snack on?"

"Food," Addison half-moaned. "Please."

Mallory smiled and waved a hand toward the dining room that connected the lounge and the kitchen. "Right this way."

Compared to the kitchen in her loft back in Los Angeles, this one was practically a closet, but it was a well-appointed closet with restaurant grade stainless steel appliances, custom hardwood cabinetry that was painted a medium charcoal, and gleaming marble countertops. "Pantry is here," she said as she opened the door to a tall cupboard nearest the dining room, "and you are more than welcome to raid the fridge as well. I'm not sure what you're in the mood for, but please help yourself to whatever you'd like."

Addison practically swooned as she made her way to the pantry. She pressed a quick kiss to Mallory's cheek and smiled as she pulled away and murmured, "You are a saint."

Mallory closed her eyes to try and stem the blush she could feel threatening, and let out a relieved sigh when the buzzer for the front door blared through the apartment. "I'll bet that's Will and Siobhan. I'll leave you to this and go let them up."

"You're sure you trust me with a cupboard full of food?"

Mallory arched a brow and tipped her head in a small nod. "For now." She smiled at the way Addison's eyes sparkled with laughter and, grateful for the lighter mood, teased, "Abuse that trust, however, and you'll be forever barred from my kitchen."

"Harsh!" Addison laughed, clasping her shirt over her heart. "But an effective threat all the same. I'd hate to never be invited back, so I won't eat you out of house and home." The buzzer rang again, and she smiled. "Go let them in. I'll be good here."

"I'll be right back," Mallory murmured. She muttered under her breath when the buzzer rang two more times in quick succession and, in a show of annoyance, did not answer the ring but simply entered the code to unlock the street door. A couple minutes later a light knock landed on her front door, and she pulled it open with a tight smile and her right eyebrow cocked in playful challenge. "May I help you?"

"Yeah, take this." Will shoved a reusable tote with four bottles of wine in it into her arms, which allowed him to readjust his grip on a larger bag that was overflowing with groceries as he pushed past her. "Now, get out of my way so I can go put this in the kitchen before I drop it all over your floor."

Siobhan laughed as she followed him inside, though she paused and pulled her into a quick hug. "How did your rehearsal go?"

Mallory sighed. "It ran long, of course, but it went really well. We only just got back not too long ago."

Will stopped at the end of the hall and turned to her with a grin. "We?"

Mallory sighed. She had talked herself out of inviting Addison to this little thing more times than she could count over the last week, convinced that Addison had to have better things to do with a free Saturday night than spend it with her and her friends who were all more than a decade older than her. But then Addison had asked if she was free to do something since neither of them had a performance that evening when they had been finally released to the showers—her eyes warm and her smile soft and hopeful—and the invitation had slipped from her lips before she could rein it in.

"Yes, we," Mallory murmured, a soft, fluttery feeling settling in the base of her throat as she remembered the way Addison had beamed at her as she accepted, her eyes bright and radiating joy. She had looked so utterly pleased by the idea of spending the rest of the afternoon together that Mallory couldn't even find it in herself to pay attention to the little voice in the back of her head that warned all of this was a mistake.

She knew it was a mistake, but it was apparently one that she was making, anyway.

"Just so we're clear, we are talking about the beautiful Ms. Leigh—correct?" Will asked.

Mallory waved a hand toward the kitchen. "She's raiding my pantry, if you must know," she explained as they made their way into the lounge.

"Is she, now? I thought ballet dancers existed on salad and protein shakes or something like that."

"Some do," Addison drawled, smirking at the *oh shit* look Will shot her as she sauntered into the reception room with a bag of pita chips and a container of roasted red pepper hummus. "But I actually have an incredibly fast metabolism, so I need way more calories than that. Hello again, by the way." She waved the food at Mallory. "Can I open these?"

"Go right ahead, darling," Mallory murmured with a smile. She saw Will and Siobhan share a look at the endearment, and she barely resisted the urge to roll her eyes. She had caught herself using it more frequently when they were together and, though she had tried to make a concerted effort to stop, apparently her subconscious liked the way Addison would soften at the sound of it, her gaze warm like melted chocolate

She hadn't meant it like *that*—except, if the increasing presence of brown eyes and pink lips and long, long legs in her dreams meant anything, there was a part of her that absolutely did—and she sighed as she cocked a challenging brow at them. "What did you bring for dinner?"

"Steak. Mushrooms. Salad. Pilaf." Siobhan tilted her head at the bag in Will's hand. "And a Banoffee pie for dessert."

"Or we could just have the pie for dinner and call it a day," Addison suggested with a grin.

Siobhan smiled at Addison. "Oh, I like you."

"That's all it takes to get into your good graces, huh?" Addison grinned. "And here I thought I'd have to work a lot harder for it."

"Nah, we're a pretty simple lot," Will replied as he took the bag from Siobhan and started for the kitchen. "Besides," he added, throwing a devilish look in Mallory's direction, "you pretty much won us over just by making that one smile again."

"I do know where you live…" Mallory threatened with a playful scowl.

"And I will totally let her in to torture you," Siobhan chimed in with a laugh. She added in a hushed aside to Addison, "But he isn't wrong."

"I hate both of you," Mallory grumbled, throwing her hands in the air in defeat. It was hard to inject too much frustration—feigned or not—into her tone, though, because of the way Addison was smiling at her.

"No, you don't," Siobhan sing-songed as she looped their arms together and she started to drag her toward the kitchen. "Was the orchestra able to keep up with you two?"

Mallory glanced back at Addison and smiled at the way her expression clearly said, *not really*. "For the most part. I had to work in quite a few changes to tempo and whatnot so I didn't stab Addy in the face or anything while we're dancing, so it'll just take a while for all those changes to be found and noted on their music."

"But you've got the whole thing sorted?" Will asked as he set the bag of groceries onto the counter beside the sink and began pulling out everything they had brought over.

"All forty-four minutes and thirty-two seconds of it," Addison confirmed with a pleased smile as she set the hummus container on the counter.

"I'm impressed," Siobhan said as she reached over to pry the lid off the hummus. "I mean, we both thought it would take longer than two months to get an entire ballet put together."

"It should have." Addison nodded as she popped open the bag of pita chips. "But that one there"—her lips curled into a soft smile as she looked over at Mallory—"is just too perfect for words."

The warmth in Addison's expression sent Mallory's pulse racing, and she shook her head as she argued, "Hardly."

Addison laughed. "As far as I'm concerned you are, so just deal with it, Collingswood."

Siobhan chuckled and held up a hand to head off the reprimand she knew Mallory was poised to direct her way. "I'm just going to get myself a glass of wine, and then I'll go up to the roof and start getting the barbecue warmed up. Will, can you prep the steaks? It looks like these girls are hungry." She looked at Mallory and added, "Did you get a new propane tank?"

"First thing this morning," Mallory confirmed. It had been a pain to carry up to the roof, too, but she hadn't been willing to suffer Will's teasing if she'd left it in the entry downstairs for him to carry up.

"Roof?" Addison asked.

Mallory nodded. "It's honestly the reason I decided to buy this flat. I had been looking for something more traditional—your more standard townhouse, if you will, with a front stoop and perhaps a small section of wrought iron fencing between a courtyard garden and the sidewalk—but the windows here and the roof were enough to convince me that this was home."

"It's a shame the weather's rubbish," Siobhan said as she uncorked the bottle. "I do love sitting up there. Who else would like a glass of wine?"

"Me," Will answered.

Mallory glanced at Addison and, when she smiled and nodded, chimed in, "And both of us, as well. Cheers."

"Here you are, lovelies," Siobhan declared as she slid two glasses their way. "Right, well, I'll be back in a jiff, then."

"Can I go up and have a look?" Addison asked.

"Of course." Mallory nodded. "Do you want to just go with Siobhan, or would you prefer I come along as well?"

Addison smiled and dipped her head in the briefest of nods as she murmured, "Would you?"

"Of course, darling," Mallory whispered.

"You birds have fun being all manly with the barbecue. I'll just stay here in the kitchen," Will dismissed them with a grin.

"You do that." Siobhan shook her head when Will winked at her and picked up the bottle of wine to pour what little bit remained in the bottle into his glass. "Good thing we brought four bottles…"

Will nodded and took a long drink. "Absolutely."

"Come on," Mallory chuckled. "Let's go get the grill warmed up."

"Do you barbecue often?" Addison asked as they made their way down the hall toward the stairs that led to the rooftop terrace.

"Only when Siobhan comes over," Mallory admitted, lifting her right shoulder in a small shrug. "No matter how many times I've tried to get the hang of the blasted thing, everything I try to cook comes out either dangerously raw or burnt, so I've given up."

"I could teach you, if you'd like," Addison offered.

"Good luck with that," Siobhan chuckled. "I've tried to teach both her and Will, and they're both complete disasters when it comes to cooking over an actual fire."

There was no point trying to argue since Siobhan spoke only the truth, but Mallory couldn't resist pointing out, "At least I didn't almost set myself on fire."

"That is true." Siobhan nodded as she pushed the door at the top of the stairs open and stepped outside. "Though, to be fair, sometimes I think he did that on purpose so I would take over the barbecuing and he could lounge about watching footy."

"I wouldn't put it past him, honestly," Mallory agreed with a laugh. "But, he's also rather hopeless on a regular stove as well, so…"

"He's so lucky he's cute," Siobhan muttered. She smiled when Addison laughed and shook her head as she hiked a thumb over her shoulder. "Anyway, I'll just go get everything warmed up."

Mallory shook her head fondly as she watched Siobhan make her way toward the outdoor kitchen that didn't see nearly enough use between London's typically dreary weather and the symphony's schedule. She could have done without the teasing, but it really was nice to be back with her good friends. She had been friendly enough with a handful of people from her section back at LA Phil to go to lunch or dinner or whatnot, but Gwen had been her only close connection, and she hadn't realized until she was back in London how much she missed Will and Siobhan's company. They were annoying at times in a way she imagined siblings would be, but they loved her as much as she loved them, and finding her way back to them was one of the few bright spots in her life over the last year and a half.

She cleared her throat as she turned to Addison, and cocked a brow as she tilted her head and murmured, "So, this is the rooftop terrace."

"You don't say," Addison teased, her eyes crinkled with her smile as she bumped their shoulders together. "It's wonderful. And so quiet!"

"On the rare sunny day, this is my haven from the world," Mallory shared.

"I can see why. Can I—" Addison waved at the shorter section of wall at the back of the terrace. The majority of the walls that framed the rooftop patio were a good ten feet, which were perfect for providing just the right amount of privacy, but there was one little section that was backside was a much less claustrophobic six.

"Go right ahead." Mallory followed Addison across the terrace as far as the outdoor kitchen where Siobhan was fiddling with the dials on the grill, and placed her hands on the black quartz that bore the telltale spots of dried raindrops. It was chilly but dry, at least, she thought as she watched Addison brace her hands on the top of the wall and push herself up to see over it.

"She's lovely," Siobhan murmured, and Mallory was grateful that she kept her voice low.

"She is," Mallory agreed just as softly, her gaze never straying from Addison.

"You look good together."

"It's not like that," Mallory sighed.

"I dunno, Mal, the way that girl smiles at you suggests that it could be. If you wanted."

Mallory opened her mouth to argue, to deride Siobhan's statement as ridiculous, but Addison—arms extended so that she was holding herself up over the edge of the building—turned around right then to *beam* at her, and she forgot how to breathe for a moment, never mind anything else.

"This view is incredible!"

It wasn't, really. The gap just opened onto the small, grungy alley the buildings shared and more buildings beyond, but she couldn't help but return her smile as she agreed, "It certainly is."

"Smooth," Siobhan chuckled.

"Oh, do shut up," Mallory grumbled as she watched Addison drop lightly to her feet and wipe her hands off on the seat of her jeans as she made her way back toward them.

Siobhan laughed loudly at that, and Mallory rolled her eyes as it prompted the inevitable question from Addison, "What's so funny?"

"Nothing, darling," Mallory lied quickly. She grit her teeth at Siobhan's knowing little finger that poked her in the side at the endearment, and shook her head as she added, "Siobhan's apparently had too much wine already—she's giving herself the giggles."

"Please," Siobhan scoffed, giving the grill one last look-over before closing the lid and starting for the door to the stairs, "we both know that you'll be tossing me out on my arse if I get to that point."

"Do I want to know why?" Addison asked. "Because you seem like you'd be a fun drunk."

"Oh, I'm the best drunk. Not that I can even remember the last time I got that pissed, but still…"

"She will flirt with anyone and anything," Mallory shared. "It's actually quite funny."

Addison smiled as she looked from Mallory to Siobhan and back again. "Has she ever hit on you?"

"She wishes," Siobhan answered.

"Hardly," Mallory scoffed.

"You could get drunk and flirt with her," Siobhan suggested, waggling her eyebrows at Addison as she pulled the door open.

Mallory could only gape when, without missing a beat, Addison winked at Siobhan and drawled, "Oh, I don't need to be drunk to want to flirt with her," before sauntering—yes, sauntering—down the stairs.

"Tell me again why you're not making a play on that?" Siobhan demanded in a hushed voice once Addison was out of earshot.

"One, that was awful. You sound like the lads down at the corner pub lusting after anyone with breasts. And two, you know exactly why that is."

Siobhan's smile turned sad as she nodded. "Yeah. But you deserve to be happy, Mal."

"I am happy," Mallory insisted.

"You could be happier."

"As could everyone, I'd imagine." Siobhan just arched a brow and crossed her arms over her chest, and Mallory sighed. "I'm not ready."

"But you like her?" Siobhan pressed.

Mallory pursed her lips as she considered lying, but she knew Siobhan would see right through her and she didn't have the energy to deal with a prolonged conversation on the matter. "Yes."

"So…someday? Maybe?"

"Someday. Maybe," Mallory agreed softly, because someday was the perfect hypothetical—always remaining safely in the future, leaving her free to never have to do anything about it.

"Good." Siobhan tilted her head toward the door that would take them back downstairs. "Shall we?"

"We shall," Mallory agreed, grateful that Siobhan didn't seem inclined to push the matter further.

Will's smile was sly, and he looked poised to throw some kind of embarrassing comment her way when they found their way back to the kitchen, but before he could open his mouth to say anything Siobhan cut him off with a shake of her head and a soft, "Leave it," murmured against his ear.

Perhaps it was the steel in Siobhan's tone or the weary slant of her own smile that convinced him to heed the warning but, whatever the case, Will simply nodded and asked, "Addison, how do you prefer your steak?"

"Medium-well."

"Excellent. Then if you lot would be so kind as to prepare the salad and sauté the mushrooms, the wife and I will head on up to take care of these." He lifted the cutting board covered in steaks and arched a brow at Siobhan. "What do you think?"

"I think that sounds like a brilliant idea." Siobhan picked up her glass of wine. "Want me to bring yours, as well?"

Will nodded. "Yeah. Ta."

"They're something of a whirlwind, aren't they?" Addison commented with a little chuckle once Will and Siobhan had disappeared from earshot.

"That they are."

"I can prep the salad if you'd like," Addison offered.

"It's fine." Mallory waved her off. "The mushrooms won't need much attention once I get them on the stove, so I'll just do it then.

You, my dear, may be in charge of keeping me company."

Addison smiled and nodded. "I can do that." She poked Mallory's wine glass toward her and added, "And I'll make sure to keep your glass full. How's that?"

"I'm afraid that after two glasses, I'll fall asleep," Mallory admitted with a wry grin.

"You're not the only one." Addison winked and dragged a hand through her hair. "But, hey, we'll just go sleep it off on the couch and leave the dishes to Will and Siobhan."

Mallory laughed. "Deal."

fourteen

How Mallory noticed that Laurent Bellamy, the twenty-eight-year-old who was doing a turn as the LSO's guest conductor as part of his graduate coursework, was about to lose his place in the piece moments before it happened was a miracle. The last three weeks had been absolutely hellish, her already grueling rehearsal schedule increased with the few free hours during the week she had taken by what seemed like a never-ending string of added rehearsals for *Evolution* because the Royal Opera House's orchestra was still struggling in places to keep up.

She made her way through her days on auto-pilot as she obeyed the many various alarms on her phone. Had she the energy to actually think about what her life had become, she would have been embarrassed by how much of her autonomy she'd given over to the scheduled alerts, but it was so much easier to follow orders. Even if those orders came by way of canned, tinny music and words on a screen. The phone told her what to do, and all she had to do was react and obey, to turn off the alarm and then go wherever the screen said she needed to be next.

She even had alarms scheduled to remind herself to eat, now, because there had been a day the week before when she had nearly passed out in Clore Studio during a particularly demanding rehearsal.

So how she realized that Bellamy was about to completely screw up was beyond her. Perhaps it was something in the pinch of his brow or the drop of his left hand that caught her attention. But whatever it was, she sat up straighter, drawing the attention of the musicians around her as she began to play with more of the physicality she used in Covent Garden. She leaned forward in her seat and lifted the scroll of her violin higher, drawing the attention of everyone with an instrument in their hands.

Her heartbeat picked up as she waited for the moment she was sure was coming, adrenaline making what had been a routine performance suddenly anything but, and she held her breath when it finally happened. Bellamy's hands swung out when they should have gone up, and she glanced around the arc of musicians to make sure they were following her lead.

They were, of course, because they were professionals. And, despite the utter seriousness of the moment, she had to bite the inside of her cheek to keep from smiling at the pride that bloomed in her chest at their skill.

Assured that things were as well in hand as they could be given the situation, she looked then to their guest conductor—whose eyes were wide as they roved wildly over the sheet music on his stand—and then to her own music. One of them needed to hold their place in the score, and it was up to her to make sure the orchestra stayed on note until he caught up.

He did, eventually, after almost a page and a half, and she blew out a soft breath, her posture relaxing by a fraction as she allowed him to take the reins once more. The rest of the performance concluded without further mishap, and when they stood at the end to receive the audience's applause, she delighted in knowing they had no idea what had happened.

Bellamy took his bow first, as was protocol, but kept it shallow and brief to quickly shift the attention to the musicians behind him with a wide sweep of his arm. They bowed as a group, letting the applause wash over them like a wave, before falling into line and filing off the stage.

Bellamy grabbed Mallory's arm the moment they were safely in the wings, and he spoke so quickly that she was barely able to make out the words, "Oh my god thank you so much you saved my arse out there."

"It happens," Mallory assured him with a kind smile. "That's why we rehearse, yeah?"

"Still." He shook his head and groaned. "I'm so sorry."

"It's fine, mate," Will assured him as he stopped at Mallory's side. "You recovered nicely, and no one in the audience is the wiser for it all, so there's no point beating yourself up about it."

"Laurent. A word?" Clara called as she made his way into the wings from the short corridor that connected the box where she had been watching the performance to the backstage area.

Laurent's shoulders slumped as his head fell forward. "Fucking hell."

"It will be fine," Mallory murmured. "She doesn't bite, and the worst-case scenario is just that you come back and have a go again sometime."

"If they let me back in the bloody building after that cockup." Laurent's lips quirked in a rueful smile as he offered Mallory his hand. "Thank you for the save, Ms. Collingswood."

"My pleasure, Laurent. Don't let this knock you down for too long, okay?"

"I'll try."

Mallory gave him one last reassuring smile before he turned toward Clara, looking quite like a man headed for the gallows. It was understandable, of course, and part of her felt bad for him, but he needed thicker skin if he was going to make a career in music. She caught Clara's eye over Laurent's shoulder and arched a brow as she motioned with her hand in a way that asked if she wanted her to stay or not. While she wanted nothing more than to stumble home and fall into bed, they usually spent a few minutes going over recently completed performances before calling it a night, just so they were on the same page going into things the next day.

Thankfully, though, Clara shook her head and waved for her to go.

"Let's get out of here, Mister Adrian," she muttered through a yawn as she nudged Will with her elbow.

"You're not doing your usual debrief?"

She shook her head. "I reckon Clara has her hands full gathering the remains of young Mister Bellamy's ego and trying to piece it back together."

Will chuckled softly as he fell into step beside her. "Poor lad. You totally saved his arse up there, though. How did you know the whole thing was about to go off the rails?"

"Honestly? I haven't the faintest idea how I saw it coming. I'm just glad I did."

Though she had her own office in the building, Mallory had taken to leaving her case with the rest of the first violins backstage to help her beat a hasty exit at the end of the night, and she smiled at the quiet applause and congratulations for the save she had made that welcomed her. "Well done tonight, you lot."

"How's he doing?" Charlie, her Associate Leader, asked as she lifted her violin case onto a nearby box and began stowing her instrument.

"Understandably rattled. But he'll bounce back." She blew out a soft breath as a ripple of murmurs floated through the group, some positive and some not so much, and added, "Clara is talking to him now."

Charlie nodded. "Good. He showed some promise. Usual time for the matinee tomorrow?"

"Usual time," Mallory confirmed.

The group took that as their dismissal, and she was left in peace to finish wiping down her violin and stowing her bow as they began filtering out the stage door. The adrenaline that had carried her through the back end of the performance faded as she snapped the latches on her case shut, and she took a deep breath as she hefted it and her bag onto her shoulder.

Will was waiting for her near the exit as he always did, and his tone and smile were kind as he pointed toward the corridor that led to the public area of the Centre and said, "Siobhan came to the performance tonight with a friend, and I'm under orders to bring you out to say hello."

"Will…" Mallory sighed.

His smile softened, and he nodded understandingly. "It's late, and you're tired, I know. We'll keep it as brief as you need, I promise. Just…please?"

"This better be an important friend," Mallory grumbled through a yawn as she allowed him to steer her down the hall with a gentle hand on her elbow. She did her best to try to blink away her exhaustion as he pushed the door to the main foyer.

"Almost there," he said as he motioned her through. "I see Siobhan just ahead."

She nodded. Siobhan was talking to whoever it was she was supposed to meet, she presumed, though she saw nothing of the woman beside a black high heel and a long, toned leg that disappeared beneath the hem of a matching black dress that fell to a few inches above the woman's knee. "Yeah, I see her. Who's the woman I'm supposed to be impressing? Or whatever it is you expect me to do…"

"Oh, you know…" His voice trailed off as Siobhan, as if sensing their approach, turned to look their way, providing a perfect view of her companion.

Mallory's eyebrows lifted as Addison's eyes found hers across the foyer, and she made no effort to break the connection as she muttered to Will, "Addy is Siobhan's friend that I'm supposed to say hello to? Really?"

Will chuckled. "Really." When Mallory didn't respond right away, he asked, "Is this okay? She wanted to surprise you."

"Oh, I'm definitely surprised." Mallory fiddled with the strap of her violin case as she watched Addison's lips curl with a soft, wholly pleased smile. "And, yes, it's more than okay. It's…"

"I know," he assured her in a low voice.

"Nice job tonight, you two," Siobhan greeted them with a smug grin.

Mallory reached out to pull Siobhan into a quick, one-armed hug. "Sneaky bugger, aren't you?" she whispered in her ear.

Siobhan laughed delightedly and dusted a light kiss over her cheek. "Well, you know me…" She winked at her as she pulled away.

"Lord help me," Mallory muttered playfully as she turned to Addison who, she only just realized, was holding a beautiful bouquet of white lilies and blue irises. It was, thankfully, smaller than the one she had ordered for her the night they had gone to watch her perform, but it was still large enough that she wasn't entirely sure she had a vase at home that was big enough to accommodate the blooms.

"I wasn't sure about the proper protocol for the symphony, but…" Addison's voice trailed off into a shrug as she offered Mallory the flowers. "I hope it's okay?"

"They're gorgeous." Mallory smiled as she took the flowers. She looked at Addison through the petals as she lifted them to her nose, and her throat tightened at the warmth in her eyes. She cleared her throat as she moved to pull Addison into a gentle hug that, she prayed, conveyed just how pleased she was. "Thank you, darling," she murmured.

"It's my pleasure, I assure you," Addison replied softly, her lips brushing lightly over Mallory's cheek, her right arm finding its way around Mallory's waist as her left hand settled lightly on her hip.

Addison's light perfume smelled of summer with a hint of ginger grass, and Mallory's eyes fluttered shut as the scent enveloped her. Her finger wrapped just that little bit tighter around Addison's shoulder as memories of that night two weeks ago when they'd ended up falling asleep together on the couch after dinner, too exhausted to keep their eyes open despite the ridiculous volume of the film Will had put on. Her pulse stuttered as she remembered the way Addison had fit so perfectly against her side, right hand fisted in the hem of her shirt as a small spot of drool dampened her shoulder. And she had been so tired, and it had felt so nice to be close to someone again, that when Addison tried to pull away in a fit of adorable embarrassment, she just wrapped an arm around her shoulders and refused to let her go.

She had tried to play it off as a joke, and Addison had played along, grumbling appropriately as she settled back into place, but the soft sigh that had tickled her neck as Addison's hand slid around her hip, holding her just as tightly, had haunted her dreams every night since.

It had been a mistake, but it was one that she couldn't quite bring herself to regret. If she wasn't on week two of running on caffeine and adrenaline, she might have had the energy to worry about that, but the more time she spent around Addison and her easy touches and gentle smiles, the harder it was to remember why, exactly, this was a bad idea.

Because whenever they were together like this, it felt like the most natural thing in the world.

"So," Will declared loudly, his voice tinged with amusement that Mallory was certain she would be suffering for the next few days until it had cleared his system, "did either of you notice the little bit of excitement we had up there tonight?"

"I didn't." Siobhan turned to Addison. "Did you?"

Addison sighed against Mallory's ear as she pulled away. There was the faintest flush to her cheeks that made her look positively adorable, and she smiled shyly at Mallory as she moved out of her embrace. "Toward the end? When Mal sat up straighter and everybody seemed to take their cue from her?"

"Did they?" Siobhan asked, looking to Will for confirmation.

"Aye, we did." He grinned and waved a hand at Mallory. "I don't know how she did it, but our fearless leader here somehow knew the poor lad was going to go off-script before he did it, and managed to save the entire performance."

"Was I that obvious?" Mallory asked Addison. It hadn't been her intention to draw enough attention to herself that the audience noticed, she had only been trying to salvage the piece.

"No," Addison whispered, her eyes crinkled with her smile as she shook her head. "I was pretty much ignoring everyone else and just watching you," she admitted in an even softer voice. "You were a vision up there tonight, Mal. I couldn't take my eyes off you."

And, oh, Addison's eyes now were full of such open wonder that her heart all but *leapt* into her throat, and she had to clear it twice before she was able to rasp, "Addy…"

"Mal," Addy murmured.

"Not that you two aren't adorable as hell," Siobhan chuckled, "but I didn't get a chance to eat before the performance, and I'm famished. Fancy going somewhere for a bite and a bevvy?"

Mallory arched a brow at Addison. "Well?"

Addison smiled and nodded as she tucked her hand in the crook of Mallory's arm. "Sounds wonderful."

"It does," Mallory agreed softly as her gaze dropped to the way Addison's fingers curled around her biceps.

"And now that *that's* settled," Siobhan drawled, "and keeping in mind that it's Saturday night, where shall we go?"

"I know of a good little place near The Royal Ballet, but I don't know if it'd be too far out of the way for you guys," Addison offered.

"We're in Notting Hill, so that would work fine for us," Will said, glancing at Siobhan who nodded her agreement. "Right, then," he looked to Mallory and Addison, "so, underground or taxi?"

"It would probably be faster on the underground," Addison admitted, "but I think, with your instruments and everything, that it would be easier to go by car."

"Brilliant." Siobhan turned toward the exit. "Shall we?"

Enough time had passed since the end of their performance to thin the crowd leaving the centre, they were able to grab the lone black taxi idling at the queue without having to wait. It was a bit cramped, trying to fit four adults, two instrument cases, and one bouquet into the back seat, but it was a far more appealing option than splitting up and leaving half the group to wait for a second car.

"Where to?" the driver asked as he pulled into traffic.

"Covent Garden," Addison answered, turning in her seat to angle her body toward the driver as she pulled her phone from her purse. "Corner of Endell and Shelton."

"On it, Miss. You lot just sit back and enjoy the ride."

Addison turned back to Will and Siobhan and tilted her head as her lips quirked in a small, hesitant smile. "I hope you guys like this place. It's one of the favorites with the company."

The hint of nerves was adorable given Addison's usual confidence, and Mallory was grateful for the darkness that surrounded them as she felt her gaze soften as she looked at her. It was easier to remember why she shouldn't allow herself to fall for Addison when she was working, or they were apart, but the moment Addison entered her orbit, her heart forgot all those valid reasons she should be keeping her distance.

They pulled to a stop at a signal, and Mallory's breath caught in her throat at the sheer beauty of the woman beside her. It was ridiculous, really, given that they saw each other nearly every day and that, by this point, there was very little of Addison's visage she hadn't all but committed to memory, but there was something different tonight. Perhaps it was the bouquet she cradled on her lap, or the hint of Addison's perfume that she swore lingered on her collar, or the memory of soft lips ghosting over her cheek, but whatever the case— she found herself wanting to reach across the space between them and take Addison's hand into her own to assure her with a touch that she had no reason to worry.

And, if they had been alone, she might have—because she was increasingly helpless to resist the pull of Addison's presence—but they weren't, so she didn't. It was one thing to accept this shift in herself in private, but it was quite another to do so in front of her friends.

So instead of reaching for Addison as she longed to do, she nudged her foot with her own and murmured, "They will."

After all, she had found the restaurant to be utterly charming when

Addison had taken her there the night she had gone to her performance.

Mallory's shoulders tensed at the way Will's gaze drifted between her and Addison, his brow pinching ever so slightly as he studied them, but his grin was genuine as he told Addison, "We're not a picky lot." He sighed as he looped his arm over the back of Siobhan's shoulders. "How's everything over at the ballet? Mal said they've finally given you a performance date?"

Addison nodded. "First Friday in January. Going to kick off the new year with a bang."

"Or a boom," Mallory drawled. She chuckled at the look of righteous indignation Addison threw her way in response. "What?"

"Hush, you. We've got a little less than two months left to prepare, still." Addison shook her head as she looked back at Will and Siobhan. "Honestly, we could probably debut it earlier, but we're gearing up for the holiday season. *The Nutcracker* brings in enough to keep the lights on for the rest of the year, so Nina wanted to wait until that run was finished."

"Makes sense," Siobhan allowed.

"We've got our media shoot Tuesday, though, so that should be fun." Addison smiled at Mallory.

"Like, brochure and website pictures and stuff?" Siobhan asked.

Mallory hummed and nodded. "And a video, apparently."

"We do short little trailer-type clips for the webpage," Addison explained. It was her turn to bump their feet together as she added, "And you'll be wonderful, Mal."

"That's debatable," Will quipped laughingly.

"Oh, sod off, you," Addison shot back. That made Will laugh even harder, and she shook her head as she leaned over to murmur in Mallory's ear, "Don't listen to him. We're going to crush it."

The tickle of Addison's breath against her skin sent a pleasant thrill up Mallory's spine, and this time she wasn't at all strong enough to resist the urge to reach out and take Addison's hand in her own as she replied, "We will."

Addison's eyes sparkled with happiness as she squeezed her hand and bumped their foreheads together. "Yeah, we will."

Mallory took a deep breath and let it go slowly as she whispered, "Addy…" Her stomach fluttered at the way Addison's eyelids fluttered shut and her breath hitched ever so softly in response, and she clenched her jaw as she forced herself to pull away.

The way Addison whimpered at the loss of contact was nearly enough to draw her back in, but she wasn't ready. Not yet, anyway. And certainly not with an audience.

She fully expected to find Will and Siobhan watching them with sly, knowing grins on their faces when she turned their way, and was pleasantly surprised to find that they were each focused intently on the glowing screens of their phones. Though, the hint of a smirk that tugged at each of their mouths told her that she would undoubtedly be hearing about this later.

The rest of the ride passed in companionable silence, and Mallory couldn't help but smile at the way Addison protested when Will insisted on paying the fare.

"Come on, darling," Mallory cajoled, reaching for Addison's hand and giving it a light tug. "Let's go see about securing a table while he settles up with the driver."

After a brief wait, they were shown to a large, empty circular booth in the back corner of the upper level of the two-story restaurant. As there were no other empty tables on which to set their things, Mallory and Will hung their instruments from the coat hangers mounted on either side of the booth, and they all piled their coats in the curve of the bench instead.

"You're not too cramped?" Mallory asked Addison as she laid her bouquet atop their coats.

Addison shook her head. "Not at all."

"This place is lovely." Siobhan looked around the restaurant. The walls were painted a soft cream, and the windows that overlooked the street below were framed by rich, pomegranate-colored drapes that were an homage to the restaurant's name.

"I'm glad you like it." Addison smiled.

Conversation flowed smoothly as they perused the menus the hostess had left for them, and continued even after their food and drinks had arrived. Even though it wasn't the first time that Addison had been around Will and Siobhan, Mallory was still surprised by how well they all got on. So much of her life anymore was spent running from one profession to the other, and it was nice to be able to enjoy having them intersect for a bit.

Nicer still, was to do it while Addison's shoulder rested lightly against her own and, every so often, she'd shift a little closer, long, lean limbs curving against her side as the late hour and the warmth of the moment and the gentle buzz of playful banter and smooth wine combined to wrap them in a cocoon of pure bliss.

"Márquez? Really?" Will exclaimed with a mischievous grin as he picked up his glass and downed the dregs of his wine. Their plates had long since been cleared and the cheque settled, but none of them were in a hurry to call an end to the evening and their conversation currently revolved around what classical music Addison had discovered.

"What's wrong with Márquez?" Addison shot back.

"Nothing. I mean, if you're into that kind of stuff…" Will sassed.

"Wait," Siobhan interrupted their playful bickering and rounded on her husband. "You love Márquez."

"Ha!" Addison cheered, pointing at him victoriously.

"Way to take the piss outta me, darlin'," Will grumbled. "What else you got?" he asked Addison.

"Why do I feel like this has turned into a pop-quiz?" Addison muttered, shaking her head. "Oh, I know one. I just found it the other day. *Symphony in Blue*. Have you heard of that one, Mr. Know-It-All?"

The smile that had been playing on Mallory's lips as she listened to Addison and Will go back-and-forth with each other fell at the mention of Gwen's work, and she clenched her jaw against the residual hurt and betrayal that she was sure would soon ice through her chest.

Only it didn't.

Not as strongly as she'd expected, anyway.

But before she could really begin to wrap her head around that, she was dragged back to the conversation.

"Aye..." Will murmured, and god, she hated the worry that flashed in his expression as he looked at her. Hated the way it reminded her of her darkest days those first few weeks after, when she was staying in their guest room while waiting to close on her apartment, and he would sit with her while she raged and then hold her tight until she fell asleep.

Hated, even more, the way Siobhan's expression mirrored his, because she had been there to pick her up and put her back together on just as many nights as he had.

But anger was good, she figured, because it had been anger and an unhealthy amount of spite that had kept her moving through those weeks and months until she could wake up and get through an entire day without thinking about it all.

Addison frowned as she looked from them to Mallory. One would have to be blind to not notice their concern, after all, and she shook her head as she murmured, "What?"

"It's nothing, darling," Mallory muttered, hating the way her voice nearly broke under the weight of the lie. God, how she wished she wasn't such a disaster that simply the mention of a piece of music could bring what had been a perfect evening to a flaming end. "He's heard of it. We all have."

Addison's frown deepened. "I don't understand..."

"I know you don't," Mallory sighed. How could Addison possibly understand when she avoided talking about that part of her life? She glanced at the tables around them. The crowd had thinned while they'd lingered in conversation, but the half-full tables were still enough to make her feel claustrophobic, and she could feel her pulse beginning to race, urging her to run, run, run. "You see, I..." She shook her head. "I'm sorry, I will explain, I swear, but I'd really prefer to not get into it here."

"I'm getting tired anyway," Siobhan offered as Will nodded beside her and made generic sounds of agreement. "So why don't we call it a night."

Addison nodded slowly, a mix of confusion and something close to fear clouding her eyes as she whispered, "Okay."

Mallory offered her friends a tight smile, assuring them that she would be okay before she turned to Addison and asked in a hushed voice, "May I walk you home?"

They were only a few blocks from Addison's place, after all. And this way she would have less time to talk herself out of doing what she knew needed to be done.

Addison's expression shifted by a fraction into something Mallory couldn't quite recognize—and *that* made Mallory's heart skip more than one beat because, after everything she had suffered, she would be damned if she lost whatever this thing was between them to it too—but, after a brief pause, she dipped her chin in a short nod. "Yeah. Okay…"

fifteen

Perspective was a funny thing, Mallory mused as she hugged the bouquet Addison had given her closer to her chest. For so long, she had thought that nothing could hurt her as much as Gwen had. Would have sworn that there was nothing, nothing that could knock her off her feet like that night.

But she had been wrong.

Because watching Addison walk beside her with her head down, shoulders hunched and rolled forward, and her hands jammed into the pockets of her coat felt, in this moment, where the past was apparently truly moving beyond the veil and out of reach, a thousand times worse. She had expected Addison to ask her about what had happened the moment Will and Siobhan were out of earshot, but the question never came, and she was too afraid of saying the wrong thing to be the first to break the uneasy silence that befell them.

After more than two months of easy conversation and playful banter, of light touches and hugs, this quiet, this distance that had spawned between them was stifling. She longed to say something that would cause Addison's shoulders to relax and replace the pensive set of her mouth with a smile, but she hadn't a clue what those magic words might be. From the day they first met, Addison had been the one to make things between them work and, without her leading the way,

Mallory was lost.

"Do you want to hang up your things?" Addison asked, her voice soft and wary as she led the way into her cramped foyer. She didn't look over her shoulder at Mallory as she shrugged off her coat and hung it and her purse on the hooks beneath the mirror mounted on the wall behind the door that served as the entryway's only bit of furniture.

Mallory's throat tightened when Addison finally, finally looked at her and she saw that the warmth and humor she was so used to seeing in her eyes was replaced with uncertainty and confusion, and licked her lips as she nodded.

"Okay. Do you want me to put those in water?" Addison motioned toward the bouquet Mallory had cradled against her chest.

"Please." Mallory handed her the flowers, and her heart leapt at the feeling of Addison's fingers brushing ever so lightly against her own.

"I'll be in the kitchen, then, when you're ready."

Mallory sighed as she watched Addison turn and walk away, and quickly divested herself of her violin, purse, coat, and heels. She had been to Addison's place a handful of times after rehearsal, on those nights when a quiet, simple home-cooked meal sounded more appealing than a less labor-intensive one out, so she knew the layout of the one-bedroom flat well enough that she didn't hesitate to make her way through the combined reception room and dining area to the small kitchen at the other end of the space.

The sound of clinking glass and running water beckoned her forward, and her stockings slid silently over slightly scarred bamboo floors. She glanced at the sitting area that fronted Addison's entertainment center, noting that there was a new Maeve Dylan book tossed idly onto the coffee table that sat in the middle of the gray patterned rug, and that nearly all of the sunshine yellow throw pillows from the two overstuffed sofas and single armchair seemed to have migrated to the corner of the larger couch nearest the light. An image of Addison curled around the pillows, one between her knees and the others in a cocoon around her sides because she always, always lounged on a sofa with her legs tucked up beneath her instead of sitting, flashed across her mind, and she swallowed around the lump it created in her throat.

Addison was standing at the sink when she eventually made her way past the small, four-person dining table to the kitchen, and she ran a hand through her hair as she looked at her. She still had no idea where to begin, and being surrounded by Addison's things made her even more afraid that this was the point in their relationship that she had been dreading—the one where she did the wrong thing and ruined the whole thing.

Mallory was standing there, quite literally wringing her hands in front of herself when Addison looked up, her dark eyes pinched at the corners and her lower lip caught between her teeth. "Oh, Addy…"

Addison shook her head. "I'm sorry," she whispered.

"Wait…what?" Mallory frowned and took a step toward her. "Why in the world are you apologizing?"

Addison rolled her eyes. "I don't know, maybe because I'm pretty sure you stopped breathing when I mentioned that stupid symphony, and Will and Siobhan looked about ready to bundle you in their arms and hustle you away to safety somewhere? I didn't mean to upset anyone; it was just the first thing that came to mind when Will pressed me for another song. And, I mean, I will be the first to admit that I don't really know anything about music, not like you, but I just…"

"Oh, Addy, no." Mallory shook her head as she reached past Addison to turn off the water that had nearly reached the top of the glass vase she'd been filling. "No, darling. You didn't do anything, wrong." Addison had already pulled the bouquet from the plastic bag that covered the stems that extended beyond the bouquet's cellophane sleeve, so she picked up the flowers and pushed them into the vase. She wiped her hands off on the dish towel sitting beside the sink, and then turned to Addison, offering her a small, sad smile. "I haven't been checking music sites for the symphony, but I'm guessing you found it on YouTube?"

Addison nodded. "Yeah. I mean, I thought it was sweet that she wrote it for—"

"Her fiancée," Mallory finished for her. "Yes. Well, it is, I guess. But it also isn't, in a way." She leaned her hip against the edge of the counter, glad that Addison just tilted her head and waited for her to continue instead of pushing for more of an explanation. She took a deep breath and let it go slowly. "Gwen, the woman who wrote the symphony, is my ex."

"Oh…" Addison blinked. "So I'm guessing from the way everyone reacted back at the restaurant that it didn't end well."

"Understatement of the year," Mallory confirmed with a huff of laughter that was dark and dry and completely devoid humor. "She… I…" She shook her head. "I don't know where to begin trying to explain all of this."

"You don't have to."

"Perhaps, but I want to." Mallory smiled at the feeling of Addison's hand covering her own and looked down at their hands. There was a lot she could say about the relationship, but it was the way it ended that truly mattered, so she decided just to start there. "I proposed to Gwen a few days after I won the audition for my position here in London."

The math wasn't difficult, less than a year had passed between her failed proposal and Gwen's much more successful attempt, and it was evident by the way Addison's eyes widened that she understood now why the mention of *Symphony in Blue* wrought such a visceral reaction. "Oh, sweetie…"

Mallory lifted her right shoulder in a small shrug. It was strange, really, how she was able to look at it all from a distance. Two months ago, the memory of that night brought her to her knees, and now… Her throat was tight and her stomach twisted and there was that familiar hollow ache in her chest and it still hurt. She had a feeling it always would. But it was no longer crippling. She could breathe, and she was still standing. Part of her had used to wonder if she would ever truly begin to heal, and she was surprised to find that she had without even noticing. "She turned me down, obviously."

"Wasn't willing to move here?"

"That was part of it, yes." Mallory looked back up at Addison. "I won't pretend the relationship was perfect, but..." She took a deep breath as Addison made a small sound of encouragement and pulled her hand from the edge of the counter to cradle it between both of hers. "I'd hoped that maybe..." She shook her head. "It doesn't matter. Because it turned out that Gwen had been seeing Dana the whole time I'd been focused on getting ready for my audition here."

"She just told you that...?" Addison gasped.

"Well, I mean, Dana was at her house when I showed up to surprise Gwen with the good news and everything, and she'd all but bolted at the sight of me, so after the whole failed proposal it wasn't too difficult to figure out that she was somehow involved."

"Seriously?"

"Gwen said she didn't want to interfere with my audition preparations, so she just..." She shrugged as familiar, icy tendrils of betrayal and heartache squeezed her chest. There it was. There was the ache she had struggled against for so long. "She let me believe that everything was fine when it was anything but."

"What a bitch!"

The absolute vehemence in Addison's voice shattered the remnants of past hurt that had threatened to overwhelm her once more, and Mallory blinked at her. "No..."

Addison's eyebrows about shot up off her forehead at that. "What do you mean, 'no'? How can you just..."

"I don't..." Mallory shrugged. "I mean..." She shook her head. "I won my audition," she whispered. "It was my dream job, and I got it. And I don't know if I would have been able to focus on my preparations like I needed to if every aspect of my life hadn't been exactly as it'd been, so... I really do think that, in her own way, she was trying to help."

"Yeah, but still."

"Believe me, darling, I know." Mallory swallowed hard and blinked against the sting of tears that threatened.

Addison sighed and pushed off the counter to loop her arms around Mallory's neck and pull her into a hug. "You deserve so much better than to be treated like that, Mal," she murmured, her voice soft and layered with so much emotion that Mallory's throat tightened at the sound of it.

Mallory closed her eyes as she welcomed the embrace, wrapping her arms around Addison's waist and urging her closer. "Thank you," she breathed as she leaned her cheek against Addison's forehead. She took a deep breath and let it go slowly. Whether it was the warmth of Addison's embrace or the exhaustion that seemed to slam into her out of nowhere, she found herself offering, "You want to know what's the worst part, though?"

Addison stiffened beneath her hands. "What?"

"I had no idea she wrote music," Mallory whispered, her voice finally cracking under the weight of what had become Gwen's ultimate betrayal. "She wrote an entire symphony, a fucking beautiful piece of music, and I'd had absolutely no idea…" Her voice trailed off, and she was grateful that instead of offering platitudes, Addison just held her tighter.

How long they stayed like that she had no idea, but eventually she felt Addison yawning against her shoulder, and she smiled as she murmured, "It's getting late, darling. I should probably—"

"There's no reason for you to head out now. Just stay here tonight," Addison interrupted in a hushed, sleepy voice as she pulled back to look at her.

Mallory held her breath as she drank in the earnestness of Addison's soft smile and gentle gaze. It was cheating, really, to turn that look on her now, when she was physically exhausted from an impossibly long day and mentally drained from painful conversation, and she was tempted, so tempted to accept, but… "I appreciate the offer, but I'm afraid my back is a little too old to sleep on a sofa," she demurred.

"Like I'd ever make you sleep on the couch," Addison scoffed. "My bed is big enough for two."

There was a rogue curl tickling the very edge of Addison's right eye, and Mallory sighed as she reached up to brush it away. Addison's breath hitched, and her eyes fluttered shut as she leaned into the touch. Unable to resist, Mallory dragged the pad of her thumb over the curve of Addison's cheek as she gently cradled her jaw. It was an undeniably intimate hold, and her heart leapt into her throat at the way Addison's lips parted ever so slightly in response. Addison was always beautiful, but never so much as she was in this moment, and it was all she could do not to lean in and kiss her.

"I'm not sure that's a good idea," Mallory whispered. And then, because she was determined to be better than she had in the past, she found the courage to add, "After everything with Gwen, I was determined to focus on my career and my friends and had convinced myself that I didn't need or want anything else. Anyone else. But then I met you and..." She sighed as she focused on the way her thumb looked as she caressed Addison's cheek. "You are talented and beautiful and so completely unfairly charming"—she smiled when Addison laughed softly at that—"and I just can't resist you."

Addison blinked her eyes open and whispered, "Oh, Mal..."

"And I hope I haven't completely misread the situation and made things—"

Addison silenced her with a finger to the lips as she shook her head. "You aren't misreading anything. I've been flirting with you pretty much non-stop from our first rehearsal." She took Mallory's free hand and cradled it against her chest as her expression softened. "And now I feel like I should explain that I didn't ask you to stay because I'm attracted to you. I asked because it's late and you're tired and, no matter what happens from here, I'm your friend, and I hate the idea of you hurting."

Mallory dipped her head to rest her forehead against Addison's.

"Thank you, darling," she breathed.

"Always," Addison promised through a yawn. "Sorry."

"It's late," Mallory pointed out, though she made no effort to move.

Addison nodded, and Mallory smiled at the way she did not pull away either. "My offer still stands, Mal. Stay here tonight. I'll find you some sweats, and we'll just sleep."

And, oh, Mallory knew that she should decline the invitation. That she should order a taxi and gather her things and go, but after too many months of struggling to do every damn thing and two-and-a-half months fighting what was happening here with Addison, she just didn't have the energy to do it anymore.

But, more than that, she didn't want to fight it anymore.

Not when this felt so goddamn right.

"If I wake up to find you cuddling me..." she mock warned.

"You'll shut up and like it," Addison sassed with a playful wink.

"Yes, I imagine I will," Mallory admitted softly.

Addison sighed and pulled away to brush the softest of kisses against Mallory's cheek that was gentle and accepting and held no ulterior motives. "I can keep my hands to myself for as long as you need me to, Mal. I promise. I just... I'm glad we're not dancing around this anymore," she whispered as she took Mallory's hand from her cheek and laced their fingers together. "Is this okay?"

Mallory looked down at their joined hands and smiled when she looked back into Addison's hopeful brown eyes. "Yes, darling. It's more than okay."

"I'm glad." Addison beamed as she squeezed Mallory's hand. "So, let's go find you something to sleep in..."

sixteen

If the standing-room-only underground train wasn't enough to remind Mallory of just why she loved her work schedule, the veritable throng of people queued to place their order at Higher Ground Tuesday morning would have done it.

As it turned out, forty-five minutes made a serious difference in the morning.

She should have expected as much, to be honest, but she had been so distracted by the incredibly vivid dream she'd been having about Addison that her alarm had rudely interrupted that trivial things like rush-hour commuters and busier-than-usual coffee shops hadn't even crossed her mind. Of course, the dream was almost to be expected after she had woken up Sunday morning to find that, despite her playful warning to Addison about cuddling, she was the one who had sought the contact and comfort of a warm body during the night.

And, oh, Addison had just *loved* teasing her about that over the lazy brunch they'd taken at a café near the opera house before she'd been forced to run home to change for Sunday afternoon's performance at the Barbican.

For as much as she wished Addison would have just pretended the whole thing never happened, she couldn't help but be thankful for the playful teasing that gently assured her that nothing had changed between them. Excluding the cuddling, that is. Or, she guessed, the more frequent hand-holding.

But otherwise, everything was the same.

They had worked their asses off in the studio the day before and enjoyed a quiet dinner at Addison's place following their massages, and though they lingered longer in their goodbye than they had in the past, she eventually took her leave with only a drawn-out hug exchanged.

In a way, it was embarrassing to be such a mess that even after all their confessions Saturday night that she was keeping them stuck in place, but she could not deny that she was glad—and more than a little touched—that Addison seemed perfectly content to wait for her.

"Earth to Mal," a laughing voice interrupted her reverie, and Mallory startled when she realized that she had somehow worked her way to the front of the queue while she'd been thinking about Addison.

"Apologies, darling," she murmured as she smiled at Lena.

"You're fine. Media day today, yeah?"

Mallory nodded. "You would think starting the day an hour earlier wouldn't be so much trouble, but…"

"I'm sure you had a late night," Lena replied with a kind smile. "I mean, Addy was looking quite rough herself, so I imagine Nina is in top form as always, yeah?"

"Addy was in already?" Mallory tried her best not to look disappointed that she had missed her. She had been hoping that she would run into her here and then they could make their way over to the opera house together.

"Yup." Lena looked pointedly toward the back of the shop. "She even ordered you your usual before she went and stole your spot."

Mallory bit her lip to try to contain her smile and, judging by the way Lena smirked at her, failed miserably at it. "Hush, you."

Lena's smirk widened as she waggled her eyebrows. "I take it the partnership is going well?"

Mallory took a deep breath and let it go slowly. "It is. Far better than I'd ever imagined, if I'm to be honest."

"Good." Lena's smirk softened to a genuine smile as she reached across the counter to give Mallory's wrist a light squeeze. "I'm glad for you. And her. I love you both, so it's…"

"Very new," Mallory shared softly. "Very, very new and, quite frankly, more than a little scary. You know, after everything…" She waved a hand in a *you know* type gesture. She'd only told Lena about the whole Gwen thing when they went to dinner before she'd left to go on tour with the LSO earlier that summer. Had it not been for her lingering foul mood and Lena's kindness—and more than a little bit of wine—she might have never shared that part of her life with her, but it had been cathartic. Besides Will and Siobhan, Lena was the first person she had shared it all with, and as she looked back at it now, she wondered if that night of vulnerability was what started her on this path to healing.

Lena nodded. "Well, I'm happy for you. And her, because I honestly can't think of anyone better suited for either of you. And I'll keep my fingers crossed." She tilted her head toward Addison. "Now, go get your girl, Collingswood. I'll have Clark bring your coffee and scone out in a minute. And I'll put the coffee in a to-go cup, just in case. Media day is a slog, you might want to ration out the caffeine."

Mallory nodded and murmured, "Cheers, Lena."

She eased her way past a trio of suits gathered around the carry-out end of the counter, and her stomach did a little flip when she saw Addison watching her with soft eyes and a warm smile. The thrill that rippled through her as their gazes locked was precisely the thing that she found so frightening, because the last person to make her feel like this was Gwen—and she was absolutely terrified of doing something that would make Addison stop looking at her like that.

She honestly didn't know if she had it in herself to recover from one more heartbreak.

And she shouldn't allow herself to want this but, oh, she loved the way Addison smiled at her like she was now, so open and happy and awed. It made her feel special and beautiful and desired and, despite her fear and her worry and her concerns, brave. Brave enough to begin to push back against the fear.

Brave enough to *want* a happy ending of her own.

Even if she wasn't quite convinced she was ready for it yet.

Once she was close enough that she wouldn't have to raise her voice to be heard, she teased, "Stealing my table now, are you?"

"Ah, well, you know, anything to get your attention," Addison drawled.

Mallory laughed as she laid her things on the floor beside the table and lowered herself into the chair opposite Addison. "I appreciate the effort, darling, but all you have to do is exist to do that." It was meant to be a joke, but there was far too much truth in the comment as well because she was always, always aware of Addison whenever she was near, and that softened what was meant to be a playful quip into a revealing confession.

Addison blinked as a light blush crept over her cheeks. "You too," she whispered as she looked up through her eyelashes.

Mallory took a deep breath as she looked back at Addison, who was watching her over her coffee cup. Her heart skipped a beat as Addison's gaze seemed to bore into her very soul, making her feel like she was flying and falling at the same time, and murmured, "I'm so very glad."

She knew it wasn't necessary to comment, but it seemed important to make sure Addison knew.

"Me too." Addison's lips curled in a smile around the rim of her mug as she took a sip of her coffee. "So, are you ready for this morning?" she asked as she leaned back in her chair and cradled the warm mug in her hands.

"Not at all," Mallory admitted with a wry shake of her head. "But I trust you'll keep me from making a fool of myself."

"Well, yeah. But only because it would reflect poorly on me. I mean, what would it look like if one of The Royal Ballet's principals had a totally inept partner?"

"Oh, shut it," Mallory chuckled.

Addison laughed. "It will be fine, Mal. I promise."

"Your order," Clark interrupted as he slid Mallory's coffee and scone in front of her. "Enjoy."

"Ta, mate," Mallory murmured as he backed away with a short bow and a smile. She picked up the fork that was lying next to her croissant and looked back at Addison. "How long do we have until we need to start heading over?"

"Well, Nina said nine, so…" She picked up her phone that had been lying face-down on the table. "Maybe twenty minutes?" She shrugged and set it back down. "No real rush."

Mallory nodded and reached for the fork that was lying on the plate next to her croissant and began cutting into it. "Did you eat already? Would you like some of this?"

"Yes. To both questions." Addison smiled as she leaned forward expectantly. She hummed happily as she took the bite Mallory offered her from the fork. "That is so much better than the oatmeal and peanut butter toast I had earlier," she sighed as she leaned back in her seat. "One of these days I'm going to have to cave and order one."

"You'd certainly burn it off."

"True, but for the same calories I could have my oatmeal and toast, plus a hard-boiled egg or two."

Mallory had to admit that Addison had a point. And, given how much she exercised during the day, the more wholesome calories were a much wiser choice, but… "Yes, but none of that is as delicious as this."

"You have a point there." Addison conceded with a little laugh.

"Another bite?" Mallory offered.

"I'm good." Addison shook her head. Her phone buzzed with an alert, and she sighed when she checked the message.

"Everything okay?"

"Yeah. It was from Serena. I guess everything is ready to go on stage now and Nina would like to start early if possible," Addison explained. "I imagine you'll be getting a similar message soon."

"Tell her we're on our way now." Mallory pulled the napkin from beneath her plate and moved what remained of her croissant into the center of it. "I can finish this while we walk."

"Are you sure? Because if I tell her I'm still at home, that would buy you enough time to at least finish your breakfast here."

"It's fine," Mallory assured her as she stood and began collecting her things.

"Okay." Addison nodded and typed out a quick reply to Serena. "Right. Done." She bounced to her feet and slung the strap of her duffle bag over her head so the strap cut across her chest. "Ready when you are, my dear."

Once Mallory had shouldered her violin and briefcase, she picked up her coffee and croissant and smiled at Addison. "Lead the way, darling."

seventeen

"There you are," Collette, the assistant wig mistress for the ballet, declared as she smiled warmly at Mallory in the lighted mirror. "What do you think?"

Mallory bit the inside of her cheek as she studied her reflection. "I think I'm going to come to you lot the next time I have an event to attend," she murmured as she turned her head from one side to the other to take it all in. Peter, the makeup artist who'd had his way with her, had gone for a smoky, dramatic look—a neutral foundation with just the faintest hint of color on her cheeks, warm, dark lids, and deep red lips—that could have been too much for her to carry off, but was softened by the loose bun Collette had twisted her hair up into. The combined effect was both elegant and romantic, and she smiled as she met Collette's gaze in the mirror. "It's lovely. Thank you."

"My pleasure." Collette pointed toward a rack of costumes and a small, curtained-off area a few meters away. "Now, it's off to Ginny for you, and then you are ready to go."

Mallory nodded and slipped obediently from her chair. She had expected to be overwhelmed by the preparation process, but everyone involved was so experienced with the whole thing that she was able to turn off her brain and just follow their directions.

"Ah, there you are. Come, come," Ginny greeted her with a smile and a beckoning wave, and Mallory ducked her head in apology as she picked up her pace. "Addy is already out there doing her solo shots," Ginny explained as she held out Mallory's dress. "So you'll be up next."

Mallory nodded as she took the dress and stepped between the flaps of the privacy curtain. "I'm impressed you finished the costumes already," she said as she unzipped the hoodie she had changed before Peter had started on her. She shivered at the rush of cool air that swept over her bare chest and hurried to shuck her sweats so she could step into her dress.

"Yes, well, Nina had told me at your last fitting that she wanted them ready for today, so I let the rest of my team worry about the costumes for the first half of this one and the corps while I finished these off. And, given that the first half and the corps are pretty traditional with the white tutus and corsets and what have you, it wasn't too difficult. Plus, this way we can focus on the final preparations for *The Nutcracker* as we've got a few new soloists stepping into roles for that one."

"It's gorgeous," Mallory assured her as she worked the dress from its hanger, taking a moment despite the less than ideal temperature of the theatre to appreciate her handiwork. Small beads just a shade lighter than the fabric of the dress had been added to the bodice, giving the dress a sense of depth and motion even on the hanger. "Honestly, Gin. It's incredible."

"I'm glad you like it," Ginny replied, sounding pleased. "But if you don't hurry and put it on, I won't be able to make any last-minute changes it might need. And if you're not perfect when you go out there, Nina will have my head."

"Sorry," Mallory apologized as she hustled into the dress. It fit like a second skin, and she wished there was a mirror in the changing room so she could see what it looked like on. "Here I am," she announced as she exited the dressing area, still fiddling with the zipper on her side.

"Here you are, indeed, dear," Ginny murmured as a wholly pleased smile tugged at her lips. She made a twirling motion with her right hand. "Look at yourself," she instructed as she pointed at the mirror set off to the side.

"Oh, wow…" Mallory breathed as she turned to the mirror. The intricate embroidery and beadwork Ginny had added to her dress were even more spectacular when she was wearing it, the lines of beads acting as embellishments to the costume as a whole while also highlighting the curves and planes of her body. If she did not know that she hadn't even laid eyes on the gown since her last fitting, she would have sworn that all of the finishing work had been done while she'd been wearing it. "Gin…"

Ginny hummed her thanks as she began tugging at the dress, getting it to fit just the way she wanted, and after a moment stepped back with a happy sigh. "Lovely. Just lovely. You are, without a doubt, the best-looking partner Addy has ever been paired with." She tilted her head toward the stage and grinned as she continued in a mock-conspiratorial whisper, "And the two of you are going to knock the ballet world on its ass."

Mallory laughed. "You're too much."

"I'm precisely the right amount of everything," Ginny sassed with a wink as she handed Mallory a pair of slippers that had been dyed to match her dress. Once Mallory had slipped them on, she clapped her hands twice and said, "Now go out there and knock 'em dead. I'll be right here so that if any problems arise when you start moving in it, we'll be able to make some quick changes on the fly so you can get through the day and I'll take care of the rest upstairs later."

Mallory smiled and nodded. "Cheers, Gin," she murmured, pausing to give Ginny's shoulder a light squeeze before she made her way toward the table just off the stage where she had dropped her things when they had arrived at the theatre.

Once she had her violin and was out of excuses to put this off any longer, she took a deep breath and made her way past the wide black curtains that hung from the catwalks overhead to shield the wings from the audience's view, and onto the stage. She held her breath as she took in the sheer grandeur of the auditorium, which was so very different from the stage than as a member of the audience. From this angle, the opulence of the amphitheater—the rich velvet seats and gilded fixtures, the ornate woodwork and breathtaking craftsmanship displayed in every nook and cranny of the building—was but a footnote to the absolute feeling of claustrophobia she felt as she stood center stage and looked out onto the seats.

There was nowhere to hide.

It was going to be her and Addison out here on their own, and every single set of eyes in the place was going to have a perfect view of their performance.

"Not a bad view, huh?" Nina drawled, interrupting Mallory's impending panic. "I've danced on more stages than I can remember, and this is still the one that I am the proudest of performing on." She took a deep breath and let it go slowly. "When the lights go down, and the audience quiets and stills, this stage becomes electric. You can barely make out anything beyond the conductor in the pit"—she motioned toward the empty pit tucked beneath the front of the stage— "and it's just...god, it's everything. Absolutely everything." Nina turned to her with a smile. "And you're going to become one of the special few who gets to experience it."

Mallory nodded. She knew the feeling Nina was describing, had felt it herself when she was younger and had done a fair bit of soloist work with symphonies throughout Europe, though never from this particular stage. "I can imagine. And I'm honored that you have so much faith in me to let me do this. I just hope I don't let you down."

"So don't." Nina smirked and then glanced over her shoulder to the side of the stage where the photographer was working with Addison for some individual shots. "It looks like Pierce is almost done with Addy and will be ready for you soon. Have you worked with him before?"

Mallory shook her head as she looked toward the photographer in question. She couldn't see much from this angle—his side was to them, and he had his camera up blocking his face—but the photographer who had done her photos for the LSO had been a petite redheaded woman and Pierce was neither petite, ginger, or a woman. He was, however, standing perfectly in the way to block her view of Addison, and for that, she was rather annoyed. "I don't reckon I have, no."

"You'll love him. He handles all our print work. We'll do a few solo shots for you, some stills of the two of you together, and then hopefully the video team will be ready to go, and we'll clear all this off and get cracking on that. Sound good?"

Mallory shrugged. "Yes?"

Nina grinned. "Brilliant." She turned on her heel and made her way back toward the umbrella flashes and black backdrop, so certain that Mallory would follow that she didn't bother to look back and check. "Pierce, this is Mallory Collingswood," she announced as she stopped at the photographer's side. "Mallory, Pierce Welker."

Pierce turned at the sound of his name, and Mallory gasped when she was finally, finally able to see Addison. She knew that she should have been making polite *pleased to meet you* type noises, but she was utterly transfixed by Addison's appearance. Where her hair had been pulled up into a somewhat traditional ballet style, Addison's was left down, leaving her natural curls free to curve around her jawline and swing with her movement. Addison's dress had similar detailing as her own, but where her beading was a shade darker than the fabric of her dress, Addison's looked to be done with thousands of tiny crystals that were less about accentuating the lines of the dress and more about demanding the attention of everyone who looked at it.

Mallory hadn't even realized she had started toward Addison until she was standing right in front of her, and dared to reach out with her free hand and touch the soft fabric at Addison's hip as she murmured, "You look stunning."

"Me? Have you seen you?" Addison shook her head. "My god, Mal…"

"Yes, yes," Nina interrupted, her tone playfully begrudged and tinged with amusement as she drew everyone's attention, "you both look beautiful. So why don't we take some pictures, yes?"

Pierce, who was watching them with a knowing twinkle in his gray eyes, nodded. "I'm done with Addy. Mallory, you're up. I'm Pierce, by the way."

"Sorry about that," Mallory apologized as she let go of Addison's side, feeling genuinely embarrassed for her behavior. "Pleased to meet you."

He grinned and waved his hand as if to brush Addy out of the way. "Ms. Leigh, could you maybe find it in yourself to move out of my frame so I can knock these out and we can get to the ones of you two together?"

Addison replied with her best aggrieved groan, and shook her head as she muttered, "Ugh. Fine. You're always ruining my fun, Pierce."

Pierce laughed and ran a hand through his dirty blond hair, making the front of it stand on end. "Whatever." He shook his head and it fell back into place. "Just move. Don't go far, though."

"If he thinks I'm going any further than I absolutely have to, he's out of his goddamn mind," Addison muttered under her breath as she gave Mallory's wrist a quick squeeze. She winked as her hand fell away and, with one last smoldering smile, finally did as she'd been asked and moved out of the way.

Mallory licked her lips as she forced herself to look away from Addison and focus on the photographer who was waiting for her. "So, what's the plan?"

"Let's start with a headshot type thing and go from there. You can leave the violin at your side for now, and just look this way..." He smiled when she complied and lifted his camera. "Beautiful. Maybe give me a little smirk? Something between a serious face and an all-out smile. You're beautiful and talented, and you know it, so let it show..."

Mallory huffed a laugh and did her best to do as he asked, and was rewarded with a flurry of flashes as he took a quick string of shots. Photos of her holding the violin were next, first looking directly at the camera as it rested on her shoulder and then playing, and once he was happy with what he'd gotten, he waved Addison back in.

"Now, let's have some fun, shall we?"

"What do you have in mind?" Addison asked as she made her way back under the lights.

"That depends..." He looked at Nina. "You've said this ballet of yours is going to throw convention out the window and, looking at them together I can see you've done just that, but how risqué do you want us to go here?"

"It's the ballet," Nina sighed, shaking her head, "so not very, I'm afraid. We can't have the mailing for this production sending our conservative ticket holders into cardiac arrest."

"Shame." He smirked as he looked at Addison and Mallory. "You're doing a video after this, yeah? Can you maybe do the bit you've rehearsed for that so I can get an idea of what we're working with and we can decide on some staged shots from there?"

"Can we move some of these lights back a bit?" Addison asked. "Maybe...six feet or so?"

"Sure." Once the last light stand was moved, he asked, "Good?"

"We can work with this," Addison assured him confidently. "Mal?"

"From the top of the video section?" Mallory asked as she lifted her violin into position.

"May as well," Nina agreed.

Mallory took a deep breath and, with one last glance at Addison, looked back at Nina who was standing beside Pierce and his camera and waited for her to count them in. Nerves, faint but distinct fluttered in her stomach as she waited for her cue to begin. It was one thing to work on a piece with members of the production team, but it was quite another to perform it for an outsider, and while Addison and Nina had both expressed confidence in her, she was painfully aware that this was the first moment that she might not live up to expectations.

Nina nodded and smiled at her. "Light and easy now." And then, in an even cadence that was a match to the notes Mallory would soon be playing, called, "Here…we…go…two…three…four…"

It was only a few heartbeats after she put bow to strings that Mallory felt Addison's fingers against the small of her back, the touch everything that she needed to center herself in the moment as she sank into it, her stance softening and her shoulders rocking back toward Addison as her body instinctively began to move with her.

Her eyes fluttered shut at the tickle of Addison's hair against the back of her neck as they leaned into one of the swooping turns that had taken her so long to get right, and she blinked them back open as they came out of it and Addison's right hand landed lightly on her hip. She planted her feet and shifted her weight to her back leg to help lead Addison into the two pirouettes that preceded the final arabesque, and as soon as Addison's right hand left her hip, she leaned back the other way, tensing her left arm in preparation for the moment Addison's left hand would come to rest on the scroll of her violin as she leaned into the arabesque, lifting her right leg well past ninety degrees as she extended her right arm in a graceful, accentuating line above it.

Mallory pulled her bow through the final note as Addison settled into that final position. It was only years of practiced stoicism on stage that kept her from grinning in triumph as she extended her right arm behind herself so that it was parallel with her extended leg, leaving the audience with the image of them staring into each other's eyes, their body positions a mirror to the other.

The air had only just begun to quiet when Nina clapped and declared, "Very nicely done. Excellent."

"Nicely done?" Pierce scoffed as he turned on her. "Bloody hell, Devereaux, you honestly expect me to do something with *that* that won't give the stuffy pensioners a coronary?"

Addison laughed as she dropped to two feet and pulled Mallory into a one-armed, celebratory embrace. "You mean that in a good way though, right?"

"I think I need a fucking cigarette after watching that," Pierce replied with a grin, shaking his head wryly. "You lot aren't just throwing convention out the window, you're absolutely destroying it. That was fantastic!"

Nina laughed, clearly pleased by his reaction. "Yes, well. Better to save that reveal for the first performance, but your reaction is exactly what I was hoping for."

"If you lot want to save the surprise, your video team is going to have to work some magic in the editing room," Pierce told her seriously. "Because if your little clip shows what I just saw, the cat will be well and truly out of the bag."

"I'm sure we'll figure out something," Nina murmured confidently.

"I'll tell you what, though, the shot you're looking for to anchor your mailer is what they did there at the end." He turned to Mallory and Addison. "Can you get back into that one without the lead-in?"

"Sure," Addison answered as she moved away from Mallory's side.

Mallory lifted her violin so Addison would know where to position herself. "Do you want the bow on the strings as well? So it looks like I'm playing? Or would you prefer the finish?"

"Both." He lifted his camera and fiddled with the focus ring. "We'll start with the pretend playing, though. Addison, I'll start shooting when you're in position. Hold as long as you can, and I'll move around you, yeah? Fall out of it when you need a break, and we'll just hit it again when you're ready."

"You got it." Addison's popped onto her toes. "Ready, Mal?"

Mallory smiled and nodded. "When you are, darling."

eighteen

Fall turned to winter in what seemed like a blink of an eye, making typically dreary days even darker with the shortened daytime hours, and suddenly there was less than a month until the first performance of *Evolution* and it was time for their first full-call.

For Mallory, trying to wrap her head around just where the time had gone was as dizzying as following the dancers on the floor in front of her who were working through the final section of the first half of the ballet. The eighteen corps dancers and the principal pair reminded her of the band from Stanford that she had seen when Gwen had taken her to a football game at the Coliseum—dressed similarly enough for one to know they were a group but so individually that they didn't look like an organized one until you saw them perform. Matt's rainbow sweatpants clashed horribly with Gabs' merlot-colored leotard and black skirt, and the corps dancers were equally mismatched.

"Hold there, please," Nina called, waving for everybody to stop, and the dancers fell to the flats of their feet as she turned to the small collection of répétiteurs and notators that were responsible for each of the performance groups that were huddled near the mirrors at the front of the room.

Mallory sighed and pushed herself to her feet. Even though Addison had warned her that the first full-call would be disjointed as the different rehearsal groups got together for the very first time to work through each section of the performance in order, she honestly hadn't expected the various groups to be stopped for their positioning or movement to be corrected so many times. She had been looking forward to getting a feeling for the flow of the entire ballet, from the first notes through to the end of hers and Addison's part, but the rehearsal so far had been fragmented at best.

Their last three weeks of rehearsals had moved at light-speed compared to what she had experienced so far and, knowing that they had only three short weeks until their first performance, she was starting to feel more than a little anxious as to whether or not they would be ready in time.

"How much longer until they get to us?" she whispered to Addison as they made their way down the short flight of bleachers at the back of Clore Studio to stretch at the barre near the back corner of the room and keep their muscles warm. It didn't matter for herself so much, but it would be reckless for Addison to get up and dance after sitting for close to two hours.

Addison shrugged and leaned into her side as she laid her left hand on the barre. "Not much, I'd imagine," she murmured. "Gabs and Matt look good—they tweaked that bit that seemed to have been pissing Nina off—and the corps' steps seem to be there, so now it's just a matter of getting them all aligned how they want for the finish. Then it's the corps' little set-up bit for us, and we're on."

"Wonderful," Mallory muttered, though it was impossible to be properly annoyed when Addison chuckled softly in her ear and wrapped an arm around her waist as she leaned in closer.

"Are you not enjoying sitting on those oh-so-comfortable wood bleachers and hanging out with me?" Addison teased.

Mallory squirmed away from the playful dig of Addison's fingers in her side. "Not at all." She laughed when Addison's fingers dug in harder and grabbed her hand to stop her tickling as she relented, "Fine. Fine. Yes, I'm quite enjoying myself. Best day ever, and all that."

"That's what I thought," Addison drawled as she turned and leaned her cheek on Mallory's shoulder.

"Oh you did, did you?" Mallory teased as she wrapped an arm around Addison's shoulders, and her heart fluttered into her throat at the way Addison melted into the embrace.

They were still on the platonic side of the line that her slowly healing heart had drawn firmly in the sand but, over the last few weeks, she had found herself increasingly comfortable reaching out for Addison when she wanted her, and letting herself enjoy the easy comfort and gentle affection that was slowly building between them. The idea of having more than this was still overwhelming, she was still re-learning what it felt like to be whole and happy, but it was so easy to be with Addison that those moments of doubt were becoming fewer and further in-between.

"Well, yeah. Because I'm awesome and completely irresistible."

"Yes, you are," Mallory agreed softly as she touched her cheek to Addison's forehead. "And, while I quite like this, aren't you going to stretch or something to keep warm?"

Addison sighed and nodded. "Yeah, probably should."

"One last time," Nina declared, clapping her hands to make sure she had everyone's attention. "And then we'll jump right into the corps for the second half. Chloe"—she looked to the pianist who had been accompanying the dancers all afternoon—"from the beginning of the pas de deux, please."

"Or not," Addison muttered. "We better get out of the way."

Mallory nodded and followed Addison back to the spot in the bleachers. They reclaimed their seats just before Gabs and Matt started dancing again, and this time the group got all the way through to their final position without being stopped.

"Good. Good. We'll work on it more next time, but that was right where I want to see it," Nina declared. "Gabs, Matt, thank you for your work. Corps, I'm afraid you have more work to do. Positions, please. Chloe, once they're in place, if you could vamp the first few bars a few times, I'll count them in."

Chloe nodded and began shuffling the sheet music in front of her as Gabs and Matt bounded across the room to the bleachers and scrambled up to where Mallory and Addison were sitting.

"So?" Gabs demanded as she all but threw herself onto the seat beside Addison.

"You sucked," Addison teased, laughing as she leaned in and dropped a loud kiss to Gabs' cheek.

"Fuck you very much," Gabs sassed, her Spanish accent making the curse sound positively musical. She playfully shoved Addison away from her, and they all laughed. "Seriously though, you two are up next. You ready?"

"Of course," Addison scoffed.

Mallory nodded in agreement as she welcomed Addison's weight against her side. "What she said."

"Please don't encourage her," Matt said as he sat down on the bench in front of them and laid his leg out along it to stretch his hamstrings. "She's bossy enough already."

"Wouldn't you be better suited doing that somewhere else?" Mallory asked.

"Probably," he agreed, turning his head so his temple was pressed to his knee instead of his forehead and winking at her. "But we want to see what you lot have gotten up to. It's been all mystery and intrigue for your half, and now we finally get to see what we're up against. I mean, with two distinct halves of the performance, one of us is going to get more applause."

"Oh, Matty my boy." Addison laughed and shook her head. "You know I love you guys, but you don't have a chance. We're going to bring the roof down with our performance."

"Fancy a wager on that?" Matt shot back.

"A hundred quid?" Addison offered.

"Two. One hundred each. You in, Collingswood?" Gabs countered, arching a challenging brow at Mallory.

Mallory smiled at the way Addison turned hopefully toward her and nodded. "Sure. I mean, it doesn't seem fair to you lot, but if you really want to give us your money like that... I'm sure we can find a way to spend it. Maybe a nice dinner out somewhere?"

"Great, she's just as cocky as Addy," Matt grumbled playfully.

Addison grinned and ignored him as she reached out to give Mallory's leg an approving squeeze. "Absolutely. Or maybe just a couple bottles of really good wine and some delivery."

"Oh, that sounds lovely," Mallory agreed as she covered Addison's hand on her thigh. "Let's do that."

"Don't you reckon you're counting your chickens before they've hatched?" Matt chuckled.

Addison shook her head. "Not at all. You'll be settling that bet after rehearsal today once you see us dance."

Matt looked poised to respond, but Chloe started playing just then, so he settled for rolling his eyes at her as he turned to watch the corps do their thing.

As the introduction for the second half of the ballet was only about four minutes, it didn't take the corps long to work through it, and Addison grinned as she gave Mallory's leg one last squeeze and asked, "Ready to go show these fools how real professionals show up for work?"

Mallory nodded and quickly shed the hoodie she'd been wearing over her tank to keep warm in the chilly studio, and she turned to retrieve her violin. "Just try to keep up, darling," she sassed, knowing it would make Gabs and Matt laugh.

"Oh, I like you, Mallory," Gabs laughed.

"Please." Addison shook her head. "You've liked her for a while now."

"Well, yeah, but that's mostly because you like her so much," Gabs retorted with a wink.

Mallory blushed, and Addison smiled as she warned, "Be good."

Gabs held a hand over her heart and batted her lashes innocently.

"Who, me?"

"Exactly. Now," Addison said as she shucked her leg warmers and hoodie, "just sit back and enjoy watching your money disappear."

Mallory didn't miss the speculative looks the corps dancers gave her as they spilled into the bleachers and she and Addison made their way down to the floor. There was a hint of jealousy in a few faces—mostly from the girls who brushed past her just a little too closely, as if challenging her right to be there—but rather than making her nervous, the barely-veiled animosity solidified her confidence. She might be new to the world of ballet, but she had decades of experience dealing with passive-aggressive challenges like these.

The hum of quiet voices questioning just what it was they were going to do was the wind at their backs as they made their way across the pale lino to where Nina waited, and the small smile quirking her lips suggested that she was very much looking forward to what was about to happen.

"Ready?" Nina asked, though it was more of a challenge than a question. She chuckled softly when Mallory nodded and Addison just smirked in response. "Excellent. Off you go, then." As they began making their way to the side of the room that acted as the wings from which they would enter, Nina called, "Chloe, can you start with the last thirty seconds of the last bit you were playing?"

Chloe tucked her mousey brown hair behind her ears and pushed her glasses higher on her nose. "Of course."

"Good. Vamp it once or twice if needed, and then when Mallory starts playing you can stop. They'll be good to do this without further accompaniment."

Mallory smiled at the surprised hum of chatter that bubbled up from the back of the room at that.

"Got it," Chloe agreed as she found her place in her music and lifted her hands to the keys.

After months of being the sole source of music in the room, it was strange being started off by a piano, especially given the fact that there was a distinct pause between when this music ended and when she would begin, but Mallory bobbed her head with the melody, letting herself get a real feel for how the pieces fit together.

She shouldered her violin at the first pause and nodded to Chloe that she would join the next time through, and cleared her mind of everything except these next forty-four minutes of music and movement. The lede neared the pause that marked her beginning, and she winked at Addison as she lifted her bow. "Try and keep up, won't you?"

Addison laughed softly and nodded. "Bring it on, beautiful."

Mallory turned her eyes forward as the music stalled and, after a couple of beats, began playing as she made her way toward the center of the room. She had long since mastered the turn-out that Nina had found missing that first day, and she bit the inside of her cheek to keep from smiling at the murmurs from the back of the room as she stopped on her mark. Then her violin soared, filling the room with the kind of sublime beauty only a life devoted to music could make, and everyone fell into a hush. Every dancer in the room had surely heard this kind of music *ad nauseam*, had perhaps even been to a performance of the LSO when Mallory's instrument was one among many. But they had never heard anyone play like this. They had never heard just *her*, pure and solo, the best of her generation. She could feel them almost straining in their seats, leaning forward like sunflowers turning their faces towards the sun, enraptured by the notes pouring from her Storioni.

Yeah, she had this.

Her gaze drifted along the strings of her violin to the mirror beyond, and her heart leapt into her throat as she watched Addison's reflection begin to make its way toward her. They had been so thoroughly rehearsed these last few months that she didn't even have to think about the music as her fingers danced along the neck of her violin, and something inside her settled when Addison's hand curled around her shoulder.

Their eyes locked in the mirror as Addison's hold tightened in a quick squeeze, and just like that, they were on the same page, equal halves of a perfectly balanced pair.

The light brush of Addison's fingertips across her upper back and along the length of her left arm was the touch that transferred the who was leading and who was following, and Mallory sighed softly as she gladly handed Addison the reins. They might not be able to pull this off without her playing the violin, but Addison was the star of the show, and she was more than happy to do whatever was needed to make sure she shone.

Where rehearsal to this point had been marked by fits and stops, corrections and repetition, they played through the entirety of their epic pas de deux from start to finish without interruption. The hush in the room was positively electric as she extended her right leg behind herself, toes pointed to draw an invisible arc on the floor as she pulled her bow across the strings of her violin for the last time, and her heart beat up into her throat as her bow arm fell away and Addison's hand curved ever so gently around her cheek. It was so, so easy to give herself over to that oh-so-soft pressure, to let it and the hand on her hip turn her and urge her closer, and she resisted the urge to grin as their foreheads came together and silence settled around them.

They had done it.

The resulting applause from the collection of dancers in the "audience" was a veritable explosion of sound, a cacophonous wave that nearly knocked her over, and she laughed along with Addison as strong arms wrapped around her neck and pulled her into a surprisingly tender embrace.

"We did it," Addison murmured against her ear.

Mallory's pulse tripped over itself at the feeling of Addison's breath against her skin, and she held her even tighter as she whispered, "Yes, we did."

It would have been so, so easy to stay like that for the rest of the night, but the applause from the back of the room was turning into hoots and hollers, and Mallory sighed as she felt Addison's hold on her neck begin to loosen.

"Take your bows, ladies," Nina cheered as she clapped a hand on each of their shoulders and turned them toward the crowd at the back of the room that, Mallory realized, were all on their feet.

Mallory offered them a small bow as Addison dropped into a regal curtsey beside her, and she couldn't keep from laughing when Matt's voice carried over the noise—"Goddamn it, I just lost a hundred quid!"

nineteen

Mallory had thought the first full-call rehearsal had been long, but it was positively expeditious compared to the four and a half hours it had taken them to get through their first wet tech a week later. It made sense, really, that it would take time to align lighting arrangements and sets—not that there were many of those in the first half of the ballet and none in the second—but as she waited in the doorway of Addison's dressing room for her to finish packing up her things, she dearly wished she had thought to throw a protein bar or something into her bag to hold her until she could get a proper meal.

"Let's get out of here." Addison tossed the strap of her duffle over her head and smiled tiredly at Mallory as she followed her into the hall and quickly locked up after herself. "Matt and Gabs better be down there waiting for us," she groaned as she dropped her keys into the side pocket of her duffle, "because otherwise, I'm going to just text them to meet us back at my place."

Mallory chuckled when her stomach growled loudly in agreement and shook her head as she draped an arm over Addison's shoulders. "I was just thinking that I should have packed a protein bar or something," she shared as they started making their way toward the lift.

"I'd fucking kill for a a protein bar right now," Addison muttered as she leaned into Mallory's side.

"Are you sorry you offered to cook tonight? Because I'm sure we can get something delivered instead."

"It's fine." Addison looped an arm around Mallory's waist as they stopped to wait for the lift. "I picked up a lasagna from Tesco the other day that I just have to pop into the oven. It's not frozen or anything, so it won't take long to heat up. And I think Matty said something about wine." She shrugged. "I dunno. I mean, it *is* a school night and everything, so he might have changed his mind on that. But I kind of doubt it. He knows Gabs loves a good Merlot, and his dad is a sommelier at some posh restaurant near the castle in Edinburgh, so he's always sending Matt crates of wine to share with 'all his starving artist friends'."

"That's nice of him."

Addison yawned and nodded as the doors to the lift began to slide open. "Yeah. Anyway, so there will probably be wine. Which means I will probably fall asleep on you at some point this evening, so I'll just go ahead and apologize for that now."

"That's perfectly fine," Mallory assured her as she steered them inside. She pressed the button for the ground floor as she passed the console, and guided Addison to the back of the car so they could lean against the wall. "I quite like when you fall asleep on me."

Addison smiled at her in their reflection in the polished steel doors. "Good. Because I'm kinda getting addicted to it."

Mallory leaned her cheek on Addison's head as she teased, "Should I be offended that you'd prefer to fall asleep on me than stay awake and enjoy my company?"

"Yes." Addison squeezed her side playfully as the lift pulled to a gentle stop and the doors began to slide open. "You should absolutely be offended that I enjoy cuddling with you so much that I'd rather drool all over you than let you go."

"Well, the drool *is* rather unfortunate…" Mallory smirked.

"Did I say that I enjoy cuddling with you?" Addison looked up to leveled a playful glare at her. "Because I take it back," she declared as she tried to pull away.

Mallory chuckled and tightened her hold on Addison's shoulders to keep her at her side. "No, you don't. And"—she hid her smile in Addison's hair because she was certain she looked positively smitten, because she pretty much was, and she wasn't at all prepared to deal with other people knowing that yet—"I can honestly think of no better way to end my day than with you curled up against me."

"And just like that, I can't even pretend to be mad anymore," Addison sighed.

"Good." Mallory pressed a hesitant kiss to Addison's temple. It was the first time she had dared to do anything of the sort and, as her heart beat up into her throat at the feeling of Addison's skin beneath her lips, a part of her looked forward to the next time she would have an excuse to do it again. She took a deep breath as she pulled away, and swallowed thickly when Addison looked up at her with warm brown eyes a small, entirely pleased smile curling her lips.

"If that's what I get for talking about cuddling, I'm gonna do it more often."

Mallory huffed a laugh and confessed softly, "If we keep cuddling, darling, I'm probably going to want to do more than that."

Addison's smile softened as her gaze dropped to drift over Mallory's lips. "I look forward to it," she whispered.

"Oh, knock it the fuck off and let's go already," Matt's voice called out from behind them, effectively shattering the moment.

Not that Mallory minded so much. Well, she could do without his roguish smirk and the knowing twinkle in his eye, but the corridors of The Royal Opera House weren't the place for conversations such as these, and she was grateful for the opportunity his appearance provided for her to become comfortable with this new facet of her relationship with Addison.

"God, Matt," Gabs groaned, "why do you have to run your mouth just when things are looking like they're getting good?"

"Things are perfect, thank you very much," Addison shot back.

"And we are not here to serve as your entertainment."

"Insists the professional performer," Gabs laughed. "Whatever. It's time for food, yes? How did your tech go?" she asked. As soon as she and Matt had finished with their part of the performance, they had been hustled off to rehearsals for *The Nutcracker,* which they would be performing the following night.

"It was tech." Addison glanced at Mallory as she pulled her arm from her waist, and arched a brow questioningly as she brushed their hands together. Her expression was gentle, the faint curve of her lips signaling that she wouldn't be offended if Mallory wasn't comfortable continuing contact while they had an audience. "We don't have any sets or anything," she continued without missing a beat, so that neither Gabs nor Matt's attention was drawn to the silent conversation they were having, "so it was just a lot of getting the lights settled."

It was one thing to open herself up when they were alone and quite another to do so around others, but a hollow feeling settled in her stomach at the idea of losing physical contact with Addison, so Mallory offered her a small smile as she turned her hand so Addison could take it.

"Like, tracking type stuff?" Matt asked as he waved goodbye to Josh, who was working the desk at the stage door.

"There was a little of that, but it was more just color changes," Addison explained as the rest of them waved to Josh as well. "You know, to help set the mood of what's happening and everything since there aren't really any sets or, hell, even breaks in the pas de deux where we get to move out of the way for a minute and catch our breath while the corps takes over for a few."

"Please," Gabs scoffed as she pushed the stage door open and held it for the rest of them, "you two could go out there in burlap sacks with the house lights on and no frills of any kind, and you'd still blow everyone away." She let the door fall shut and fell into step beside her so they were walking four-across down the narrow street. "But, whatever. I'm not here to prop up your already inflated egos."

Matt laughed. "She's right, you know. We're going to be completely overlooked when the reviews come out on this thing."

"Or just barely mentioned as the reviewer rushes to swoon over what they did," Gabs added, her tone light and playful and her smile proud as she looped a hand around the crook of Mallory's arm and gave it a light squeeze, letting her know that she was teasing. "Really, Addy, you're just lucky we love this new partner of yours so much that we're willing to let it slide."

"Cheers, darling," Mallory murmured.

Addy squeezed Mallory's hand and smiled at her as she asked, "So, Matty. What's the wine selection for the evening?"

"Oh, you're gonna love it." He grabbed the straps of the large backpack he was wearing as he bounced on the balls of his feet in excitement and winked at Addison. "We're going American tonight, just for you. My dad just discovered this new vineyard in the Pacific Northwest that he can't stop raving about."

"Did you bring a Merlot?" Gabs asked.

"Of course. And a bottle of their Pinot Noir from their reserve selection that he says is the best of their line. I hope you like reds, Mal. Because Addy said we were having lasagna, I didn't bring any whites."

"I'm perfectly fine with either," Mallory assured him with a smile.

"Excellent."

Addison bumped shoulders with Mallory as she asked, "So, did anything particularly exciting happen while we were stuck in tech?"

"Maybe? I heard a rumor that Tania is talking to a headhunter about a spot that will be opening in Paris after the season."

"I heard that, too," Gabs chimed in.

"No way? Seriously?" Addison shook her head.

Mallory dragged her thumb over the back of Addison's hand as she allowed herself to tune out the dancers' gossip. She had no idea who this Tania was, and she honestly wasn't all that pressed to find out.

It was nice, though, to just be able to walk and let the rise and fall of their voices drown out the sounds of the city around them. Even though it was her day off from the symphony, she had still been in her office by nine to work on the bowing notations for the next set of performances and to meet with a second violinist whose ego wasn't equipped to handle not being grouped with the firsts, and she had run out of there to make the tech rehearsal in time. There had been so much to see and learn whilst she had been sitting in the audience watching the first half of the ballet that she hadn't had time to decompress from her morning, and so this was really the first time all day that she'd had to just zone out and not focus on anything in particular.

Before she knew it, they were at Addison's place, and she reluctantly let go of her hand so she could tend to the doors to let them all in. The group all but scattered the moment they were inside and out of the cold, Addison ducking down the hall to toss her bag into her bedroom as Matt wandered toward the kitchen with his backpack, leaving Mallory and Gabs in the small entryway.

Mallory glanced at Gabs as she hung the strap of her violin case over her coat on what had become her usual hook in the entryway, and set her briefcase on the floor beneath them. "Here, allow me to move out of your way," she murmured.

"No need." Gabs dropped her tote onto the floor beside her briefcase with little regard for its contents as she hollered toward Addison's bedroom, "What does the oven need to be at?"

"Three seventy-five," Addison called back.

"On it," Gabs declared, winking at Mallory as she skipped off toward Matt in the kitchen.

Mallory shook her head as she watched her go, feeling far older than she had all day when faced with the amount of energy Gabs still had even after a long day of rehearsals, and was about to follow when she saw Addy making her way toward her with a gentle smile.

"Oh good, they haven't scared you off."

"Oy, Addy!" Matt yelled. "Where's your wine opener?"

Addison sighed. "How about we leave them here and go over to yours for tonight instead?"

Mallory laughed and arched a brow as they started for the kitchen, where far too many cabinet doors were being slammed to be anything but a ruse to get them to hurry up. "Do you reckon the place would survive them being here unsupervised?"

"Good point," Addison agreed regretfully. She motioned to the sofa as they passed through the sitting area. "You want to just grab a seat? Once the lasagna is in, it'll be about an hour until it's ready. I figured I'd just bring snacks out here and we can hang out while me and Gabs ice our feet."

"I can do that while you and Gabs get your ice sorted. What are you thinking about for snacks?"

"You're sure?"

"Of course." Mallory smiled and bumped Addison's arm with her elbow. "Besides, this way your feet will have defrosted before they wind up on my lap later."

Addison laughed. "Oh, I see how it is."

"See how what is?" Matt asked.

"Nothing," Addison told him. "The corkscrew is in the drawer to the right of the range." She smiled at Mallory and added, "For snacks, I've got veggies and hummus, and I picked up a couple whole grain baguettes the other day that should be nice and crunchy now that we can slice up to dip in the hummus too. Oh, and there's a little jar of sun-dried tomato pesto in the cupboard we can put on the bread if we want."

"Oh, we definitely want," Matt interjected as he spun the corkscrew on his finger and bumped the drawer shut with his hip. "I'm starving."

"You're not the only one," Mallory muttered as her stomach grumbled in agreement.

"I got the oven going already," Gabs said as she set four stemless glasses onto the counter beside the sink. She picked up one of the bottles he had set on the counter and smirked when she turned it so

Addison and Mallory could see the rainbow-hued outline of a grasshopper on the matte black label. "Look, it's a gay grasshopper."

Addison arched a brow as she looked at it, and opened a narrow cabinet beside the fridge to pull out two plastic tubs. "You really shouldn't label the grasshopper like that, Gabs," she lectured playfully as she worked the tubs apart and handed one to her, "maybe it just likes the colors."

Gabs chuckled wickedly and shook her head. "If we hadn't promised to be on our best behavior tonight…"

"Seriously," Matt agreed as he began working on uncorking the bottle of Merlot.

"But you did," Addison reminded them both as she handed Gabs one of the tubs, "so you're going to just keep whatever inappropriate quip you got there in your head all to yourself."

"You can tell me later," Matt assured Gabs in a loud whisper.

Addison rolled her eyes, but otherwise didn't rise to the bait.

Mallory smiled at her and gave her wrist a light squeeze as she slipped past to open the fridge. "Let me get the lasagna out, and then you two can start filling your buckets." She shook her head when she lifted it from the shelf, the aluminum pan it was in felt dangerously flimsy, and hurried to set it on the stove as she went to grab a baking sheet to put it on.

Addison's kitchen wasn't nearly large enough to accommodate four adults, but it didn't take Addison and Gabs long to get their ice baths sorted, and once they had moved to the lounge, it was much easier to move about. Mallory was pleasantly surprised by how easy it was to work with Matt as they prepared the various snacks Addison had mentioned earlier, and by the time they, too, retired to the lounge to wait for dinner to be ready, she felt like she was in the company of old friends.

"The lasagna should be ready for the foil to come off in forty minutes or so," Mallory told Addison as she set the cutting board she and Matt had arranged the food on onto the coffee table.

"You two are amazing," Gabs groaned as she traded her wineglass for one of the larger pieces of baguette that she dragged through the hummus.

"You say that like it's a surprise or something," Matt shot back, winking at Mallory as he dropped to the sofa beside her.

"Definitely not a surprise," Addison murmured, running a light hand over Mallory's thigh when she sat beside her. "Thank you."

Mallory looked down at Addison's hand on her leg, and a soft smile curled her lips as a feeling of absolute *rightness* enveloped her. "My pleasure, darling."

twenty

Mallory lifted a tired hand when she spotted Will at a table toward the back of The Barbican Kitchen, a small restaurant on the ground floor of The Barbican Centre. The restaurant was mostly empty as it was still two hours before their concert was set to begin, and she was grateful for the empty tables and chairs that allowed her to walk without worrying about accidentally hitting anyone with her violin or briefcase as she wound her way through the narrow aisles between tables.

"You look like hell," Will teased as Mallory set her things on the floor and dropped into the chair opposite him.

"Cheers," Mallory muttered as she laid her head on the table and seriously considered whether it would be possible for her to steal a few minute's sleep like that.

"Well, on the bright side, it's Friday, which means tomorrow we pull a triple, Sunday's a double, and then we get two days off for Christmas and Boxing Day. Of course, then we're back to daily doubles until New Year's, so…"

The upcoming days off were good news, indeed, but she flipped him off anyway. He could have left it at that and not reminded her of all the performances still to come before things settled back to their usual pattern. The holiday season was the busiest for the LSO, with twice-a-day concerts for the fortnight leading up to Christmas and then through New Year's. It was a grueling time of year normally, but she now looked back on last year's stretch with an aching fondness rooted in the knowledge that she truly hadn't realized how good she'd had it.

Will laughed. "Love you too, Mal. Anyway, why are you so tired? I thought you had the afternoon off from the ballet?"

Mallory nodded, rather liking the way it made the cool, hard table massage her forehead. She had been fighting a headache for the last couple of days, and this was actually the first measure of relief she had found for it. "'Off' is a relative term, I'm afraid. Nina still made us run through it twice without a break before she dismissed us. And the only reason we got off that easy was because Addy's dancing tonight and she needs to rest."

He made a small sound of sympathy and patted her arm. "So no nap for you, then?"

Mallory shook her head, noting that the massage wasn't quite as pleasant when she moved it in this direction. "I would club a baby seal for a nap at this point," she groaned. "I mean, Addy and I went down to the physio suite for some recovery work after our shortened rehearsal, which was nice, but by the time we'd finished there, I had just enough time to shower, run home to collect my blacks for tonight, and get over here to meet you."

"You could have canceled, you know. We didn't have to get dinner beforehand."

Mallory waved him off. She had considered it, of course, just for the hour's sleep she might have gotten, but she couldn't remember the last time they had spent any time together, just the two of them, and even tired as she was, she missed her best friend. "I need to eat anyway."

"So are you ready to go up and choose something?" The restaurant was more of a canteen, really, a super-casual place where one selected plates from different stations and then paid before finding a seat. "Or are you going to just sit there and hope the food magically arrives in front of you?"

She shrugged. "Honestly haven't decided yet."

He laughed. "Well, at least Max gave you last night off though, hey? So you got one night off this week—which is more than the rest of us got."

Forehead still firmly planted on the tabletop, Mallory allowed herself a small smile as she acknowledged his statement with another nod and a low hum. She should have taken that gift of a night off to catch up some much-needed sleep, but she had lingered at Addison's long after Matt and Gabs had called it a night, knowing that they wouldn't get to really see each other again until Boxing Day. And, even as exhausted as she currently was, she could not find it in herself to regret those few extra hours spent lounging on the sofa with Addy curled against her side as old *Grey's Anatomy* episodes played on the television.

And she certainly didn't regret the way Addison had smiled at her when she had kissed her cheek whilst saying goodnight.

"Yes, at least I didn't have to work last night," she agreed.

He hummed and then offered in a hopeful tone, "Well, Devereaux will have to back off on your rehearsals leading into the actual performance though, right?"

Mallory sighed and forced herself to sit up. "One can only hope."

"Excuse me," a new voice spoke up hesitantly. "Are you Ms. Collingswood?"

Mallory looked over at the girl who was standing a few feet away from their table. She was young, perhaps in her final year of primary school or somewhere near there, with positively wild strawberry blond curls that Mallory doubted would ever submit to being tamed. Her dress had that department store crispness to it that suggested it had been recently bought, and there was a determined set to her jaw that made Mallory smile, especially once she noticed the way the girls' fingers were rubbing nervously over the back of a glossy leaflet she held loosely in front of her stomach so as to not wrinkle the paper.

"Indeed I am. But you can call me Mallory. And who might you be?"

The girl took a deep breath and squared her shoulders. "Ellie Brighton."

Mallory smiled and offered the girl her hand. "It's a pleasure to meet you. This is my friend Will Adrian. He plays the bassoon in the symphony."

Ellie offered him a polite smile and shook his hand as well. "Mr. Adrian."

Will laughed. "Will is fine," he assured her with a wink.

"Yes, sir," Ellie murmured.

Mallory chuckled and arched a brow at him as she mouthed, 'Sir?', before she crossed her legs and turned to face Ellie more directly. "So, what can I do for you, Miss Ellie Brighton?"

"Is this really you?" Ellie carefully unfolded the mailer in her hands and turned it to show Mallory the large picture inside the fold. It was the one Pierce had directed them into immediately following their brief performance for him the day of the pictures—the one where Addison was in a full arabesque, supported by her fingers on the scroll of Mallory's violin. "There? With the violin?"

Mallory's smile softened automatically at the sight of her and Addison together. Their expressions were professionally neutral, focused, but there was a light in Addison's eyes that made her heart flutter with joy. "That's me."

"So you're a dancer, too?"

Will guffawed, and Mallory shot him a glare before returning her attention to Ellie. "I have only ever been properly trained in the violin, I'm afraid. But Addison Leigh, the ballerina in the picture there"—she tapped the child's mailer—"has been helping me learn just enough so that we can do that one dance. Do you enjoy the ballet?"

"Oh, yes." Ellie bit her lip, looking positively sheepish, and added, "It's my favorite. I've been taking lessons ever since I was three, but my mum says I have to play the violin as well."

"Do you not enjoy the violin?" Mallory asked.

"It's okay. I mean, it's fun to learn new songs, but I would much rather dance," Ellie admitted softly, her eyes darting nervously toward the restaurant entrance where her mother, at least, was no doubt waiting on her.

"Well, there's no reason you can't be amazing at both, right?" Mallory offered gently. She was not a fan of forcing children into activities they had no interest in, but at least Ellie sounded like she didn't actively hate her music lessons. She tilted her head and leaned forward to add in a playfully conspiratorial whisper, "And, I mean, who knows—if this new ballet Addison and I are going to be performing in the new year is well-received, they might very well need a talented musician to perform it in the future who knows ballet. Do you think that might be something you would be interested in?"

"Dance and music?" Ellie murmured, her eyes widening.

"Dance and music," Mallory confirmed with a wink. "If you want to see videos of someone who does just that—not ballet, exactly, but she absolutely dances whilst playing her violin—ask your parents if you can look up some Lindsey Stirling videos on YouTube."

"I will," Ellie enthused, nodding eagerly.

"Ellie!" a voice called from somewhere near the entrance to the restaurant. Ellie's mother, Mallory was sure.

Ellie blushed and offered Mallory her mailer. "Sorry. I was just, um, wondering if…well, if you maybe could sign this for me?"

"Of course." Mallory smiled as she took the mailer and spread it on the table in front of her. Nina had shown her and Addison the finished product the day they had been sent out, and she had seen this picture of her and Addison on posters around The Royal Opera House advertising the upcoming release, but she still got a thrill every time she saw it. "Do you have a pen?"

Ellie nodded and handed her a silver sharpie that would stand out perfectly in the black space above their heads. "Sorry."

"No worries, dear," Mallory assured her gently as she signed her name with far more care than she usually did above her half of the photograph, just in case the girl managed to track down Addison as well. "Here you are," she murmured as she handed Ellie back the mailer and her pen. "Are you staying for the concert tonight?"

Ellie nodded. "And then Friday I get to see Ms. Leigh dance at the ballet!"

She was clearly more excited for the ballet than the symphony, and Mallory chuckled softly under her breath because, really, who could blame the child for that? Certainly not her. She would much rather watch Addison dance than be at the symphony—and she was playing in it. "Lucky you."

Ellie beamed and nodded in agreement. "Thank you for signing my picture. My parents are waving at me to hurry along now," she shared with a small roll of her eyes that would undoubtedly become much more impressive in a few years, "so I gotta go."

"Have a wonderful evening," Mallory murmured. "I do hope you enjoy the performance tonight."

Ellie nodded and, with one last sheepish smile, turned and skipped off in the direction of her parents who, Mallory saw, stood waiting at the restaurant's entrance.

"Addy's performing twice in three days?" Will asked once Ellie had gone.

Mallory shook her head. "Well, yes. But she's actually performing tonight, Friday, and Sunday. Tonight and Friday were on her schedule originally, and she offered to take the Christmas Eve performance so people with family within commuting distance might be able to go home for the holiday since hers is over in America."

"That was sweet of her."

"Yes, well…" Mallory smiled as she remembered the way Addison had told her about the change in her schedule. *And, well, I mean, you're going to be performing that night anyway, so I might as well take one for the team so that I'm not just sitting at home wishing I was with you.*

"That's quite the smile you've got there, Mal." Will smirked and waggled his eyebrows. "Care to share with the class what it's about?"

"Not at all," Mallory retorted with a wink.

Will laughed. "Fair enough. So besides work stuff, how is everything going with the marvelous Ms. Leigh?"

"It's wonderful," she confessed with a happy sigh.

"Mallory Collingswood!" he gasped, clutching the lapel of his suit jacket. "Have you been holding out on me?"

"Hardly," she chuckled. "It's not like anything's happened, really. I mean, cuddling doesn't count, right?"

He nodded emphatically, and then brushed away the hair that had flopped into his eyes from the exuberance of the gesture. "It most certainly does."

"Well, then I guess you'd think a kiss on the cheek is significant as well, then?" she ventured with an amused smile.

"Who did the snogging?"

"There has been no snogging." She rolled her eyes when he just arched a brow and crossed his arms over his chest, waiting for her to answer his question. "It was a perfectly chaste and proper kiss on the cheek, thank you very much. We went back to hers with Gabs and Matt after tech last night, and I kissed her cheek when I was leaving."

"Just the cheek?"

"Just the cheek."

"Well, that's at least something, yeah?"

"It's definitely something. And I..." She took a deep breath and let it go slowly as she ran a hand through her hair. "I do think about kissing her properly. I want to. I just..."

He leaned his arms on the table and smiled encouragingly as he waited for her to either find the words she wanted or just give up on the train of thought completely.

"I'm afraid of moving too fast with this, I guess. I really like her, Will, and I don't want to mess it up."

He frowned. "How would you mess it up?"

"By being me? I mean, I don't have the best track record with women and, well, I've been trying to work on the things Gwen claimed to find so insufferable, and Addy and I certainly talk more than Gwen and I ever did, but…"

"You can't keep thinking like that, Mal. It takes two people to make a relationship work, or not work, and that one was just…" He sighed. "Not ideal. And what's this thing you're afraid of rushing, exactly? Because you've been spending practically every day with Addison since September…"

She shrugged. "I don't know. I guess just…moving on in general? I mean, we both remember what a mess I was in June when I saw that video…"

He nodded slowly. "Yeah, that was definitely rough. But do you also see how much happier you've been these last four-ish months?"

"No, I do, it's just…"

When she didn't continue, he reached out to take her hands into his own with a small, almost heartbroken smile. "You don't have to stay hurt forever, Mal. What happened with Gwen…" He shook his head. "It was awful. It fucking sucked and it was awful and sometimes when I look at you and I see just how much you still *feel* that betrayal I wish you had given me the okay to fly out there and give her a piece of my mind about what she did. I know you don't think she was being malicious by leading you on like that while she started up with Dana, but she didn't just break your heart, Mal—she broke something inside you by lying to you like that. And I…" He looked up at the ceiling and blinked rapidly. "I hate it. I hate her. I honestly fucking hate her for what she did to you."

Mallory sniffed and pulled a hand from under his to wipe at her eyes. He had supported her and tried to get her back on her feet ever since she had arrived utterly heartbroken on his doorstep, but their conversations had never been *this* honest. She had known, of course, that more than her heart had been broken, but he had never let on that he knew it, too. "Why haven't you told me this before?"

He shook his head, and there was a hint of tears glistening in his eyes when he pulled his gaze from the ceiling to look at her. "You made it through last season by the skin of your teeth, and you needed me to look like I believed you when you insisted you were fine—so I did. But you don't need that now. Gwen might have broken you, but…" His voice trailed off into a sigh, and he smiled. "Even utterly knackered by your workload, you are happier than I remember you being in years. Not just recently, but *years*. Like, since before you went to America to try and make a name for yourself. And maybe it's just London's wonderful weather or time working its magic or whatever, but I think it's Addison. I think being with her is helping you fix what Gwen broke, and I fucking love her for it."

Mallory huffed a teary laugh and nodded because, yeah, when he put it that way, she loved her for it, too. "So what do I do?"

He smiled and gave the hand still nestled beneath his own a squeeze. "Let yourself be happy. Let yourself heal and move on, and for fuck's sake take that goddamn photograph Gwen gave you off the wall in your lounge and burn it or something."

Mallory smiled. "But I actually do like that photograph."

"Find a different one that you like more," he retorted as he pulled his hands away. "Oh, and one more thing…"

She nodded. "What's that?"

"If you think being with Addison will make you happy—don't fight it. Don't talk yourself out of it. Just…be happy."

Mallory nodded as she pushed herself to her feet. A rogue tear rolled down her cheek when he hopped up and pulled her into his arms, and she took a deep, shuddering breath as she clung to him.

"Let Addy make you happy, Mal" he murmured against her ear. "Okay?"

She held onto him tighter and nodded against his shoulder, and she could feel his smile when he brushed a scratchy kiss across her cheek.

"Good," he husked as he pulled away. "Now, how about we go get some food?"

"Food sounds wonderful," she agreed softly as she wiped at her cheeks.

"So when are you going to see her again?" he asked as they began making their way toward the food stations.

Mallory shrugged. "She's going to come over on Boxing Day, and we're planning on just spending the day hanging out, trying to recover from the pre-Christmas performance insanity. But I don't know if we'll find a way before then."

"You know, could always bring her over to Siobhan's parents' place for Christmas. They wouldn't mind."

Mallory smiled. During her time in America, her own parents had become used to traveling for the holiday as their only child wouldn't be around. They had stayed home the year before and hosted a lavishly formal Christmas dinner at their house in Kensington, but this year, at her insistence that she genuinely didn't mind if they went, they had decided to spend the holiday in Greece. Will and Siobhan had invited her to their family get-together the moment they had found out she'd be alone, and she was honestly looking forward to spending the day with Siobhan's very laid-back family in Cambridge than suffering through another formal affair at her parents' place like she had the year before. "Thanks, but Addy's doing something with Gabs and the other dancers who aren't heading home for the holiday. Maybe next year?"

He nodded and handed her a tray. "Okay, yeah. Next year." He looked up at the clock on the wall and groaned when he saw the time. "We better get moving. We've only got forty minutes or so until the half-hour call, and I will need to warm up."

Mallory glanced at her watch to double-check the accuracy of the centre's clock, and nodded. She didn't need to warm up, she had already played more than she should have for one day, but Clara liked to do a quick meeting at the half-hour just to make sure they were on the same page for the upcoming performance. "Right. I think I'm good with this." She held up her tray of chicken, veggies, and a salad. "You?"

"I'm going to grab a piece of pie. Meet you at the table?"

"Sure." And then, before he could scamper off in search of dessert, added, "And, Will? Thanks."

He smiled and nodded. "Always."

twenty-one

Will groaned and stretched his arms against the steering wheel as he waited for the traffic signal to change. "Tell me again why we didn't just take the train?"

"Because the trains don't run on Christmas?" Mallory offered from the backseat. The streetlights shining through the window made the glitter still trapped to her sweater sparkle, and she sighed as she tried to discreetly brush it onto the floorboards.

Not that it made much difference. They were all covered in the stuff, thanks to Siobhan's brother Colin who thought filling the Christmas crackers with glitter was a marvelous idea. And, the car hadn't fared much better, as nobody had been able to completely rid themselves of the menace. Of course, if the glitter bombing had been restricted to the crackers, the mess might have been manageable, but an all-out glitter fight had ensued after the initial quasi-explosions, and she feared Siobhan's parents' dining room might never actually recover from it.

Glitter had gone *everywhere* as everyone gathered at the table, regardless of chronological age, channeled their inner hooligan and flung handfuls of the sparkly bits at Colin in retaliation for the initial dousing. The entire scene devolved from there, with parents dumping piles of glitter onto their kids' heads and siblings and cousins trying their damnedest to shove handfuls down the backs of each other's shirts. Even her status as a guest hadn't exempted her from the melee, as Will and Siobhan had taken great pleasure in teaming up against her to make sure she did not escape un-glittered.

As if anyone could, even without the glittery free-for-all. The paper crowns that had been inside the crackers were, predictably, equally coated in the festiveness, and tradition meant they *had* to put the paper crowns on for the meal, so… Yeah. It was definitely a holiday they would all remember.

"What she said," Siobhan echoed through a yawn as she tugged at her jumper, which sent a small shower of glitter flitting into the air. "I'm going to kill Colin for this." She sighed and brushed the glitter toward the floor in front of her. "I mean, if I'm going to be *this* covered in glitter, I should at least get a lap dance out of the deal."

Mallory laughed as Will offered, "We can totally arrange that if you'd like."

"A lap dance?" Siobhan asked.

He nodded, and even from the backseat, Mallory could see he was grinning. "Oh yeah. Totally."

He must have waggled his eyebrows at Siobhan or done something equally suggestive because she laughed and smacked his leg. "I don't want a lap dance from you. I want someone who knows what they're doing!"

Mallory caught Will's eye in the rearview mirror and smirked. "Women are much more adept at it, anyway."

"Right?" Siobhan sighed. "We need to go to a club again, sometime." She turned in her seat to smile at Mallory as the signal finally changed and Will refocused his attention on the road. "I don't think you enjoyed our last trip out as much as you could have, but I bet now you would totally get into it."

"I really don't think I would," Mallory argued gently, because she knew Siobhan's heart was in the right place and she didn't want her to think that she didn't appreciate the offer. "I've never been especially comfortable in situations like that."

"Yeah, she's more of a one-naked-woman-at-a-time kind of woman, aren't you?" Will jumped to her defense. "And she totally just wants Addison, so…"

"Oh! I didn't realize you two were there already!"

Okay, maybe he wasn't jumping to her defense at all.

Mallory shook her head and, in what she could admit was a childish bit of retaliation, raked her hands through her hair to shake just a little more glitter out of it and onto the back seat. "We're not." Siobhan pouted, and Mallory couldn't help but smile as she began collecting her things. They were only a couple minutes from her apartment and, as it was getting late, she didn't want to make them wait for her once they got there. "You're ridiculous."

"Maybe, but at least I don't make glitter bombs."

"Excellent point," Mallory agreed as the car began to slow. "You are going to get him back for that one, right?"

Siobhan nodded. "As soon as I come up with a good enough idea, I absolutely will be doing that. You want in on it?"

"I think I'd rather stay out of the retaliation loop."

"You're no fun," Siobhan huffed.

"Wise decision, my friend," Will countered with a laugh.

"You'll be helping me," Siobhan told him.

"Yes, well, I chose to marry into the crazy," he retorted. "Poor Mal just kind of got adopted into it all because of me."

"Nah, she's basically your sister. Which means she's my sister-in-law." Mallory smiled. This wasn't the first time Siobhan had laid claim to her like that, but it still blew her away sometimes that her best friend had managed to marry such a wonderful woman. "So she's stuck with us whether she wants to be or not."

Before Mallory could speak up for herself in the matter, however, her phone began playing Addison's ringtone—*Balance*, the final piece from *Evolution*. They had traded more texts than she could count over the last five days, but their schedules hadn't ever aligned in a way that allowed them to actually *talk*, and her heart leapt at the idea of hearing Addison's voice.

"You gonna answer that?" Will asked, winking at her as he turned in his seat.

"Absolutely." Mallory arched a brow at his expectant expression and shook her head as she added, "Just as soon as I get out of the car."

He sighed dramatically and gave her a little pout. 'Ugh, fine. I see how it is. Tell Addy we say 'hi,' then."

Mallory nodded as the music continued to play, pitting her desire to speak to Addison against her need to make sure Will and Siobhan knew just how much she appreciated their including her in their holiday plans. "I shall. And thank you for allowing me to tag along today. Even with the glitter, it was a wonderful day."

"Our pleasure," Siobhan insisted with a smile. She waved at Mallory's phone and added, "Now, go answer that before it goes to voicemail. You should never keep a beautiful woman waiting, after all."

Mallory tilted her head in agreement as she leaned through the gap between the front seats to brush a quick kiss over each of their cheeks. "I'll talk to you later."

She tapped the icon to answer the call as she fell back into her seat, and lifted it to her ear as she reached for the door. "Hey, you," she murmured, as she stepped out onto the sidewalk.

"Hey," Addy sighed.

Mallory frowned at the hint of melancholy in Addison's voice and offered Will and Siobhan a distracted wave as the car door closed with a hollow *thud*. "What's wrong, darling?"

"What? Nothing... I just..."

Mallory hummed encouragingly as she unlocked the entry door, and couldn't contain the shiver that rolled through her when she stepped inside. She hadn't been in the cool night air for long, but there was a definite bite to it that made her glad to be inside again. When Addison didn't elaborate, she prodded gently, "Are you okay?"

"Yeah. Of course," Addison murmured. *"I just miss you and wanted to*

hear your voice, I guess."

"I miss you too," Mallory confessed as she began climbing the stairs to her flat. She hadn't seen Addison since their abbreviated rehearsal the week before, and texts—while better than nothing—did very little to alleviate the ache of longing that settled in her chest whenever she thought of her. "How is your orphan Christmas going?"

"Drunkenly. Very, very drunkenly." Addison chuckled softly. *"I think Ben and I are the only ones here who are sober. You should see them all right now. Matt and Gabs split everyone into teams, and they're having a gigantic Just Dance competition for an empty bottle of vodka that Gabs filled with water and glitter because they, and I quote, 'needed a fucking awesome trophy.' Somebody is going to end up pulling a hamstring or something with the way they're going at it, and then Nina's going to lose her shit."*

Mallory smiled as she rounded the curve at the first floor and started up the final flight of stairs. Nina absolutely would lose her shit if one of her dancers returned from their holiday break injured—especially if that injury was acquired playing a video game. "So I take it you've left the room, then, since I can't hear them?"

"Yeah, I'm on the fire escape. It's so much calmer out here."

"And freezing. Please tell me you at least have a coat on."

"I do. And I stole the blanket from the back of the couch, so I'm nice and warm. How was your holiday? Are you still at Siobhan's family's thing?"

"It was nice. But we left just after tea to make the drive back. I'm actually unlocking my front door as we speak," Mallory shared as she twisted her key in the lock and pushed the door open. She set her purse onto the apothecary credenza that anchored the wall across from the door and sighed at her reflection in the mirror above it as she shrugged off her coat. She had no idea how it happened, but she looked like she had even more glitter on her than she had when they'd left Cambridge.

"Oh…"

There was no mistaking the hitch in Addison's voice or the longing that imbued what was little more than a soft exhale, and Mallory closed her eyes against the ache that bloomed in her chest at the sound of it.

She had thought she could wait until the following day to see Addison again, and she could if she absolutely had to, but she didn't want to wait. Didn't want to cross one more day off the calendar where she didn't get to spend even a brief fraction of a moment of it with her.

If she had a car, she would drive out to Richmond and pick Addison up herself, but she hadn't seen a reason to buy one when her apartment was so close to the underground and she could get to anywhere from there. On the rare occasion she needed to go where the trains wouldn't take her, she had gone and rented one, but there was no way she would be able to do that on Christmas night.

"Does Ben drive, by any chance?"

Addison huffed a quiet laugh that trembled with relief and happiness. *"Yeah."*

Mallory closed her eyes and lifted her face to the sky. "What would it take to get him to drive you over here right now?"

"God, that would be…please tell me you're serious."

Mallory's heart fluttered into her throat at the unabashed hope in Addison's voice, and she nodded as she murmured, "I don't think I have ever been more serious about anything in my life. I would come collect you myself if I could, but—"

"Hold on and let me go ask him?"

"Of course, darling." Mallory chewed her lip as she opened the narrow closet to the right of the console table to hang up her coat while she waited for Addison to return. Even though she had never visited the house in Richmond that a bunch of the dancers shared, she imagined she could picture Addison's progress as she went in search of her friend. There was a slamming door followed by a hum of noise that grew louder as Addison neared the heart of the party, and she smiled at the sound of pop music and laughter and jeers that came through the phone.

"Mal?" Addy asked just as Mallory closed the closet door.

"I'm still here, darling."

"He's going to give me a ride. Said it should take us around forty minutes or so

to get there."

Mallory's smile turned into a full-blown grin. "Wonderful. I can't wait."

twenty-two

Mallory checked the time on her phone as she used her foot to push the drawer that held her hairdryer closed. Odds were good there wouldn't be much traffic due to the holiday, but she probably still had at least another ten minutes or so before Addison might arrive.

And, while she dearly wished Addison was already there, she was glad for the time it gave her to tidy up, as the glitter she had brought home with her dusted her path from the front door to the shower desperately needed to be hoovered so that it wasn't tracked any further. She had given the apartment a thorough cleaning that morning as she waited for Will and Siobhan to pick her up so there wasn't much else to do, and after she started a load of laundry with her clothes from the day to hopefully banish the sparkly menace from her home forever, she found herself hovering near the window that overlooked the street.

The lights from the small, artificial tree she had put up earlier that morning reflected in the glass as she peered into the night, waiting for a car to stop in front of her building and a familiar lithe form to emerge, and she had to force herself to resist the urge to constantly check the time on her phone. Of course, that didn't stop her from squinting to see the time on the blu-ray player beneath the television. Eventually, a dark, compact sedan pulled up to the curb, and her pulse stumbled over itself as she watched Addison climb out of it and loop the straps of a small bag over her shoulder. She tightened her grip on her phone as Addison ducked down to wave goodbye to her friend before slamming the car door shut, and there was no containing the smile that broke free when it began to ring.

"Hey, you," Addison murmured. *"I'm here."*

Mallory's heart fluttered at the sound of Addison's voice, and she couldn't resist resting her forehead against the glass to watch her stride gracefully toward the door below. "Do you remember the code for the door?"

"Yep. Be up in a jiff," Addison promised before disconnecting the call.

Mallory stayed at the window until she was sure that Addison made it inside. Once she had disappeared from sight, she hurried to the front door, not caring about how desperate it made her seem. She clearly wasn't the only one who couldn't wait, however, because not long after she opened the door to wait for Addison, she saw her jogging up the stairs. Much like herself, Addison was dressed for warmth and comfort in a pair of leggings and an oversized hoodie beneath her coat, and the feeling of something being just that little bit off that had niggled at her since the week before settled at the sight of her.

She laughed at the way Addison slowed to a more restrained walk the moment she spotted her, and held out a hand and beckoned her onward with a playful, "Don't stop now."

The light blush that colored Addison's cheeks as she ducked her head before resuming her earlier pace was absolutely adorable and, though it was soft, Mallory still heard her mutter to herself, "Busted."

Mallory smiled as she stepped out of the way to allow Addison inside. Her pulse beat heavily in her throat as Addison's eyes swept slowly over her face as if recommitting it to memory, and she swallowed thickly to try and force it back into place as she shoved the door shut behind her.

Whether it was their time apart or the faint echo of Will's advice from the other day or both she honestly wasn't sure, but she was struck positively breathless by just how much she wanted this.

Wanted her.

Needed her, really, if the nearly overwhelming urge to reach out and take Addison into her arms was any indication.

She had been painfully aware of how much she had missed Addison, but it was different now—stronger, almost, as if she could not fully appreciate just *how much* she had missed her until they were reunited. She had missed her, yes, but she hadn't understood why she had felt the separation so acutely. Hadn't realized until just this moment that it was because it was only when she was with Addison that she felt whole.

There was a gentle affection in Addison's eyes that hinted she felt it too, that the shared attraction they had confessed to weeks ago was actually something much more significant, and Mallory blinked back the sting of tears that threatened as she took a small step forward, closing the distance between them as her hands settled lightly on Addison's hips. She marveled at the way Addison moved to meet her—the shift so instinctive and confident, like they had done this dance a thousand times already and were destined to do it over and over again for the rest of their lives. She drew a shaky breath as Addison's bag fell to the floor with a quiet *thud* and strong arms looped around her neck to urge her even closer.

"Darling," Mallory whispered as Addison melted into her, and she ran her right hand up the length of her spine to press between her shoulder blades, cradling her against her chest. Her eyes fluttered shut as she leaned her cheek against Addison's forehead, and she sighed as she felt herself completely relax for the first time in almost a week.

Oh, how she'd missed this.

She smiled at the way Addison burrowed closer, one arm dropping to her waist as the fingers of her other hand slipped up into her hair, and hummed as she pressed a kiss to her forehead.

"God, I've missed you," Addison breathed.

A delicate shiver rolled down Mallory's spine as the soft confession landed in gentle waves against the sensitive hollow of her throat, and her pulse beat an irregular rhythm as she pulled back just enough to dip her head and murmur against Addison's cheek, "Me too." She sealed the confession with a tender kiss, and her heart fluttered at the way Addison sighed and tilted her head invitingly. "Oh, Addy," she moaned as she dragged her lips lower to press a kiss to the corner of Addison's mouth.

Addison whimpered and pulled back just enough that their breaths mingled between their lips, waiting, offering, and willing but not pushing, and warmth bloomed in Mallory's chest as she dipped her chin to brush the softest of kisses over Addison's lips once, twice, three times before finally, finally capturing them in a sweet kiss.

After so many weeks and months of wanting this but being so, so afraid that she would do something to screw it all up, Mallory's head spun at the feeling of Addison's lips moving against her own, and her eyes stung with tears when a gentle hand curved around her jaw, holding her like she was the most precious thing in the world. Addison kissed like she danced—deliberately, confidently, passionately, holding nothing of herself back—and it was positively intoxicating.

Mallory clung to Addison as their kisses deepened and slowed, the euphoric rush of that first brush of lips smoldering into genuine affection and emotion, and their breaths were equally ragged when they finally broke apart.

"Wow," Addison hummed, her smile pure sunshine as she gazed up at Mallory. "Had I known that was what was waiting for me, I would have asked Ben to break the speed limit getting over here even more than he already was."

"I didn't..." Mallory blushed. "I hadn't *planned* on kissing you like that. This wasn't... I mean..."

Addison chuckled and pushed herself up onto her toes to save Mallory from her rambling with a soft kiss. "I really don't mind." She brushed another feather-soft kiss over her lips. "I liked it. A lot."

Mallory smiled as she tucked a rogue curl behind Addison's ear.

"Me too." She shook her head at how much noticeably rougher than usual her voice was, and swallowed back the lump in her throat as she dipped her head to murmur against Addison's smiling lips, "Would you like to actually come inside, now?"

"Are there more kisses inside?" Addison retorted, her playfully serious expression belied by the twinkle of laughter in her eyes.

Mallory nodded and ran a tender hand along the line of Addison's jaw. "Darling, you can kiss me whenever and wherever you'd like," she promised as she dragged her thumb over Addison's lips.

Addison shrugged off her coat and dropped a quick kiss on Mallory's lips before turning to hang it on the doorknob of the coat closet. "Oh, I really like the sound of that."

Mallory smiled and inclined her head in a way that clearly said *I do, too*. She took a deep breath as she reached down for Addison's bag, and let it go slowly as she stood back up, took her hand, and laced their fingers together. She cleared her throat as they started down the hall, and swung Addison's tote bag in front of them as she asked, "Guest room, or mine?" She blushed at the low, suggestive chuckle and arched brow Addison responded with. That was absolutely not at all what she was asking. "I just want you to be comfortable."

"I was just messing with you." Addison laughed and squeezed her hand. "I will never turn down a chance to cuddle with you, sweetie, so your bedroom would be wonderful. However, I do," she added as she let go of Mallory's hand and took her bag, "need to get something out of that."

Mallory huffed a soft laugh when Addison pulled a small package wrapped in festive snowman patterned paper and brandished it with a triumphant grin, and shook her head as she leaned in and kissed her. "Sorry, you were just too adorable to resist," she murmured when she pulled away.

"I am definitely not complaining," Addison hummed as she tossed her bag into Mallory's bedroom. Her eyes crinkled with happiness as she pushed up onto the balls of her feet to return Mallory's kiss with one of her own. It was slow and sweet and perfect, and she sighed as she dropped her heels. "You are so good at that."

"I'm glad you think so," Mallory murmured as she guided Addison toward the lounge with a light hand on the small of her back. "I'm afraid I didn't have much time or energy to worry about decorating this year," she apologized as she waved a hand at the rather scrawny artificial tree in the corner that was bare of decorations save the fairy lights it came pre-strung with. It was a pitiful attempt, honestly, and as she looked at it now, she wondered why she had even bothered. Which was stupid, really, because the reason for her admittedly half-arsed attempt was standing right beside her. God knows she hadn't had a proper tree or decorations of any kind in her home for years, but she had wanted to do *something* to make it feel like a real holiday for when Addison came over.

"It's more than I did at my place," Addison assured her as she waved a hand at the sofa on the far wall. "What happened to the picture you had up there?"

Mallory shrugged as she stared at the wall that had been blank since the morning after her talk with Will. It had actually been harder than she'd anticipated to take the picture down, knowing it would be forever, but also incredibly freeing as she committed to leaving that part of her life firmly in the past. The picture was stashed away in the back of the closet in the study, but she had plans to take it to the local charity shop in the new year, once her work schedule returned to a more humane pace. "It was time to take it down."

"And move on."

Mallory blinked in surprise at Addison's insight—she had never told her exactly where the photograph had come from. A soft smile curled her lips as she reached for Addison's hand, and she nodded as she gave it an affectionate squeeze. "Yeah."

"I'm glad," Addison whispered.

"Me too."

Addison smiled and lifted their joined hands to press a lingering kiss to Mallory's knuckles. "So, do you want to open your present?"

"Of course, darling." Mallory waved her toward the sofa. "Just let me get yours from beneath my Charlie Brown tree."

Addison laughed and shook her head. "It's a cute tree. And, can I just say that I'm so impressed you know that? It seems like nobody from here does!"

"I did spend close to a decade in the States, you know," Mallory pointed out as she knelt down to retrieve the package she had carefully wrapped in elegant silver paper and set beneath the tree that morning.

Addison smiled at her as she made her way to the sofa. "It's just more evidence as to how special you truly are."

"I beg to differ, honestly, but I'm pleased you think so." Mallory shook her head as she sat beside Addison, spinning her present between her hands. "Happy Christmas, darling," she murmured as she held it out to her.

"Merry Christmas, Mal," Addison echoed as they exchanged gifts. She bounced a little in her seat and insisted, "You first."

Her excitement was adorable, and Mallory smiled as she slipped a finger beneath the fold of the wrapping paper to pry it open. "Wow, a plain white box," she drawled, winking at Addison as she wadded up the paper and tossed it onto the coffee table. "Thank you, darling. It's perfect."

Addison laughed and shook her head. "Smartass. Shut up and open it."

"Fine," Mallory sighed as if she was being asked to complete the most impossible task in the world, and made a show of struggling with the flap on the side of the thin, rectangular box for a moment before she finally flipped it open and reached inside. She knew from the feel alone that she would soon be looking at a picture frame, and she bit the inside of her cheek as she guided it from its box. The frame was simple, a plain black wooden number that matched the others scattered around her apartment, and Mallory's breath hitched in her throat when she saw the photograph Addison had chosen to give her.

It was the two of them in their costumes at center stage, the final moment of their pas de deux captured in time forever.

"Oh, Addy," she breathed as she ran a light finger over the glass, caressing Addison's hand that was wrapped around her jaw, utterly enraptured by the way each of their professional masks were completely lost as they stared at each other with such open affection that it made her heart ache. "When...?"

"First dress rehearsal," Addison whispered, scooting closer to lean her head on Mallory's shoulder so they could look at the picture together. "I had originally talked to Pierce and gotten him to send me a copy of the shot they're using in the brochures, but then Gabs sent me this and I just..." She shrugged and reached out to touch their faces. "I knew it was a little...much, I guess you could say, given our situation before tonight, but it made me smile, and I just wanted you to have a copy of it, too."

It was, without a doubt, the most romantic photograph Mallory had ever seen. Not because she was in it, but because of the composition of the shot. The lights and the shadows. The way the background was blurred, giving the impression that nothing in the world existed outside the two of them. The unfiltered adoration that was so plainly written in each of their expressions. It could have been two complete strangers in the shot and she would have been struck by it, but knowing it was the two of them brought tears to her eyes.

"It's beautiful," Mallory murmured, blinking back her tears as she smiled at Addison. "I love it. Thank you."

Addison's lips curved in a gentle smile and her eyes crinkled with affection and understanding as she gave Mallory's hand a light squeeze. "You're welcome, sweetie."

"Okay. Now it's your turn," Mallory murmured, tapping the package on Addison's lap with the edge of her picture frame.

She held her breath as Addison's finger slipped beneath the edge of the fold, and couldn't help but smile at the way the paper was summarily torn away from the shirt-sized box that had been nestled inside it.

"Oh, look a white box," Addison drawled, her eyes twinkling with mirth as she began working at the lid.

"I can take it back, you know…" Mallory playfully reached for the package. Honestly, part of her wanted to. There were actually two gifts inside the box, and while she knew the first would make Addison laugh, it was the smaller, second present she had purchased on a whim Saturday afternoon whilst on her way to Saint Luke's for their midday performance that had her feeling anxious. It had been too perfect to resist but, much like Addison's picture, even with the recent shift in their relationship, she worried it would be considered a bit too much.

"Like hell, you will," Addison sassed. She wiggled the top of the box free and laughed as she set it on the table. "I love it," she declared as she pulled out a folded, heather gray hoodie and lifted it up to look at it properly. "This is so awesome," she enthused as her eyes roved over the phrase printed on the front of it—*If ballet were easy, it would be called football.* "And so fuzzy! I'm going to live in this from now on!"

Mallory smiled, utterly pleased that the sweatshirt had gotten exactly the reaction she'd hoped for. "It seemed like something you would like."

"I love it." Addison pressed a quick kiss to her cheek. "Thank you."

"My pleasure, darling," Mallory assured her softly. She cleared her throat and added, "There's one more gift in there."

"There is?" Addison's eyes widened as she spotted the narrow, rectangular velvet box that had been tucked beneath the sweatshirt that left only the exact type of jewelry that was hidden inside to the imagination. "Mal…" she breathed as she picked up the velvet box and shifted her legs so the one that had been holding it fell to the floor.

Mallory held her breath and nervously smoothed her thumbs back and forth over the edges of the picture frame that was still on her lap as she watched Addison pry open the hinged lid.

"Oh, Mal," Addison breathed when she finally saw the necklace.

She carefully, oh so carefully lifted it from the box, and Mallory smiled at the look of genuine awe on her face as she studied the white gold ballerina captured in an arabesque. The edges of the ballerina's tutu glittered with tiny diamond chips, and further up the chain, an infinity symbol embedded with slightly larger diamonds held the length of chain the dancer dangled from.

"I couldn't resist when I saw it in the shop's window the other day," Mallory confessed softly. "I just had to buy it for you."

"It's…" Addison blinked and shook her head, and Mallory was afraid that she was about to say that it was too much, too expensive of a gift even though it was something she could easily afford. But instead, she just whispered, "It's beautiful. So, so beautiful."

There was no mistaking the emotion behind Addison's smile when she turned to look at her, and Mallory sighed with relief as a gentle finger hooked beneath her chin and guided their lips together in a tender, lingering kiss.

"Help me put it on?" Addison murmured the request against Mallory's lips.

"Of course, darling." Mallory smiled and, suddenly acutely aware of the way her heart thudded heavily in the base of her throat, took the necklace from Addison.

"Let me take this off real quick." Addison pulled her hoodie off and tossed it onto the table. "I want to be able to see what it looks like on."

The clasp took a bit more effort than Mallory had anticipated because there was the faintest hint of a tremble in her hands, but she managed to secure it without too much fumbling. "There you are."

"What do you think?" Addison smiled shyly as she turned.

Mallory licked her lips as she nodded. The infinity symbol was balanced perfectly on the point of Addison's defined collarbone, and the dancer lay against the flat of her chest an inch or so below it, suspended above the collar of her heathered scoop-necked tee, the white gold of the necklace further enhanced by Addison's olive-toned skin. "Perfect."

"Come with me to look." Addison took Mallory's hand and tugged her off the couch.

Mallory laughed as she padded after, her feeling utterly smitten. "There's the standing mirror in my room, or the vanity in the bath—" she cut herself off as Addison veered into her bedroom with a little skip. She shook her head as she followed behind her, and her heart lodged itself in her throat as she watched Addison's expression in the mirror shift from playful to struck to awed as she lifted a hand to touch the foot of the dancer. Addison's throat bobbed heavily as she released her hand and stepped closer to the mirror, and though the answer was clear by the look on Addison's face, Mallory couldn't resist asking softly, just to make sure, "Do you like it?"

"I love it," Addison breathed.

Mallory's heart fluttered in her chest as she stepped up behind Addison, wrapping her arms around the dancer's narrow waist as she rested her chin on her shoulder. "I'm so very glad."

Addison smiled and covered her hands at her waist as she leaned back into her, their gazes locked in the mirror, confessions too powerful to be put into words just yet conveyed by a look.

A comfortable silence fell around them, gentle and warm and without expectation, and Mallory tightened her hold on Addison's waist as she tucked her chin to press a kiss to the delicate chain that drew a precious line across the slope where Addison's neck and shoulder met. She smiled at the feeling of Addison shivering in her arms. "Cold?"

"A little. But that was for the kiss."

Mallory hid just how happy that made her by kissing that same spot again, and then sighed as she relaxed her hold on Addison's waist. "Let's go get you back into your hoodie. Can't have you falling ill. Nina will have my head."

Addison laughed and nodded. "Okay. Can we cuddle on the couch and watch a movie?"

"Of course, darling," Mallory all but purred as she ghosted a kiss over Addison's lips. "I would like nothing more than to hold you in my arms for the rest of the night."

twenty-three

"I'm going to go stretch."

Mallory smiled at the feeling of Addison's fingers curling around her waist and the tickle of breath against her ear. She nodded as she barely resisted the urge to turn her head, thread her fingers through Addison's hair, and capture her sweet, sweet lips in a lingering kiss. After a positively blissful thirty-six hours of lounging about and making out like teenagers, they had been thrust immediately back into their hectic, often conflicting schedules a week and a half ago, and though they had managed to find slices of time here and there where they could be together, it wasn't nearly enough for her liking. The last week and a half had been exciting and wonderful and absolutely, positively hellish with the LSO's two-concerts-a-day holiday schedule that still had four days left to go and the exacting, demanding rehearsals for *Evolution*, which would finally premier the following evening.

It was like the entire world was on edge—stressed and frantic and borderline hostile—and she dearly wished the calendar had remained stuck on Boxing Day so she could still be her couch with Addison laying on top of her, trading slow, deep kisses that made her heart flutter and a pleasant warmth settle low in her belly as their wandering hands became increasingly bold in their explorations.

The only good news in her inability to stop time, she figured, was that things would return to normal on Monday and then they would have more time to themselves. But for now, they were little more than pawns to their careers.

Addison's hands slid around her waist to press against her stomach and pull her closer, and her eyes fluttered as a playful, husky voice whispered against her ear, "If we were alone right now I'd totally kiss you, by the way."

Mallory laughed and covered Addison's hands with her own, selfishly enjoying this moment of unprofessionalism. "I would let you," she confessed softly.

Addison groaned and headbutted her shoulder. "And on that note, I'm actually going to go stretch, now. It looks like Gabs and Matt are about to start their final pas de deux, we'll be on in twenty-five or so."

Mallory nodded. She had done a thorough warm-up with Addison up in the studio before the first act had taken the stage and, since her part was more musical than physical, she trusted the track pants she wore under her dress to keep her muscles limber enough to perform. "Have fun."

"Always," Addison drawled.

Mallory shivered at the feeling of Addison's lips brushing a furtive kiss across the back of her neck as she pulled away, and shook her head as she watched her skip toward the portable barre that was set up near the rear of house entrance to the wings. A gentle, easy smile curled her lips as she watched Addison slip her wireless earbuds into place before pulling her phone from her left leg-warmer and selecting whatever playlist it was she was in the mood to warm up to that day.

She sighed as she forced herself to look away.

They were at work, after all, and it wouldn't do to be caught staring at Addison like she wanted to push her up against the wall and kiss her senseless. And, besides that, they were taking the stage soon. It was time to focus and prepare.

She hummed along with the now-familiar music from Gabs and Matt's pas de deux as she turned toward her violin to triple-check that everything was as it should be. She tightened the knobs on her shoulder rest to make sure that it would hold—she would make sure it was in-tune during the "intermission break"—and had just begun to rosin her bow when her phone began to vibrate and dance on the table beside her case.

Joseph Hayes?

A delicate frown creased her forehead as she stared at the name of the Managing Director of the LSO Board on her screen. She could think of no reason he would call her—Max was the one who was tasked with dealing with the Board, after all, not her. If he was calling her directly, it had to be for something at the LSO that was far more drama than she could even begin to deal with at the moment, and so even though she knew that she *should* take the call, she sent it to voicemail.

Judging by the time, her LSO colleagues should be beginning to arrive at St. Luke's for their early evening performance. Which meant that whatever the problem was that prompted Hayes to call her wouldn't be able to be properly dealt with until afterward, by which time she should be done with rehearsal and able to take his call.

The music from the theatre faded into silence, leaving nothing for her to listen to but the erratic beat of her heart, and she took a deep breath as she tried to refocus her thoughts on her upcoming performance. Nina would have her head if she wasn't completely dialed-in for this final dress rehearsal.

Before she could even begin to do that, however, her phone buzzed again.

"Bloody hell," she muttered as Hayes' name flashed on her screen again.

One call she could ignore and blame on faulty technology or whatever, but she couldn't ignore two—especially when they were so close together. Only a true emergency could prompt something like this, and her stomach twisted as she tried to figure out just what was going on.

Mallory turned to signal to Addison that she was going to duck out for a call, but she had her headphones on and her eyes closed as she worked through her stretches on the portable barre that was set up closer to the backstage entrance. The last thing she wanted to do was disturb her preparations, so she just sighed and moved to a quiet corner where she hoped her talking on the phone wouldn't disrupt the rehearsal.

"Hello?"

"Ms. Collingswood, this is Joseph Hayes. I need you to report to St. Luke's immediately."

She shook her head. "I'm sorry, sir, but I'm in the middle of a dress rehearsal in Covent Garden at the moment. I have actually snuck off just to take this call."

He sighed, clearly exasperated that she didn't immediately kowtow to his command. *"The deal we made was that the LSO would be your priority."*

"And it is, sir," Mallory replied evenly, keeping the flash of anger that she felt from her tone. It wouldn't do to lose her temper. "I have missed only one performance before today since I began this collaboration project, and Max cleared all of them well in advance." And, really, if the evening performance hadn't been scheduled so unusually early—especially given that it was a Thursday—she might have been able to make it back to St. Luke's for it. "As I'm sure you can understand, *Evolution* premieres tomorrow night and this rehearsal—while unfortunate in its timing—is a necessary part of the preparation process. Have you spoken with either Max or Clara about this? They both assured me the LSO would be fine for today without me."

"Yes, I spoke to Max earlier, even though he's at a conference in Barcelona," Hayes snapped, sounding even more disgruntled. *"And I would agree with his assessment that one day wouldn't be a problem, except Clara was in a car accident on her way back to the Barbican this afternoon."*

Mallory's eyes widened in surprise. "Oh my god, is she okay?"

"She says that she should be fine, but she is at Princess Grace getting checked

out for whiplash and a possible concussion. Thad is in Chicago until the middle of January, so the Bellamy kid from the Royal Academy coming in to lead for the day."

"I'm glad it sounds like she's going to be okay." Mallory nodded slowly as she finally understood what was going on. It was certainly less than ideal to have the LSO's musical director, conductor, and leader unavailable for a performance. "Charlie, the assistant leader, knows that I'm with the Royal Ballet today, and is more than capable of assuming my chair for this one performance, sir, even with a guest conductor."

"Yes, I know. He did a decent job covering for you this morning, but he just called in sick. Thinks it's either food poisoning or the stomach flu, but either way he isn't at all sure he'll be able to perform tonight. We also had to send Alex home this morning because she couldn't stop coughing, and when Johan went to his doctor's appointment between performances today he was ordered onto bed rest effectively immediately. This leaves the first violins disastrously sparse."

Mallory looked up at the ceiling and felt a headache coming on. "Disastrously sparse" was not exactly an understatement. Besides Max, Clara, and herself, the LSO was also at risk of missing her top three first violins. Of course, out of all of that, her mind selfishly latched onto the information about Charlie. He hadn't seemed ill the night before, and she prayed that whatever it was he was suffering from was just food poisoning. Forget going into rehearsal not in the right mindset, if she fell ill before their first performance Nina might actually kill her. "Right," she muttered after a time. "Then if Charlie can't make it, I recommend that Robyn assume the role for today. She's been with the orchestra for years and knows this particular arrangement inside and out." Robyn might lack the confidence to lead for an extended period of time, but Mallory was sure that she would be able to manage this one performance.

"I'm afraid that just won't do."

Mallory pinched the bridge of her nose as her pulse began to race at the prospect of telling the man in charge of her contract what he didn't want to hear. "Well, I'm sorry sir, but it will have to. I can't leave my rehearsal here." She blinked her eyes open at the feeling of a gentle hand curving around her elbow, and offered Addison a small smile as she held up a finger and mouthed, "One minute."

Addison nodded and took a step back to give her some privacy as she glanced over her shoulder, and when she looked back at her, there was an apologetic grimace twisting her lips. "We're up," she whispered. "Nina's looking for us."

Mallory nodded and, heart pounding in her throat, reported, "Sir, I'm afraid I must go now. I'm needed on stage."

Hayes muttered something under his breath that she was absolutely certain she was glad she couldn't make out before he demanded, *"I will see you at the matinee tomorrow, yes?"*

"Of course."

"We will discuss this more. I expect you in my office an hour before the orchestra's call." He hung up.

Mallory winced at the palpable anger in his tone and let her hand fall from her ear. She felt mildly sick to her stomach, but she forced it down as she apologized, "Sorry about that."

"Is everything okay?"

"Not really." Mallory shook her head. "But I can't do anything about it at the moment," she muttered as she turned toward the table where she had left her violin. She couldn't see Nina anywhere, but that didn't mean she wasn't nearby and counting the seconds until they presented themselves to her.

Addison grabbed her hand. "Are you okay?"

"It doesn't matter."

"Hey…" Addison pulled Mallory to a stop and stepped closer, her eyes shining with concern. "Talk to me."

"It's just…" Mallory shook her head. If she started to explain what just happened, she might very well lose it, and they didn't have time for that. So instead she tried to brush it all off. "Nothing. It's nothing. Just LSO stuff that I can't do anything about because I'm here, so—" The rest of her half-formed protest was silenced by a gentle kiss. She whimpered and lifted a hand to Addison's neck as she kissed her back, desperately chasing the comfort she so desperately needed. One kiss turned into two, then three, and her riotous thoughts calmed as her pulse evened out, racing fear and anxiety slowed to a slow, steady, heavy beat that matched Addison's beneath her thumb.

"I thought we weren't doing this at work?" Mallory murmured when, after one last lingering kiss, Addison pulled away.

Addison shrugged, her expression at once concerned and entirely unrepentant. "You looked like you needed it."

Mallory glanced around to see if anyone was paying them much attention and, when she was assured that they weren't, smiled and confessed softly, "I did. Thank you."

"Anytime, sweetie. Are you going to be okay?"

Mallory took a deep breath and let it go slowly before murmuring, "I think so, yes." Things at the LSO would undoubtedly be tense for a while, but Hayes had had a hand in pushing her to do this collaboration, and she knew that, once Max returned, he would support her decision. She spotted Nina emerging from between dark curtains, brow pinched and her lips pressed in a tight line, clearly displeased, and tilted her head toward her as she said, "Nina's looking ready for blood."

"When isn't she?" Addison chuckled darkly as they started making their way toward her.

"Am I keeping you from something important?" Nina drawled when they were close enough to be addressed without her having to raise her voice.

"Sorry. Minor disaster at the LSO," Mallory apologized as she hurried to grab her violin. "Clara was in a car accident."

"What? Is she okay?" Nina asked. Her foul mood seemed to evaporate in an instant as alarm pulled at her features.

"It sounds like she will be fine. She's at Princess Grace getting checked out now," Mallory said reassuringly. She met Nina's piercing stare without blinking, and relaxed ever so slightly when she was rewarded with a short nod.

"You're on in three."

"Got it," Mallory confirmed as Addison nodded beside her.

Nina muttered, almost fondly, "Of course you do." She took a deep breath and let it go in a quiet huff. "I'm going to watch from the audience." Her phone was already in her hand as she exited the stage.

Once Nina had disappeared, Mallory allowed Addison to turn her with a light hand on her hip. She smiled as soft hands framed her face and took a deep breath as Addison pushed up onto her toes and touched their foreheads together.

"Hey." Addison smoothed her thumbs over Mallory's cheeks. "I know that phone call sucked and that the timing couldn't have been worse, but I need you with me now, okay? I need you right here with me"—she took Mallory's free hand and cradled it against her chest, right over heart—"for the next forty-four minutes..."

Mallory closed her eyes as she focused on the feeling Addison's heart beating beneath her palm, and let that steady *thump, thump, thump* chase away what lingered of the quiet anxiety that was buzzing at the back of her mind. It was surprisingly easy, really, to push her worries away and focus on Addison instead, and she dipped her head in a small nod as she blinked her eyes open. "I'm all yours, darling."

twenty-four

Mallory chewed her lip as she looked out the window of the town car that had picked her up half an hour earlier. The car service was an extravagance she didn't usually bother with because the underground got her from point A to point B in the city faster than a car ever could, but all of London seemed to have fallen ill with something or another and, with *Evolution* premiering that evening, she wasn't willing to risk her health by taking public transportation. She ran her thumb over the rubberized grip on the side of her travel mug that was full of an organic herbal immunity tea Addison swore by, and took a small sip as the car slowed in front of The Barbican.

The warmth of the drink did nothing to chase away the unease that had haunted her from the moment she had ended her call with Hayes, and she set her jaw as she placed the mug between her knees to begin gathering her things. While she appreciated the small smile Noah, the driver, gave her when he caught her eye in the rearview mirror as he threw the car into park outside the Silk Street entrance, she couldn't quite summon one to match, and she was glad that he didn't seem offended as he just dipped his head in a small nod and undid his seatbelt so he could hurry around to get her door.

She shivered at the rush of freezing air and pulled her scarf tighter as she waited for Noah to get her door. Part of her felt ridiculous waiting when she was capable of doing it herself, but he had acted so perfectly scandalized on Monday when she had tried to assure him that it wasn't necessary—*"I'm sorry, Miss, but my wife would have my head if she heard I let a woman open her own door."*—that she relented.

"Got you as close to the entrance as I could, Miss Collingswood," Noah declared as he pulled open her door.

Mallory arched a brow at him and shook her head at the cheeky smirk she got back in response. She had tried several times throughout the week to get him to call her by her first name but, much like his insistence on opening her door, he continued to have his own way with things. "Thank you, Noah," she murmured as she climbed out of the car. She hunched her shoulders against the biting wind that swept her hair into her face, and asked, "Is it okay if I leave my ballet bag in here?"

"Of course. I won't go far, so just give me a bell when you're done"—he pushed the door closed and shoved his hands in his pockets to protect them from the cold—"and I'll meet you right back here."

She nodded and started making her way across the sidewalk to the door so that he would stop standing around on formality waiting for her and get back into the car where it was warm. There was no earthly reason anyone should suffer this weather any longer than absolutely necessary, and she would feel awful if he caught a cold, or worse, because of his chivalry.

Her footsteps echoed ahead of her as she made her way past the golden statue of The Barbican Muse in the main entryway, the sound quietly ominous given the reason for her early arrival, and she straightened her posture as she began to mentally prepare herself for the dressing-down she was about to receive.

She was confident, at least, that she wouldn't end up paying for her insubordination with her job. Hayes had agreed to the collaboration, after all, and posters promoting both *Evolution* and her role in the ballet were plastered around the Centre to such a degree that she could hardly turn around without being confronted with a picture of herself. But his reputation as a ruthless and often vindictive businessman had followed him into retirement and onto the Board, and she knew that he wouldn't lose any sleep over making her life a living hell for a while.

"Oi, Mallory!" Max's voice called from behind her.

Mallory tightened her grip on her tea as she turned toward him. "I thought you were in Barcelona…" Her voice trailed off when she spotted a familiar figure at his side. "Clara!" She had spoken to Clara only briefly the night before to check up on her and, while she didn't have a concussion, she did have a broken nose and a severe case of whiplash that should have kept her sidelined until at least the following week.

Clara waved. "You look like you're going off to war, mate."

Mallory shook her head. Clara had a bruise across the bridge of her nose that was beginning to extend under her eyes, was wearing a rather imposing neck brace, and she carried herself stiffly, but she appeared otherwise fine, and Mallory couldn't help but smile as she retorted, "And you look like you've just come home from one."

"She does, doesn't she?" Max agreed. "And I was. I grabbed the first flight out of there this morning, landed at Heathrow, picked up this one"—he tilted his head toward Clara—"and we came right here."

"Not that I don't appreciate it, because I do, but why are you lot here?"

Clara and Max shared a look, and Max shrugged as he answered, "Clara called me last night after she spoke with Hayes. He's always been a controlling pain in the arse, but he's off his rocker on this one, and we couldn't let you suffer his wrath alone. Yesterday was a total cock-up, but none of it was your fault."

"You're good friends." Mallory smiled at them both. "But I could have handled this on my own. You could have stayed at your conference, Max, and lord knows you should be at home recuperating," she told Clara.

Max shook his head. "The conference isn't going anywhere. And, at any rate, I was flying back this afternoon anyway so I could be at the ballet tonight for your premiere, so it's not like I missed much more than a few hours' sleep."

"And, this isn't really that bad," Clara added as they continued across the foyer toward the lifts. "Besides, the docs gave me some really good drugs."

"Clara…" Mallory huffed a laugh.

"Deal with it, Mal," Clara sassed as she pressed the button to call the lift. The doors slid open immediately, and as they filed inside, she added, "You have enough going on, especially today, of all days. We want to help."

"Are you ready for tonight?" Max asked.

"I think so." Mallory pressed the button for the second floor, and sipped at her tea as she turned toward them.

"You 'think so'?" Clara huffed a laugh when she took another sip of tea instead of rising to the bait. "Well, then I guess I'll just lower my expectations for the performance."

Mallory arched a brow in surprise. "Are you still coming?"

"Of course. I bought a new suit, and all of this"—she motioned toward her face—"isn't going to keep me from showing it off."

"Ah, well, as long as you're doing it for you," Mallory drawled as the lift stopped at the second floor and the doors opened. She was pleased, though. While she had given her guest tickets to her parents and Will and Siobhan, it was nice to know that there would be other friendly faces in the crowd later.

Max chuckled at their banter and started down the corridor to Hayes' office.

"Oh, you spoke?" Mallory grinned. As opening night approached, the artistic director had been keeping her and Addison longer after each rehearsal to dissect their performance, but last night she had dismissed them along with the rest of the company, much their surprise.

Clara glanced at Max's back before she stuck her tongue out briefly.

"Fine," she muttered with a light blush, "Nina called just as I was being discharged, and overheard the nurse reminding me to watch out for symptoms of concussion. Next thing I knew, there she was on my doorstep insisting that I shouldn't be alone. She took one scathing look at the TV dinner thawing in the microwave and ordered me confined to the couch while she cooked 'real food.' The woman is frighteningly competent."

"Tell me about it." Mallory hid her smile. The Clara she knew was notoriously independent, used to going it alone since her studies had seen her moving halfway across the globe in her youth, while the present demands of her career took her to several countries in any given year. But beneath the grumbling, she sensed that Clara was pleased this time. It was also nice to know that there was more to Nina than the hard-driving martinet that relentlessly drilled her and the rest of the Royal Ballet. Now if only Hayes proved to be more than an arse and a half… She slowed as they approached Hayes' open office door. "Hey, seriously, thanks for this."

"You're welcome." Clara took a deep breath. "You ready?"

"For this? Not at all," Mallory admitted with a wry smile. "But I've got things to do today, so I guess there's no time like the present…"

Max, who had paused to wait for them, winked at her. "There's the swagger I like to see. Keep your chin up, Mal. We got this," he said as he rapped his knuckles on the frame of Hayes' door and strode in ahead of them.

Hayes was in the process of heaving himself upright behind his desk when they followed on Max's heels. He looked comically surprised at their presence. "Max? Clara? I wasn't expecting to see you here this morning…"

"Yes, well," Max drawled as he shook the Hayes' hand, "I figured it was more important for me to be here than spending a few hours listening to Gerald extol the virtues of a varied programming schedule. Especially since it's not a problem for us because Clara always makes sure we mix up the established classics with lesser-known, contemporary compositions, anyways."

"Right…right…" Hayes murmured. He cleared his throat and turned to Clara. "How are you feeling?"

"I've been better," Clara admitted as she shook his hand. "I know you said that I needn't worry about this meeting, but I was feeling well enough when I woke up this morning that I decided to come in for an hour or two just to help clean up the mess from yesterday."

"Ah…" Hayes' eyes darted to Mallory as she stepped between Max and Clara. "I see."

Mallory dipped her head in a small nod. "Director Hayes."

"Ms. Collingswood."

"Shall we get on with it, then?" Max asked, his tone light, as if he wasn't perfectly aware of what he was doing. "As everyone here knows, Mallory does have quite the schedule today…"

"Right…" Hayes muttered. He cleared his throat and seemed to gather himself as he waved a hand toward the sitting area at the front of his office. "Would you care to sit?"

"I think I'll stand, if you don't mind," Clara replied. "It's easier this way, you know, with my neck and everything."

"Works for me. I've been sitting too much all week anyway," Max chimed in.

Mallory bit the inside of her cheek to keep from laughing at the owlish way Hayes blinked at them. It was clear that none of this was going according to his plan. "I'm fine standing too, if you are, sir."

Never one to back down from a challenge—especially it if meant surrendering a position of authority—Hayes nodded. "Of course…"

"Excellent," Max replied. "So, let's get down to business. Yesterday was pretty much a disaster on all fronts, but everyone I spoke with last night said that Robyn managed admirably given the short-notice and that young Bellamy handled himself like a pro. Is that your assessment as well, Director?"

Though it looked like it caused him great pain to do so, Hayes nodded. "It would have been better if Ms. Collingswood had been there—"

"But she was busy preparing for the collaborative project with The Royal Ballet that we approved before the season started," Clara cut him off.

"Well, yes, but that was on the grounds that the LSO would remain her priority. It was unprofess—"

"With all due respect, sir," Max interrupted, the fire flashing in his eyes a startling change from his usual affability. "Mallory Collingswood is, without a doubt, the most professional musician I've had the honor to work with, and I will not stand here and listen to you attack her character."

"I agree completely," Clara echoed.

Mallory had to grit her teeth to keep from gaping at them, but neither seemed to notice.

"All of this"—Max motioned toward the four of them—"is nothing more than a power play on your part because you're mad she didn't drop everything and come running when you called."

"Excuse me!" Hayes protested. "This is not... As the leader of this orchestra, she—"

"Do I need to repeat the part where I pointed out she was doing the job we all agreed she should do?" Max droned, looking almost bored. "You can't publicize how TRB needed one of ours to make this ballet happen, then turn around and interfere with her performance. I took the liberty of reaching out to Gianna, Brad, and Vaughn after we spoke last night, and all of them seemed to understand that yesterday was just a confluence of unfortunate events."

Mallory held her breath as she watched Hayes' eyes widen. Max hadn't just called Hayes out on what he had been trying to do, he brought back up. Gianna Ngo, Brad Abbott, and Vaughn Wosczyna—the Chair, Vice Chair, and the LSO's largest donor, respectively—had been vocally displeased with Hayes' leadership style for a while, and even she had heard rumblings of a coup within the voting membership that would oust Hayes from his position.

"Furthermore," Max continued, his tone carrying an unmistakable edge, "not one of them seemed to feel that Mallory was in the wrong for staying at her dress rehearsal."

Hayes glowered at Max. "I won't forget this, Cole."

"Neither will I," Max promised. "You seem to keep forgetting that anything that impacts on the performance of the orchestra falls within my purview as Music Director, not yours. So you can come at me with these little power moves any day of the week, Hayes, but you will not pull this shite with my musicians. Are we clear?" When Hayes just pursed his lips and continued to glare at them all, Max nodded. "Excellent. Now, if you'll excuse us, Mallory needs to get back to Covent Garden to prepare for tonight's performance, I am sure I have a mountain of emails to sort through since I was playing hooky all week, and Clara needs to get back to her sofa so she can begin to recuperate."

Mallory opened her mouth to point out that she had planned on playing in the midday concert, but was silenced by a look from Clara. Part of her marveled at how she had been ousted to the role of a spectator at what should have been her own flogging, but she was beyond grateful for the unexpected help.

"Right," Hayes grumbled after a moment. "Good luck tonight, Ms. Collingswood."

"Thank you, sir," Mallory replied with her most polite smile. "I hope you enjoy the show."

Hayes nodded curtly in a way that suggested he wouldn't be attending, and Mallory was honestly glad for it as she dipped her head and followed Max and Clara out.

Once they were back in the elevator and safe from their voices being overheard, Max looked at her and Clara with the most mischievous smirk she had ever seen and drawled, "So, that went well…"

"Very well," Clara agreed. "That was more fun than I've had in a meeting with that man in years."

Mallory laughed as she pressed the button for the ground floor. "I can't believe you lot did that."

Max waved her off. "He's had his way around here for too long. I can deal with his posturing and schoolboy bully bollocks, but he should have never come after you like that. Especially after Clara and I both cleared it."

"I appreciate it." And she did. She had known he would support her, but she had never expected Max to do what he just did. "But if you get flak for it, I will never forgive you."

Max scoffed. "Even if Hayes had the guts to try to take action against me, the rest of the Board would never support it. My job is perfectly secure. As are both of yours," he added, flashing her a small smile as the elevator doors opened to the main lobby. "So get out of here. Clara, rest. Mallory, go rest your legs or stretch or whatever it is you need to do to get ready for tonight."

"But the concert…" Mallory protested.

"Is going to be covered by the orchestra from the Royal Academy today." Max laughed at her obvious surprise and explained, "I floated the idea by Marcus Apps over at the school yesterday when I inquired after Bellamy, and he agreed. It's a win-win for everyone. You all get a break, and his kids get to take to the big stage for an hour or two."

"But the tickets. What are you going to do when people complain that they paid to see the LSO?"

"I'm so glad you asked. This was Gianna's idea, and I actually love it. Everyone who bought tickets expecting to hear us will be able to come back toward the end of the season for an outdoor performance here in the Centre courtyard complete with complimentary food and drinks."

"Do you think Hayes will sign off on that?"

Max's shoulders twitched in a shrug, and he ran a hand through his hair. "I don't reckon he'll be around to protest anything we do by then."

"So you, Gianna, Brad, and Vaughn are really going to push to vote him out?" Clara asked. "It's not just rumor anymore?"

He nodded. "Hayes was never happy that I was signed over his personal candidate at the time, and he's chosen to show that by second guessing every decision I've made since. The players are increasingly unhappy about the situation, and several have complained to Gianna and Brad about it. This little power-play of his was the last straw so far as they're concerned. So, don't worry about it."

"Well, be that as it may... Thank you," Mallory murmured earnestly. "For having my back like that up there."

"Any time, Mal," Clara assured her.

"Of course," Max echoed with a gallant little bow. "Now, seriously, get out of here and go rest up so you can take the stage in Covent Garden tonight and show the world just how bloody talented you are."

"Okay. Thank you." Mallory smiled. "Clara, can I give you a ride home? I've hired a car service for the week so that I don't risk catching any rogue germs on the tube."

"A ride home would be wonderful." Clara nodded. "Cheers."

"Brilliant." She nodded as she reached to pull her phone out of her bag. "I'll just call Noah, and then we can be on our way. Max, thank you again."

"Any time, Mal. Now, go."

Mallory huffed a laugh and snapped off a little salute. "I'm going..."

twenty-five

"Hey." Addison opened her door with a smile. She looked rested and ready to perform with her kit bag slung across her chest, and the black dress bag dangling from her left hand said she was prepared to celebrate at the party Nina was hosting for the cast, crew, and the ballet's biggest donors once the curtain came down. "You know, you could have just texted me or something, and I would have come down."

"Yes, well," Mallory murmured as she took a step back to give Addison room to close and lock her front door. She held her hands out to take Addison's things, but when Addison didn't hand them over, she shoved her hands into the pockets of her coat and lifted her right shoulder in a small shrug as if to say, *I have better manners than that.*

Addison arched a brow at her as she pulled her key from the lock and dropped it into the side pocket of her bag. Her right hand found the crook of Mallory's elbow as they began making their way toward the stairs. "You're spoiling me, you know. Going back to having to walk to and from work every day is going to be brutal after this."

Mallory covered Addison's hand on her arm and gave it a light squeeze. "This isn't spoiling, darling." She glanced over at her as they started down the stairs and flashed a small smile. "This is simply me making good use of the car and driver I have at my disposal. If I were to make a genuine attempt to spoil you, it would be with fancy dinners out, weekend holidays, and so many other things I wish we had time for."

Addison slid her hand down to lace their fingers together in Mallory's pocket. "Someday we'll have time for all of that." She gave Mallory's hand a squeeze. "But you do spoil me. In so many little ways that I don't think you even notice it most of the time. And sending your driver to take me to and from work every day very much falls into that category."

A small wrinkle furrowed Mallory's brow as she pushed the gated door that guarded the entry to the upstairs apartments open. The car and driver thing, she understood, but she couldn't think of anything else she had done for Addison that could even remotely be considered spoiling. Part of her wanted to ask what it was she had done, but what mattered more was that Addison wasn't bothered by it. "Is that okay?"

"Yes, sweetie." Addison smoothed her thumb over the back of Mallory's hand reassuringly. "It's never a bad thing to show me you care." She gave Mallory's hand one last squeeze before removing her hand from the pocket and slipping it into her own. "Hiya, Noah," she greeted the suited driver who was standing beside the car, waiting to get the door for them.

"Miss Leigh. I'll put your things in the boot." He smiled and gave a small bow as he pulled the door open. "Big night tonight. You ready?"

"We'll find out soon enough," Addison drawled playfully as she handed him her bags before slipping into the back seat. "It is very weird to only be heading over there now, though," she observed with a smile once Mallory had joined her in the car and Noah had closed the door. "Usually I'm there by five at the latest on performance days. I have to keep reminding myself that I'm not actually running late."

"I'm sorry. I thought this was—"

"We're not on until after eight thirty," Addison interrupted, placing her hand on Mallory's knee. "There's no reason for us to get to the theatre that early. We'd be going apeshit with nerves if we had to sit around and wait for Gabs and Matt to work through the first act."

"I've been nervous all day," Mallory confessed. "I can't remember the last time I was this nervous for a performance."

"Me too," Addison replied quietly as Noah climbed behind the wheel. She smoothed her thumb over Mallory's knee in a light caress as the car pulled away from the curb to merge with traffic headed toward the theatre.

Driving from Addison's to the theatre took longer than it would have for them to walk the same distance, but the car was warm and quiet in a way that the city outside certainly wasn't, and Mallory was grateful for the calm that surrounded them as they made the ride in companionable silence.

Noah handed them their bags once they were standing on the sidewalk outside the stage door entrance, and doffed his cap as he bid, "Break a leg, ladies."

"Ta, Noah," Mallory murmured as she slid the strap of her violin case over her shoulder. "There's a party after the show, so it will be late when we're done here."

"That's fine, Miss," Noah assured her with a smile as he slammed the lid of the boot. "My wife is in Hull visiting our daughter this weekend, so I've got nowhere to be. Just enjoy your party and give me a bell when you're ready to head home."

Mallory nodded and turned to Addison as Noah made his way back to the driver's door, and heaved a soft sigh as their eyes locked. "Shall we?" she asked as she pulled open the stage door.

Addison took a deep breath, and her lips curled in a small smile as she let it go slowly. "We shall."

"Addy, I have autograph req—" Josh began the moment they stepped inside.

"Not before the show," Addison cut him off, though not unkindly. "I'll be down afterward to deal with all of that."

He ducked his head in apology as he shifted the stack of programs to the side of the counter. "Right. Sorry."

Addison nodded and started making her way down the hall to the lift.

Mallory arched a brow as she jogged to catch up. "Superstition?" she asked knowingly.

"Yep." Addison pursed her lips as she pressed the button to call the lift. "Surely you do the same?"

Mallory chuckled and shook her head. "Autographs of orchestral musicians aren't particularly sought after. The last time I signed anything was for a little girl back before Christmas, and it was because of the mailing for my role here."

"That's too bad. You guys are incredible."

"Thank you," Mallory murmured as the doors to the lift opened and they made their way into the car. Her nerves returned with a vengeance as the doors slid shut and the lift began to move. The ride to the second floor was silent as the weight of their impending performance settled around them, and that silence wasn't broken until Addison reached for her hand once they had stopped outside the dancer's dressing room.

"Hey, Mal."

Mallory's hummed as she turned to Addison and arched a brow in silent question.

Addison sighed and pushed up onto the balls of her feet to lay the softest of kisses to Mallory's lips. "I'm going to be lost in my own head here for the next few hours," she murmured, her voice heavy with apology as her heels touched back down. "I won't talk much, if at all, and I'm going to seem like I don't want to be bothered," she elaborated as she stroked Mallory's shoulder, "but just know that it's not because of anything you've done. Okay? It's just how I am before performances."

"The same goes for me, darling." Mallory smiled reassuringly as she took Addison's hand from her arm and kissed her knuckles. "You just do whatever it is you need to do to get yourself ready."

Addison smiled, clearly relieved. "The wig mistresses prefer you to have your make-up done before they arrive, which will be in about thirty minutes."

Mallory nodded. They had gone over all of this the day before and, should her nerves return to the point she couldn't think clearly, she had the pre-show schedule written down and tucked away safely in her bag. "After hair, it's time to warm up." She frowned as a thought she hadn't considered before this moment occurred to her. "Is that something you would prefer to be alone for?"

"It is," Addison confirmed, her eyes soft with apology. "It's late enough that the studios upstairs will all be empty for the night, so I'll take Ashton, and you can use Fonteyn. I talked to the stage manager, and he'll be running separate calls for us—basically treating the ballet as two separate, back-to-back performances—so there will be a half-hour call to remind us of where we are on the clock. I won't get dressed until the quarter—about eight twenty or so on this schedule—and then I'll head down to the stage."

"The curtain comes down on the first part at a quarter past eight," Mallory continued. "Intermission runs until eight thirty-five."

Addison smiled. "Exactly. Quarter call is at twenty, the Five at the half-hour, and then the tabs go out again. The corps does their thing, and then it's all us."

"And then it's all us," Mallory echoed as she lifted a hand to gently cradle Addison's jaw. She sighed as she traced the curve of her cheek with a tender thumb, savoring this last moment of togetherness, and blinked as she let her hand fall away. "I'll see you in a couple hours."

Addison nodded and pushed herself back up to steal one last kiss. "See you in a couple hours."

Mallory waited until Addison disappeared inside her dressing room before heading for her own. She had never arrived at a venue so early before a performance, but because this was the first time she was doing anything like this, she figured it was best to follow the house traditions.

And, as it turned out, it was a good thing she did.

Two hours had *seemed* like an excessive amount of preparation time in the abstract, but it turned out to be precisely enough time to allow her to get everything done. She had seen Addison only once in the time since they'd separated, and she had looked so focused with her eyes on the floor and her headphones on that Mallory doubted she even noticed her.

Mallory waited until the quarter call before making her way downstairs with her violin case in one hand so it wouldn't rub against her costume and a stainless water bottle in the other to help ward off dehydration from nerves. Gabs and Matt offered her thumbs ups and broad smiles when she saw them backstage but didn't try to talk to her—respecting her preparation process while still obviously pleased with how their own performance had gone—and she returned their smiles with a small one of her own before she made her way toward the small table where she would leave her things.

She took a slow, deep breath as she opened the lid of her violin case, the click of the latches drowned out by the sounds that filtered through the heavy curtains that separated the stage area from the auditorium, and let it go slowly as the stage manager called the five. The call seemed to usher the corps back to the wings, and Mallory kept her attention on the dark wood of her violin as she did her best to ignore their murmured conversations and the whisper of fabric being adjusted after the quick change.

She lifted her bow and violin from its case and, heart thudding heavily in her throat, turned to soak in these last final moments before taking the stage. She had a feeling all the details would be later lost due to her nerves, but it seemed important to try to commit it all to memory. Her gaze drifted over lithe dancers in gold- and silver-hued dresses and matching shoes, looking out onto the stage with a confident set to each of their frames as they awaited the call to take their places, bodies warm and legs already limber from the first act.

The call of, "Beginners, please!" reverberated through the wings, and Mallory watched as the corps sprung into motion, moving as one through the drapes and onto the stage.

The stillness that descended on the wings in their absence was palpable—certainly more than enough to send the faint-hearted running—but she barely noticed it because just then, as if she somehow knew when things would quiet, Addison arrived backstage. Her brow was smooth, carrying no hint of stress, though her expression was focused, her shoulders beneath the zip-up hoodie she wore over her dress were relaxed, and her gait even and confident. She looked poised and prepared and ready to conquer the stage, and Mallory was struck breathless as she looked at her, utterly amazed that, out of everyone in the world, she was the one blessed enough to see her like this.

Brown eyes locked onto hers, and her pulse sped as soft lips curled in an even softer smile and an arched brow beckoned her closer.

Yes, she was so very, very blessed.

Music swelled from the orchestra pit just as she reached Addison's side, and she licked her lips as a hand on her hip pulled her closer. Their breaths mingled in the finite space between their lips as the dancers on stage began to move, and then the world fell away as a warm, firm hand pressed against the skin above her heart. She mirrored the touch, and felt her pulse automatically slow to match the steady beat beneath her palm.

I need you here with me, Addison's pulse seemed to command; while hers answered unabashedly, *I'm all yours, darling.*

The music from the pit began its slow descent into the silence that heralded her entrance, and Mallory smiled at Addison as she backed away.

She was ready.

They were ready.

She shouldered her violin as she turned to the stage, waiting for the action to still and the music to stop, and then took a deep breath as she started toward the lights, the sweet sound of the violin heralding her entrance as she made her way toward center stage. She was vaguely aware of the dancers breaking apart behind her and hurrying with an enviable amount of grace toward the wings, but only vaguely. Beneath the heat of the lights, standing in front of a veritable wall of blackness that hid the audience she knew was watching, she welcomed the zen-like state of being that consumed her when she performed.

It was just her and the music.

And then Addison's hand was on her shoulder, and her awareness expanded just enough to include her, as well.

Step for step, note for note, turn for turn they danced like they were born to do it together. It was easy and natural and *fun*, and when she extended her right leg, toes pointed to draw an invisible arc on the floor as she pulled her bow across the strings of her violin for the last time, she *knew* they had just done something incredible. Her heart beat up into her throat as her bow arm fell away and Addison's hand curved ever so gently around her cheek, and she melted eagerly into that oh-so-soft pressure to let Addison urge her closer until their foreheads came together and silence settled around them.

They had done it.

She bit her lip to keep from smiling at the absolute triumph that shone in Addison's eyes, and then the lights went out and the curtains dropped, and there was no containing the smile that broke free as Addison laughed and kissed her as the crowd beyond the curtain erupted in applause. It was the perfect end to a flawless performance, and she sighed as the rush of activity behind and around them forced them apart well before she was ready.

"We did it," Mallory murmured, wrapping her arms around Addison's waist and pulling her into a fierce embrace as two assistant stage managers sprinted past them to catch the heavy tabs of the curtain to make sure they didn't bounce apart.

"Yeah we did," Addison agreed, pressing a smile of a kiss to the side of Mallory's throat as the lights came back on and the stage came alive with dancers rushing about to find their position for the calls.

They finally broke apart for good when Holly, the member of the tech crew assigned to seeing her instrument safely off stage and back into its case, approached and called out, "Ms. Collingswood. The violin, if you'd please."

"Case is on—"

"The table just there," Holly finished for Mallory with a smile as she carefully took the instrument. "I'll make sure it's properly stowed," she promised before hurrying away.

Because of the unusual structure of the ballet, the structure of the general call consisted of the two of them flanked by Gabs and Matt in the front line with the corps behind them, and Mallory couldn't contain her smile as their friends crushed them in a happy, bouncing hug.

"You were fucking amazing!" Matt declared, his voice deep and booming in Mallory's ear.

"So good!" Gabs agreed, squeezing them tight.

"Quick as you can, please!" the stage manager called out, interrupting their celebration.

Matt's huff of annoyance was adorable, and Mallory laughed as they broke apart, assumed their proper positions, and linked hands.

The curtains swept into the proscenium arch as if they weighed nothing, and the full force of the audience's applause was a tidal wave that washed across the stage. They advanced in a line toward the front of the stage, their steps finding the rhythm of the applause, and took their first bow as a unit before Gabs and Matt broke away, pointing at Mallory and Addison before they, too, began to clap.

The rest of the call was as much of a blur as the pre-show preparations had been. Despite having rehearsed this part of the performance on three separate occasions, she still felt like she was scrambling to keep up as she followed Addison back and forth across the stage, doing her best to gracefully manage the absolutely gigantic bouquet she was handed. She had a chance to catch her breath as they gave way for the corps to take their call as a unit before stepping back up into the spotlight so Addison could collect Henry Walker, the conductor and music director of the Royal Opera House's orchestra, for his curtain call.

Usually, the conductor marked the end of the main curtain call, but with it being the premiere of a brand new ballet, there was one more person to be recognized, and Mallory did her best to applaud with the rest of the theatre as Nina Devereaux strode out of the wings to take her place at center stage. Her black gown was elegant and perfectly understated, and when she lifted a hand to acknowledge the crowd, their applause almost blew the roof off the building.

The queen of London ballet was back, if only for this night, and the audience more than made sure she knew just how much they loved her as the stage manager emerged from the wings with a bouquet that made the one Mallory was holding look like a cheap prop. Nina balanced the behemoth in the crook of her left arm with ease as she dipped into the most elegant curtsey Mallory had ever seen. She waved again as she straightened, and then backed into the spot Mallory and Addison had shifted to open between them as the entire cast and Nina Devereaux took one last bow before the curtain came down and an assistant stage manager bolted from the wings to catch the tabs before they could swing open again.

Nina turned to the group and smiled as she offered them a small bow. "You were all brilliant tonight. Job very well done."

Judging by the way everybody around her seemed to puff up at the compliment, Mallory wasn't the only one who felt like she was flying at the high praise. Nina was tough and exacting and impossibly demanding, so if she thought they had done that good of a job, they must have absolutely crushed the performance.

"Corps, you're dismissed. I'll see you at the party in Hamlyn Hall. Class tomorrow is pushed back until one so that you all have time to recover from your celebrations." Everyone cheered at the announcement that class would be delayed, and Nina shook her head as the corps dashed off the stage. "You four were perfect tonight," she declared as she turned to Mallory, Addison, Gabs, and Matt. "Truly perfect. I could not be prouder of the way each of you performed. No post-mortem needed for anyone, we will go over everything at our next regularly scheduled rehearsal."

And, oh, if Mallory thought she was flying before, it was nothing compared to the high she was riding now, and she could only tip her head in thanks for the compliment because her throat was too tight to speak.

Matt, however, didn't seem to have that problem, and he made them all laugh as he cooed, "Aww, you love us! Group hug!"

"Nice try, Mr. Magnusson," Nina chuckled. She took a deep breath and let it go in a quiet huff as she smiled proudly at them all. "Take your runs, soak up the applause because you more than earned it tonight, and I shall see you all next door at the party."

They all straightened before responding with small bows, and Addison sighed as she sank into Mallory's side. "You two are up first," she told Matt and Gabs as she nodded at the curtain. "Have fun."

"Oh, we will," Gabs retorted with a wink as she slipped gracefully through the curtain Matt pulled open for her.

With the stage now clear except for the four of them, a thinner curtain fell in a whisper behind Mallory and Addison, hiding the stage from view so the crew could begin breaking it down and setting up for the next day, and a mischievous smile curled Addison's lips as she wrapped her free hand around Mallory's neck and pulled her down into a searing kiss.

Mallory reached for Addison with her free hand and pulled her closer as she slanted her mouth over Addison's to deepen the kiss, and her heart fluttered into her throat at the way Addison melted into her as their tongues stroked against each other. After the rush and the high of the performance, kissing Addison like this was like adding gasoline to a flame, and Mallory moaned as desire licked its way over her skin and smoldered low in her belly.

"Jesus, Mal," Addison whimpered when Mallory pulled back just enough to flick her tongue over her lips.

The naked desire in Addison's voice set Mallory's pulse racing, and she groaned as she forced herself to restrict her next kiss to a chaste peck. Her stomach clenched at absolute want that was shining in Addison's dark, dark eyes, and she dipped her head to brush a tender promise of a kiss across her lips. "Later, darling."

Addison nodded, but before she could say anything in response, the curtain between them and the theatre fluttered, and Matt and Gabs reappeared looking flushed and happy and so very done for the night.

Gabs smirked when she saw them standing so close together, and arched a brow as she drawled playfully, "Well, I'm glad you two found a way to amuse yourselves while we were out there." She laughed when Addison flipped her off and looped a hand over Matt's arm as she tipped her head toward the curtain. "They're all yours."

Addison nodded and arched a brow at Mallory as she reached for the overlap in the curtains. "You ready, beautiful?"

Mallory brushed a kiss over Addison's cheek as she reached for the opposite opening in the fabric. "Lead the way, darling."

The applause that had begun to soften after Gabs and Matt's departure roared back to life as they stepped into view, and Mallory smiled as she and Addison linked hands to curtsey their thanks. She laughed as they stood back up, and followed Addison's lead as she began waving and gesturing to the crowd in a way that hopefully said *thank you so much* and *you are all incredible*.

The noise didn't dissipate once they had made their way back behind the curtain, and Mallory shook her head as she listened to the cheers and applause that seemed to grow in volume in their absence.

"They're not slowing down." Addison smiled wryly. "We're going to have to go back out there."

"How many more times do you reckon we'll have to do this?" Mallory asked as she parted the curtains and followed Addison back into the spotlight.

"Who knows!" Addison laughed as she began waving to the crowd again. "Just relax and enjoy it, Mal! We did it!"

twenty – six

Mallory finished putting on her earrings and took a step back from her dressing room mirror to give herself one last once-over. She had twisted her hair up into a loose chignon to better show off the halter-strap neckline of her dress, and her make-up was simple and classic, in tones that complimented her fairer coloring and her dress. She nodded at herself as she ran her hands over the dress' sleek, cream-colored pencil skirt that hugged her hips and was too mature, perhaps, to be considered playful, but she thought the billowy black bodice did well to keep the overall effect from being too formal.

A knock on the door drew her attention away from her reflection, and she smiled at the way her heart fluttered into her throat as she hurried to answer it. There was only one person who would be knocking on her dressing room door an hour after the show had ended, and she very much couldn't wait to see her. They had yet to go on a proper date since everything between them changed due to work and life and the universe seeming to conspire against it, but this felt like the beginning of one, and instead of being nervous about messing it up, she was excited to see what the rest of the night held in store.

A half-dozen playful, flirty greetings ricocheted across her mind as she reached for the door, but all of them were instantly forgotten when her eyes landed on Addison. There was rarely a moment when she wasn't aware of her beauty, even in workout clothes and drenched in sweat she was a vision to behold, but she was absolutely breathtaking in a slinky cranberry red slip dress that didn't come close to reaching mid-thigh and stilettos so high that, had she not spent the majority of her days on her toes, she might have been at risk of tipping over. Her make-up was minimal—her flawless, olive-toned complexion accentuated only by a faint, smoky shadow on her eyelids and burgundy lipstick—and her naturally wavy hair was artfully teased into playful disarray.

Mallory licked her lips as she remembered the way Addison had pushed her against the wall of the lift after they had finally left the stage and kissed her so thoroughly that, in the time it took them to rise two floors, she had all but forgotten her own name. Then, like when they had been on stage, the flowers she held had kept her from holding Addison like she wanted to, but she had no such encumbrance now, and her stomach flipped as she imagined threading her fingers through those loose waves and kissing her senseless.

But then Addison shifted just enough to cause the lights to catch on the glint of white gold and diamonds balanced on the point of her collarbone and the silhouette of a ballerina that lay delicately against her sternum, and Mallory was struck breathless as the urge to take Addison to bed was instantly softened and compounded. Desire, warm and molten rippled through her as she imagined laying Addison out and worshipping her so slowly and thoroughly that the sun would break the horizon long before she had finished. She blinked, breaking the spell that had befallen her just enough to drag her eyes away from the delicate dancer, across the angular hollow of Addison's throat and the distinct, heavy beat of her pulse, past plump, soft lips that were parted enticingly, until she was finally staring into Addison's eyes. "God, you're beautiful..."

"You are." Addison shook her head as she stepped closer, and Mallory was struck by the way her hand shook as she lifted it to cradle her jaw. "Oh, Mal..." she whimpered, her voice breaking ever so slightly as she guided their lips together in a kiss so tender that it made Mallory's knees weak.

Mallory reached for Addison, one hand finding its way up into her hair as the other grabbed desperately for her waist, pulling her closer, needing to feel the warmth and the press of her body as she melted into the kiss. Their kisses on stage had been euphoric, the ones in the lift playful and coaxing and fun, but this…oh, this was so much more.

This was a kiss that promised everything.

"Come here," Mallory murmured between kisses she pulled her back into her dressing room. She nuzzled Addison's cheek and brushed the softest of kisses over her lips as she pushed the door shut, and let her hand that had been wrapped in Addison's hair drift down to cradle her cheek as she eased her back against the door. Strong hands wrapped around her waist to pull her closer as they came together again, every kiss so full of emotion that Mallory thought her heart might burst.

Hands began to wander as their kisses became deeper, tongues sliding together as the need to be closer, to give more, to surrender to this magic they'd found overwhelmed them, but three sharp knocks on the door shattered the moment before they could lose themselves in it completely.

"Please tell me you're dressed," Gabs hollered.

Even though she was startled by the interruption, Mallory couldn't help but smile when Addison groaned against her lips, "I'm going to kill her."

Mallory pressed a chaste, apology of a kiss to Addison's lips as she dragged her thumb over the nipple she'd been playing with as they'd kissed one last time before sliding her hand down to rest on Addison's waist, instead. "I'm dressed," she called out.

"And Addy?" Matt asked loudly.

"Of course they're together," Addison grumbled.

"Like you're in any position to talk," Matt sassed.

"How did you even hear that?" Addison demanded more loudly.

Gabs laughed, and two lighter knocks landed on the door. "Let's go, you two. Devereaux is looking to show you off to everyone down there, so touch up your make-up, fix anything else that needs fixing, and let's go."

Mallory sighed and leaned her forehead against Addison's. "I wish we could just skip the party and go home," she confessed, her voice rough with longing as she brushed their lips together.

Addison's breath hitched, and she pulled her closer, holding her tighter as if that alone would keep the world that was literally knocking at the door at bay. "Me too."

"Soon," Mallory murmured against Addison's lips. She kissed her again softly as she nuzzled her cheek, lingering in the moment even though they didn't have the time to do it, letting herself savor the feeling of the angular lines of Addison's body beneath her own and the way her breath landed lightly against her lips.

"Don't make me come in there," Gabs warned, knocking on the door again for emphasis.

Addison groaned and let go of Mallory's hip to bang her right hand on the door in frustration. "I hate you!"

Mallory smiled and ran a light finger over Addison's lips. "Five minutes, okay?" she bartered through the door. "We'll meet you at the lift, and you can escort us down to the party from there."

"Deal," Gabs hollered.

Mallory chuckled at the look of annoyance on Addison's face and kissed away her pout. "The sooner we finish things here, the sooner we can go home."

Addison nodded, looking adorably resigned. "I know. I just…"

"Believe me, I know," Mallory assured her. She shook her head as she resisted the urge to lean in a steal one last kiss, knowing that it would make all of this even more difficult, and sighed as she forced herself to pull away. "Come on, darling," she murmured, half-turning toward the mirror.

Addison smiled as her eyes raked over Mallory's body. "That really is a great dress."

The open adoration in Addison's expression made Mallory's stomach flip, and she swallowed back the lump in her throat as she replied softly, "As is yours."

They shared one last lingering look, and then sighed in tandem as they turned to check their appearances in the mirror. No matter how much they wished otherwise, the world wasn't quite done with them for the day.

"Shall I leave my things here?" Mallory asked as she smoothed a thumb over the edge of her mouth. Thankfully, their lipsticks were of complimentary shades that blended well together and didn't need to be retouched.

"Yeah. We'll pop up and grab it all on our way out." Addison blew out a loud breath and raked a hand through her hair. "You almost ready? I swear I can feel them gearing up to charge through the door..."

Mallory nodded and offered Addison her hand. "Lead the way."

"I really wish we could just go home," Addison muttered under her breath as she turned to the door.

Mallory squeezed her hand in understanding. "Soon, darling."

Addison sighed and nodded. "Yeah."

"God, finally," Matt declared in mock exasperation when they finally made their way to the lifts.

"Wow, you two look incredible." Gabs nodded as she gave them a thorough once-over, a slow, wholly mischievous smirk tugging at her lips. "I mean, this totally isn't the best night to finally indulge your little dressing room fantasy, Addy, but I definitely understand why you'd be tempted because goddamn..."

Mallory stared at the gleaming steel doors of the lift, knowing that any reaction on her part would only egg Gabs on, and filed the information away for a point in the future where she might be able to do something with it.

Addison blushed and shook her head as she pressed her thumb to the lift's call button. "We really need to find you two boyfriends."

Gabs laughed. "Like me getting any would stop me from teasing you."

"I hate you," Addison muttered as she tucked herself into Mallory's side.

Mallory hid her smile by pressing a kiss to Addison's forehead.

"No, you don't." Matt stretched his arms over his head and smirked as they fell to his sides with a slap. "Because we're going to keep you stocked with champagne while Nina drags you around to chat with reporters and donors and stuff, and when you're done with that we're going to run interference while you disappear out the back door."

"I thought this was a cast party?" Mallory asked as the doors began to slide open.

"It is. Mostly." Gabs shrugged as they filed into the car. "Honestly, I think there are only like five or six reporters down there—all old friends of Nina's from when she was the star here—and maybe a few dozen of the company's biggest donors."

"You know," Matt chimed in with a knowing little nod, "to let them feel like they had a part in what happened tonight so they'll keep writing the cheques."

"Isn't the business side of all of this grand?" Mallory drawled.

"Sure, we can go with that," Matt muttered, winking at her as the lift glided to a stop and the doors opened.

It only took a few minutes for them to make their way through the building and into Hamlyn Hall, the iconic steel and glass atrium adjacent to The Royal Opera House, and Matt and Gabs made vague noises that amounted to *be back in a minute* before they disappeared into the crowd.

Mallory smiled as she and Addison hovered at the edge of the hall, taking a moment to absorb the sight that welcomed them. Gabs and Matt had made her think the whole thing would be pure drudgery, but there was upbeat instrumental music playing through the speakers throughout the hall, and the bar was bustling with beautiful people dressed to the nines. Waitstaff wove through the crowd with trays of champagne glasses and hors d'oeuvres, and though they would apparently be working for a bit, it was still very much a party ripe with the air of celebration.

"Are you ready to go mingle?" Addison murmured in her ear, her tone apologetic as she pulled her hand away.

Mallory missed the touch immediately, but she smiled as she nodded so that Addison would know she understood. "As I'll ever be."

They hadn't taken more than a handful of steps before Matt appeared in front of them with a tray full of champagne glasses, and he grinned at them as he broke into a graceful pirouette before dropping to one knee as he held up the tray in offering. "Champagne. As promised."

"Did you mug a poor waiter?" Addison took two glasses and handed one to Mallory.

"Please. Gabs winked at her, and she handed it over. Probably would have given her more than that, too, if she'd asked," he shared with a laugh as he got back to his feet.

Addison shook her head as she scanned the crowd. "Where is she?"

"Playing nice with Nina's guests." He downed a glass of champagne, set the empty on the tray, and picked up another. "So knock those back and grab a fresh one, ladies, because we're up."

Mallory laughed, thinking that he was kidding, but when she saw Addison tilt her head back and empty her glass, she quickly followed suit before trading her empty glass for a fresh one.

"Nicely done, you two." Matt winked at them as he set the tray onto a nearby empty table. "Now, let's go save poor Gabs. Leave no man behind, and all that—right?"

"Exactly," Addison agreed, and smiled when Mallory nodded.

"Did you two invite anyone to this shindig?" Matt asked as they started toward the cluster of people hiding Nina and Gabs.

Addison shook her head. "No point, really." She bumped her

shoulder against Mallory's and smiled. "Everyone I want to celebrate with is already here."

"Yeah, yeah. You two are so cute it's gross, really," Matt teased, throwing a brotherly wink over his shoulder at them. "Mal? How about you? You had people at the show tonight, yeah?"

Mallory nodded and looked around the room. "My parents and Will and Siobhan were at the show. Will and Siobhan said they might stop by, but I don't see them, and my parents begged off. They're getting older, and it's just too late for them." She shrugged. Honestly, it was easier this way. She knew they cared and were supportive, but whether it was because both her parents were particularly "British" or simply a result of her leaving home at nine to become a year-around boarder at the music academy, their relationship was closer to extended family than anything else. "My mother did text me after the show though. She said they both loved the performance and sent their congratulations."

"Of course they did," Addison declared. "We kicked some serious ass out there tonight."

Matt rolled his eyes. "Yeah, whatever," he grumbled as they stopped just outside the perimeter of people surrounding Nina. He cleared his throat to get the artistic director's attention and tipped his head when she looked their way.

"Ah, here they are," Nina declared, her smile warm as the crowd parted to allow the three of them to join Nina and Gabs at the center of it. "You've all had the chance to meet Gabriella, but here are the rest of our stars from tonight. May I introduce Matt Magnusson, our wonderful male lead from the first act"—she motioned to Matt, who bent at the waist in a small bow, and then to Addison and Mallory— "and the two women who performed the, dare I say, most technical pas de deux to ever grace a ballet stage, Addison Leigh and Mallory Collingswood."

Mallory smiled politely as her eyes swept over the group that had turned to stare at them, and then froze when her gaze landed on the familiar face to Nina's right. She had known, of course, that Clara would be coming—they had discussed it earlier, after all—but seeing her standing beside Nina Devereaux, a glass of water in her right hand while her left rested lightly on the small of Nina's back, looking far more comfortable and familiar than she had ever let on definitely threw Mallory for a loop. She covered it well, though, she thought, as she nodded to her conductor. "Hello, Clara."

Clara winced a little as she offered her a playful grin and lifted her glass in a toast. "Mallory."

"Clara is the conductor at the London Symphony Orchestra," Nina explained to the group, "and she graciously allowed me to solicit Ms. Collingswood's participation in *Evolution*." She smiled at Clara. "It's turned out to be quite the collaboration, I'd say."

"Okay…are they, like, a thing?" Addison whispered in her ear as Clara smiled warmly at Nina and expressed her agreement with the statement.

Mallory shrugged. They certainly *looked* like they could be, and there was no denying that they cut quite the pair with Nina in her elegant black gown and Clara in a waistcoat and tails. The extent of Clara's injury was masked by artfully applied makeup that covered the worst of the bruising on her face, and Mallory was willing to bet that the strikingly absent neck brace was against her doctor's orders. Though, she couldn't blame her for it. A neck brace was not the type of accessory one chose to wore to an event like this if they could avoid it.

"No idea," Mallory murmured out of the side of her mouth. But, before she could wonder too much about it, they were surrounded by smiling faces wishing to offer their congratulations.

Word must have spread about their arrival, because soon everyone who wasn't a member of the ballet company seemed to be jockeying for position to speak to them. The surge of well-wishers flowed around the four of them like they were boulders in a stream, surrounding and isolating them from each other in their haste to be seen.

Mallory plastered on her most polite smile as she shook hands and allowed the people seeking her attention to guide their brief exchanges of conversation. It was easiest that way, because she forgot whatever it was they were talking about every time her eyes landed on Addison, who always seemed to be looking her way at that same moment with soft eyes and a wistful smile.

It was torture to be so close, yet so far from the only person she wanted to be spending this evening with, and every lingering look, every small smile exchanged made her heart ache. And every time it happened she became more and more tempted to break off whatever conversation she wasn't paying much attention to, push her way through the crowd separating them, and take Addison into her arms.

"Ms. Collingswood," a new voice spoke up, drawing Mallory's attention from Addison.

Mallory swallowed back a sigh and forced a smile as she turned to the woman. Her accent was distinctly American, she wore a designer gown, and her ears and neck were adorned with a collection of tasteful yet undoubtedly expensive diamond jewelry.

"Elizabeth Sloan," the woman introduced herself, extending her hand. "You were wonderful out there tonight."

"Thank you, ma'am." Mallory dipped her head in a small bow, unable to keep her gaze from drifting to Addison who was, of course, looking right at her. Her stomach fluttered and dipped at the open longing in Addison's expression, and she cleared her throat as she forced herself to look away. "I'm glad you enjoyed the performance."

"I'm a big Halonen fan. I knew the moment my office got the announcement about this special performance that I had to get tickets," Sloan explained.

"So you work here in London, then?" Mallory asked politely as she had to will herself to not look at the warm brown eyes she could feel watching her.

Sloan puffed up a little as she nodded. "I'm the American Ambassador to Britain."

It was clear that Ambassador Sloan was expecting some kind of reaction at the title, but Mallory could only manage an arched brow as she murmured, "Well, I'm glad you were able to take time out of your schedule to come see our show, then."

"Ambassador Sloan!" a booming voice called out cheerfully from the left, and Mallory almost sighed with relief when the woman's attention shifted to see who was calling her.

"Eldon!" Sloan beamed at him. "I'm sorry," she apologized as she turned back to Mallory. "But I need to speak with Lord Batham about something. Again, thank you so much for such a wonderful performance this evening."

"Of course, ma'am," Mallory murmured, shaking the Ambassador's hand one last time.

With the Ambassador gone and no new well-wishers waiting for her attention, Mallory let that sigh of relief she had been holding back slip free as she looked for Addison. It didn't take long for her to spot her not far from where she'd seen her last—lips quirked in a small smile around the rim of a champagne flute and dark eyes smoldering with desire—and she sucked in a sharp breath as that one look sent a delicious shiver down her spine. Her feet began carrying her toward Addison without any conscious effort on her part, and it took every ounce of self-control she possessed to not lean in and capture her lips in a searing kiss when she finally reached her side.

"Champagne?" Matt offered.

Mallory shook her head as she stepped that little bit closer to Addison. It would have served as a decent enough distraction for her hands and mouth, something to occupy both until they were alone, but she knew that the alcohol would make it that much harder for her to not surrender to the ardor coiling low in her belly that she was already barely resisting. Her pulse stumbled over itself at the sound of Addison's breath catching as she ran a finger along the back of her hand, and she swallowed thickly when Addison's hand slipped into her own. She couldn't look away as Addison angled toward her, moving close enough that their linked hands were hidden between them, and the air that was already thick with longing became even more difficult to breathe.

"Jesus Christ, you two. Get a room already," Gabs teased as she appeared at Matt's side with a flute of champagne and a plate of canapés balanced in her right hand.

Mallory's heart skipped a beat when Addison turned into her, flipping Gabs off with the hand that held the nearly-empty flute of champagne, and held her breath as a light, barely-there kiss that left her skin tingling was dragged from the corner of her mouth to her ear. She grabbed for Addison's hip with her free hand as a ragged breath cascaded over her ear, and her eyes fluttered shut as Addison's husked, "Take me home, Mal," short-circuited her brain.

Mallory nodded as she blinked her eyes open, and then it sounded like someone else was asking with her voice, "Are we done here?"

"You're so done," Matt chuckled. "Get out of here."

Mallory squeezed Addison's hand and ducked her head to whisper against her ear, "Lead the way, darling."

twenty – seven

"Finally," Addison breathed when the car stopped in front of Mallory's building.

Mallory nodded. The short, thirteen-minute ride from the theatre had been pure agony, the air between them so charged with anticipation that they hadn't dared to even look at each other, knowing that it would only take one look to shatter the tenuous hold they had on their self-control, and it was all she could do to not vault from the car now that it had stopped. "Exactly," she agreed as she reached for her door, not willing to waste any more time by entertaining Noah's gallantry.

Noah shot her a playful glare over the roof of the car as he opened the rear driver's side door and offered Addison his hand to help her out, and then hustled to the boot to help them retrieve their things. He handed Addison one of the bouquets and asked in a concerned, fatherly tone, "Everything okay?" as he held out the shoulder strap of her bag for her to slip her arm through it.

Mallory wasn't surprised that he picked up on the tension that simmered between them—considering they were usually touching in some way, even if it was just holding hands, the distance they had kept from each other had been impossible to miss—but she was glad, at least, that he didn't seem to understand it.

Addison huffed a quiet laugh and shook her head. "Everything's perfect," she assured him as she moved out of the way so Mallory could collect her things.

"Just tired," Mallory lied as she slipped the strap of her kit bag over her shoulder. Her violin had ridden in the back with them, as she would never dream of transporting it in a crumple-zone. She motioned toward the bouquet Noah was reaching for, and added, "Take that one home with you. Surprise your wife with them when she returns from her trip."

"Oh, I couldn't—"

"You absolutely can," Mallory interrupted as Addison's hand slid down her forearm to tangle their fingers together. Her heart leapt at the way Addison tugged her away from the car, and she shook her head to ward off his next protest as she allowed herself to be pulled toward the door to the building. "I insist."

Noah looked between them—Addison none-too-subtly dragging Mallory toward the front door with Mallory following willingly even as she tried to not bring an abrupt end to their conversation—and a slow smile of understanding lit his face as he nodded. "Right. Cheers, Miss."

"Ta, Noah," Mallory replied with a grin as she heard Addison enter the code for the main door. "I'll ask for you next time I hire the service?"

"I look forward to it, Miss," he assured her with a chivalrous tip of his hat as he slammed the lid to the boot shut.

Mallory barely avoided tripping over the threshold as Addison tugged her inside, and she laughed softly as she pulled her close to claim her lips in a slow, deep kiss that left them both flushed and breathless by the time they eventually broke apart. "It was all I could do to not kiss you like that in the car."

"God, I know," Addison murmured, pressing as close as the massive bouquet in her arms allowed as she kissed Mallory again.

Mallory sighed into the kiss and cupped Addison's jaw in her free hand to keep it from becoming too much. After a night of starts and stops, intrusions and obligations, she wanted more, and the promise of complete, uninterrupted privacy waited for them at the top of the stairs. "Come on, darling," she whispered against Addison's lips as she began slowly backing toward the stairs. She smiled at the way Addison huffed in protest even as she followed, and squeezed her hand. "I know."

The encumbrance of bags and instruments and that bloody bouquet was enough to put a damper on the desire pulsing between them long enough for them to make it up the two flights from the street to her front door, and Mallory sighed with relief when she shoved it open. "Finally," she muttered, echoing Addison's sentiment from the car earlier.

Addison just hummed in agreement as she dropped her bag and the bouquet on the floor and turned to grab the lapels of Mallory's jacket and pull her into a scorching kiss. Mallory barely had the self-awareness to set her violin on the apothecary's table in the entryway before Addison pushed her back against the wall beside the front door, though she let her kit bag slip carelessly from her shoulder as she grabbed Addison's hips and urged her closer, delighting in the soft sounds of pleasure that Addison made as they kissed and the way she arched against her.

Coats were shed between increasingly desperate kisses and left in forgotten puddles in the entryway as Mallory let the press of Addison's lips and the touch of a hand on her side steer her backwards down the hall toward the bedroom as they continued trading deep, hungry kisses that made her head spin. Trusting Addison to lead, she let her hands wander over soft fabric and subtle curves, coaxing soft sighs and moans and whimpers from Addison's lips.

The light from the hall and the soft glow of the city beyond the window were more than enough to guide them to the bed, and Mallory shivered when Addison pulled her to a stop beside it. Their next kiss was so slow and full of longing that it made Mallory's knees weak, and she could only nod when nimble fingers toyed with the single clasp at the back of her neck as Addison whispered, "Please?" against her lips.

"I've been wanting to do this all night," Addison confessed in a breathy whisper as she pinched the clasp open. She guided the straps slowly over Mallory's shoulders before letting them fall, and a look of pure adoration softened her expression as she cradled Mallory's breasts in her hands.

Mallory gasped as she felt the swipe of Addison's thumbs over her nipples tug between her legs, and her back curved to leave room for those wonderful, wonderful hands between them as she took Addison's face in her own and pulled her into a searing kiss.

"You are so beautiful," Addison breathed, squeezing Mallory's breasts as she dragged her thumbs over her nipples.

"Addy..." Mallory's voice trailed off into a groan as Addison's fingers closed around her nipples.

"I want you," Addison moaned against Mallory's lips as her fingers relaxed, leaving Mallory's nipples throbbing. "Please let me have you?"

The tenderness in Addison's plea and the fact that she even thought to ask for permission sent a pleasant warmth through Mallory's chest, and she nodded as she captured Addison's lips in a slow, deep kiss. Addison's hold on her breasts became firmer as she used that hold to turn her until the backs of her thighs hit the side of the bed, and her hands fell to Addison's hips, holding her close as Addison's lips began burning a delicious trail across her cheek.

She turned her head as Addison's mouth moved lower, dragging a wet, breathy kiss over the hinge of her jaw, and her eyes fluttered shut at the feeling of dull teeth nipping at her pulse point. Her hold on Addison's hips tightened as she continued to tease the sensitive spot, long fingers tweaking and rolling her nipples in exquisite harmony with every kiss and suck and bite, leaving her a gasping, trembling mess. "Please, Addy..."

Addison blew out a ragged breath and dragged the tip of her nose over the spot she'd been teasing, and blinked as if trying to stir herself from a fog as she lifted her head to capture Mallory's lips in a searing kiss.

"Please," Mallory repeated, taking Addison right hand from her breast and pulling it around her back to the lone zipper holding her dress in place.

"Oh, Mal," Addison murmured as her fingers pinched the small tab.

Mallory ran her hand along the length of Addison's arm as the zipper began to loosen, and tangled her fingers in Addison's hair as their lips came together once more. Their tongues slid sensuously around each other as the Addison tugged the zipper slowly lower, and a light shiver traveled up her spine when the dress finally fell to the floor, and cool air washed over her skin. The skirt of her dress had been so tight that only the flimsiest of thongs wouldn't show beneath it, and she groaned at the feeling of Addison's hand caressing her ass. Her stomach clenched when the light touches turned into a firm hold drawing their hips together as Addison's mouth slanted over her own, and she dragged her fingers from Addison's hair to the zipper nestled between her shoulder blades.

A breathy whimper of encouragement spurred her onward, and she flicked her tongue over Addison's lips as she eased the thin straps from her shoulders. Addison fell into her arms before the dress had even hit the floor, and quiet moans tumbled against parted lips at the first heavenly feeling of skin against skin. Desire blazed between them as the last of their clothes were pushed to the floor, and Mallory's breath caught in her throat when a firm hand on her hip pressed her back onto the bed.

Her right hand found Addison's side as they moved, holding her close, asking her with a touch for what she needed. She sighed at the feeling of Addison's body pressing her back into the mattress as one long, long leg slid between her own, and her hand on Addison's side drifted lower to grab and squeeze and pull her closer. The press of Addison's thigh against her clit was exquisite, and she delighted in the moan that rumbled in the back of Addison's throat when she arched against her.

"God, Mal," Addison husked as she ground their hips together, and a small, pleased smile curled her lips at the way it made Mallory whimper. "So beautiful…"

"You are," Mallory whispered. She wrapped her free hand around the back of Addison's neck and guided their lips back together as she rocked her hips to meet Addison's next slow grind.

They fell into a rhythm that was theirs alone as they arched against each other, trading slow, deep kisses that had them gasping against each other's mouths as their bodies sought the closeness their souls desired. They came together again and again and again, hips rolling, chests arching, thighs flexing in a simple, sensual dance that was the most beautiful thing Mallory had ever experienced, and the absolute *rightness* of the moment sent her heart fluttering into her throat.

Addison seemed to feel it too, because her voice trembled ever so slightly as she murmured, "Look at me," against her lips.

Mallory blinked with the effort it to comply, and then her breath caught when their gazes locked and she saw the absolute love shining in Addison's eyes. "Oh…"

Addison smiled and brushed a kiss over her lips. "That's it, sweetie."

"Oh, Addy…" Mallory ran her hand through Addison's hair as they continued to move together, the roll of their hips becoming slower and more deliberate as they stared into the other's soul. Never in her life had Mallory experienced such a powerful connection with a lover, and as she stared into dark, fathomless eyes that seemed to glow with the heat of a hundred suns, she knew it was because this was the soul that was meant for her.

She stared into Addison's eyes, utterly transfixed as she rocked against her, mouth open, breath coming hard and fast and ragged as she rode the wave of ecstasy building inside her, and bit her lip as she struggled to stay her own release long enough that they could fall together.

"Mal…" Addison pressed a hard kiss to her lips. "Please…with me…"

Mallory clung to Addison even tighter as their hips pressed together in a continuous grind, and groaned when it became too much to resist any longer. She whimpered as the universe tilted and she tumbled into ecstasy, her broken cry of pleasure echoed by Addison as she trembled against her with release.

She cradled Addison in her arms as their heartbeats slowed, and when the haze of orgasm finally began to fade, twisted her hips to roll them over. A gentle, awed smile curled her lips as she stared down into Addison's eyes, and she sighed as she dipped her head to capture her lips in a tender kiss. "That was…" her voice trailed off as she struggled to find even a single word that could possibly come close to describing what they had just shared.

Addison's eyes softened with her smile as she ran a light hand over Mallory's jaw. "Perfect. It was absolutely perfect."

Mallory's eyelids fluttered as she leaned into the touch, and she nodded as she brushed an adoring kiss over Addison's lips. "It was." She kissed her again. "You are," she whispered as she pressed her lips to the corner of Addison's mouth. "So perfect," she breathed against Addison's cheek. She sealed the words with another kiss before she moved lower, taking her time to taste and savor and worship, delighting in Addison's soft sighs and quiet moans, reveling in the knowledge that she was the one coaxing such incredible sounds from her perfect lips.

She cupped Addison's breasts as she teased her nipples to tight points with light licks and heavy sucks that had Addison writhing beneath her. Long before she was ready to move on, a gentle hand against her head, shifting hips, and gasped pleas urged her onward, and she moaned softly as she shifted to slide her other leg between Addison's as she dragged her lips over twitching abdominals that flexed beneath the touch, and used her knees to guide Addison's legs open as she nipped at the sharp point of Addison's hipbone.

"So beautiful," she murmured as she dragged the tip of her nose along the line where Addison's leg and torso met, and she couldn't contain the whimper that escaped her when soft curls brushed against her cheek.

"Please, Mal," Addison moaned, her hips lifting pleadingly as Mallory settled between her legs.

Mallory wrapped her arms around Addison's thighs and tugged her open wider, and her heart fluttered into her throat as she dipped her head to breathe, "Oh Addy…" against sensitive nerves before laying a soft, reverent kiss to the spot. Her eyes rolled back in her head at the sound of Addison crying out in pleasure as she arched against her mouth, and she nuzzled closer as she sought to find out what other heavenly sounds she might be able to coax from her lips.

twenty-eight

Mallory came awake slowly, the light flooding her bedroom coaxing her from sleep even as she snuggled closer to Addison. They had traded places while they'd slept, so that instead of holding Addison she was curled into her side, her head pillowed on the plane of Addison's chest with her right arm thrown over her waist and their legs tangled together. It shouldn't have been nearly as comfortable sleeping position as it was, and she smiled at the sound of Addison's strong, steady heartbeat beneath her ear. Happiness bloomed in her chest as memories from the night before flashed across her mind, and she sighed as she brushed a kiss over the subtle swell of her breast.

"That feels nice," Addison whispered.

Mallory hummed as she curled her hand around Addison's waist and pressed a lingering kiss to her breast. It felt pretty incredible to her, too. "I'm sorry, darling. I didn't mean to wake you."

"You didn't. I was dozing…" Addison stretched her legs beneath the sheet that was puddled near their waists. "The light woke me up," she elaborated as she relaxed. "Otherwise I think I could have slept all day."

Mallory's eyelids fluttered at the feeling of Addison's fingers combing through her hair, and she caressed Addison's side as murmured, "Do you want me to close the curtains?"

"No." Addison groaned and arched her back so her breast was lifted in front of Mallory's mouth. "I'll sleep later. Please, continue what you were doing."

The smokiness of Addison's voice sent a pleasant shiver down Mallory's spine, and she pushed herself up onto her left forearm to give herself a better angle nuzzle Addison's breast as she asked playfully, "This?"

The hand in her hair tightened for the briefest of moments as Addison's back bowed just that little bit further, and then relaxed as she sank back into the bed. "Oh, yes..." she purred, her left leg sliding out invitingly as her arm fell at an angle off to her side, leaving herself completely open to Mallory's touch.

Mallory's pulse tripped over itself at the sight of Addison's submission, and she dipped her head to drag the tip of her tongue over Addison's nipple. Her right hand slid from Addison's hip to her left breast as she fluttered her tongue against the hardening nub, and her eyes fluttered shut at the way Addison whimpered her name when she sucked the nipple between her lips. The sounds of Addison's pleasure were as much of a turn-on for her as the physical evidence of it, and Mallory eagerly lost herself in both as she sucked and nipped and pinched and rolled Addison's nipples, her mouth and hands switching back and forth with the ebb and flow of Addison's gasps and moans until an insistent hand urged her to move on.

She framed Addison's ribs with her hands as she began laying a trail of wet, reverent kisses along the defined line of her abdominals, loving the way they flexed and twitched beneath her lips. Her hands found Addison's waist as she dragged her teeth over a protruding hipbone, and she couldn't contain the soft moan that tumbled from her lips when she finally eased between her thighs.

"God, you're beautiful," she murmured as she lowered her mouth to slick, swollen folds, and her eyes fluttered shut at the breathy, ragged cry that spilled from Addison's lips when she pressed a lingering kiss to her clit.

She wrapped her arms around Addison's legs as she settled onto her stomach and began coaxing the sensitive bundle from hiding with the tip of her tongue, bathing it with light licks and slow swirls to match the roll of Addison's hips. Her touch became firmer as the speed and the force of Addison's movement increased, kissing and licking everywhere Addison's body asked her to, and her stomach clenched at the feeling of Addison's hands curling around her own as she pressed her tongue inside her.

"Please…" Addison moaned, her back bowing off the mattress as she strained against Mallory's mouth, muscles clenching, trying to draw her deeper.

Mallory groaned as she pulled herself closer, using her upper arms to support Addison's ass, holding her off the bed as she and thrust into her again and again and again until Addison's hips stilled and she came with a shuddering moan that made Mallory's eyes roll back in her head.

Mallory pulled back just enough to ease Addison through her release with soft licks and tender kisses, and when Addison went lax in her arms, spent and boneless, she pressed a reverent kiss between her legs before lowering her back to the bed. She dragged the back of her hand over her mouth as she shifted her weight to her knees and smiled at the utterly blissed-out look on Addison's face as she leaned in to capture her lips in a slow, deep kiss.

"Please wake me up like that every day for the rest of my life," Addison murmured as she pressed a hand against the small of Mallory's back and urged her closer.

Mallory moaned at the feeling of warm, slick arousal against her skin as her hips settled between Addison's thighs, and she nuzzled Addison's cheek as she confessed, "I would love nothing more."

Addison's eyes crinkled with happiness as she curled a hand around Mallory's neck and guided their lips together. "Good."

The kiss started tender and sweet but quickly became something much more heated and serious, and Mallory sighed as she allowed the hand on her neck and the legs hooked around her hips to guide her over onto her back.

"I want you," Addison whispered against her lips as she eased her knees between Mallory's thighs and guided them open wider.

Mallory groaned and lifted her chin to capture Addison's lips in a searing kiss as a light hand swooped down her side and over her hip. "I'm all yours, darling," she breathed as nimble fingers dipped between her legs.

Addison's eyes softened with her smile as she brushed a kiss over Mallory's lips. "Oh, Mal…"

Mallory gasped as Addison's fingers began gliding in soft circles over her clit and hooked her knees around her hips. Her heart felt like it was trying to fly out of her chest as Addison's nipples dragged over her own, and she whimpered softly when fingers dipped lower, pushing lightly as a playful tongue flicked over her lips. "Please, Addy."

"What do you need, sweetie?"

Mallory grabbed Addison's wrist beside her head as she used her legs to pull her closer as she rolled her hips pleadingly. "You."

"You have me." Addison brushed their lips together. "You have me," she repeated as she kissed her again.

A broken sigh tumbled from Mallory's lips as Addison's fingers eased inside her, and she relaxed her hold on Addison's hips as she opened herself to her touch, wanting to take her as deep as she possibly could. She stroked Addison's side with her free hand as they fell into an easy rhythm, letting it drift down to the top of her ass with every thrust and higher along her ribs with every retreat, and smiled into their kiss as Addison's touch became stronger, more demanding until she abandoned her slow caress to hold on to Addison's hip as the fire in her belly began to spread.

"That's it, beautiful," Addison encouraged huskily, nuzzling Mallory's cheek.

Mallory to Addison as the fingers inside her curled and light flashed behind her eyes, and she gasped Addison's name as she came, her orgasm washing over her in waves as Addison's stroke gentled and slowed to ease her through the length of her release.

"Forget what I said earlier," Addison murmured against Mallory's lips when she finally relaxed beneath her. "I want to wake you up like this every day."

Mallory laughed and looped her arms around Addison's neck to pull her down on top of her. "Whatever you want, darling," she breathed as she lifted her chin to capture Addison's lips in a deep, searing kiss.

twenty-nine

After a week of butter-soft leather and warmth and *quiet*, the tube was a rather jarring experience, but Mallory was almost glad for it. Part of her wished that Noah had been waiting at the curb to drive her to the Barbican just so she would be able to avoid the cold and the noise and the crush of people on the tube, but at least this way she had something to focus on other than how much she wished the world hadn't been waiting to force Addison from her arms.

She stared at her reflection in the window behind the person seated opposite her on her train to the Barbican station, and she shook her head at the sadness she could see in her expression. Knowing that she was being ridiculous did little to ease the ache that had settled in her chest when, with one last lingering kiss and a promise from Mallory that she would come to Addison's apartment that night after her concert, Addison slipped out the door to head into Covent Garden for class. It seemed cruel, really, to have to put those feelings of happiness and security and affection on hold to deal with real-world obligations, but as her phone buzzed with an incoming text, she was glad, at least, that she wasn't alone in her ridiculousness.

I miss you.

Mallory smiled at the way her heart fluttered into her throat when she saw the message, and she ducked her head further to try to keep it somewhat hidden from any curious eyes around her as she replied, *I miss you too, darling. I take it your class over?*

Little ellipses in a gray bubble appeared immediately. *Yep. Am on my way down to Eve for a massage now. Oh! And I thought you'd find this interesting—rumor has it that Nina never came in today.*

Mallory arched a brow. *Very interesting. Did Matt or Gabs say anything about what happened at the party after we left?* She hit send as she felt the train began to slow, and looked up to spot the signage in the tile beyond the window that identified her stop.

She slipped the phone into her coat pocket as she began gathering her things—besides her violin and briefcase, she had also packed her kit bag with things for the next day since she would be staying at Addison's—and grabbed the bar beside her seat as she braced for the train to stop. Her phone buzzed with another alert as she was exiting the train, but she didn't dare try to look at it until she was aboveground and had enough room about her to not have to worry about accidentally hitting anyone with her bags.

Lots and lots of drinking. Mallory chuckled when she saw Addison's response to her question. *And apparently, your conductor and Nina left at the same time. They think. Like I said: lots and lots of drinking. It's hangover city around here today.*

Mallory glanced up at the crossing signal and then turned her attention back to her phone as she stopped at the corner to wait. Honestly, from the way they were acting around each other during the little bit of time she saw them together at the party, she wasn't all that surprised. Nina and Clara being a thing, as Addison had put it, wouldn't be nearly the scandal it would have been even fifteen years ago, but it just didn't seem Nina's style to do something so openly when investors and reporters were around. *Did they, now?*

The signal chirped that it was safe to cross, and she fisted her phone in her pocket to keep her hand warm as she let the wave of people around her carry her across the street and toward the main entrance of the Barbican. Her phone buzzed again just as she stepped inside, and she nodded hello to the security guard as she pulled it from her pocket.

She began making her way toward her office on autopilot as she reopened her message thread with Addison. *M & G both admit they were pretty wasted, but they're not the only ones whispering about it, so I think so, yeah. Anyway, enough about them. I'm going to have to get on Eve's table soon…do I need to worry about her commenting on any unusual scratches or bruises? ;)*

Mallory pursed her lips as she pressed her thumb to the call button for the lift. Not all of their encounters had been as gentle as their first, but she also didn't recall seeing any marks on Addison's body when they had lingered in the shower that morning. Granted, she had been more focused on touching than looking, but she didn't think any of the little bites she had rained on Addison's neck and shoulder as she took her against the wall had been rough enough to mark. *I think you're safe, darling.*

She stepped into the elevator and was glad she was alone in the car when Addison's reply came through because she couldn't keep from laughing when she read, *Shame. I was hoping for an excuse to brag about how amazing you are.*

"You're the one who is amazing," Mallory murmured as she typed those exact words. "I don't know what I did to deserve you," she added to herself under her breath as she hit send, "but I don't ever want to lose you."

Addison's response was quick. *Guess we're just gonna have to agree to disagree. ;)* There was a pause, and then a new message appeared just as the lift stopped at her floor. *I wish I could kiss you right now.*

Mallory smiled as a gentle warmth bloomed in her chest. *Me too.*

"Now that's a smile," Will teased.

Mallory glanced up through the doors that were still sliding open and sighed. "Sod off," she muttered as she flipped him off.

He laughed as he used his foot to push himself off the wall he'd been leaning against. "What?"

She shook her head as a new message from Addison appeared on her screen. *I wish we could keep going with this, but Eve's ready for me and I don't want to keep her waiting. Come over as soon as you're done there. I'll leave the door unlocked so you can just come in.*

"Just…" Mallory held up a different finger to tell him to give her a minute and brushed past him toward her office as she tapped out a quick reply so Addison would hopefully see it before her massage. *I'll be there as soon as I possibly can, darling. I promise.*

She smiled at the heart emoji she got in response not two seconds after her text went through, and took a deep breath as she forced herself to close out the app and put her phone away. She let the breath go slowly as she turned toward Will, who hovered a couple meters away to give her some privacy, and arched a brow as she drawled, "Do I want to know why you were laying in wait to ambush me?"

He laughed and shook his head as he closed the distance between them and pulled her into a fierce hug. "You were fucking brilliant last night, Mal. I'm so proud of you." He squeezed her tighter and then sighed as he relaxed his hold and took a step back. "I'm sorry we didn't stay for the party, but it was late, and Siobhan was completely knackered, and—"

"It's fine," Mallory interrupted as she pulled her keys from her bag and opened her office door. "You didn't miss anything, really. Nina had us playing nice to their donors, and then Addy and I buggered out of there as soon as we could," she said as she shoved the door open.

"We noticed," a new voice replied, and Mallory shook her head as she turned to see Clara striding down the corridor in her trademark black suit with a folded newspaper clutched in her right hand. The bruises on her face were more pronounced than they'd been the night before, but it was clear that she was intending to conduct their performance that evening.

"What are you doing here? You should be at home recuperating." Mallory shot back as she made her way into her office, knowing the two of them would follow.

"You know I don't sit still well. I'll just have to reign in my movements a little, but I can stand up there and wave my arms around a bit."

Mallory nodded as she set her things on her desk. Clara was notorious for always having at least a half-dozen projects going at any given time so that she wasn't bored. "Still…" She ran her hands through her hair as she turned toward her friends. The mischievous slant of Clara's smile made her nervous, and she had a feeling it had something to do with her and Addison leaving the party early. "Should we be offended that we don't warrant the tails you were wearing last night?" she asked, hoping to change the subject.

Will dropped into one of the four small armchairs that made up a cozy sitting area at the front of her office and crossed his legs. "You have to admit the tails were pretty awesome."

"Cheers, William," Clara drawled. "At least one of you has taste."

"I never said the tails weren't handsome," Mallory pointed out. "I was simply—"

"Avoiding commenting on the fact that you and Addison hightailed it out of Hamlyn as soon as you were done sucking up to Nina's donors?" Clara interrupted.

Mallory arched a brow at Clara as she leaned back against her desk. "Yes, well, according to Addison, we weren't the only ones people noticed leaving together last night, so…"

Clara's smirk softened into a sad smile, and Mallory instantly regretted snapping at her. "Yeah," she muttered as she unfolded the newspaper she was holding. "That's…I don't know. Complicated, I guess. You know, still."

Mallory sighed. "I'm sorry, Clara." If they had been alone, she might have asked her about what had happened because, according to Addison, the ballet was awash with gossip about Nina and Clara, but she knew Clara wouldn't want to talk about it in front of Will. "I shouldn't have lost my temper like that."

"I'm sorry, too." Clara nodded. "I actually didn't come up here to give you a hard time, though. We didn't get a chance to really talk last night, and I wanted to congratulate you on your performance. You and Addison were incredible, Mal. Truly amazing. I knew Nina could work miracles, but watching you two together..." She shook her head as her voice trailed off, and offered Mallory the paper. "Have you seen the reviews?"

"No. We honestly forgot about them," Mallory confessed as she took the paper from Clara.

Will snorted. "I bet you did, mate."

Mallory rolled her eyes at him, but quickly forgot to be annoyed when she saw the picture of her and Addison beneath the *Times'* Arts banner that filled the entire space above the fold. The shot was of one of their many spins, where Addison was pressed against her back, one hand on her hip and the other on her elbow, their heads so close that it looked like their cheeks were touching as they moved. It wasn't the flashiest shot the photographer could have gotten, but it captured the emotion of the ballet perfectly, and she took a deep breath as she unfurled the paper to see the article that accompanied the photograph. "Oh, wow..." she breathed as she saw Will jump to his feet in her periphery.

They knew they had crushed the performance, of course, but knowing something was different from seeing it recognized in print.

"The future of ballet is now. Leigh and Collingswood are flawless in the premiere of Nina Devereaux's latest original masterpiece," Will read aloud over her shoulder. He gave her side a squeeze. "I couldn't agree more, Mal."

"Me too." Clara smiled, the lingering hint of sadness in her eyes fading as she pulled Mallory into a hug. "You two are beautiful together," she whispered. "I'm so happy for you."

"Thank you," Mallory murmured as she wrapped her arms around Clara's waist. She held her close and added quietly against her ear, "Addison mentioned that Nina hasn't been to the theatre today. I understand that things between you two are complicated, but the kids over there are talking about it and..."

Clara sighed. "I'll check on her."

"Let me know if there's anything I can do?" Mallory asked as they separated.

"I will." Clara pulled her phone from the inner pocket of her blazer. She gave it a flick to wake up the screen, and pursed her lips as she nodded slowly to herself. "Right. I'm going to head down to my office. Mal, pre-show meeting in thirty?"

"I'll be there," Mallory promised.

"I'll let Max know, as well." Clara slipped her phone back into her pocket as she turned to leave. "Be good, you lot," she called over her shoulder as she walked out the door.

"Who? Us?" Will called after her. "Never!" He grinned at the sound of Clara's laughter from the corridor and blew out a loud breath as he turned to Mallory. He tilted his head toward the door and asked in a low voice that wouldn't carry beyond the room, "Everything okay there?"

Mallory shrugged and made her way over to the sitting area. She still had to change into her blacks, but she could do that right before heading down to Clara's office. "No idea," she admitted as she lowered herself into one of the chairs.

"Well, that sucks," Will grumbled as he took the chair across from her. He raked his hands through his hair and then let them fall to his lap with a slap. "You and Addy really bailed early on the party last night, huh?"

Mallory sank back in her chair and nodded. "Yeah."

"That's it? That's all you're going to say?" Will demanded with a grin.

Mallory laughed. "You asked if we left the party early and I said yes. What else is there?"

He rolled his eyes. "Did you go home together?"

"We did." Mallory smirked.

"What is this? Twenty bloody questions?" He threw his hands in the air. "And?"

"It was…" Her voice trailed off into a sigh, and she shook her head as she murmured, "Perfect. It was perfect."

"Yeah?" Will arched a brow and smiled.

"Yeah."

"Good." He stretched his leg out to give her foot an affectionate kick. "So when are you seeing her again?"

"Tonight, actually. I'm going to head over to her place after the concert."

He laughed. "Can't get enough of her, eh?"

Mallory lifted her right shoulder in a small shrug. "I could spend every minute of every day with her, and it still wouldn't be enough. She's…" She took a deep breath and let it go slowly as the truth she had been avoiding admitting to herself made her heart beat slow and heavy in her chest. "She's everything, Will."

Will nudged her foot again and smiled. "Yeah?"

A small smile curled Mallory's lips as she nodded. "Yeah."

thirty

"Go ahead and get that." Addison tilted her head toward the foyer where Mallory's mobile was ringing inside her briefcase as she grabbed Mallory's breakfast plate and stacked it atop her own. "I'll clean up."

Even though Mallory could tell from the ringtone that it was Clara calling, she still asked, "Are you sure? I can always call her back later."

"Very sure." Addison smiled and pushed herself to her feet. She waggled her eyebrows as she leaned in to steal a quick kiss, and murmured, "I have plans for you later," as she pulled away.

Mallory laughed. "Again, darling? You're insatiable."

"You know it." Addison winked. "But seriously. I got this. Go see what's so important that Clara needs to call you six hours before your performance."

Mallory arched a brow in surprise as she got to her feet. "How do you know it's Clara?" she asked as she started toward the foyer at a pace somewhere between a walk and a jog to try to catch the call before it went to voicemail.

"Because it's Beethoven's Ninth," Addison called after her, and Mallory swore she could hear the smile in her voice. "I know I'm just a dancer, but give me a little credit here, huh?"

"All the credit in the world, darling," Mallory replied loudly as she dug in her bag for her phone. It had stopped ringing, of course, the moment she grabbed it, but she pressed her thumb to Clara's name on the screen as she made her way back through the living room. She might not be able to help with the breakfast dishes while on the phone, but she figured she could at least enjoy the sight of Addison bopping about the kitchen with an epic case of bed-head in a pair of tie-dyed patterned leggings and the hoodie she had given her for Christmas. "Sorry, I just missed your call," she said when Clara answered on the second ring. "The phone stopped ringing the moment I got to my bag."

"Please, don't worry about it. I'm not interrupting anything, am I?"

Mallory smiled and shook her head as she reclaimed her spot at the table. "We just finished breakfast. If there was anything to interrupt, I wouldn't be speaking to you right now," she added, smiling at the way Addison laughed at the comment.

"Fair enough," Clara chuckled.

Mallory relaxed back in her chair and crossed her legs as she watched Addison begin dancing lightly in place at the sink, shoulders and hips swaying elegantly to the melody that was playing in her head. "So what's up?"

Clara sighed. *"Nothing."*

Mallory frowned. That sigh certainly didn't sound like nothing. "What's wrong, Clara?" She shook her head when Addison turned to shoot her a curious look. "Did something happen? Do I need to come to the Centre early today?"

"No. No. It's nothing like that," Clara replied quickly. *"I was actually…god, this was a bad idea. I'm sorry. I shouldn't have bothered you."*

Mallory shrugged at Addison, who was still watching her for some sign of what was going on, and pursed her lips as she tried to figure out what would have prompted Clara's call. If everything at the LSO was fine, that left… "I know you said you couldn't get ahold of Nina before the concert last night. I'm guessing you spoke to her after?"

If she weren't so worried about Clara, she would have laughed at the way Addison's eyes widened in surprise at the mention of her boss.

"Yeah."

Mallory closed her eyes and pinched the bridge of her nose as she asked gently, "What happened?"

Instead of answering, Clara asked, *"How do you and Addison do it?"*

"How do Addison and I do what?"

"I don't know," Clara muttered, sounding more frustrated than Mallory could ever recall hearing her. *"Everything? Is the age-difference thing a problem for you two? Do the conflicting schedules really make things impossible?"*

Mallory nodded as she began to understand what was going on. "Things are still complicated, huh?"

Clara huffed a hollow laugh. *"Yeah."*

Mallory let her hand fall to her lap as she blinked her eyes open to look at Addison, who had given up on the dishes and was leaning against the sink watching her with an adorably confused and worried look on her face.

She offered her a small, reassuring smile as she told Clara, "Surprisingly enough, the age thing hasn't been a problem." Affection bloomed in her chest at the way Addison gave her a look that clearly said she thought the very idea of their age-difference being an issue was ridiculous. She knew, of course, that it could have been one—hell, it should have been; fifteen years was nothing to scoff at—but she was so, so glad that it wasn't. "As for time…we've just kind of been stealing it where we can. We've been talking about how to handle our schedules when we're no longer working together. We know it won't be easy, but we're determined to do it." It helped that Mallory was determined not to repeat past mistakes on this point, too. When Clara didn't respond, she asked carefully, "Did something happen?"

"Yes. No. I mean…" Clara sighed. *"Everything is the same as it's always been. It's all chemistry and fear, and which one wins with her depends on the moment. God, she really just…"*

"Drives you crazy?"

"Like it's her bloody calling in life," Clara grumbled. *"And yet we both keep coming back for more, so…"* She groaned softly, and Mallory had no

problem imagining the way she was undoubtedly tugging at her hair and shaking her head in frustration.

"Do you want me to chase her down and knock some sense into her?" Mallory smiled at the way Clara chuckled softly at the suggestion.

"While I would love to see that, I don't think that's going to do me any favors. This helped, though. I just needed to vent, I think. Though if your girlfriend could get the rest of her buddies to stop gossiping about us over there in CG, that might help." Clara sighed. *"I swear, it seems like she wants this, but she's just…"*

"I'll talk to Addy about it. Can't make any promises that she'll succeed, but…"

"Anything is better than nothing. Thank you. And I'm sorry for interrupting your time together."

"Any time, darling," Mallory murmured. "Meeting in your office at four?"

"Yep. I'll see you then. Enjoy the rest of your day, and please apologize to Addison for me for this."

"It's not necessary, but I will," Mallory assured her. "I'll see you at four. Let me know if you want me to bring a bottle of tequila."

"God, I wish," Clara snorted. *"Maybe once I've recovered from this stupid car accident. I'll see you later, Mal."*

Mallory shook her head at the quiet click of the call disconnecting, and sighed as she set the phone onto the table. "Your boss is driving Clara insane," she shared as she got to her feet and started for the kitchen.

"My boss is your boss too for a few more months," Addison pointed out, "and she drives everyone insane. That's kinda her thing." She grinned when Mallory laughed and nodded. "But what did she do this time?"

Mallory shrugged and wrapped her arms around Addison's waist. "It kind of sounded like something might have happened between her and Clara, and then she freaked out about it." She pressed her lips to Addison's temple and added, "Again."

"That's not good." Addison looped her arms around Mallory's

neck. "So what are you going to ask me about?"

"Clara was wondering if you could try to put a lid on the speculation about them with your colleagues. The gossip isn't going to help Nina's reaction with all this."

"Totally. I mean, I can try, but realistically..."

"Believe me, darling, I know," Mallory sighed.

"I'll call Gabs and Matt later after you leave for work and see if we can't come up with some kind of plan for tomorrow."

"You're the best," Mallory murmured as she hugged Addison tighter. "Thank you."

"I am," Addison hummed as she nuzzled Mallory's pulse point. "But you're pretty amazing, too, you know..." She brushed her lips over the spot she'd been teasing and let her breath cascade over it in a trembling wave. "Do you like this?"

Mallory chuckled softly and nodded as she turned her head to offer Addison more skin to ravish. "You know I do," she breathed as she slipped her hands under Addison's hoodie. "Do you like this?" she countered as she let her hands drift up over Addison's ribs to her breasts.

"Not at all," Addison groaned as Mallory tweaked her nipples. "God, Mal...Take it off," Addison instructed as she arched into Mallory's hands. "Please..."

Mallory smiled and quickly lifted the hoodie up over Addison's head. "Better?" she asked playfully as she let it fall to the floor at the feet.

Addison nodded and tangled a hand in Mallory's hair to pull her closer. She flicked her tongue over Mallory's lips and murmured, "It's a good start."

Mallory laughed and darted forward to capture Addison's lips in a deep, searing kiss as she dropped her hands to Addison's waist and began working her leggings down over her hips. It took a bit of effort to get them all the way off, but it was more than worth it when she was able to caress the long, long legs she so adored before grabbing

Addison by the ass and lifting her up onto the counter. She smiled at the taste of Addison's laughter, and stroked the backs of her fingers along her inner thighs as she moved between her legs.

"Better?" she asked as her left hand drifted up over Addison's hip and her right dipped between slick, soft folds.

Addison's hips rocked beneath her fingers as she tangled a hand in Mallory's hair and pulled her close. "Fucking perfect," she gasped against Mallory's lips as two fingers slipped deftly inside her.

Mallory kissed Addison softly as she curled her fingers and pulled out slowly, more than willing to draw this beautiful moment out for as long as possible. "Yes, you are," she breathed as she let warm velvet draw her touch deeper once more.

thirty-one

"Hey, you."

Mallory looked up from the zucchini she was slicing and smiled at Addison as she made her way into the kitchen. "How was your rehearsal?"

Nina had backed their *Evolution* rehearsals down to only a few times a week now that their first performance was successfully in the books, and while it should have been a relief to no longer be running herself ragged every day, she found her newly free hours in the afternoon burdensome. It gave her time to resume her usual practice schedule, which was nice, and her body certainly appreciated the break, but the rest of her wanted nothing more than to spend that time in Fonteyn with Addison.

Of course, Addison was granted no such break, as the gap in her schedule had been replaced with preparations for her role in the company's next show.

"It was fine. I danced *Don Quixote* last season, so it's more refreshing my memory about what I'm supposed to be doing than actually learning a whole new ballet." She smiled as she slipped around the edge of the counter. "I would have rather spent the time with you, though."

"Me too." Mallory laid her knife on the cutting board and turned to pull Addison into her arms as she captured her lips in a sweet, lingering kiss. She sighed happily when they eventually broke apart, and nuzzled Addison's cheek as she savored the feeling of holding her close. "You have to admit that getting to do this is better than working, though," she murmured as she dipped her head to kiss her again.

"This is better than pretty much everything," Addison breathed as she lifted her chin to meet Mallory's next kiss.

Mallory hummed at the feeling of Addison's fingers in her hair and melted into her as their tongues stroked idly together in tender kisses that overflowed with so much emotion that by the time they finally broke apart she was left feeling dazed and completely breathless. She licked her lips as she blinked her eyes open, and smiled as she ran a gentle hand over Addison's jaw.

The corners of Addison's eyes crinkled with her smile as she leaned into Mallory and whispered, "God, please don't ever stop kissing me like that."

"I won't." Mallory kissed her again as her heart swelled with so much affection that she thought it might burst. No, she would gladly do this for the rest of her life if Addison let her. "But for now," she added with a little laugh as Addison's stomach growled loudly, "I think I should get back to preparing dinner."

"I'm sorry."

"Don't be." Mallory caressed Addison's cheek with her thumb. "We'll have time for more of that later."

"I know, but…"

Mallory interrupted her with a kiss. "It's fine, darling. I promise." She smiled as she pulled back to drop a playful peck to the tip of her nose. "You may have your wicked way with me later if you'd like, but for now you need food."

"What if I said I need you more?" Mallory arched a brow as Addison's stomach immediately argued that point rather definitively, and laughed when Addison grumbled, "Fine. Whatever. Cook me dinner if you must."

"Thank you." Mallory brushed a kiss over Addison's cheek. "Could you get the salmon out of the fridge?" she asked as she turned back to the zucchini she had been slicing when Addison arrived. She picked up her knife and waved it at the refrigerator. "It's on the top shelf."

"You want a glass of the Sauvignon Blanc that's in the door, here?" Addison asked as she set the salmon beside Mallory's cutting board.

"If you would," Mallory demurred as she ran her knife through the remainder of the zucchini and pushed it into a pile in the corner opposite the squash she had sliced up earlier. She stiffened ever so briefly in surprise at the feeling of Addison's hands on her waist and braced her knife hand on the cutting board so she didn't accidentally cut herself as she turned to look at her over her shoulder. "May I help you?"

Addison flashed a mischievous grin as she gave Mallory's sides a squeeze, and she laughed when Mallory squirmed away from the touch. She pushed herself up onto the balls of her feet and pressed a kiss to the side of Mallory's throat. "Would you like a glass now, or would you rather wait for dinner?"

Mallory shivered at the feeling of Addison's lips and tongue against her skin, kissing, nuzzling, licking, teasing all the little spots that drove her wild as she waited for her answer. "Wait," she muttered. She cleared her throat and added, "I'm fine waiting for dinner."

"Okay." Addison dropped a smackeroo kiss to Mallory's pulse point and gave her sides one last squeeze before she pulled away. She laughed at the disbelieving look Mallory shot her and shook her head. "I need food, remember?"

"You need something all right," Mallory grumbled playfully. "Am I going to have to kick you out of my kitchen?"

"No." Addison smiled. "I just couldn't resist. Do you need help with that?"

Mallory looked down at the piles on her cutting board and shook her head. "It's basically done. I just need to get these set"—she reached for the roll of parchment paper at the back of the counter and ripped off two medium-sized sheets—"and then it's just a matter of putting everything into the parchment, folding them up, and throwing them in the oven for twenty minutes or so."

"You're sure?"

Mallory smiled. "Positive, darling. You can ice your feet in the meantime if you'd like."

"I wouldn't like at all, but I need to." Addison shook her head. "You're sure you don't mind?"

"Why would I mind? Besides, this way they'll have maybe thawed out by the time we've finished eating, and you won't use my legs as a means of warming them back up."

"Well, so long as I'm doing this for you," Addison sassed as she retrieved the plastic tub at the bottom of the pantry that she used for ice baths whenever she was at Mallory's and set it on the floor in front of the refrigerator. "So how was your afternoon off?" she asked as she pulled the container from beneath the automatic ice maker and dumped it into her tub.

Mallory shrugged. "It was an afternoon off. It was nice to be able to get most of my errands for the week done, but it was otherwise unremarkable." She smiled to herself as she laid a sheet of parchment paper beside her cutting board and began piling a small mountain of carrots, squash, and zucchini in the middle of it and, knowing that it would make Addison laugh, confessed, "I did accidentally get off the tube in Covent Garden, though."

"Really?" Addison chuckled as she dumped the entire container of ice into her bin. When Mallory nodded, she said, "Well, you should have come by. You could have brought me a coffee or something."

"You don't drink coffee in the afternoon," Mallory pointed out as she seasoned the veggies.

"Could have been decaf," Addison sassed playfully as she closed the freezer door. "Or hot chocolate."

Mallory laughed and moved out of the way so Addison could move her tub of ice to the sink. "Right. Anything else, darling? A sandwich?

Salad?"

Addison's shoulders shook with laughter as she flipped on the tap. "You are so lucky I like you."

"Believe me, darling"—Mallory smiled as she leaned over to drop a quick kiss to Addison's lips—"I know." She kissed her again and sighed as she pulled away. "Do you like dill?" she asked as she turned back to the packets she was preparing.

"Not as much as I like you." Addison winked at her as she slapped the tap off.

"I'm very glad of that," Mallory retorted as she opened the salmon and sprinkled the fillets with salt and pepper.

Addison laughed as she gave the bin a shake to break apart any ice cube that had frozen together when the water hit and hefted it from the sink. "I'm okay with dill. If you could maybe throw a few extra slices of lemon onto my salmon, though, I'd love you forever."

"Oh, well, if that's all it takes, then here..." Mallory gathered the entire pile of lemon and laid it on top of one of the fillets. "How's that?"

"Perhaps a little excessive, but I appreciate the sentiment." Addison kissed her cheek. "You're adorable, you know that?"

"Hardly," Mallory scoffed as she felt her cheeks warm with an embarrassed blush.

"Absolutely adorable," Addison argued softly, and the earnestness in her voice made Mallory's blush that much worse. "And brilliant." She kissed her cheek again. "Ridiculously talented." Another kiss. "Kind."

Mallory sighed. "Addy..."

"And so, so beautiful." Addison nuzzled her cheek.

Mallory yelped in surprise as ice water splashed against her side and reflexively jumped away from the cold. "And wet," she muttered, tugging at her sweater.

"Mmm, my fav—"

Mallory silenced whatever quip Addison was about to let loose with a finger to her lips. She huffed a laugh at the playfully annoyed look she got in return, and shook her head as she replaced her finger with a tender kiss. "Thank you."

Addison smiled. "Always."

"If we keep this up, we're never going to eat dinner," Mallory pointed out as Addison leaned in for another kiss.

"Okay, fine." Addison sighed dramatically. "Guess I'll stop trying to be romantic and just go plunge my feet into some ice water," she muttered as she eased past Mallory to exit the kitchen.

Mallory shook her head as she watched Addison make her way to the dining table and set her bucket onto the floor in front of the chair that had become hers over the last few months. "I'll go get you a towel once I get these into the oven," she told Addison, who looked like she was about to go searching for one. "Just get going on that."

"You're sure?"

"Positive," Mallory assured her with a smile. "This is actually nice," she added as she moved the salmon fillets to on top of the veggies she had arranged earlier.

"What's nice?" Addison asked, her voice just that little bit strained as she eased her feet into their nightly torture.

Mallory lifted her right shoulder in a small shrug. "Having a relaxed dinner together on a weeknight. Being able to actually have something of a work-life balance."

"That is always preferable to a work-work imbalance." Addison raked her hands through her hair and then grabbed the back of the chair over her shoulders.

"That is true," Mallory agreed with a little laugh. She glanced up at Addison as she continued to roll the end of the packet she was working on closed. "But you know what I mean."

"I do." Addison arched forward to stretch out her shoulders. "And I think we need to try to arrange our schedules so we have more nights like this, because I really like being able to end my day with you."

Mallory blinked as her heart fluttered into her throat at Addison's words. "Me too."

"Lucky me." Addison smiled as she sighed happily and relaxed back in her chair. "So, do you wanna hear all about the tinder guy both Gabs and Matt matched with today at lunch?"

Mallory arched a brow and nodded as she refocused her attention on her work. "Oh, absolutely."

thirty-two

Mallory covered her cough with her elbow and offered Max's secretary, Leanne, a tired smile as she made her way toward the music director's open office door.

"You okay?" Leanne asked, her brow beneath her soft gray curls pinched with concern. "Do you need some ibuprofen?"

"Took some before I came in. I'm fine," Mallory lied. The cold she had been keeping at bay all week by sheer force of will had finally overwhelmed her weakened defenses that morning, and she dearly wished she were back in bed in her comfiest clothes instead of dressed in her blacks and heels at work. "Just a cold. Are Max and Thad already inside?"

Leanne nodded as she dug a cough drop out of her top desk drawer and she shook her head as she offered it to Mallory. "It won't do much, I'm afraid, but it might help."

"Ta, Leanne," Mallory murmured as she took the proffered medicine.

Her fingers were sluggish as she tried to unwrap the cough drop, and she sighed as she popped it into her mouth. It wasn't going to make her feel any more alert, but she hoped that the menthol would clear the stuffiness in her head enough that she could at least get through the concert. Then she could go home and grab a few hours rest before she was supposed to pick Addison up for dinner. With the way she was feeling, she would have begged off for the night under normal circumstances, but this was the only night they both had off before Valentine's Day on Wednesday, and she would be damned if she missed their first one together.

"No offense, Mal, but you look like shite," Max greeted her as she entered his office.

He and Thad were sitting across from each other in the sitting area in front of his desk, and both of them were eyeing her with such obvious worry that she didn't even bother to try to lie like she had with Leanne.

"I feel like it, too," Mallory admitted with a little shrug. "But I'll live. Are there any changes to the program for this afternoon?" she asked as she set her things on the floor beside the chair closest to the door.

Max shook his head. "No. Well…" His voice trailed off as he glanced at Thad, who nodded almost immediately, and Mallory cursed her foggy brain for not allowing her to follow the silent conversation happening in front of her as she took a seat between the two men. She didn't have to wait long, however, to find out what she was missing because Max continued in a gentler tone, "Go home. Charlie can handle first chair for this one."

"I'm fine," Mallory protested weakly.

"Then you can be fine tomorrow night," Max argued, his expression kind but firm in a way that told her he wasn't going to change his mind. And, honestly, if she weren't feeling so awful, she would have kissed him for it. "But if you're not feeling better, for the love of god, just call in sick. When is your next performance with The Royal Ballet?"

"In a fortnight."

"All the more reason to rest while you can," he declared with a definitive nod. "Have Leanne order you a car and try to go get some rest."

Mallory blinked slowly and, too worn-out from the journey into the Centre to put up even a half-arsed argument, nodded. "Thank you. I'm sorry."

"Nothing to be sorry for," Thad assured her with a kind smile. "We're not going anywhere here, so you just worry about you for right now."

"Right," Max agreed. "Do you want help getting your things downstairs?"

"No, thank you. I'll manage," Mallory said as she grabbed the straps of her violin case and briefcase so she could shoulder them as she got to her feet. She had lost her balance when she had tried to get to her feet on the tube earlier, and didn't trust herself not to get lightheaded if she were to bend down to gather her things. Forget having Leanne call her a car, if that happened he'd have his poor secretary escort her all the way home just to make sure she got there safely. "Sorry, again."

"It's fine," Max said as he got to his feet. He followed her to the door and cleared his throat to get his secretary's attention. "Leanne, could you order a car to pick Mallory up at the main entrance as soon as possible?"

"Of course," Leanne confirmed as she reached for the phone on her desk. "Is there anything else?" she asked as she began punching in a phone number from memory.

"Not right now," Max said. He gave Mallory's shoulder a squeeze. "Ring Leanne when you get home so we know you made it back okay. Okay?"

"Okay," Mallory rasped as Leanne murmured something she couldn't quite understand into her phone.

"Car will be outside the main doors in ten minutes," Leanne shared as she hung up her phone. "The driver you had last time is on assignment, so she couldn't get him for you. Said she's sending over a driver named Curt instead. Insists he's just as amazing as Noah, and that he has a full ginger beard that can't be missed, so you'll know it's him."

"Ginger beard," Mallory repeated as she adjusted the straps over her shoulder. "Right."

Leanne eyed her critically for a long moment and then looked at Max. "I need to stretch my legs a bit. All right if I kip out for fifteen minutes or so? I think I'll stop for a tea on the way back—would you like anything?"

Max smiled. "Not a problem at all. And no, thank you. I think we're good for now."

"Brilliant." Leanne grabbed her purse and arched a brow at Mallory as she waved a hand toward the door. "I'll walk down with you, then, if you don't mind?"

Mallory shrugged. Even her fogged brain could connect the dots of what was happening around her, and she murmured, "Not at all," as she started for the door. She had yet to win a battle of wills with Leanne when she was in peak form, so she knew she didn't stand a chance right now. And, truthfully, it was nice to know that she had people looking out for her. "Thank you," she added softly.

"Of course," Leanne replied simply. There was a protectiveness to the way Leanne walked beside her that made Mallory's lips twitch with a small smile, and she fiddled with the strap of her violin case as they stepped into the lift. She was thankful that Leanne understood that she didn't have the energy to walk and talk at the same time, and she only broke the silence that settled between them when the coffee cart in the lobby came into view. "Let me get that tea real quick. Your car won't be here for another five minutes or so, anyway."

Mallory just nodded as she followed her to the cart. It was warmer here in the middle of the building than just inside the doors anyway, so she was fine staying under the secretary's watchful eye for a few more minutes.

"Hello Fiona," Leanne greeted the woman working the cart with a warm smile. "Can I get a decaf black tea and one of your special immunity teas, please?"

Fiona's keen green eyes sized Mallory up immediately, and she nodded as she began pulling little airtight containers from beneath the counter. "Good call," she said as she added an empty tea bag and a jar of honey to her collection. "Coming right up."

"I have tea at home," Mallory protested as she watched Fiona begin measuring different leaves into the disposable tea bag. All the other times she had stopped for a cup on her way into work she'd been given a cup of hot water and a tea bag she could have bought at the store, and she wondered if this kind of treatment was always available, or just for Fiona's best customers.

"Not this tea, you don't," Fiona quipped without looking up from her work.

Too tired to argue and realizing that it wasn't worth the effort anyway because she was clearly outnumbered, Mallory simply nodded and unzipped her bag to get her wallet.

"I got this," Leanne murmured, placing a hand on Mallory's arm.

Mallory shook her head. She was fine being mothered into submission about the tea, but she was more than capable of paying for it herself. "Leanne…" Her argument trailed off at Leanne's determined expression, and she sighed. "Thank you."

"Good girl," Fiona chuckled. "So, Lee, how's your husband doing?"

Mallory took a step back to not completely eavesdrop on the women's conversation and pulled out her phone. She debated texting Addison to tell her that she was heading home from work early, but eventually decided against it. Addison was meeting Gabs, Matt, and a few of the other dancers from the ballet for lunch, and she didn't want to interrupt their fun. Plus, by sneaking home for a nap, perhaps it would allow her to rally enough to make it through the evening she'd planned without letting on just how awful she felt.

Addison deserved a romantic night out and, sick or not, she wanted nothing more than to spoil her silly on the one night of the year where over-the-top romantic gestures were perfectly acceptable.

She didn't have the energy to bother scrolling through Twitter or playing any of the mindless games on her phone, so she just slipped it back into her bag and made her way to a nearby bench to wait for Leanne and Fiona to wrap things up. It was nice to not have to think for a few minutes, and she closed her eyes as she slid down on the bench so she could rest her head on the back of it.

"Here you are, dear," Leanne interrupted her quietude a few minutes later.

Mallory sighed as she blinked her eyes open. "Ta," she murmured as she sat up to take the paper cup from her.

"Fi says to give it five minutes or so to steep, and then it'll be ready to go."

"Five minutes," Mallory confirmed as she got to her feet. She hefted the straps of her bags higher onto her shoulder and nodded to assure Leanne that she was okay.

"Right, then. Off we go," Leanne declared as she turned toward the corridor that would take them to the Centre's main entrance. "Your car should be here soon."

A sleek black Town Car was pulling up to the curb just as they exited the building, and Mallory offered Leanne a weak smile as the driver—who did, in fact, have a most impressive ginger beard that made him look like he was plucked straight from the Highlands—climbed out of the car.

"Ms. Collingswood?" he asked as he hustled to the back of the car to lift the hatch on the boot.

"That's me," Mallory confirmed. "I'm good just keeping this with me."

"All right, then." The driver nodded as he slammed the lid. "My name's Curt, if you need anything, Ms. Collingswood," he said as he opened the rear passenger door for her.

"I'll call in the morning to check-in and see how you're feeling," Leanne said as Mallory made for the car.

Mallory nodded. "Thank you for the tea. And walking down here with me."

"Of course, dear," Leanne replied kindly. "Get some rest, okay?" she added as she half-turned back toward the building.

"I shall try," Mallory promised as she offered her a wave. She slipped her things from her shoulder and bent down to lay them far enough inside the car that she could safely climb in after them. Curt held his position by her door and waited for her signal that she was ready to go and, once she was situated, she gave him a small nod.

She sighed as he pushed the door shut and relaxed into her seat as she folded her hands around the warm cup of tea on her lap. Traveling by car like this was so much nicer than dealing with public transportation. It was truly a shame that she couldn't possibly justify the expense to make it an everyday thing.

"Where to, Miss?" Curt asked as he slipped behind the wheel. He typed her address into his GPS as she rattled it off, and nodded when a route popped up on the screen. "We're good to go," he announced as he buckled his seat belt. "Will have you home in a jiff."

"Thank you." She took a sip of her tea as the car pulled away from the curb and let her head fall back onto the headrest as the warm liquid worked its way down her throat. She couldn't make out just what kind of tea leaves Fiona had mixed in the brew, but it was delicious. And if it indeed ended up to be some kind of immunity booster to help her get over this virus she was suffering faster, she would be stopping by Fiona's cart every morning for a cup.

Especially given the fact that their second performance of *Evolution* was only a fortnight away.

It was easy to let herself drift off a bit as the car made its way through traffic, and she was genuinely surprised when Curt announced, "Here we are."

"Brilliant." Mallory blinked her eyes open and sat up straighter in her seat as she reached for her briefcase. "Just let me get my card to settle the fare."

"It's already been covered, Miss." He smiled at her in the rearview mirror. "It was handled when the reservation was called in."

"Of course it was," Mallory murmured, shaking her head.

He chuckled. "Just let me hop on out, and I'll come get your door for you."

Mallory nodded. After riding with Noah for a week, she had been properly trained to wait but, even if she hadn't, she didn't have the energy to argue with him about it. She slipped the straps of her violin and briefcase over her shoulder when he opened her door, and murmured, "Cheers, mate," as she eased past him.

"Have a good day, Miss," he replied cheerily as he slammed the door shut.

She glanced over her shoulder at the car as she pushed the door to her building open, and smiled when Curt doffed an invisible cap at her before pulling away from the curb. She had no idea where the car service found drivers like him and Noah, but if the rest of their ranks were as thoughtful, it was a wonder that any other company managed to survive competing against them.

Her apartment was delightfully warm after the chill of the stairs leading up to it—she had turned up the heat a few notches before she'd left despite the hit her gas bill would take for it just so she could come home to a warm house—and she hummed softly to herself as she set her things on the apothecary's table inside the door. Because she would be needing her coat later, there was no point putting it away, so she just shrugged it off and folded it atop her things on the entry table. She kicked her heels off and left them on the rug in the foyer— she'd be needing those later, too—and raked her hands through her hair as she started down the hall for her bedroom.

Once she'd changed out of her blacks and into her comfiest sweatpants and a faded henley she'd had since her final year at the Royal Academy, she set her alarm clock for an hour before she needed to leave to pick up Addison for dinner and climbed into bed. She grabbed the pillow from Addison's side of the bed, burrowed beneath the duvet, and sighed as the familiar scent of her lover enveloped her.

Fully relaxed for the first time since she had gotten out of bed earlier, it wasn't long before she fell into a deep, dreamless sleep.

The steady beep of her alarm clock pulled her awake some hours later, and she yawned as she rolled onto her back and stretched her legs. Her head was a little clearer, and she felt marginally better than she had earlier which, she figured, was as much of an improvement as she could reasonably expect. Only the allure of seeing Addison was enough to coax her from the warmth of her bed, and she shivered as she threw back the covers. A glance in the mirror in the corner of her room was enough to confirm that her hair had been thoroughly ruined by her midday nap, and she shook her head as she turned toward the bathroom to see if she couldn't salvage it without having to shower again.

The low hum of Addison's voice, which seemed to be coming from her kitchen, gave her pause, and she blinked in confusion as she turned away from the bathroom and instead padded toward the rear of the apartment.

"Yeah, everything here is going great," Addison said, her voice quieter than usual, in a way that made Mallory think she was trying not to wake her. "Really, Mom. You guys are going to love her as much as I do." She laughed. "No, it's not too cold. It's definitely warmer than that one year you guys flew up to New York."

Mallory's pulse stuttered at the warmth in Addison tone when she said "as much as I do" and she combed her fingers through her hair to tame the worst of her bedhead as she rounded the corner to the kitchen area. Even though she was beyond confused by Addison's presence, she could not help but smile when she spotted her sitting atop the counter beside the stove.

"Oh!" Addison grinned at her as she rounded the corner into the kitchen. She looked as beautiful as ever in a pair of skinny jeans and an ivory sweater, and Mallory arched a brow at the sight of her largest pot boiling away on one of the burners. "Mal just woke up, so I gotta go. I just have to let this simmer for another hour or so, pull out the chicken, shred it, strain the liquid to get out the gunk and add everything back into the pot to cook…right?" She nodded along with whatever it was her mother said in response as she beckoned Mallory closer. "Perfect. I will definitely call you back if I have any more questions. Thanks for your help. See you in a week. I can't wait to show you guys around some more. Love you, Mom," Addison said before she pulled her phone away from her ear and disconnected the call. She shook her head as she set her phone onto the counter. "Sorry, I didn't mean to wake you."

"You didn't." Mallory smiled at the way Addison hooked her legs around her waist to pull her in closer. "I had set an alarm before I fell asleep."

Addison wrapped her arms around Mallory's neck and pressed a kiss to her forehead. "How are you feeling?"

"Fine," Mallory lied automatically as she sank into Addison's embrace and took advantage of Addison being taller for a change to lean her head on her shoulder. She sighed at the feeling of Addison's fingers scratching the back of her neck and snuggled just a little bit closer. "That feels nice."

"Good," Addison murmured. She leaned her cheek against Mallory's forehead and let her right hand drop to drag up and down Mallory's spine. "When was the last time you took some Tylenol?"

Mallory shrugged. "Before I headed in to work."

Addison hummed and pressed another lingering kiss to her forehead. "You should probably take some more. You're warm."

"Yeah." After a long pause, Mallory added, "Not that I don't like this, but dare I ask why you're here?"

Addison gave her a light squeeze before pulling away enough to look at her. "Will texted me that Max sent you home. And when you didn't answer your phone when I called to check on you, I decided to come over just to make sure you were okay."

"Will texted you?" When Addison nodded, Mallory asked, "Why?"

"The real question, sweetie, is why didn't you?"

"I didn't want to interrupt your lunch."

Addison shook her head as she ran a light hand over Mallory's forehead and down her cheek to cup her jaw. "You wouldn't have interrupted anything. You are a million times more important to me than anything in the world, and I would much rather have you tell me that you've been sent home for being ill than to hear it from Will."

There was a hint of steel beneath the gentleness of Addison's tone that warned her not even to try to argue, and Mallory nodded. "Okay."

"Good." Addison dipped her head to brush a soft, chaste kiss over Mallory's lips, and her eyes shone with affection as she pulled away. "I love you."

Mallory couldn't contain her smile as she murmured, "I love you, too." She groaned as she felt a sneeze coming on and turned her head just in time to avoid letting it go in Addison's face. "Sorry."

Addison shook her head. "It's fine, sweetie. Why don't you go take some Tylenol or something to help with your fever, and then we'll go cuddle until it's time for me to get back to this soup."

"But I made a reservation—"

"I called and canceled it." Addison smiled unrepentantly as she dropped a kiss to Mallory's forehead. "And I'm making you my mom's famous homemade chicken noodle soup to help you feel better."

"It smells wonderful," Mallory assured her as she peered into the soup pot on the stove. Sure enough, a whole chicken was boiling away in there. "But how did you even know where I made the reservation?" She shook her head as she realized the answer to her question the moment she finished asking it. "Never mind. Will told you, didn't he?"

"Yup."

"Traitor."

Addison smirked. "Would it make you feel better if I told you I had to threaten to tell Siobhan that he hadn't even ordered flowers yet to get him to tell me?"

Mallory chuckled. "You don't mess around, do you?"

"Not when it comes to you."

Mallory sighed as her heart fluttered at the absolute conviction in Addison's voice. "I love you."

"Love you, too." Addison pressed a gentle kiss to the corner of Mallory's mouth. "When you're feeling better," she murmured as she nuzzled Mallory's cheek, "we will celebrate this properly. But, for now, it's Tylenol and cuddles. Couch or bed?"

"Whichever you'd prefer," Mallory replied as she slipped from Addison's hold.

"I want you to be comfortable. Come on, babe. What would you rather do?"

Mallory sighed. She would be more comfortable in bed, but she didn't want to fall asleep again and risk not being able to sleep later. "We can do the couch in the lounge. That way we're close to the kitchen in case anything needs monitoring."

Addison nodded as she slipped gracefully off the counter. "Okay." She tilted her head toward the bathroom. "Go take some medicine while I give this a stir, and then I'll meet you out there."

When Mallory returned to the lounge, Addison was already stretched out on the couch scrolling through Netflix, and she smiled as she laid down between her legs and rested her head on her chest. "Thank you for coming over," she murmured as she settled her ear over the steady beat of Addison's heart.

Addison draped an arm over Mallory's ribs to hold her close as she promised, "Always, my love."

thirty-three

"This, here, is where Thad tends to get a little too into the piece and loses some of his control." Mallory drew a small mark above the section of music she was going over with Charlie, who would be taking her spot in that evening's performance while she was on stage in Covent Garden. "So you'll need to step up a bit to hold the group until he comes back around…" She pursed her lips as she scanned the music and made another small mark where things had gotten back on track in the performance they'd just finished. "Here."

Charlie chuckled and made similar notes on his own sheet music. "He's a little different from Clara, huh?"

"Just a little." Mallory nodded. Thad was fun to work with—he was energetic and enthusiastic and genuinely loved his job, which translated into his performance at their concerts—but it definitely required more of her position as leader than when Clara was at the helm. Thankfully, Charlie had been in the business a good decade longer than her, so he was more than up to the task. "But you'll be fine."

"Of course we will. Are you ready for your big show tonight?"

"As we'll ever be. I'm just glad that the cold that knocked me out two weeks ago didn't linger. And that Addy didn't catch it. Devereaux upped our rehearsal schedule this week to make sure we were prepared, and if I'd still been ill…" She shuddered. "It would have been awful."

"Do you even have an understudy for it?"

"No."

He nodded. "Really good thing you got over it after a few days, then."

"I know you can't come tonight, obviously, but if you and Keiko would like tickets to one of the other two shows we're going to do, just let me know, and I'll get you guys tickets."

"That would be great, thanks. I'll talk to her about it and then have a look at our schedule."

Mallory reached blindly for her phone, which had begun vibrating against her desktop, as she replied, "Perfect." She flipped it over to look at the screen and grimaced when she saw the time and Addison's name. She was late. "Oh, bugger," she muttered as she accepted the call and lifted the phone to her ear. "Hello, darling."

"Hey, beautiful. Mom and Dad's tour this morning ran a little late, so we're just leaving the theatre now to head over to Persephone. Are you there already?"

"Not yet." Mallory pinned the phone against her shoulder and began gathering her things. "Charlie and I were just going over some notes for the performance tonight, and I didn't realize how late it'd gotten, so I'm actually still at the office. If I leave right now, I can be there in maybe thirty minutes? Are you walking over?" she asked hopefully. Not that it was a long walk from the Royal Opera House to the restaurant, but it would give her a few more minutes than if they were taking a car.

"Yeah. There's no point trying to track down a taxi since it's so close. And if you need to do a little more work, that's fine. I know you don't like missing concerts."

"It's fine, darling. I promise. And I think we're good here." Mallory was relieved that Charlie nodded in agreement and flashed him a grateful smile as she began shoving her things into her briefcase. "Persephone, right?"

"Yeah. I need a good bowl of pasta to get me through the performance tonight. Do you want me to order for you?"

"If you lot are too hungry to wait, sure. That'd be lovely. You know what I like." Addison's answering chuckle was positively salacious, and she shook her head as she murmured, "Behave, you."

Charlie laughed and got to his feet. "And that's my cue to leave. Break a leg tonight, Mal."

Mallory angled her phone away from her mouth as she replied, "Thank you, Charlie. Send me a text later to let me know how it went here?"

He shook his head as he slung his violin onto his back and picked up his briefcase. "It'll be fine. Don't worry about us here. You just focus on what you've got going on. We'll go over it all before the concert tomorrow night."

"You're the best."

"That's what my wife tells me," Charlie quipped. He gave a little wave and added, "See you tomorrow," before he sauntered out the door.

Mallory lifted her phone back to her ear. "Sorry, darling. Are you still there?"

"Nope," Addison teased, her smile evident in her tone.

"I'm on my way out the door now. See you soon?"

"I can't wait." Mallory smiled at the sound of what had to be Addison's father mocking her response in the background. *"My dad thinks he's funny,"* Addison muttered, confirming Mallory's suspicions. *"Come save me?"*

Mallory laughed softly and nodded. "I'll be there as soon as I can."

"Good." Addison huffed a breath, and Mallory could just imagine her rolling her eyes at whatever antics her father was up to now. *"I'll see you soon, sweetie. Bye."*

Mallory sent a quick text to Noah, whom she'd once again hired for the week leading up to their performance, to let him know that she was ready to leave, and then she slipped her phone into the outer pocket of her briefcase. She pulled on the coat she had left draped over the back of her chair when she'd arrived earlier, and shook her head as she buttoned it over her dress. She had hoped to sneak home and change out of her blacks and into something more appropriate for a casual meal before heading over to the restaurant, but that plan was out the window now.

Because she and Charlie had lingered to discuss the performance she was going to be missing, the halls of the Centre were nearly deserted, and she was able to hustle out the door without having to politely beg off any kind of conversation with anyone. Twenty-eight minutes after she left her office, Noah had pulled up to the curb in front of Addison's favorite restaurant in Covent Garden, and she checked the time on her phone as she waited for him to get her door.

Which was ridiculous, really, because she had been checking it obsessively for the entire trip, but it was easier to fixate on the time and her progress than worry about what would happen if Addison's parents didn't like her.

"Here you are, Miss," Noah declared as he opened her door and offered her a hand. "Do you want to leave your things in the car? I had lunch earlier, so I'm just going to head over to the car park and wait."

Mallory pursed her lips thoughtfully for a moment before nodding. "I'll leave my violin," she said as she set the instrument back onto the seat, "but I'll take my briefcase."

"Aces. Just ring when you're done, and I'll be here in a jiffy," he promised as he helped her out of the car.

"Ta, Noah," Mallory murmured as he let her hand drop. "I'll text you in a bit, then. Keep your fingers crossed for me that this goes well, yeah?"

He smiled and crossed the index and middle fingers on both of his hands. "But you won't need it. Enjoy your lunch, Miss."

Mallory smiled and nodded as she turned to the door. "See you in a bit."

"Welcome to Persephone," the girl working the front counter greeted her before the door had even fully closed behind her.

"Hiya. I'm meeting my friend and her parents. Leigh?"

The girl nodded as she glanced at the laminated seating diagram on her podium. "They're upstairs. Would you like me to show you to the table?"

"No need." Mallory shook her head and fiddled with the strap of her violin case as she looked toward the stares. "I'm sure I'll be able to find them," she added as she turned away from the podium.

Because tea time was still a good couple hours away, the restaurant was nearly empty, and it wasn't difficult at all for her to spot Addison and her parents the moment she reached the restaurant's upper level. Her fingers rubbed faster over the strap she'd been playing with as she approached their table on legs that felt increasingly unsteady, and she forced what she prayed passed as a genuine smile when Addison's mother noticed her.

"I'm terribly sorry I'm late," she apologized as she stopped beside Addison's chair. "I was going over some things with a colleague and lost track of time."

Addison beamed up at her as she got to her feet and pulled her into a quick hug. "Breathe, sweetie," she whispered against her ear, her voice tinged with amusement. "Everything's fine."

Mallory huffed a weak little laugh, embarrassed that her unease was so obvious, and nodded.

"Good." Addison brushed a kiss over her cheek and took her hand as she turned to her parents. "Mom. Dad. This is Mallory."

"Figured as much," Addison's mom chuckled as she stood to offer Mallory her hand. She had the same build and coloring as Addison, though her auburn waves were flecked with gray, and her smile was so warm and genuinely pleased that Mallory felt her nerves begin to ease. "Celine. It's wonderful to finally meet you."

"You, as well," Mallory murmured as she shook her hand.

"Robert," Addison's father said as he, too, stood to greet her. He was tall—easily six and a half feet—with a lean build, dark hair, and kind hazel eyes that sparkled with an oh-so-familiar mischievousness behind his wire-framed glasses. "Addy did tell you that you didn't have to dress up for us, right? I mean—"

"Bob," Celine interrupted, rolling her eyes.

"Dad," Addison groaned as she leaned her head on Mallory's shoulder.

Mallory laughed when he winked at her, looking utterly pleased that he managed to embarrass his daughter and make her laugh at the same time, and dipped her head in a short nod as she replied, "It's a pleasure, sir."

"The pleasure is all ours, dear," Bob replied with a sincere smile. He motioned toward the empty chair to Addison's right and added, "Sit. Sit. Lord knows you're going to be on your feet enough later tonight."

Mallory dipped her head in a short nod as she slipped her things from her shoulder and set them carefully on the floor beside the spot they'd saved for her. She shrugged out of her coat and draped it over the back of the chair as Addison and her parents retook their seats and cleared her throat softly as she sat beside Addison. She bit the inside of her cheek at the feeling of Addison's hand settling reassuringly on her thigh, and took a deep breath as she turned her attention to Celine and Bob. "Did you enjoy the Globe Theatre tour?"

"It was wonderful," Celine answered, nodding. "I wish we'd have done it on a nicer day, but it was still an amazing experience. How was your concert?"

"It went well. It's always a bit of an adventure when Thad is at the helm, but it keeps things interesting, at least," she elaborated as she gave the tabletop a quick glance and noted that it was devoid of menus.

Addison saw this, and gave her thigh a squeeze as she said in a low voice, "I ordered you the capellini fresco that you got last time."

Mallory covered Addison's hand with her own and rubbed her thumb along the backs of her knuckles. "Perfect. Cheers."

"Thad is your conductor?" Celine asked, bringing the conversation back to music.

"One of the two we have employed to lead during the season, yes,"

Mallory answered, straightening slightly in her seat. "Our other conductor is Clara Martin. She led the first half of the season, but she's in San Francisco at the moment working with the symphony out there. She'll return in May to close out the season with the LSO."

"She's also going to conduct our final performance, right?" Addison chimed in.

Mallory nodded. "I believe that's the plan. Though if complications get any more complicated…"

"Yeah," Addison sighed.

Mallory curled her fingers between Addison's and gave her hand a gentle squeeze as she asked Addison's parents, "I know we're meeting you for lunch tomorrow, but do you have any other plans while you're here? Addison said you fly home on Tuesday."

"Tuesday morning," Bob confirmed. "And, not really. Just wandering the city."

"He's an architect," Celine explained, rolling her eyes fondly at her husband. "So he loves the juxtaposition of the different architecture styles in European cities."

"So is my friend Siobhan." Mallory smiled. "Her firm does a lot of the modern skyscrapers around the city. Are you in commercial or residential design?" she asked, glad to turn the conversation in a direction that would allow her to sit back and listen instead of being the center of attention.

Bob seemed pleased to be able to talk about his work and his observations of London, and he carried on until well after their food had arrived. The rest of the meal was spent in friendly conversation that bounced from one topic to another, not terribly unlike when she was with Addison, Will, and Siobhan, and by the time their plates had been cleared away and Bob had insisted on covering the bill, she felt like she had known Addison's parents for years.

"Are you girls going to rest before your performance this evening?" Celine asked as they all pulled on their coats.

"As much as we can, I think," Addison answered, looking to

Mallory for confirmation. When Mallory nodded, she added, "We need to be back at the theatre by half-past six, so we don't have too much time, but it'll be enough."

"Well, we appreciate you two letting us take you out to eat," Celine said, looking every bit the proud mother as she gave Addison's arm a squeeze. "Mallory, it was an absolute pleasure to meet you."

"You, as well."

"Are you going to hang out after the show later?" Addison asked as they started for the stairs, giving Mallory time to send Noah a quick text to let him know they were on their way out the door now.

"I doubt it," Bob answered after looking to his wife to see what she was thinking. "We'll leave the stage door to your fans. We'll just gush about how incredible you were at lunch tomorrow."

"Don't jinx us, Dad," Addison warned.

"Are your parents going to join us tomorrow?" Celine asked.

Mallory shrugged. "I honestly don't know. I know my father's been in Belgium for a work thing and that my mother went with him, but I don't know when they're coming back. I did leave a message on my mother's voicemail the other day when Addison mentioned it, but I haven't heard anything yet."

"Well, if they can't make it, we'll just double-up on the gushing, then," Celine replied.

"Or you could just focus on Addison," Mallory suggested with a wry smile.

Celine laughed. "Nice try, dear." She wrapped an arm around Mallory's shoulders and the other around Addison's and pulled them into a hug. "But from the way my daughter talks about you, I think it's safe to say that you're pretty much stuck with us. Break a leg tonight, girls."

"Thanks, mom," Addison murmured.

"Thank you," Mallory echoed as she gave Celine's waist a light squeeze.

"Come on, Celine, let them go so they can rest a bit," Bob teased when Addison and her mother—and Mallory, by proxy, though she couldn't help but smile at how accepted and included the Leighs made her feel—lingered in the embrace.

"Okay, okay," Celine muttered as she gave them both one last squeeze. "We'll see you two tomorrow at noon," she said as she pulled away. "Addy gave us the address of the restaurant you suggested, so we'll meet you there. And if you sleep in and it looks like you're going to be late, just let us know, and we'll change plans. Okay?"

Addison laced her fingers with Mallory's and nodded. "Thanks, mom."

"We will see you tomorrow," Mallory added. She offered Bob her right hand—glad that Addison was holding her left—and said, "It was lovely to meet you. Thank you so much for the meal."

"Our pleasure, kiddo," Bob assured her with a smile. He tilted his head toward the street, where Noah's gleaming black Town Car had just pulled up to the curb, and added, "Now, get out of here. We'll see you in the morning."

"Can we give you a ride?"

"Thank you, but it's not necessary, dear," Celine insisted with a smile. "We are more than capable of finding our way back to the hotel." She looped a hand around Bob's arm and waved the other at the car. "You girls just worry about doing what you need to get ready for tonight."

"Bye, guys," Addison said, offering her parents a smile and a wave as she tugged Mallory toward the curb.

"Are they not coming with us?" Noah asked when they reached the car.

Addison shook her head as she ducked into the back seat. "Not this time."

Noah nodded. "Right, then. Where to, ladies?"

"My place, please," Mallory said as she handed Addison her briefcase before sliding in after her.

Noah tipped his head and shoulders in a small bow and smiled at them both before he slammed the door shut.

"I think you've replaced me as their favorite daughter," Addison shared as Noah hustled around the back of the car to his door.

Mallory chuckled and shook her head. "You're ridiculous."

"Maybe," Addison agreed as Noah climbed behind the wheel. "But yet here you are, so what does that say about you?"

Mallory glanced at Noah, who had turned up the radio to a volume that sufficiently drowned out their conversation, and smiled as she leaned in to capture Addison's lips in a slow, sweet kiss. "I love you."

"I love you too, sweetie," Addison whispered, a soft smile curling her lips as she nuzzled Mallory's cheek for a long moment before pulling away. She glanced over the seats to the clock on the dash and sighed. "We're not going to have much time to rest before we have to be back at the theatre."

"Are you going to be okay?"

"Oh yeah. I've pulled harder days than this," Addison said as she pulled their joined hands onto her lap. "I mean, more time would have been nice, but…"

"Spending the time with your parents was worth it?"

Addison smiled and nodded as she lifted Mallory's hand to her lips and placed a lingering kiss to her knuckles. "Yeah. Getting to finally introduce the most important person in my life to them was absolutely worth it."

thirty-four

"Mmm," Addison purred. "Good morning."

Mallory ran her fingers up Addison's spine and smiled at the way she snuggled closer. "How did you sleep, my love?"

"God, like the dead." Addison murmured as she kissed Mallory's throat. "I'm sorry I basically passed out on you as soon as we got home."

"Don't be." Mallory continued to stroke up and down the length of Addison's back as she turned her head to look at her. "It was an incredibly long day at the end of an even longer week." Incredibly long was something of an understatement given the size of the crowd gathered outside the stage door when they'd tried to leave the theatre. She had been completely thrown by the sight of them and had followed Addison's lead as they worked through the crowd, signing programs and taking pictures with the hardy souls willing to suffer a brisk February night just for the chance to meet them. By the time they had finally made it home, it was well after midnight, and it had taken all the energy she had left to strip off her clothes before climbing into bed. "And, besides," she added as she wrapped her hand around Addison's waist and pressed a kiss to her forehead, "I wasn't far behind you."

"That makes me feel better." Addison stretched against Mallory's side and groaned. "What time is it?"

"A little after nine," Mallory answered without looking at the alarm clock beside the bed. Between rehearsals and concerts and Addison spending time with her parents, moments like this had been completely absent over the last week; and so, even though she had woken up roughly half an hour earlier, she had been more than content to enjoy the quiet of her apartment and the feeling of Addison curled against her side. It was her favorite way to start the day regardless of what else was happening in her life, but even more so after a week like the one they'd just had. She pulled her hand from Addison's side and resumed rubbing her back as she added, "I honestly was expecting you to sleep longer. I know how much more demanding *Evolution* is for you than your usual performances."

"Oh, it definitely is." Addison braced her elbow on the mattress above Mallory's shoulder and smiled down at her. "But there is no one else in the world that I would want to do it with."

"Me neither." Mallory lifted her chin to capture Addison's lips in a slow, sweet kiss. "I love you."

"Love you," Addison murmured. "So, so much." She ran a gentle hand along Mallory's jaw as she stared at her with so much affection that it stole the breath from Mallory's lungs. "I've missed not being able to do this all week," she confessed as she dipped her head to capture Mallory's lips once more.

Mallory hummed her agreement as Addison's tongue dipped past her lips, and moaned softly at the feeling of Addison's right leg slotting between her own as they traded deep, unhurried kisses that made her heart beat slow and heavy in her chest. She let her left leg fall open wider as the tenor of their kisses began to shift from soft and adoring to gently arousing, and a feeling of serenity settled over her as she surrendered to the heavenly feeling of Addison rocking lightly against her in time with their swirling tongues.

"Oh, Addy..." she whimpered when Addison's thigh pressed against her in a way that sent a jolt of pleasure rippling through her, and grabbed onto Addison's ass to hold her in place.

"Yes?" Addison hummed as she dropped her head to press a kiss to the point of Mallory's chin.

Mallory turned her head to the side at the gentle pressure of Addison's kiss, and swore she could feel her smile against her throat as her lips moved lower, painting the length of her throat with soft, soft kisses as she stilled above her. "Please don't stop."

"Never." Addison nipped at her pulse point and then soothed the spot with a long, heavy lick. "I will never stop loving you," she murmured as she dragged her lips over Mallory's jaw.

The absolute ardor in Addison's gaze when she stared down at her made her breath catch in her throat, and she swallowed thickly as Addison shifted above her and her right hand ghosted over her side to draw swooping circles around her breasts in a lazy figure-eight. She sighed as Addison's caress spiraled slowly higher until she was teasing her nipple to an even tighter point with every deliberately exquisite circuit, and she mewled as she arched her chest into Addison's touch.

"I know, sweetie." Addison brushed a gentle kiss over Mallory's lips and cupped the breast she'd been teasing in her hand, giving Mallory the firmer touch she craved as she dragged a heavy thumb across her nipple. "You are so beautiful."

Mallory dragged her right hand up Addison's back to thread her fingers through soft auburn waves. "You are," she whispered as she pulled her down and claimed her lips in a kiss that was soft and deep and full of pure surrender. She gasped at the feeling of Addison's fingers closing around her nipple and then groaned when that delicious touch almost immediately disappeared as Addison's hand ghosted over her stomach and past her hips to dance along her inner thigh.

"I've got you," Addison promised as she slid her touch higher.

Mallory's eyes fluttered shut at the feeling of long, nimble fingers dipping between her legs, and she rolled her left leg out wider as her hips lifted to match the leisurely movement of Addison's fingers.

"That's it, sweetie," Addison encouraged as her touch slid higher to rub broad, oh so soft circles over Mallory's clit.

A trembling moan caught in Mallory's throat as Addison's lips slanted against her own in a deep, passionate kiss that left her utterly breathless. She melted into Addison as one kiss blended into another, their tongues sliding together at the same exquisitely languid pace as the touch between her legs. Her hand drifted from Addison's hair to stroke idly up and down her back as they moved together, Addison offering quiet words of love and encouragement as her breaths came harder and faster, soft gasps of pleasure falling from her lips as the heat coiling low in her hips began to tighten. She squeezed her eyes shut as she tried to delay the inevitable, but there was no way to hold back when Addison murmured, "Please come for me," against her lips. Her release was as gentle as the touches and kisses that brought it on, and she clung to Addison as waves of pleasure rolled through her.

She blinked her eyes open when her orgasm finally eased, and her heart skipped a handful of beats at the love she saw shining in Addison's eyes. "Addy…"

Addison smiled and dipped her head to brush a kiss over Mallory's lips. "I love you."

"I love you," Mallory whispered as she lifted her head to capture her lips in another lingering kiss. Affection bloomed in her chest at the way Addison whimpered as she sank into the kiss, and she smiled against her lips as she guided her onto her back. "My turn," she murmured as she settled her knees between Addison's legs and guided them wider.

"Oh, god, please…"

Mallory flicked her tongue over Addison's lips as she eased her legs open wider, and nuzzled her cheek as she asked, "What would you like?"

"You."

"You have me, darling," Mallory murmured. She kissed her softly and added, "For as long as you want me, I'm yours."

"Good. Because I don't ever want to let you go." Addison smiled and ran a light hand over Mallory's jaw. "So I guess you're stuck with me forever."

"Sounds like heaven," Mallory confessed, unable to keep her smile in check as she captured her lips in a deep, searing kiss. "But, for now," she added when the kiss reached its inevitable end, "I would very much like to make love to you."

Addison hummed and pulled her down into another kiss. "Please…"

thirty-five

"So, what do you reckon our better halves have been up to while we've been slogging away at work?"

Mallory glanced back at Will, who was following her up the stairs to her apartment, and shrugged. "No idea. I know Addy was looking forward to a lazy day at home, though."

"Wait, she's officially moved in? When did that happen?"

"It hasn't. Officially, anyway," she added as she led them around the second-floor landing. Officially was the key word in that statement, however, because Addison had been spending the night more often than not for the last month or so.

"Ah, so it's just an unofficially kind of thing…"

Mallory pulled her key from her bag and opened her front door. "Yeah. It's an unofficially kind of thing." She set her bag and violin case on the apothecary table and turned to look at him as she slipped off her coat. "I don't know. Maybe in a few months we'll do it properly but, for now, this is working, and I don't want to rock the boat."

"I don't think you'd be rocking any boats, mate." He leaned his oboe case between the apothecary table and the corner of the wall and shrugged out of his coat. "Has she said anything? Siobhan kept dropping hints left and right when we were dating—that's how I knew it was time to do it."

"Yeah, well, considering *she* was the one who actually proposed to *you*"—Mallory handed him a hanger for his coat—"I'm not especially surprised that it took her dropping hints like that for you to catch on."

"Okay, first of all, that was rude." He scowled at her playfully as he reached past her to hang up his coat beside his wife's. "And second of all, don't think I didn't notice you never answered my question."

Mallory offered him an unapologetically enigmatic smile and shrugged. In truth, she had noticed that Addison had begun referring to her apartment as home, but she wasn't about to give him that kind of ammunition to use against her. She knew that all she had to do was ask to make their unofficial situation to become official, but she wasn't quite ready to make that jump yet, and she knew that Addison was willing to wait until she was. "Sucks to be you."

He nodded. "It usually does, yes."

"Cheater!" They both turned to look down the hall at the sound of Matt yelling. "How'd you do that?"

"You got owned!" Gabs laughed.

"Sounds like Matt and Gabs are here," Mallory observed.

"It's not cheating," Siobhan retorted, punctuating the statement with a triumphant whoop. "It's skill. And you just don't have it, ballet boy."

Will huffed a laugh and shook his head. "And that sounds like we should go put on our 'adult' hats and make sure everyone is behaving themselves."

"Probably a good idea," Mallory agreed as the sound of raucous laughter and Gabs chanting "ballet boy" filtered down the hall.

"Hey! You're home!" Addy grinned at them from her spot on the sofa that faced the hallway. She was leaning against one arm while Gabs had claimed the other, and their legs were tangled together in the space between them. Above the sofa, on the wall that had fluctuated between being bare and holding the photograph Gwen had given her, hung the piece of art that Addison had surprised her with a week ago—a positively giant canvas that was filled with the music for the end of their pas de deux. The gray-black notes and staffs and the aged parchment color of the canvas background brought a warmth to the room that she hadn't realized it had been missing and, combined with what the music represented, it was a strikingly romantic piece of art.

"We are." Mallory smiled. She glanced around the room, noting Matt and Siobhan perched on the edge of the sofa that faced the television and the pale gray controllers in their hands. It appeared that Matt had brought along the plug-and-play game system he had been telling her about the other day while she and Addison waited for their studio to become available. "Dare I ask what's started this latest round of name-calling?"

"His wife cheats," Matt declared, pointing an accusing finger at Siobhan.

"Well, yeah," Will drawled. "Why do you think I burned our Monopoly set?"

"Okay, look." Siobhan pointed a warning finger at Will. "It's not my fault you suck at that game. And two, I'm still pissed about that. But"—she rounded back on Matt—"I can't cheat at a video game when you're playing the bloody computer."

"Super Mario Brothers," Addison explained, answering the questioning look Mallory shot her.

"Really?" Will's eyes widened with excitement as he hurried to loosen his tie and pop the top button on his shirt. "Can I have a go?"

Mallory shook her head. "And on that note, I'm going to go change out of my blacks," she announced as she turned toward around. She smiled when a familiar hand wrapped around her hip just as she turned into the bedroom. "Can I help you?"

"The question is, can I help you?" Addison murmured against her ear, her voice tinged with amusement. "I mean, I don't want to brag or anything, but I am really good at getting you undressed."

"Believe me, darling, I know," Mallory chuckled. "Were you able to relax at all whilst we were gone?"

"A little bit." Addison closed the door behind them, cutting the volume of the playful bickering in the room next door to a low hum. "Until Gabs and Matt showed up about an hour ago, anyway," she continued as she crossed the room to where Mallory was standing beside of the bed. "Then, you know, circus."

Mallory pulled Addison into her arms. "I'm sorry you didn't get the lazy day you'd hoped for."

"It's not like I had to do anything to keep them occupied. They've all been taking turns on Matt's little Nintendo the whole time. I just laid on the couch and laughed at them." Addison kissed her softly. "Now, how about you turn around so I can help you out of that dress." She laughed at the disbelieving look Mallory shot her and shook her head. "Not for *that*. Geez. I just meant I can do the zipper for you."

Mallory smiled as she turned away from Addison. "Thank you, darling."

"Thank you," Addison countered as she swept Mallory's hair over her shoulder. "I seriously love unzipping you," she breathed as she pressed her lips to the base of Mallory's neck. "It's like unwrapping present every single time."

Mallory's eyes fluttered shut at the feeling of Addison brushing soft, soft kisses over her back as she unzipped her, and a delicate shiver rolled down her spine when strong arms wrapped around her waist to hold her close once she'd finished. "I love you," Mallory murmured as she lifted Addison's left hand to her lips and pressed a kiss to her knuckles before placing it over her heart.

Addison pressed her palm to the heavy beat of Mallory's heart as she held her tighter. "I love you."

Raucous laughter and swearing exploded in the sitting room, shattering the bubble of gentle affection that had surrounded them, and Mallory sighed as she gave Addison's hand over her heart a squeeze.

Addison rubbed her cheek between Mallory's shoulder blades. "Can we just kick them out so I can keep holding you like this?"

No matter how much she wished she could say yes, Mallory shook her head. "I don't think so."

"Stupid friends and their stupid games," Addison grumbled. "Why did we invite everyone over, again?"

"You thought it would be fun to get everyone together for a casual evening of friends and food since things are going to get crazy leading into our next performance," Mallory reminded her.

"Oh yeah… God, that was a stupid idea, wasn't it?"

In light of their current situation, Mallory was inclined to agree, but it was also nice to have their home so full of happiness and love. A year ago she would have never imagined her life would look anything like this, and she offered up a silent thanks to whatever deity had seen fit to bring Addison into her life. "If you'd like, we can absolutely kick Gabs off the couch and claim it as our own, though." She turned in Addison's embrace and smiled as she touched their foreheads together. "How does that sound?"

Addison huffed a playfully aggrieved breath and nodded. "Fine. But I call dibs on being the big spoon."

"I'm taller, though."

"Doesn't matter. I called dibs," Addison sassed. She reached down to grab Mallory's ass and gave it a firm squeeze. "So, you lose."

If this was losing, Mallory would gladly do it every day for the rest of her life. "Fine. You win."

Addison dropped a smile of a kiss to Mallory's lips. "Damn right I do." She winked as she pulled away and turned toward Mallory's dresser. "Now, let's get you changed so we can cuddle the shit out of each other and drive them all crazy. What do you want?"

"Jeans and a shirt is fine," Mallory answered as she slipped off her dress and draped it over the bed so it wouldn't wrinkle. She'd only worn it for a few hours, so it didn't need to go to the dry cleaners just yet.

Addison turned from the dresser with the requested items in hand and smiled as she looked at Mallory standing beside the bed in nothing but a bra and panties. "Goddamn, you are gorgeous."

A soft smile curled Mallory's lips at the open appreciation in Addison's gaze, and she blinked back her happiness as she reached for the clothes that dangled forgotten in Addison's hands. "Thank you, darling," she hummed, unable to resist leaning in to steal a quick kiss.

"If you keep kissing me like *this* when you're wearing nothing but *that*," Addison murmured against her lips, "I will totally march out there right now and shove the lot of them out the door."

Mallory laughed as she took a step back. "Sorry."

"No you're not," Addison huffed, smiling as she handed Mallory her clothes. "So get dressed before I lose what little self-control I've got left. I'll hang your dress back up for you."

Mallory dressed quickly as Addison returned her dress and heels to the closet and smiled as she offered Addison her hand when they met at the door. "Shall we?"

Addison threaded their fingers together and nodded. "Yeah. Sure. I guess. Why not…"

"God, finally," Siobhan declared, throwing her hands in the air dramatically when they rejoined the group.

"Sod off," Addison drawled, squeezing Mallory's hand as she led her to the couch. She laughed along with Siobhan and flicked her free hand in a *shoo* motion at Gabs. "Up you get, Ms. Calvente."

"Why? Maybe I want to cuddle, too."

"Sorry, Gabs, but she's all mine." Addison shook her head. "I'm not sharing."

Gabs sighed dramatically and tossed the magazine she'd been reading onto the coffee table, the pages bent open to an advertisement for a private catamaran charter in the Virgin Islands. "Fine. Whatever. I'll just go cuddle with Siobhan, then. Will, you'll share her with me, right?"

"Knock yourself out, mate," Will replied distractedly as he smashed a turtle and picked it up. "Less work for me."

Matt laughed. "And who's going to cuddle me, then?"

"Guess you're stuck with my husband." Siobhan flashed him an apologetic smile as she wrapped her arms around Gabs' waist and pulled her down onto her lap.

Mallory smiled as she allowed Addison to guide her between her legs, and sighed happily as she laid her head on her chest.

"You comfortable?" Addison whispered against the top of her head.

Mallory nodded and snuggled closer. "This is absolutely perfect, darling."

thirty – six

"So, what are you going to do with yourself next season when you're not running around like a chicken with your head chopped off?" Will asked as they surveyed the crowd gathered in the Barbican courtyard from the windows in the corridor outside her office three floors above.

Max had pushed out the make-up performance for the one they'd rescheduled during the lead-up to the first performance of *Evolution* until the very last day of May so the weather would be nice enough to accommodate an outdoor concert, and Mother Nature had actually played along by giving them an absolutely glorious evening for their performance. Although, everything seemed to be coming up roses for the LSO ever since the Board successfully ousted Hayes the month before. The running joke in the building was that it was the Gods' way of rewarding them for getting rid of him.

"I have no idea," Mallory replied as she turned her back to the gathering crowd and leaned against the window. She took a deep breath and let it go slowly as she tilted her head back against the glass.

It was almost hard to believe that in ten days her tenure at The Royal Ballet would be over. Though they still had one performance left in their short run, *Evolution* was securely the juggernaut Nina had hoped it would become, and she honestly didn't know how she felt about the whole thing being almost over. On the one hand, she quite liked the idea of not running around like a chicken with her head cut off, but on the other...

She wouldn't get to work with Addison anymore.

And then there was the fact that, with the success of *Evolution*, symphonies from around the world were jockeying for a place on her calendar for the coming season, offering compensation packages that were at least twice, and in some cases close to four-times what had been her standard rate for such appearances. So, even though she wouldn't be dashing around London like a madwoman, it was looking like she would be keeping an equally hectic schedule on a more global scale the following year.

Though, at least Addison's schedule was such that, if the trip was short enough, she could travel with her. There wasn't a ballet company in the world that wouldn't love having her crash their classes for a few days, and the idea of traveling *with* Addison instead of away from her took a significant weight from her shoulders. In all her years as a professional, she had never hesitated to take any job that would further her career, but when that first offer from Berlin came through three weeks ago, her initial reaction had been to turn it down simply because Addison was in London and not Berlin and the idea of being a continent away made her feel physically ill.

Will bumped her with his shoulder as he turned to mirror her posture. "Kinda crazy how different everything is compared to how it was at the beginning of the season, huh?"

She nodded. "It is that, yes."

"Hey, there you are."

Mallory smiled as she turned her head to look at Clara, who was bounding down the hall toward them with a wide grin. Clara had returned to London at the beginning of the month not only to finish out the season with the LSO, but also to begin studying Mallory's performance in *Evolution* so that she could better conduct the ballet's final performance. "Here we are. Did you need something?"

Clara yawned as she took up a position similar to theirs so that she and Will were flanking Mallory. "I'm hiding from the Board members prowling the halls downstairs. Between everything here and then working with you lot at the ballet, I just need a few minutes of peace and quiet."

"Welcome to my life," Mallory chuckled.

"True," Clara conceded. "You two looking forward to this summer's tour?"

"Sure," Will agreed amenably.

Mallory pursed her lips and shrugged because, truthfully, she wasn't looking forward to it at all. Firstly because she didn't understand why they were doing North America again when they were there last summer, but mostly because The Royal Ballet would be touring Asia and Australia during that same time. It was the reality of their professions, of course, but spending over a month away from Addison was definitely not something she was looking forward to. The only positive to the whole thing was that the Board had listened to Will's reports from the players that seven weeks was too long to be on the road, and that they'd made this year's tour much shorter.

Clara laughed at Mallory's non-answer and leaned into her side. "Just wait, Mal. We've got exciting things planned for this one."

"Yeah?" Mallory side-eyed her. "Like what?"

"Can't tell you yet," Clara replied. "We're still working on polishing up the details, but I think you'll actually enjoy this tour if we can get everything hammered out."

"Are we still ending in Los Angeles?" Mallory countered. It didn't matter what Clara, Max, and the Board were planning—if she had to return to L.A. on top of everything else, it was going to be an absolute shite trip.

"Well, yes. The stops aren't what we're playing around with. Those were set last August. But trust me on this one, okay?"

Mallory smiled at the faint entreaty in Clara's voice. "You, I trust. Everything else, not so much."

"I'll take it." Clara groaned and pulled her phone from the inner pocket of her tuxedo jacket. She sighed as she checked the screen and pushed herself upright. "Max beckons. Shall I offer to bring you along?"

"Please don't," Mallory chuckled. "We're quite all right here until it's time to queue up."

"Fine. Abandon me like that. I see how it is," Clara muttered playfully as she typed out a quick response to Max's text. She re-pocketed the phone. "Right, well, I'll see you lot down there in about twenty minutes, then. Enjoy hiding from the world whilst I suffer untold horrors downstairs."

"We will," Will assured her with a grin.

"And make sure you warm up properly," Clara added. "This one's got to be perfect so we can keep our season ticket holders happy."

Mallory smirked. "I thought that's what the alcohol was for?"

Clara laughed. "True." She gave Mallory's wrist a tap with her finger. "You good?"

"Perfect, Clara," Mallory assured her. "We'll knock this one out of the park."

"Bloody right we will," Clara sassed with a confident smirk.

"We should probably warm up now," Will murmured once she was out of earshot.

Mallory nodded and tilted her head toward her office. "Yeah. Let's go."

thirty – seven

The first thing Mallory saw when she made her way into Fonteyn for their final rehearsal was Addison sitting on the floor, leaning against the mirrors with her legs stretched out wide in front of her. It was a sight she had become accustomed to over the course of their rehearsals, and she was surprised by the way her heart clenched with regret that this would be the last time she ever saw her like this.

Addison must have been feeling the same, because the soft smile she turned her way was just that little bit dimmer than usual. "Last one. You ready?"

"For the rehearsal, yes…" Mallory's voice trailed off as she looked around the studio. It was one of those rare sunny days in London, and the light pouring into the room from the skylight overhead made everything from the barres to the walls to the pale linoleum on the floor look positively radiant. She could distinctly remember how nervous she had been for her first rehearsal, how frustrated she'd been when nothing had seemed to go right, and how perfectly lovely Addison had been. Though she didn't know it at the time, that was the day that her entire life changed, and she was so, so grateful for everything her time in this studio had given her. "For this to be over…no. I'm not ready for this to be over."

Addison nodded and leapt gracefully to her feet. "I know," she murmured as she wrapped her arms around Mallory's waist. "I feel the same way."

"Last rehearsal," Nina declared as she strode into the room with a wide grin. "Are you ready?"

"Of course," Mallory confirmed as Clara slipped quietly through the door after Nina. She had been attending as many of their rehearsals as her schedule allowed over the last fortnight to better acquaint herself not only with the music, but also the way Mallory performed it so that she would be ready to take the helm of the Royal Opera House's orchestra for their final night on stage. "Hello, Clara."

"Hiya, Mal." Clara smiled and nodded at them in turn. "Addy."

Addison waved. "Hey. And, yes, Nina," she continued as she propped her heel on the barre beside Nina and bent forward until her cheek was resting against her knee, "we're ready."

"Good." Nina leaned against the barre at the front of the studio, and her posture softened when Clara took a similar position at her side. Mallory wasn't sure where, exactly, things stood between them, but there was an easiness to their interactions that suggested they might eventually find their way beyond "complicated." Before Mallory could overthink it, however, Nina tilted her head toward the center of the room indicatively. "From the top, then, Mallory, if you would…"

Mallory nodded and turned to go retrieve her violin as Addison pulled her leg from the barre. She watched Addison give it a little shake before leading into a series of quick little jumps in place.

"Everything okay?" Nina asked.

Mallory's eyes jumped from Nina to Addison in the mirror.

"Yeah." Addison rolled her head in a slow circle and swung her arms across her body. "I'm just a little tight from yesterday. I'm fine, though."

Nina pursed her lips thoughtfully as she gave Addison a slow once-over, as if she could visually diagnose the degree of muscle tightness Addison was experiencing. "If you start feeling like you need us to call this early so you can go to the recovery suite, let me know immediately."

Addison responded with her most exaggerated grin and two thumbs up.

"Bloody Americans," Nina grumbled. She rolled her eyes at Addison's answering laughter, but it was clear from the quirk of her lips that she was satisfied by her dancer's self-assessment. "Cheeky buggers, the lot of you."

Mallory bit her lip to keep from laughing as she pulled her violin from its case, but lost the battle when she turned to look at Addison, who was standing in the middle of the room with her hands on her hips glaring playfully at her. "Yes?"

"Do not agree with her!"

Clara, at least, had the grace to cover her laughter with an impromptu coughing fit, while Nina made no such effort to hide her amusement.

Mallory tilted her head and gave Addison a look that said, *Who, me?*, and shouldered her violin. "I'll cook you dinner later to make up for it."

Addison gave up the act and grinned. "Awesome."

"I believe you were just played, Ms. Collingswood," Nina observed.

"I believe she doesn't mind at all," Clara added in a faux whisper.

Mallory shook her head at them. "It's fine. I'm used to it." She arched a brow at Addison as she lifted her bow and played a series of quick, jaunty notes to loosen up her fingers. "Are you ready?"

"When you are, Collingswood," Addison sassed, throwing in a little wink for good measure as she made her way to the side of the room to wait for her cue.

Mallory shook her head and, instead of replying, closed her eyes and took a deep breath to center herself.

Flirty banter was fun, but now it was time to work. They were to take the stage together for the final time the next night, and everything needed to be absolutely perfect.

When she was ready, she blinked her eyes open. She caught

Addison's gaze in the mirror across the room and, when Addison gave her a small nod to signal she was ready, began to play. Their steps had gone through some minor changes over the last few months, and though very few people would probably notice just what they were doing differently, the result was striking. In the beginning, Addison's paths around her were wide enough to allow plenty of room for swinging arms and legs and Mallory's bow, but over time those circuits had become tighter and tighter until it was only their understanding of each other and their movements that kept them from crashing into each other.

It was a relatively simple change in the grand scheme of things, but there was no ignoring the way it drew each of their talents into sharper focus and highlighted just how perfectly in sync they were.

Mallory was vaguely aware of Clara's hands waving minutely at her sides as they worked through their performance, but the majority of her attention was focused on Addison's warm brown eyes as she leapt and twirled around her, and the enchanting quirk of her lips every time the choreography called for them to touch.

Knowing this was the last time they would rehearse together, Mallory didn't bother to contain her instinct to lean into Addison's touch as she played, and she was only vaguely aware of the way those touches lingered just that little bit longer, turning striking postures designed to accentuate Addison's talent into something much more intimate. She poured her heart into her playing as Addison's fingertips dragged sensuously along her arm and waist, and moved fluidly with every small hold or press of Addison's hands against her body.

It was not, as Nina had suggested during their first meeting all those months ago, simply a dance between a musician and her Muse. For those not looking for anything more profound, of course, that story would suffice; but if one were to look more closely, they would see that it was a story of two souls finding their way to each other.

She allowed herself a small smile as they eased into the coda of their pas de deux, and sighed at the feeling of Addison's hand curving ever so gently around her cheek, drawing her closer. Her arms fell to her sides as she dipped her head to touch their foreheads together, and her heart felt like it was trying to leap from her chest as she stared into Addison's eyes.

It hadn't been the easiest journey to get from where they had started to where they were now, but she knew beyond a shadow of a doubt that this was precisely where she was meant to be.

She quirked a brow at the mischievous spark in Addison's gaze, but before she could ask what it was about, soft lips ghosted briefly over her own as Addison melted into her.

"I don't remember that being part of the choreography," Mallory murmured against Addison's ear as she wrapped her arms around her waist. It wasn't a part of the choreography they shared with the audience, anyway. It had certainly become a part of their personal routine after the lights blinked out and the curtain dropped.

"God, could you imagine?" Addison nuzzled Mallory's cheek, clearly in no hurry to pull away despite the fact that they were very much not alone. She sighed as she dropped to the flats of her feet and leaned her head on Mallory's shoulder as she whispered, "I wish we could."

Mallory closed her eyes and leaned her cheek against Addison's head. "Yeah…"

They broke apart slowly at the sound of a throat being cleared, and Mallory licked her lips as they turned toward the front of the room.

"Incredible," Clara declared with a proud smile. "Bloody brilliant. Truly."

"Thank you," Addison replied as she tucked herself into Mallory's side. She arched a brow at Nina and dared, "So…anything we need to change before tomorrow night?"

Nina shook her head. "I don't think so. That was…" Her voice trailed off, and she smiled. "Breathtaking. Absolutely beautiful. If you two dance like *that* tomorrow night, you'll have everyone in the theatre in tears as they applaud you."

Addison beamed. "Yeah?"

"Yeah," Clara answered. She touched Nina's wrist and added in a quieter tone, "I'm sorry, but I've got a meeting back at the Barbican I need to get to."

"I'll…" Nina blinked as she turned to look at Clara. "I'll walk you out."

"Yeah?" Clara replied softly.

Nina nodded and leaned forward to whisper something against Clara's ear that had the conductor looking unabashedly pleased, and chuckled softly as she glanced at Mallory and Addison. "There's nothing left to practice or change. You are perfect. Addison, I'm going to have Serena clear your calendar tomorrow except for class in the morning. I want you rested and ready to set the world on fire tomorrow night."

Addison wrapped her left arm around Mallory's waist and snapped off a playful salute with her right. "Yes, boss."

"Why don't you ever salute me?" Clara asked Mallory playfully.

Mallory arched a brow and countered, "Why don't you ever salute me?"

"Fair enough," Clara conceded with a smirk. She took a deep breath and let it go in a huff. "Right, well. Meeting time for me, unfortunately. Mal, I know we wrapped our season last night, but don't forget we have a meeting with Max and Gianna Monday morning. It's looking like those changes to the summer touring plans have worked themselves out…"

"Wonderful," Mallory muttered.

Clara chuckled. "I think it's pretty safe to say that you'll love what we've done. But, for now, rest up, and I will check in with you tomorrow night before the show."

Mallory nodded as Clara turned toward the door, and bit the inside of her cheek to keep from smiling at the way Nina moved to follow.

"Do you think they're…" Addison asked in a low tone as the door closed after them.

"No idea." Mallory shrugged. "Clara hasn't said anything."

Addison sighed as she turned to pull Mallory back into her arms. "That was fun."

"It was," Mallory agreed as she looped her arms around Addison's waist. She smiled as she dipped her head to touch their foreheads together. "I am going to miss dancing with you every day."

"If you think you're done dancing with me just because we won't be rehearsing every day, you've got another thing coming," Addison murmured. "We will dance at home," she added as she lifted her head to capture Mallory's lips in a tender kiss. "Where we can do this all we want, too."

"Oh?"

Addison hummed in the affirmative and flicked her tongue over Mallory's lips before she claimed them with her own once more. "And, as I'm sure you've noticed by now, dancing with you is something of a turn-on for me."

Mallory blew out a soft breath as her body instinctively curved toward Addison. "God…"

"Do you want me to stop?" Addison whispered, her voice taking on the low, rough tenor that never failed to send a pleasant thrill down Mallory's spine as she moved just that little bit closer.

Mallory whimpered. They should. She knew they should, but Addison's left hand had dropped low enough that firm fingertips were pressing encouragingly against her ass and she couldn't deny just how very much she wanted her to continue—the risk of someone walking in on them be damned. "Please don't."

"I love you…" Addison breathed, her eyes crinkling with her smile as she wrapped a hand around the back of Mallory's neck and guided their lips together once more.

thirty-eight

"Thank you." Addison squeezed Mallory's wrist as she slipped through the stage door Mallory was holding open for her.

"Hiya," Yvette, the woman who had been working the stage door desk since Mallory's first trip to the Royal Opera House, greeted them with a little wave as the door closed behind them.

Mallory smiled and tipped her head in greeting as Addison replied, "Hey, Yvette."

"Before you go up, could you maybe…" Yvette motioned toward two stacks of playbills and photographs on the counter in front of her.

Before Mallory could respond, Addison shook her head and said, "After the show. We're not jinxing this one."

"Figured as much," Yvette chuckled. "But is there a show you're ever willing to risk jinxing?"

"No," Addison admitted with a little laugh.

"Fair enough." Yvette turned to look at the clock mounted on the wall behind her. "There's about an hour to go until tabs go up on the first act, so the rehearsal studios should be clearing out soon as everyone begins finalizing their preparations."

"Perfect," Addison replied.

Mallory nodded and murmured a similar sentiment, and reached for Addison's hand as they started down the hallway to the lift. The rear of house area of the theatre was quiet, but a tech hand exited the door to the backstage area as they waited for the lift, and the air on the other side of it felt like it was charged with electricity.

"Do you feel that?" she asked, her voice barely louder than a breath as the lift arrived and the doors in front of them slid open.

Addison squeezed Mallory's hand as they stepped into the lift. "Yeah." She glanced at her as she pressed her thumb to the button for the second floor. "I take it this doesn't happen at the Barbican?"

"No." Mallory shook her head. "I haven't felt anything like this *anywhere.*"

"How funny. Maybe it's just a theatre thing? I don't know how to explain it, but it's always like this on the final night of a run. Like the ghosts of this place are wired, or something." Addison leaned into Mallory's side. "You'll feel it more when we get down to the wings in a bit. The trick is to not let the energy in the air throw you off your game."

Mallory smiled at the way Addison curled into her. "Wonderful," she drawled as she pressed a kiss to her temple. She was used to nerves—hell, at this point in her career, they were almost a welcome old friend—but combating this extra-normal adrenaline or whatever it was would be an entirely new experience.

"It's not that bad," Addison murmured.

Mallory nuzzled Addison's ear. "If you say so, darling."

The lift stopped at their floor, and Addison laughed as the doors slid open. "You'll see."

"I'm sure I will," Mallory agreed quietly as she followed Addison off the lift. She ran her thumb over the back of Addison's hand as they made their way along the corridor, enjoying these last few moments of togetherness before they were forced apart. "See you in the wings?" she asked when they stopped in front of Addison's dressing room door.

Addison seemed to weigh her answer for a long moment before finally nodding with a heavy sigh. "Yeah. That'd probably be for the best." She smiled at the confusion that furrowed Mallory's brow, and shook her head as she elaborated, "I would like to spend these final moments with you, but at the same time…"

"You don't want to jinx anything," Mallory finished for her with an understanding smile. She leaned in and captured Addison's lips in a sweet, lingering kiss, and murmured, "I understand, darling," when she finally pulled away. She lifted her free hand to cradle Addison's cheek as she kissed her again. "And I agree on both counts, so… I shall see you in the wings in a couple hours."

"I love you."

"I love you," Mallory murmured. There was something in the way Addison was leaning into her that told her she would have to be the one to put an end to this, but she couldn't resist stealing one final kiss before she pulled away. "Soon, darling," she promised as she took a step back.

"Soon," Addison echoed, her voice warm and resigned but not exactly sad. She tilted her head toward Mallory's dressing room and winked. "Go make friends with the ghosts."

Mallory laughed. "I shall try my best."

"Good."

Mallory waited until Addison had disappeared into her dressing room before turning toward her own, knowing that she needed to get her makeup sorted before the wig mistress arrived to do her hair. The next two hours passed in a blur of makeup, hair, stretching, warming up, and getting into costume, and she couldn't help but smile at the sound of Addison singing inside her dressing room when she made her way to the lift at the Half so she could meet with Clara before the second act. It was a departure from what had become her usual routine, but they had agreed to touch base quickly during the break to make sure they were on the same page for the half of the ballet that would leverage the most significant weight on their skill.

Matt and Gabs were just finishing their final pas de deux for the first act when she peeked onto the stage through the curtains in the wings, and she applauded along with the audience as the lights dimmed and the tabs fell.

"You're down early," Gabs noted a little breathlessly as she skipped off the stage with Matt trailing behind her. "Nervous?" she asked as she reached for her hoodie that was draped over one of the portable barres that were closest to the stage.

"No more than usual," Mallory admitted. "The ghosts, as Addison called them, seem to be a bit harder to ignore, but I'll manage." She smiled as Gabs chuckled and tipped her head in a way that said she understood, and added, "Clara wanted to touch base before the second act."

"She's amazing," Matt said as he joined them. "Not to knock Henry or anything, but that is the tightest the orchestra has played for this thing in the entire run."

Mallory laughed and nodded. "That's Clara, for you."

They chatted amenably as Gabs and Matt pulled on the layers they'd shed before performing, and Mallory couldn't help but arch a brow in surprise and appreciation when she spotted the conductor making her way toward them in a positively dashing tuxedo that she'd paired with a high-collared white shirt that had the top two buttons undone, leaving the very top of her throat exposed. It was a simultaneously demure and sexy combination, and if Mallory had to guess, she'd wager the buttoned-up look was chosen for Nina's benefit. "Speak of the devil," she teased once Clara was within earshot. "How'd it go?"

"Good." Clara nodded and smiled at Gabs and Matt. "You two were incredible."

"Cheers, mate," Matt drawled, buffing his fingernails on his shoulder.

Gabs laughed and replied more sincerely, "Thank you." She elbowed Matt as she smiled and winked at Mallory. "Break a leg out there, Collingswood."

"I shall try my best," Mallory promised with a small, half-bow.

"Good. We'll see you afterward, then. Time for us to go cool down properly before Nina finds us chatting and rips our heads off."

Mallory smiled at the way Clara's gaze drifted across the backstage area at the sound of Nina's name, but didn't press the matter, instead bidding Gabs and Matt a cheery farewell before turning to her friend. "Truthfully, how did the first act go?"

"Fine." Clara shrugged. "They're good. Not as good as you and Addy, obviously, but still quite good. How are you? Ready?"

"As I'll ever be," Mallory confirmed.

"Good enough," Clara murmured, a proud smile quirking her lips. She tilted her head toward the backstage entrance nearest the lifts. "Here comes your girl."

"We're at the Five!" the stage master's voice rang through the wings.

"And that's my cue to get back to the pit," Clara declared. She held up a fist. "Break a leg, Mal."

"You, as well," Mallory countered with a little laugh as she lightly bumped Clara's knuckles with her own.

"Like I'd have it any other way," Clara chuckled.

"Are you two planning trouble?" Addison joked as she joined them.

"Of course." Clara winked. "Take good care of our girl out there—yeah?"

Addison smiled. "Always."

"Excellent." Clara grinned and offered them a jaunty little wave as she turned on her heel and called over her shoulder, "I shall see you lot after you've brought the roof down on this place, then."

"She's definitely different than working with Henry," Addison murmured as they watched Clara disappear around the corner that led to the pit entrance.

"Working with her is different from working with anyone I've ever come across," Mallory agreed as she slipped her violin case from her shoulder and laid it on the table behind her. "In a good way, of course.

She's truly one of a kind."

Addison hummed in agreement as a trio of corps dancers stopped a few feet away, looking out onto the stage with a confident set to each of their frames as they awaited the call to take their places. In deference to the dancers' preparation, Mallory didn't seek to continue their conversation, and the silence that settled around them drowned out the rustle of fabric and quiet scrape of shoes that surrounded them as she shed her layers and pulled her violin and bow from their case.

"Beginners, please!"

Mallory smiled at Addison as the corps took the stage and the wings around them cleared. As had become their tradition, Addison's right hand settled on her chest over her heart just as the orchestra began to play, and she licked her lips as she mirrored the touch. She felt her pulse falter for a moment before it fell into sync with Addison's, and her eyes fluttered shut as she let that slow, steady *thwump, thwump, thwump,* ground her.

"I love you," Addison whispered.

Mallory dipped her head to touch their foreheads together. "I love you, darling."

They stayed like that until Clara guided the orchestra into the slow descent to silence that heralded her entrance, and she dared to steal a quick kiss before she surrendered herself to the task at hand. She smiled as she pulled away to shoulder her instrument, savoring the softness in Addison's gaze for the space of two heartbeats before turning toward the stage, her smile was replaced by a mask of concentration.

The air seemed to reverberate with anticipation as the theatre fell silent, waiting for her entrance, and she took a deep breath as she made her way onto the stage. She bit her cheek to keep from reacting to the rattle of applause that flittered through the darkened auditorium before it was quickly silenced, and then she forgot about the audience altogether when Addison's hand landed on her shoulder.

The music had long since become a part of her in a way that

allowed her to play without having to give too much thought to the notes, and she surrendered herself to the emotion that swelled inside her as they moved together fluidly, circling and spinning so closely together that it was as if they were two halves of a whole. The dance was theirs and theirs alone, so perfectly choreographed to highlight each of their strengths that while others might try to imitate it in the future, none would be able to duplicate it. Her eyes stung and her vision blurred as she extended her right leg, toes pointed to draw an invisible arc on the floor as she pulled her bow across the strings of her violin for the last time, and her throat tightened with affection at the shimmer of tears in Addison's eyes.

Her heart beat slow and heavy in her chest as her bow arm fell away and Addison's hand curved ever so gently around her cheek, and she didn't bother to try to contain the soft smile that curled her lips as she melted into her touch, letting Addison urge her closer until they had settled into their final position.

"I love you," Addison breathed against her lips as the silence in the theatre was shattered with an explosion of applause.

"Oh, how I love you," Mallory whispered, only dimly aware of the lights around them blinking out and the tabs whooshing down in front of them as she surrendered to the moment and captured Addison's lips in a kiss that held all of the love and admiration and devotion she felt for her.

"I don't remember this being part of the choreography," Addison teased softly, her breath cascading over Mallory's lips with the weight of butterfly wings.

Mallory smiled and, ignoring the flood of dancers pouring onto the stage to take their position for the curtain call, kissed her again. "Do you want me to stop?"

Addison's eyes glowed with joy and love and everything that was wonderful in the world as she murmured, "Never."

"Not that I can blame either of you for this," Gabs interrupted with a laugh as she carefully took Mallory's violin and bow from her hands and passed them off to the stagehand who would see them returned to their case, "but you need to stop with the whole making out on stage thing and line up."

"That was so hot," Matt chimed in. "Shite, I'd make out with Mal if she played like that for me."

Mallory laughed. "Matthew, we are both far to gay for that to ever happen. But cheers, mate."

He grinned and tipped his head in a way that clearly said, *Yes, well…*

"Quick as you can, please!" the stage manager called out, drawing their attention back to the task at hand.

They hurried to take their places, and Mallory smiled at the feeling of Addison's hand slipping into her own as the curtains swept dramatically up into the proscenium arch. She laced their fingers together as they advanced in a line toward the front of the stage to acknowledge the deafening applause that welcomed them, and her heart swelled at the way Addison refused to let go even when it was their turn to address the audience on their own.

Once the back-and-forth of the main curtain call had finished, Mallory made her way to the side of the stage to collect Clara for her turn in the spotlight.

"Pretty sure this is supposed to be Addison's job, yeah?" Clara laughed as Mallory offered her her hand.

"She thought this would be a more fitting end to the evening," Mallory shared as she gallantly led Clara to center stage. "And besides," she continued as she spotted Addison turning toward the opposite wing, "this way it left her open to collect Nina." She laughed at the way Clara's eyes widened. "Breathe, Martin."

"Sod off, Collingswood," Clara murmured out of the corner of her mouth as she turned toward Nina, who was crossing the stage toward them in a stunning black gown.

Mallory fell back a step to stand beside Addison as they gave Clara and Nina their time in the sun. Once Nina and Clara had sufficiently basked in the audience's applause, they fell into position at their sides—Clara to Mallory's left and Nina to Addison's right—and bowed one last time before the main curtain cascaded back to stage and the assistant stage manager rushed to catch the tabs to hold them shut.

"Corps, dismissed," Nina called with a smile. "I shall see you lot Tuesday morning for class. The season might be done, but that's no excuse to not be in top form for our tour this summer."

A chorus of, "Yes, Nina," echoed around the stage as the corps dancers took their leave.

Nina turned to her four stars as the stage began to empty. "You four were wonderful. Enjoy these runs—you have earned them."

Mallory expected Nina and Clara to take their leave at that—as performers, their obligations were not quite met for the evening, but there was no reason for them to stay any longer—but they lingered in the liminal space between the curtains as Matt and Gabs slipped through the tabs.

"Well, Clara…" Nina asked once it was just the four of them.

Clara grinned. "Absolutely. It would be my honor."

"That's what I thought," Nina chuckled. Mallory and Addison shared a confused look, which made Nina laugh harder. "It's good news, I promise."

"Brilliant. Am I going to be clued-in as to what that good news is?"

Now it was Clara's turn to laugh. "Yep. You both will be fully briefed Monday morning at eleven when we meet in Max's office." She looked at the tabs that fluttered open, and added, "But, for now, just enjoy this. Lord knows you've earned it."

"And on that note, we shall leave you to your adoring public." Nina smiled as she looped a hand around the crook of Clara's arm. "Do not disappoint them."

"Of course not, Nina," Addison deadpanned as Clara led Nina into an elegant spin and led them toward the wings.

"What was that about?" Matt asked.

"No idea," Mallory murmured.

"Sounds like they're not done with you yet," Addison added,

grinning at her friends as she tipped her head toward the amphitheater.

"Let's do it together," Gabs suggested.

Addison laughed. "So you can leave us to god knows how many runs while you disappear?"

"Bloody right. We're not the stars of this show. All of that applause"—Matt winked at them as he slipped a hand through the gap in the tabs and pulled the curtain open—"is for you. So go soak it up. I don't know if you quite realize how incredible you were tonight, but you deserve this moment. Go enjoy it."

Mallory arched a brow at Addison and smiled when a sure hand slipped into her own and tugged her forward. The audience's applause swelled as the four of them emerged, and Mallory laughed when Gabs and Matt broke away almost immediately to applaud them alongside the crowd.

"And there they go," Addison murmured, her tone amused as they ducked through the tabs with one last wave.

Mallory would have responded, but the noise inside the opera house rose a good half-dozen decibels at Matt and Gabs' exit, so she instead just squeezed Addison's hand in solidarity before letting go so she could wave to the audience that was on their feet applauding their effort. Later, they could plot their revenge but, for now, there was nothing left to do but smile and wave and enjoy the moment.

thirty – nine

"Siobhan wants us to bring a salad for toni—" Mallory grabbed onto Addison's waist to keep from knocking her over as the dancer stopped suddenly in front of her as she was reading the text she had just gotten from Siobhan. "Sorry."

"It's fine, love." Addison shook her head as she pointed to a black and white framed photograph hanging on the exposed brick wall of Higher Ground that certainly hadn't been hanging there the last time they had stopped in.

Mallory gasped softly as she drank in the sight of her and Addison on stage at the Royal Opera House. She was braced on her left leg with her right extended in a line behind her, while Addison seemed to hover on the pointe of her shoe in front of her, fingertips resting lightly on the scroll of her violin and her left leg lifted behind her in a line that continued the angle of Mallory's extended leg. It was the hold Nina had chosen for the mailers at the beginning of the campaign and, while that shot had been incredible, the months of rehearsals that had happened since then was clearly evident in the sharp lines of their bodies and the seemingly effortless way they pulled it off. "Wow…"

"Ah, damn," Lena's laughing voice interrupted them. "I was hoping to see your faces when you saw it for the first time. It's brilliant, right?"

"It's incredible," Mallory murmured. She stepped closer to Addison and wrapped an arm around her waist as she murmured in her ear, "I almost can't believe that's us." Addison laughed, the sound light and awed and happy, and Mallory smiled as she kissed her cheek. "You look like you're floating…"

"I always feel like I am when I'm with you," Addison whispered as she sank back into her. "God, Mal…look at us…"

Lena cleared her throat softly. "Is it okay?"

"It's the most beautiful photograph I've ever seen," Mallory assured her as she finally tore her eyes away from the frame.

Addison nodded in agreement as she turned in Mallory's arms to look at Lena. "What would it take for us to get a copy of that?"

Lena grinned. "I've got it behind the counter for you already."

"Of course you do." Mallory chuckled fondly. "Seriously, though, how were you able to get a copy? Doesn't the ballet hold the rights to his photographs?"

"They do." Lena nodded as she led them toward the register with a little wave. "But Pierce and I go way back, and Nina doesn't have a problem with him slipping me a picture to put up on the wall here every now and again. It's not like I'm selling the prints and, besides, it's free publicity."

"Fair point," Mallory agreed as Addison took the large manila envelope Lena offered them.

There was a sparkle in Lena's eyes that suggested there was more in the envelope than the photograph they'd been discussing, and Mallory peered over Addison's shoulder as she opened it. "That's more than one print," she observed as Addison reached into the envelope.

"It is," Lena confirmed, her tone light and playful, with just a hint of *oh my god just hurry up already.*

There were four copies of the print they'd been admiring when Lena found them—two in color and two that were black and white—but that wasn't the end of their surprise. "We weren't sure if you'd prefer the artsy one or the color one, so he included both. And then there's the—"

"Oh…" Addison's breathy exclamation interrupted her as she fanned through the stack of prints and saw the additional shot that had been slipped into the pile.

Mallory echoed the sentiment as she wrapped her arms around Addison's waist and rested her chin on her shoulder. She had been so, so wrong when she'd said the picture of them dancing was the most beautiful one she'd seen. This one was. It was a simple candid of the two of them sharing a tender kiss in the liminal space between the main curtain and the less glamorous drop curtain that hid the working part of the stage from the audience during encore curtain calls, and the combination of the dimmed lights and the dark crimson curtains and their dresses created the most romantic image she had ever seen. The shot of them dancing was striking and beautiful and artistic, but this was soft and warm and open and unguarded, and it stole the breath from her lungs. She squeezed Addison's waist and whispered against her ear, "I love you."

She smiled at the way Addison melted into her as she replied softly, "Love you."

"God, you are so cute," Lena laughed. "I'm glad you like the pictures."

"Why so many copies?" Mallory asked as Addison tapped the pages into a block so they'd slide easily back into the envelope.

Lena shrugged. "Figured you'd both want them."

"Besides, this way I can put them up in my dressing room and then the others can be put out at home," Addison chimed in.

Lena's eyebrows lifted as she waved a finger between them. "Wait. So does that mean you're…"

Mallory nodded and held Addison just that little bit tighter. "After we're both back from touring, but before next season."

They'd only broached the subject the day before but, for all her fretting about moving too quickly or messing things up, it had ended up to be an entirely unremarkable conversation. She had planned on bringing up the idea of Addison moving in with her once she had returned from her summer tour, but Addison had made a comment while they had been lounging on the couch binge-watching *Warehouse 13* about how she wished she had an artifact that would teleport her clothes from one apartment to the other when she needed them, and it had just…happened. Much like everything in their relationship, deciding on this next step had been so natural and organic that it wasn't scary at all—it just felt right.

So beautifully, wonderfully right.

Lena arched a brow knowingly as a mischievous smirk quirked her lips. "So how much blood will be spilled in the halls next door vying for your soon-to-be old place?" A donor had left the apartment to the Royal Ballet in their will close to fifty years prior, and it was up to the company's acting artistic director to decide who got the apartment with a killer location and rock-bottom rent.

"Probably far too much," Addison admitted with a wry laugh.

Lena tilted her head in a way that said, *Yes, well…,* and sighed as she glanced behind them at the door. "A couple just came in, so for as much as I'd love to continue this… Your usuals?"

"Minus the pastry," Mallory confirmed. "And to-go, unfortunately. We've got a meeting at the Barbican."

"Both of you?" Lena asked as she grabbed a pair of paper cups and scribbled their names on the sides with a Sharpie so they wouldn't get mixed up.

"Yep." Addison nodded as Mallory finally released her hold and moved beside her to complete their transaction.

"No idea what it's about though," Mallory elaborated as she reached for her wallet.

Lena shook her head as she refused to take Mallory's card. "Your money is no good here today, Collingswood. This one's on me. And that's bloody strange."

"Extremely," Mallory agreed. "But whatever it's about, Clara is giddy with excitement over it all—so I don't imagine it will be *too* awful. It is a little unsettling that we've both been summoned, though."

"I'll bet," Lena drawled as she started making their drinks.

"Can you put these in your bag?" Addison handed her the pictures.

"Of course." Mallory opened her briefcase and slid the envelope between her iPad and the folder of music she had yet to purge after the end of the season. Her eyes drifted back to the image of the two of them on the wall as they waited for their coffees, and she smiled as she zipped the bag shut.

"Let me know how it goes?" Lena asked as she handed them their drinks.

"We will," Mallory promised. She glanced at her watch and shook her head. "I'm sorry, Lena, but we've got to get going if we're going to be on time."

"Go, go." Lena shooed them off with a smile. "Good luck."

Addison lifted her coffee in farewell. "Thanks."

The underground was busy but navigable—the real rush would happen in a few hours at the close of business—and they made it to the Barbican with relative ease. Although the LSO wasn't the only occupant of the Barbican Centre, the halls felt deserted as they made their way up to Max's office, a fact Mallory was most grateful for as it meant they wouldn't run into anyone who would ask about the meeting. She had been trying her best to play it cool and act like she wasn't worried, but there was no silencing the little voice in the back of her head that wondered if this was the shoe that was destined to drop since everything else in her life was going so well.

Mallory motioned toward the door to Max's suite so Addison would know they had arrived before she turned into it, and she forced a tight smile when she saw Leanne look up from her computer.

"They're waiting for you," Leanne greeted them with a smile that was far more genuine than the one Mallory had managed.

"Cheers," Mallory murmured as her right hand found the strap of her briefcase and began worrying it.

While she hated showing any sign of weakness, she wasn't

surprised that Addison had noticed, and she was nevertheless calmed by the gentle hand on the small of her back as they made their way through the open door to Max's office.

She had expected Clara and Max to be at the meeting, but the sight of Gianna Ngo, Nina Devereaux, and an older gentleman with silver hair and sharp blue eyes in a three-piece pinstripe suit she didn't recognize gave her pause. Everyone she knew how to read *seemed* relaxed—Clara was perched on the arm of Nina's chair and, though they weren't touching, there was no mistaking the familiar way Nina was angled ever so delicately toward her, and Max was all but slouched in his seat with his heels propped on the small table that anchored the sitting area—but the entire scene sent a feeling of *déjà vu* rippling through her.

"Ah, there they are," Clara drawled with a grin as she spotted them.

"Right on time," Nina added with an approving nod. She motioned to the man on her right, "This is Charles Neiman, one of the Governors of The Royal Ballet," she added for what was clearly Mallory's benefit.

"Pleasure to meet you, sir," Mallory nodded at him as she stepped further into the room to shake his hand.

Charles pushed himself to his feet to greet her. His handshake was firm but far from crushing, and his voice was much softer than she'd expected as he replied, "Likewise, I assure you." When he released her hand, he turned to Addison. "Ms. Leigh. Another spectacular season."

"Thank you." Addison tipped her head in a small bow.

"Yes, yes," Nina drawled, waving a hand in a *let's get on with it* kind of way. "So, I'm sure you're both curious as to what's happening here?" she added as she motioned them toward the two empty seats between herself and Max.

"Just a little," Addison admitted as she took the seat closest to Nina and Clara.

"Terribly," Mallory echoed as she sat beside Max, who dropped his feet to the floor as he straightened in his chair.

"Well, then we shan't keep you waiting any longer," Nina murmured with a smug smile as she turned to Max.

"As you both know," Max picked up the conversation as if being handed a baton, "the LSO is doing another North American tour this summer and, as I'm sure you're equally aware, The Royal Ballet is doing Asia and Australia." He paused, waiting for them to acknowledge his statement, and grinned when Mallory and Addison nodded. "What you don't know is that the LSO and The Royal Ballet have been in talks for at least a couple months, now, about those tours."

"And I'm sure you're also aware," Charles Neiman chimed in, and there was no mistaking the fact that this entire conversation had been choreographed before their arrival, "that *Evolution* has created quite the stir." When Addison and Mallory nodded, he continued, "So, obviously, both our companies would like to capitalize on the hype you've created."

Mallory held her breath as she waited for the punch line that was surely coming soon.

Gianna leaned forward in her seat as she took over. "Obviously, there's no way for you two to be in two places at once, so we've all agreed that the best solution is for you to split your time between the companies this summer."

Mallory let the breath she'd been holding go in a whoosh as she looked at Addison. Her heart leapt at the idea of not having to spend any time away from her, and she bit her lip to keep from mirroring the wide grin that curled Addison's lips when their eyes locked.

Max chuckled. "You'll do two weeks in Asia with the Ballet and then fly over to meet us in Southern California for the final fortnight of the LSO's tour. With Nina, it'll be the entire ballet being performed, but with us, it'll just be your part, as the Royal Ballet can't spare *all* their dancers and the venues we're to play are not equipped to handle an entire ballet production."

Addison nodded slowly, her brow furrowing ever so slightly as she processed the timeline that had just been presented to them. She turned to Nina. "Am I to rejoin the company in Melbourne for our last week, then, after we wrap with the LSO?"

Nina smiled and shook her head. "You've put in plenty of work this season. Goodness knows you've earned the extra week off."

Addison took a deep breath and let it go slowly. "Thank you."

"Thank you," Nina replied. "And you, Mallory. I knew when I called Clara back in August that you were the only one who could have possibly brought *Evolution* to life, but your performance exceeded my wildest dreams. Both of you."

"You'll probably be dusting this one off at least once a year for the rest of your careers," Max chimed in with a little laugh.

Mallory let the smile she'd been holding back finally break free as her eyes locked with Addison's. "I think I can handle that."

Addison laughed. "Me too."

epilogue

Mallory balanced the carrying tray that held hers and Addison's coffees and celebratory pastries against her stomach as she slipped her sunglasses back into place. They had wrapped their final performance in Los Angeles the night before, and she was looking forward to surprising Addison with breakfast in bed before they set about enjoying a lazy day lounging around the hotel's rooftop pool before their flight home tomorrow. She adjusted her grip on their morning treats as she eased the shop's door open with her shoulder, and smiled when a hand reached in to hold the door for her. "Cheers, mate."

"Mallory."

Mallory's heart stopped beating at the painfully familiar sound of that voice murmuring her name. But it didn't make sense. Gwen couldn't *be* in Los Angeles. She was supposed to be in Europe with the rest of LA Phil for the final leg of the summer tour. Hell, knowing that Gwen was thousands of miles away had been the only thing that had allowed her to breathe easy the whole time she'd been back in Los Angeles.

There was a hesitant smile on Gwen's lips as she met Mallory's stunned gaze. "Um, surprise?" she said weakly. "I'm sorry for ambushing you like this. I just...can we maybe talk, you know, for a minute or something?" She tilted her head imploringly.

Mallory grit her teeth as she stared disbelievingly at Gwen. Her first impulse was to brush past her with a curt, *no fucking way,* but there was something in the way Gwen's shoulders bowed, as if preparing to be rebuffed, that made her relent with a terse nod. Even now, it seemed, she could not find it in herself to deny Gwen what she wanted.

"Thank you," Gwen breathed. She motioned toward an empty table just inside the door. "Would you like to sit, or…?"

Mallory's hands were starting to shake as the reality of the situation that *should not have been happening* began to sink in, and she didn't trust herself to remain calm enough not to drop the coffees onto the sidewalk. She turned and abruptly made her way back inside the coffee shop. "What are you doing here?" Mallory asked brusquely as she set the cardboard carrying tray onto the nearest table. She was glad, at least, that her voice didn't tremble. She pushed her sunglasses back up onto the top of her head as she sat down. "You should be in Brussels."

"I flew back into town last night," Gwen explained as she took her seat across the table from Mallory. "Dana's due any day now, so they gave me leave to come home so I'd be here when she goes into labor."

"That's…" *Quick,* Mallory thought. Hell, it wasn't even a full year ago that the video of Gwen's symphony debut and proposal hit the internet, and they were already expecting a child? And, more than that… "I didn't know you wanted children."

"I didn't think I did, either," Gwen agreed with a little shrug. "But last September we were at the beach with Luke and Jay, enjoying the last bit of summer. Dana pointed to this little girl digging near the water, and said something about how she couldn't wait to bring our kids to the beach and teach them how to build sandcastles and surf. And I just… All of a sudden I realized that I wanted that."

"With her."

"Yes." Gwen ducked her head. "It was supposed to take a few tries for the IVF to take, but it worked on the first try, so…yeah."

"And you chased me down to tell me this?"

"No, I…" Gwen shook her head. Her eyes shone with remorse as she looked up through her lashes and added, "When I found out you were still here, I just felt like I needed to find you and apologize again for the way things ended between us. And I guess I wanted to see if you were okay. I handled everything so badly that night, and I'm so, so sorry—"

"It's fine, Gwen," Mallory interrupted. Then, more softly, "Really, I'm fine. I wasn't at first, but I am now." She took a deep breath and held it for a moment before letting it go, using the time to consider whether or not it was worth wading back into these muddy waters. A couple of months ago she wouldn't have, but now she realized that she had truly moved on. Besides, in the end, she knew that if she didn't bring it up now that she'd always wonder, so she asked, "Do you know what hurt the most though? Aside from the cheating and the lying and everything else?"

Gwen seemed to shrink in her seat as she asked in a quiet voice, "What?"

"I had no idea you wrote music." Mallory shook her head. "You wrote a fucking beautiful symphony, and I had no bloody idea..." Her voice trailed off as emotion tightened her throat, and she swallowed thickly to clear it so she could ask, "Was I truly that awful? That you felt you had to hide that part of yourself from me?"

"No!" Gwen's hands shot across the table to cover hers, and it took Mallory everything she had to not pull away. "No, Mal. It wasn't anything like that."

"Then why?" Mallory hated the way her voice cracked, but was glad that the tears she could feel welling up stayed put.

"I didn't..." Gwen sighed. "It was just something I messed around with when my head was too full and I needed to relax. It wasn't just you—I didn't tell anyone about it."

"And yet..."

"And yet," Gwen agreed. "Dana came over to the house unexpectedly one day, and I'd had my papers spread over the coffee table. She asked what it was, so I had to tell her because it was right the hell there, and then she just randomly kept asking about it. You know, asking how it was going, if I'd play a bit for her, stuff like that. I never expected to actually finish the damn thing, but eventually I did, and then she said something to Luke about it, and he mentioned it to Rhode, and it just snowballed. I honestly hadn't planned on it being a *thing*, but all of a sudden it was and I just kind of buckled in for the ride."

Mallory bit her lip as she looked at the woman she had once loved with her whole, imperfect heart. Maybe it was the rambling explanation, or the way Gwen's eyes were open and honest and begging to be believed, but Mallory found that she did believe her. And, more than that, she felt she could forgive her now. In the end, the only thing that mattered was that they were both where they belonged. She let her lip slip from her teeth as she turned her hands to return Gwen's hold. "It is a beautiful piece of music. I'm glad you found the courage to share it with the world."

"Thank you." Gwen squeezed her hands. "I haven't seen it yet, of course, but rumor has it that your ballet is incredible, too. I was so surprised when I heard you were collaborating with the Royal Ballet."

"It was too good of an opportunity to pass up," Mallory confessed. "To work with Nina Devereaux, who kept drilling me on it until I got it right, and with Addy, who's the perfect partner..."

Gwen smiled. "She's a beautiful dancer."

"She is. And she's an even more wonderful human being. She's...she's everything I never knew I needed."

"She makes you happy?"

Mallory nodded. "Very happy."

"I'm glad."

Mallory smiled. "Me too." Making peace with her past was nice, but she had left her future back at the hotel and her heart was suddenly racing with the need to hurry back to it. She murmured apologetically, "I'm sorry, but I should be getting back. I left a note, but Addy is going to worry that something's happened to me if I linger much longer."

"Of course." Gwen pulled her hands away as she got to her feet. "Thank you for talking to me."

"Thank you for searching me out."

"You mean ambushing you? Yeah, totally," Gwen laughed. She smoothed her hands over her thighs and tilted her head as she added, "May I...hug you goodbye?"

Mallory nodded and opened her arms, and her eyes fluttered shut as Gwen sank into her. They held each other for a long moment, and Mallory couldn't resist brushing a kiss over the soft spot in front of Gwen's ear as she pulled away. "Goodbye, Gwen."

"Goodbye, Mal," Gwen whispered, her eyes gentle and warm with the peace they had finally won.

With nothing left to say, Mal smiled at Gwen as she picked up the cardboard tray with hers and Addy's coffees. They would probably need to be reheated by the time she walked the two blocks to their hotel. Hang on, there were dozens of hotels in downtown Los Angeles, so how... "Wait a second. How did you find me?"

Gwen chuckled sheepishly and shoved her hands into the back pockets of her shorts. "I had someone in the front office at Phil look into it for me. When they gave me the name of the hotel where the LSO was staying, and I didn't find you there, I remembered how much you liked the coffee here. I almost turned around when I saw you coming out... I didn't know if you'd want to even see me, but I needed to try. For both of us."

"Thank you."

"Any time, Mal. Be happy."

Mallory smiled and lifted her tray of coffee in farewell. "You too."

The walk from the coffee shop to the hotel was a blur of cars and sunshine and more people than should have been walking around downtown Los Angeles. She tapped her foot anxiously as she waited for the lift that would take her up to their floor. She could hear the television through the door as she tapped her key to the lock, and her heart lodged itself in her throat as she stepped inside. "Sorry, darling," she apologized as she set the tray with their drinks onto the small desk beside the dresser that held the television. "I had every intention of getting back before you woke up."

"It's fine," Addison hummed as she stretched beneath the downy white comforter. Her skin was bronzed from days spent soaking up the sun both in Australia and here, and something inside Mallory settled as she stared at her. "Your note said you'd be right back."

Mallory smiled as she left their drinks on the desk and crawled onto the bed. "I love you," she swore as she dipped her head to capture Addison's lips in a slow, sweet kiss. "So much."

"Love you, too," Addison murmured as her hands worked beneath the hem of Mallory's tee and began pulling it off. "But you have way too many clothes on if you're going to be in bed with me."

Mallory laughed and continued to lavish Addison's lips with as many kisses as she could while she undressed her, and she sighed happily as she kicked the comforter off the foot of the bed and stretched out on top of her. "Better?"

"So much better," Addison confirmed, her voice deliciously rough as she tangled a hand in Mallory's hair and guided their lips together.

Kissing Addison was wonderful, but Mallory forced herself to pull away so she could tell her, "I saw Gwen just now. At the coffee shop." She hated the way Addison stilled beneath her, but she had promised herself that she would never keep anything important from her and, well, running into her ex certainly fell into that category. She started to pull away because this seemed like more of a sitting up type of conversation, but a firm hand on the small of her back held her in place.

Addison slid her hand from Mallory's hair to gently cradle her face as she asked, "Are you okay?"

"I am." Mallory smiled and brushed her lips over Addison's. "It was unexpected, of course, but, at the same time…it was nice." She kissed her again. "Loving you helped me get to a point where I didn't particularly need that closure anymore, but I feel like it's all properly settled now, if that makes sense."

"You feel free."

Mallory nodded. "And blessed to have you in my life. You are everything in the world to me, Addison. I love you so very, very much."

"Love you more," Addison teased as she lifted her head to capture Mallory's lips in a sweet kiss.

"That's just not possible, darling," Mallory countered as she pinned Addison back against the bed and endeavored to do her very best to show her with soft touches and reverent kisses just how much she cherished her

The phone on the bedside table exploding to life just as she bit Addison's hipbone was a most unwelcome distraction, but the hand in her hair urging her downward was all the encouragement she needed to ignore it. They both sighed with relief when the ringing finally stopped, but when the phone started up again, Mallory swore, "I'm going to kill him."

"Not if I beat you to it," Addison replied as she rolled to grab the handset that would undoubtedly keep ringing until they answered. "Really bad timing Will."

Mallory was debating continuing with what she was doing despite Addison holding the phone to her ear, when Addison sat up and held the phone out to her with a half-strained, half-amused, "He says it's important."

Mallory rolled her eyes as she relented and reached for the phone. "What do you want, Will?" she demanded as she pushed Addison back down onto the bed. She was not finished ravishing her yet, and she'd be damned if even her best friend's impeccably awful timing ruined this for her.

"Well, a merry good morning to you, too, darling!" Will replied in an annoyingly chipper, sing-song voice.

"Sod off."

He laughed. *"Are you always this cheerful in the morning? How does*

Addison put up with you?"

"Addison wakes me up a hell of a lot more nicely than ringing my bloody phone off the hook," Mallory told him as she dipped her head to tease Addison's nipple with the tip of her tongue.

"I bet she does," he drawled.

Mallory nuzzled Addison's breast and hummed at the feeling of long, long fingers tugging at her hair. "Seriously, mate, what do you want?"

"For you and your beautiful girlfriend to roll your arses out of bed and get down here. Since Max and Clara are playing nice with the Phil higher-ups building international professional goodwill or whatever, we've decided we're going to spend our last day in California enjoying this ridiculously warm weather and amazing sunshine. So grab your bathing suit and sunscreen, fearless leader. It's family day, and you and Addy are coming with us whether you want to or not."

"Oh really?" Now it was her turn to laugh. She winked at Addison as she added, "What if we have something else planned?"

She could practically hear his smirk in the silence that crackled over the line before he replied, *"I've got twenty musicians down here with me, and we will absolutely storm the corridor outside your room with our instruments and play the loudest, most annoying music we can think of until you come out."* His laugh was positively demonic as he added, *"Todd is really liking the idea of that, by the way."*

Mallory pursed her lips to keep from smiling in spite of her annoyance. Of course the tuba player would be looking forward to making an insane amount of noise. "And then everyone in the rooms around us will complain to the front desk, and you lot will be forced to stop."

"In a normal situation, yes," he conceded. *"But as I'm calling from the hotel manager's phone and she's trying very hard to not laugh her arse off at all of this, I think we'll win this round. Up and at 'em, Collingswood. The bus we hired will be here in thirty minutes, so that means you have exactly that much time and not a minute longer to get down to the lobby before we force you out."*

"I hate you."

"You love me," he countered, complete with a smackeroo kiss to the phone. *"See you soon!"*

"I need a new best friend," Mallory grumbled as she hung up the phone.

"I'll be your best friend," Addison murmured as she arched her chest toward Mallory's mouth.

Mallory smiled and gave her nipple a playful bite. "You are my everything, darling."

"Ditto," Addison moaned. "What did Will want?"

"To inform us that we are going to the beach, apparently. And that the bus he arranged will be downstairs in thirty minutes."

"And I'm guessing from your half of the conversation that he doesn't care if we have other plans?"

"Not one whit," Mallory confirmed as she smoothed her hands over Addison's sides. It was a touch designed more to soothe than arouse because there was no denying that the mood had been most effectively killed.

"And the bit about complaining to the front desk?"

Mallory pressed a kiss to the hollow of Addison's throat. "He threatened to assemble a group of musicians to play outside our door until we relent and come out."

Addison laughed. "Sorry, but that's kind of genius."

"It's annoying." Mallory smiled as she brushed Addison's hair from her eyes. "I would much rather spend the day right here with you," she breathed as she dipped her head to capture Addison's lips in a sweet kiss. "Just like this." She kissed her again. "I am so looking forward to being able to wake up like this every day."

"Me too," Addison hummed, wrapping a hand around the back of Mallory's neck to guide their lips together again.

Despite Will's threat of musical eviction, they lingered in the moment, trading slow, adoring kisses as they welcomed-in the day on their terms. Their days over the last month had been hectic and gratifying, but the open and the close of each one had been theirs and theirs alone. "I love you."

"I love—" Addison's response was interrupted by a foghorn-esque honk from a tuba. She laughed and shook her head. "Has it really been half an hour?"

Mallory glanced at the clock. "It hasn't even been ten minutes."

"Sure doesn't sound like it."

"No, it certainly doesn't," Mallory agreed. She held her breath as an ominous silence descended on the floor for a long moment, and let it go with a huff as the group assembled outside their door launched themselves into the final piece from *Evolution* with a ridiculous amount of enthusiasm. She shook her head as she rolled off Addison to sit up and stare at the door. "Wow..."

Addison sat up beside her and cocked her head as she listened. "Is the tuba covering your part?"

Mallory nodded. "He's trying, anyway." Honestly, she was rather impressed at how successful as he was with it. "I think we should probably get out there before they get themselves arrested."

"Good thing we showered after the show last night," Addison noted as she gracefully rolled out of bed. "And that it doesn't exactly require any effort to be presentable for the beach."

"That is true," Mallory agreed. "Will you throw my bathing suit on the bed? I'm going to grab a robe out of the bathroom and then stick my head out the door to let them know we've heard them and will be downstairs by the time our original thirty-minute window will have ended."

"Or you could just leave them out there." Addison tossed Mallory's blue bikini onto the bed and stepped into the bottom half of her own. "You know, for a little mood music while we get dressed."

"Yes, because there is nothing sexier than the bleating of a tuba," Mallory drawled as she watched Addison work the scrap of red fabric up her legs.

"It's more a matter of making them stick it out," Addison countered as she reached for her top. "You know, they wanted to be annoying so…let them put in the work for it."

Mallory chuckled and shook her head as she crossed the room to where Addison was standing. "Whatever you want, darling."

Addison stopped fiddling with the straps on her bikini top and smiled as she grabbed Mallory's waist to pull her close. She laughed at the sound of Todd letting rip a particularly awful attempt at a high C—though Mallory was willing to bet that he messed it up on purpose, just to be even more annoying—and Addison's eyes sparkled with laughter softly as she pushed herself up onto the balls of her feet to kiss Mallory softly. "I love you."

"I love you, too, Addy," Mallory breathed as she ignored the noise designed to smoke them out and she cradled Addison's face in her hands and dipped her head to capture Addison's lips in a searing kiss that said better than words ever could just how very much she loved her.

"How long do you think they'll keep going?" Addison murmured between kisses.

Mallory smiled and threaded her fingers in Addison's hair. They could stand out there playing all bloody day long for all she cared—she was quite content to stay right where she was. "Does it matter?"

"No. I just…" Addison's voice trailed off into a laugh as the music faded to silence for one glorious moment before Will and his merry band of music makers began a new song. "Wow. The wedding march? Really?"

Mallory sighed and pursed her lips as she turned to glare at the door. "I have no doubt that one was Will's idea. He's probably laughing his arse off out there right now."

Addison made a small sound of agreement as she hooked a finger under Mallory's chin and gently guided her attention back to her. "He probably is," she agreed softly. "Because he loves you just as much as he loves teasing you."

"I'm sorry," Mallory apologized.

"For what?"

Mallory shrugged. "All of that? I mean, I don't want you to be uncomfortable. We haven't even properly moved-in together yet, and—"

Addison shook her head as she interrupted Mallory's rambling with a gentle finger to her lips. "I'm not uncomfortable. I think it's funny." She smiled at the way Mallory arched a brow at her in disbelief. "I know we're not there yet, sweetie, but we will be." She let her hand drop to cradle Mallory's neck as she leaned in to whisper against her lips, "And when we are, I will buy a ring and get down on one knee to ask you to be mine forever. And you will make me the happiest woman in the universe if you choose to say yes."

Mallory's heart fluttered with joy as she touched their foreheads together. "I will say yes. I can't imagine a future that doesn't have you by my side."

"Me either." Addison's eyes crinkled with happiness as she lifted her chin to brush the lightest, most adoring of kisses over Mallory's lips. "I love you."

Mallory couldn't contain her smile as she chased Addison lips to claim them in a sweet, lingering kiss. "I love you, darling. So, so much."

acknowledgements

As always, I must thank all of you, my readers, for continuing to take the time to actually sit down and read something that I wrote. Being able to do what I love every day is a gift that I cherish, and I can't thank you all enough for your support.

Thanks also go to my amazing, incredible, wonderful betas. To Lou, whose insightful notes and observations kept the finer details of the story grounded in reality when I spiraled too far into the land of make-believe—as always, I could not have done this without you. Thanks also go to Jade for the idea of how to fit a Veritas reference into this story and for going through embarrassingly rough drafts looking for typos and missing words, and to Sarah for taking the first-draft of this thing for a test drive and letting me know how I could make it better.

Made in the USA
Middletown, DE
19 February 2022

61545632R00234